ANNA*CAINE..........JUNE.6.42......GARY INDIANA.
BOX.243.   373HARRISON,STR:

SECOND HAND WIFE.

BOOKS BY
KATHLEEN NORRIS

Manhattan Love Song
The Angel in the House
Wife For Sale
Walls of Gold
Treehaven
Younger Sister
Second-Hand Wife
Belle-Mère
The Love of Julie Borel
Hands Full of Living
Beauty in Letters
The Lucky Lawrences
Margaret Yorke
Passion Flower
Red Silence
Storm House
The Foolish Virgin
What Price Peace?
Beauty and the Beast
The Fun of Being a Mother
My Best Girl
Barberry Bush
The Sea Gull
Hildegarde
Mystery House
The Black Flemings
Little Ships
Mother and Son
Home
Noon
Rose of the World
The Callahans and the Murphys
Butterfly
Certain People of Importance
Lucretia Lombard
The Beloved Woman
Harriet and the Piper
Sisters
Josselyn's Wife
Undertow
Martie, the Unconquered
The Heart of Rachel
The Story of Julia Page
The Treasure
Saturday's Child
Poor, Dear Margaret Kirby
The Rich Mrs. Burgoyne
Mother
Maiden Voyage

KATHLEEN NORRIS

Second Hand Wife

TRIANGLE BOOKS
NEW YORK

COPYRIGHT, 1931, 1932, BY KATHLEEN NORRIS
All rights reserved

TRIANGLE BOOKS EDITION PUBLISHED FEBRUARY 1941

REPRINTED FEBRUARY 1941
REPRINTED MARCH 1941
REPRINTED APRIL 1941

TRIANGLE BOOKS, 14 West Forty-ninth Street,
New York, N. Y.

PRINTED AND BOUND IN THE UNITED STATES OF AMERICA

SECOND HAND WIFE

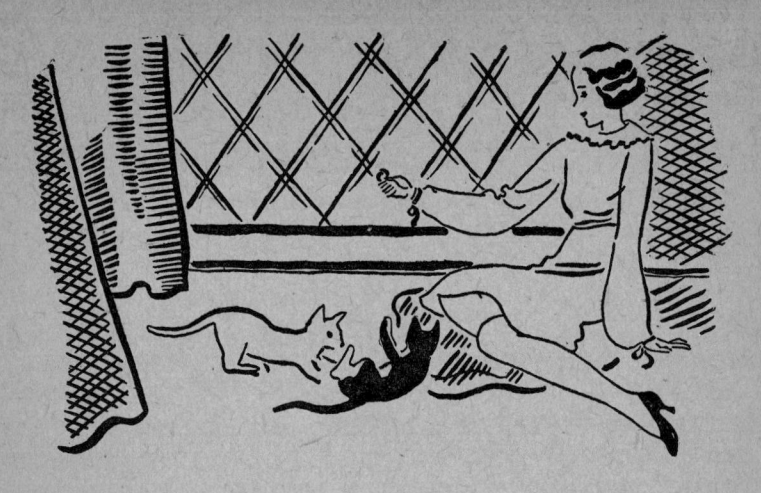

CHAPTER ONE

ON SATURDAY NIGHTS they always went to the theater on passes, Alexandra and her mother never called it the theater; they spoke of it merely as "some show." It usually was a show that was not successful; the passes were easily gotten then.

Alexandra's mother, fat and soft and still pretty and confiding at fifty, would slip up to the box office at some quiet moment and murmur to the clerk, "What's the chances, Lew?" And Lew either slapped down two torn checks instantly or murmured in return, "Come back in a little while, will you, Mrs. Trumbull?"

In the twenty-one years of her life Alexandra Trumbull had as little thought of paying for her theater seats as for the air she breathed. Movie seats were different. The audiences were different; they drifted in and out at all hours. There was never any papering of the movie houses. Alexandra and her mother did not care. They saw all the big films, anyway. Some man took Sandra and gallantly included her mother in the party; or Mrs. Trumbull and a woman friend went to the movies during the long dull empty afternoons when Sandra was at the office.

Sunday was the Trumbulls' lazy day, their happy day, even though deep somewhere in Sandra's being was a feeling that there was something all wrong about the way she and Flossy spent Sunday. She had always called her mother Flossy; had been indeed the "mother" of them both since her tenth or twelfth year. Mrs. Trumbull had been Flossy O'Brien Belleau, adored little singer of the cabarets and after-theater shows, only twenty-two years ago. She was shrewd, suspicious, shrill little Flossy still, in many moods. Her mind remained what it had been at fifteen, on that memorable occasion when she had come shyly forth to sing at "Amateur Night" at the Chutes, and men had thrown money at her before she finished "My Wild Irish Rose" and "When I Walks Dat Levee Roun'."

Half Irish, half French, all San Franciscan Bohemian, Flossy loved idleness, gossip, loved lying abed for half of Sunday. But Sandra's father had been English-born, and Sandra inherited some queer, uneasy Victorian instincts about order and thrift and energy. She was usually tired on Sunday after the workday week and the Saturday night's dissipation, but still she sometimes wondered if she and Flossy ought not to be up early, and go to church somewhere, and come back to open windows and tear beds apart, wash shining dishes and put the apartment in order.

It was all vague. They belonged, mother and daughter, to no church. Flossy at the age of nine had attended a mission for married women, with her mother. But her mother had died after that, and some Roumanian acrobats had taken the little girl into their care, with scanty spiritual results. Sandra's father had been a tall, lanky, fair man, who spoke with a crisp English accent. when he spoke at all. He had emigrated rather mysteriously from his native country at the age of forty-odd, had lived precariously on a quarterly remittance from home, and had affected a half-hearted interest in a small prune ranch near San José which he had bought, and for which he had partially paid. He had greeted his daughter's arrival in this world with a pitying "Poor little devil; why not drown her?" and had presently died without ever having mentioned even to his plump, fussy, singing young wife his family connections, if he had any, or his personal history, of which obviously he had had much. If Rodney Trumbull had ever joined any church or attended one he never gave anyone a hint of it in his later years.

So Flossy and Sandra never went to church. As to housekeeping, the outlook was poor too. They had one large room at the back of a lodging house in the second block of Ellis Street, right in the very heart of the theater, hotel, restaurant, business district. Flossy, upon retiring perforce from the field of cabaret and vaudeville entertainments when Sandra was seven, had opened this house as a theatrical hotel. But this had not succeeded; now a Mr. and Mrs. Bevilaqua were lessees of the place, and Flossy, much of whose furniture they had taken over as a consideration, had to show for her adventure only the fact that she got her room rent-free.

With the best of intentions Sandra could not seem to see their one big room as a home. It did not encourage domestic effort. It was on the second floor, but the lower room was half a basement, and the Trumbulls' room only some seven or eight feet higher than a cemented pit at the back. Great buildings, garages, the sides of a movie house, dark commercial hotels hemmed it in; there was no chance for sunshine, even in summer. Sometimes a pallied reflection of light flickered there when the sun, directly overhead, caught with a blaze on the opened skylight of the café next door. Down in the bricked and cemented pit there was one heavy basement door, usually barred, the gate to a narrow path that was wedged between the buildings leading to the street, and a great deal of rubbish—dead flowers, cigarette butts, browned drifting newspapers, flower pots holding the shriveled stalks of Easter lilies.

Sandra and her mother were not concerned with the view; they rarely glanced out of their two tall windows, unless to see whether or not the rain was falling. There were long dangling Nottingham lace curtains at the windows, and over them other draped curtains of brown burlap stenciled in darker brown and red *fleur-de-lis*. This dashing note had been introduced by Flossy years ago; Sandra used to lie in bed wondering what to do about the curtains. If she took down the limp, dusty lace ones the brown ones would look unutterably dingy and forlorn. If she took away the brown ones the white ones alone would be worse. She solved the problem in the usual Trumbull fashion by doing nothing.

"Flossy, burlap curtains ought never be draped. They belong in studios or country cabins."

"That's right."

"And as for the others, they ought to be in some elegant, old-fashioned place with a colored butler and a couple of rich old maids——"

"That's right, too." But Flossy's tone would be a little less secure this time; she had not her daughter's imagination. "I'll tell you," she had once volunteered. "Everyone was getting that stenciled burlap and Mission chairs when I took this house, and it sort of appealed to me." And after long thought she had added, "What would *you* put at those windows, Sandra?"

Sandra had studied them awhile from her sodden heap of piled sofa and bed pillows. Her long body had been stretched in Sunday comfort under the limp quilts and blankets, her long arms locked behind her head, her long strange eyes narrowed.

"Well, I don't know," she had presently admitted with the rueful slow smile that lighted her face when she was amused at the general absurdity of life. "You'd have to do so much—to everything——

"Move out completely in the first place," she sometimes thought. But of late years she had not said this often; it distressed Flossy. Nice little clean apartments with electric refrigeration and bay views did not appeal to Flossy. The smoky, sooty, shadowed downtown world in which they lived was the only possible world for her. The gossip of night clubs and vaudeville teams and cabaret entertainers was the breath of her body. She passionately clung to the neighborhood of Ellis Street, Powell and O'Farrell and Geary Streets. She did not want to become respectable and conventional and domestic.

Sandra made no issue of it; perhaps the situation was none too clear in her own mind. She would have to be different and Flossy different and the world different before they could take a bright, clean, open apartment on Sacramento Street, or move into a Spanish bungalow down the Peninsula.

The room in which they lived was large; it might have been a back room in a restaurant once or the back parlor of a pretentious residence. It was steam-heated, but there were besides a heavy black marble mantel and a grate where a coal fire was laid. It was never lighted; scraps of paper and hair, matches, dark brown frills from candy boxes, and pink string were thrown in on top of the dusty coal. An onyx clock, stopped, and a ticking alarm clock, two large imitation Sèvres vases, and a photograph of Flossy Belleau in a Dolly Varden dress shared the shelf with the litter of letters that were stuck behind the clock, a tiny pot of artificial pink flowers, a copper ash tray, and various other small articles picked up by Flossy or Sandra at café openings and amusement-park contests as souvenirs. To the left of the fireplace was the big brass bed upon which, when it was made, Flossy always put all the little lace pillows and the long-legged Spanish and Pierrette dolls.

Opposite the windows, across the dark room, were three doors. One led into the dark, carpet-scented hall, one opened upon the bathroom, with its tin tub, its old-fashioned, odorous plumbing, its eternal bead of gas which a jerked string brought to full light. The third door gave the suite a kitchen no larger than a large closet, dark, but complete with a tiny ice box, a sink, some shelves, an opening upon a fire escape for vegetable boxes and garbage pail, and a two-ring gas stove.

A closet had actually been sacrificed for this convenience, and Flossy and Sandra kept their clothes in an old-fashioned cumbrous wardrobe that absorbed the center of the third wall. Its great doors had originally been paneled with mirrors, only one of which remained. But with the looming mirror above the mantel, and the pier glass in maplewood that was her mother's chief treasure, Sandra had sometimes been embarrassed in childhood to see so many angles of her little half-dressed self; she never regretted the empty wooden spaces where the wardrobe mirrors should have been. The sofa, the wardrobe, the pier glass, and one collapsed old Morris rocker on a stationary base filled this wall. The fourth wall was broken by the high windows; a sewing machine, a chair, and a radio were ranged in the spaces between windows and wall.

For the rest there was a crowded center table on which Sandra and her mother cleared casual spaces for their informal meals; there were a few mismated chairs; there were one or two small stands from which sewing, playing cards, theater programmes, sheet music were in a continual state of sliding. Flossy's ukulele, the slippers she was gilding, her camera, her strip of tapestry work, her book from the circulating library at the corner never had appointed or regular places. Sandra used to wonder sometimes how she and her mother accumulated so many things they did not want. They were not acquisitive folk, but Flossy would never throw anything away if she thought she might ever use it, or if it was "cute." Of plaster Kewpies, dressed in feathers, of red glass diminutive steins lettered in white, of paper dolls made in the likeness of Norma Talmadge or Ann Pennington, Flossy said with equal fondness that they were "cute." Flossy bought all the theatrical and movie magazines every month, and they took up room, too, especially as she kept them for months. And if any generous friend, departing after a vaudeville engagement, offered Flossy a garment—a maribou-trimmed wrap in blue satin or a pair of gaudy hunting breeches in red and black—she always accepted it enthusiastically, with the intention of "making it into something." She ripped long strips of fur from old coats; she carefully cut brown and creamy lace from outworn nightgowns; she saved remnants of silk. These she rolled into balls and put into large cardboard boxes and shoved them under the sofa. Inasmuch as neither she nor Sandra was clever about making garments, the boxes were rarely disturbed.

More than this, out of the goodness of her heart Flossy often offered to store the possessions of her friends for various periods ranging from days to years. Roped boxes and leather trunks stenciled with the names of theatrical teams accumulated dust in corners; "May's box"—"Lil's things"—"all that stuff of Frank's"—helped to complicate Sandra's domestic problem.

"God knows I never threw down a friend!" Flossy would

state, tears of emotion in her eyes, when the talk lingered on over some dinner at Solari's or La Favorite. Sandra had felt very proud of such a mother when she was quite small.

"Does anyone ever throw down a friend, Flossy?"

Flossy would glance lovingly at the child, glance significantly at the group.

"Hear her! You wait until you're older and you'll know."

The path of mother and daughter had diverged somewhere back in Alexandra's youthful days. Neither had known it. Flossy had sunk comfortably deeper into her lazy life, "working" the men she knew for dinners and little presents of stockings and hats, but giving generously, too, of her company and her friendship. She was all affection. Sandra had withdrawn, even in grammar-school days, further and further away from it all. As Flossy grew soft and fat, Sandra had grown tall and firm and slender, a quiet, proud, self-contained child whose love was shyly, rarely given, whose affection, as deep as her mother's, was confined almost exclusively to that same mother. Sandra loved little cats, excitedly adored all dogs, was marvelously tender and motherly and murmuring with babies. But except for these she had few affiliations.

Flossy had wanted her splendid Juno of a daughter to go on the stage; Sandra shook her fair head. Completely puzzled by her child's decision to go to a secretarial school, her choice of plain dark clothes, her finicky passion for hot water and unscented powders and soaps, Flossy gave her her way. The theater to Sandra was a place of simple amusement; she did not want to play with grease paint and wigs even as a child; she smiled absently at managers who threw out hints of schools of the drama; she never wanted to go back-stage and talk to performers. Her first job was with an advertising firm; her second and present one was with Cavendish & Bartlett, successors to the Polk, Cavendish

Company of San Francisco, investment bankers, who did at the same time a large business financing other concerns and individuals. Sandra worked hard, held herself somewhat aloof from the other clerks in the office, and at twenty-one was paid a round hundred a month.

This was incomprehensible to Flossy. Sandra could have had the run of all the theaters, the greenrooms, the movie houses. She could have had walking-on parts by this time, could have been immersed in the delicious intimacies, the gossip and exchange of the theatrical world.

But Flossy loved her too much to criticize her; she even stood faintly and secretly in awe of this superb, tall, full-breasted creature who was so inexplicably her child.

"Sandra and me's different—but she's all right, at that!" Flossy told her friends.

Flossy awakened first in the dark back bedroom on a certain October Sunday. Sandra, twisting the long roll that was herself under the covers, blinking, dragging another pillow or two under the tousled mass of her chestnut hair, lay staring at her mother for a moment or two, yawning and smiling. Coffee scented the air; Flossy had a coat on—she had been to the bakery.

"I woke you," Flossy stated, regretfully.

"No, I think it was the bells. It isn't—" said Alexandra—"it isn't noon?"

The bells had stopped, but the sparse Sunday whistles were proclaiming it.

"Yep," the older woman confirmed them. "You had a good sleep," she added, in satisfaction.

"I was going to wash my hair this morning."

"It's terribly cloudy. The paper says rain."

Sandra lay still. After almost twelve hours of sleep she felt exquisitely rested, at peace with the world. What if her holiday were half gone, there remained this best part of

Sunday, this lazy hour with Floss and breakfast and the newspapers. The rest was apt to be duller to Sandra than any office day.

"Where'd you go, darling?"

"Butter——" Floss answered briefly from the kitchen.

"Foggy?"

"No. But I think it rained in the night."

Sandra dragged herself up, disappeared into the bathroom for casual ablutions, came back to establish herself again in bed with the bulk of two great newspapers beside her.

"You don't have to do that," she protested absently, as her mother brought her a black tin tray.

"I love to!" the older woman asserted, also without much feeling. They understood each other; they were always waiting on each other.

Now Mrs. Trumbull pushed a light table to the bed and brought her own toast and coffee to it, sitting so near that Sandra could move her own paraphernalia to the table, drop the tray on the floor between wall and bed on the other side, and comfortably rustle the sheets of the paper.

"Ted Hovey's act is called off on account of his illness," Floss announced, reading.

"Oh, too bad."

"You know just about how ill he was!"

"You mean he wasn't?"

"Of course not. That new girl he got in poor Ethyl's place just ran away with the act."

A long wordless space, when the papers crackled and the toast was broken and the hot coffee lowered in the cups. Mist filled the dreary shaft outside the windows, but the room was pleasantly warm. Sandra's droplight made a gold aureole of the hair that tumbled about her face. Flossy dragged a tall lamp behind her own chair and sat in her own pool of light.

Suddenly the girl sprang out of the free side of the bed and was in the kitchen.

"Oh, darling, why didn't you let me——"

"It's nothing—I'm not going to toast it." Sandra came back with the coffee pot and the sliced French bread and a little wooden basket with figs and tomatoes and one banana in it.

"Have an egg, darling?"

"Oh, heavens, no! This is all I want."

The reading, the rustling went on in the crowded dusty room with its staring Kewpies and manikins, its ukulele and unlighted, littered coal fire.

"There—that's Carter Cavendish," Sandra presently said, in an odd, quiet voice.

Her mother looked up alertly and took the sheet of brown rotogravure that the girl extended.

"Which one?"

"The one in the circle with the horse."

Mrs. Trumbull, chewing a scrap of toast, considered him. She set down her cup without glancing away from the picture.

"Look like that?"

"Well, yes; only of course—in office clothes——"

"He's handsome," the older woman observed, after further study. "Is he the president, Sandra?"

"No; his older brother, Peter Cavendish, is. I don't see him very much. His office is upstairs. He doesn't play polo."

"This is the one that plays it, hey?"

"Marvelously." Sandra's voice dropped from enthusiasm to flatness. "They say," she added. "I've never seen him play."

"You're just as good-looking as you can be," Mrs. Trumbull told the paper portrait.

"Are you in his office, dearie?" she presently asked.

"No. I'm in what they call the main office, but I go into his sometimes. But Miss Curtis is his regular secretary; she was with the firm before he went to college even. They say she knows more about the business than anyone else."

"I'll bet," Floss ruminated aloud—"I'll bet she's in love with him."

Alexandra laughed shortly.

"Oh, *is* she?" she echoed ruefully.

"No, is she, Sandra?"

"Why, of course she is, Flossy!"

"You don't mean it!"

"I do mean it. Everyone knows it."

"Isn't that awful?" Mrs. Trumbull said idly, handing back the paper.

Sandra, a smile twitching at the corners of her wide, well-molded mouth, returned her eyes to the picture and shrugged faintly.

"He's thirty-two, say," she offered, noncommittally. "Miss Curtis is about—oh, thirty-five or six. She knows he's married."

"She tell you she liked him?"

"She didn't have to. No; she never says anything about it—it's one of the unwritten—well, facts in the office. We all know poor Gertie is languishing in secret. The way she looks at him! The way she answers him!"

"Well, that's too bad. That's hard on her," the older woman commented.

"I suppose it is. But she gets a lot out of it, Flossy," the girl observed, flinging the paper away. "She sees him every day, she knows all his affairs, what he allows his wife, and who writes to him—everything. If he has a cold she mixes him things to take, and if anyone annoys him she has the pleasure of saying that Mr. Cavendish is out just at present."

A subtle irony in her smile, the big even teeth faintly biting her full lower lip, she lay back in her pillows, long arms locked behind her head.

"Do you suppose he knows it?" Flossy presently asked, from a brown study.

"Knows what?"

"Suppose Carter Cavendish knows that his secretary is crazy about him?"

"He must. But he's always very nice and simple and businesslike in the office, and you can't tell. . . . It's very hard for a girl to see a man every day, if he's attractive and she's attractive," Sandra went on, presently, "without some sort of feeling developing."

"*You* see him every day," her mother observed.

"Yes, I know. But I only go in and out once or twice. She sits right beside him—they have jokes about the bores that come in, signals—things nobody else knows."

"Do you think him so attractive, Sandra?"

Sandra was dreaming. She brought her eyes to earth with a start.

"What did you say, darling?"

"Do you think he's so attractive?"

"Mr. Cavendish?"

"Yep."

"I can imagine," Sandra answered, in a carefully impersonal tone—"I can imagine that in his own home—playing polo, I mean, tennis, swimming pools—all that—he might be very—nice."

There was a silence. Then the older woman said:

"You didn't ever get a crush on anyone in the office, did you, Sandra?"

"You would have known it if I had, Floss."

"I mean—comparing your looks to Miss Curtis——" Flossy began and floundered.

"Well, you see, the main office is a great big loft, with thirty or forty desks, out in the open," Sandra explained. "Miss Curtis and the other private stenographers are—slightly different. We don't have much chance for—affairs."

Her mother's attention had already wandered. She was deep in the paper again. Sandra presently got up and began preparations for Sunday's luxurious leisurely bath. She wandered to and fro in her faded shabby pajamas, gathering the few dishes in the kitchen sink, cold-creaming her face.

"Didn't hear you, Floss."

"I asked if he wasn't married, Sandra."

"Who, darling?"

"Cavendish."

"Oh? Oh, yes; certainly he is. His wife was—it was before I went into the office—his wife was an Eastern girl, Betty Finchley. He's got a little girl named Patsy. Patricia, probably. The little girl telephones to him, Miss Curtis says."

Sandra was balancing on the edge of the tin tub, bent sidewise to test the water with a long, slender hand. She had abandoned the pajamas and was wrapped only in a scanty Japanese crêpe jacket of deep blue dragons on a white ground. Her long slim legs, her long slim arms were bare, her head was strained back on the slender column of her neck. The sharp firm curve of her breasts lifted the cheap cotton fabric into a line of beauty.

"I wonder," her mother, herself in a wrapper and wandering aimlessly about as the girl had been, came to the bathroom doorway to say—"I wonder if you're ever going to fall in love, Sandra? It seems to me that at your age I had had half a dozen beaus."

"You're different, Flossy. You have them now."

"Because they buy me dinners!" Flossy agreed, and laughed suddenly and apologetically.

"Aren't you ashamed of yourself—you with a grown daughter?"

The smile died from the fat, soft, childish little face.

"No, I'm not, Sandra. A lot of these boys," her mother began earnestly, "come to town on business for a few days. They're lonely—they have no friends here. They want to talk to someone and go to a show, and they know they're safe with me."

There was much more of this, Flossy arguing away seriously and with feeling. Sandra only laughed as she slipped into the hot water. There was small danger of her misunderstanding her warm-hearted, limited, good little mother.

"I think you're straight, Floss," she told her mother.

Their conversation diverged; Mrs. Trumbull did not think of Carter Cavendish again until the next day, when in the endless stretches of a Monday afternoon she and a neighbor were getting ready to go to a movie. Mrs. Booley, who had been one of the Whirling Waynes a few years ago, happened to ask where Sandra worked, anyway.

"Wait a minute," Flossy answered. "I've got a picture of her boss here—Carter Cavendish."

She ruffled through the mass of newspapers that were piled on the lower shelf of the center table and heaped in a corner on the kitchen floor.

"It's funny, it doesn't matter, but he's a handsome feller, and I would like to have you see what he looks like," Floss had finally to apologize. "I can find everything else but that sheet. It must be here—but I can't lay my hand on it now. No matter. Only it's funny, for nobody's taken anything away to-day."

They went out of the dark room together, talking of the movies.

CHAPTER TWO

SANDRA TRUMBULL had recently had the astonishing experience of being voted the most popular girl in the offices of Cavendish & Bartlett. The honor had come upon her absolutely without warning; she had been but languidly, but indifferently, amused by the proceeding. Her own vote had been cast, without much reflection, for little Myra Byrnes, who was in fresh mourning and always appeared to have been weeping. The contest, to Sandra, was just one of those "office stunts."

But whatever Sandra did, everyone else in the office took the popularity test in deadly earnest; nothing else was discussed for many a noontime. Girls reflected and giggled and struggled over filling in the long blanks when the actual balloting came.

"Is she kind?" "Is she tidy?" "Is she prompt?" ran some of the questions. "Does she use good English?" "Is she fond of outdoor sports, books, music, cards, games?" "What do men who have business associations with her think of her?"

"It's vivisection!" Sandra had murmured to her nearest neighbor.

"I don't think it's supposed to have anything to do with sex at all," Laura Files had answered primly.

When her own name had been called as the winner, Alexandra Trumbull had experienced an astonishment amounting almost to vertigo. It had been extremely difficult for her to come forward from the assembled group in the main office, where they had their weekly "Better Service" talks. She had all but forgotten the balloting, now some days past. She had been sitting in her usual dreamy silence, only now and then bringing her long, strange, hazel eyes to the earnest face of old Runyon, who was maundering on about efficiency and organization spirit. Sandra felt some little contempt for the salesmanship patter of the day; she had been but half attentive.

"Miss Alexandra Trumbull, of the main office . . . " The name had jarred her confusedly to her feet; the clapping of hands, the laughter and pleasure all about her had made her feel humbled and ashamed.

"Oh, no—not I!" she had stammered in all honesty. All the speaker's kindly words had come back. . . . "fellowship, willing work, eagerness to help anyone in trouble, kindness, sweetness . . . "

"Oh, no, truly——" she had protested, being pushed forward by generous hands, somehow, to the front of the room, and facing the white smile in the brown face of Carter Cavendish.

"Congratulations!" he had said. Her own hand had felt the grip of his big fingers, and with his left hand he had tendered her the little box of flowers and the slip of an envelope. A check for a hundred dollars, and violets, and the girls clapping until she awkwardly pinned on the flowers.

"Here, don't lose that check!" Carter had said, laughing, as it fell, and with a swift movement he had recovered it.

"I shouldn't have it, Mr. Cavendish," Sandra had continued to protest, bewilderedly. Not that he cared, one way or the other. It had been a mistake, she had thought a thousand times since, to draw him into it at all. It had been too heavy a note; it didn't make any difference to him, anyway. He had only bowed and smiled, perfunctorily and kindly, and had murmured a few quite indifferent words: "Oh, I think you must let the other young ladies decide that."

And then it had been over; Mr. Cavendish and Miss Curtis and Mr. Runyon suddenly had disappeared to their own sacred offices, and the girls, bubbling with laughter that they had taken Miss Trumbull so completely by surprise, had gathered about to examine flowers and check. Somehow their artless, affectionate pleasure had given Sandra more pain than pride; she did not like them really—she had only been decent to them, kind to them, because her own native good manners dictated it, and it was too bad to have them praising her, claiming her, storming her citadel for that.

The episode had left her only a prickling sensation of shame; she did not quite like to remember it. She wanted very much to send the entire hundred dollars to old Jim Huchinson, the janitor, who had been taken to the city hospital a few weeks before. But that would look like a further bid for popularity and enthusiasm.

The real sting for her lay not in the girls' choice of her name and their absurd and embarrassing enthusiasm. It lay in that memory of a brisk, well-dressed, important young man, who had spared a scant five minutes to give the winning young lady the prize and a glimpse of the Cavendish smile. Carter Cavendish! What had *he* ever done to be so handsome, so sure of himself, so kindly approving and superior?

She, Alexandra Trumbull, who held herself quite as good as any Cavendish of the lot, had bungled over some deprecatory, modest remark, and he had brushed it aside—had hardly heard it. "Oh, I think you must let the other young ladies decide that," he had said, with indifferent conscious superiority.

"I hope he had sense enough to know that I wasn't talking to *him!*" she would think, many a time, writhing, in the days that followed. And under the spare paper in the side drawer of her desk she would uncover the newspaper picture of him, laughing, in a loose-collared white silk shirt that showed the modeling of his big arms and shoulders, the horse's long, mild head close to his own. Sandra would study the photograph somberly.

She tried to stop thinking about him; it was no use. He was always in her mind. When she and her mother sat gossiping over their breakfast Sandra was wondering if he would come into the main office this morning, wondering what he was doing, down in the Cavendish home in Burlingame. When she was in the office every step was his step, every tingle of her house telephone his voice. And when he went away in the late afternoon all the interest and life of the place seemed to go with him.

She was not conscious of liking him or of disliking him. It was just that she could not get him out of her mind.

"How can Carter Cavendish afford polo ponies—aren't they terribly expensive?" she asked Miss Curtis at a noon hour, when they were having their lunch together at the Maple Leaf Cafeteria.

The name brought a flash of pleasure to the eyes behind the strong glasses.

"Oh, he doesn't," the older woman answered eagerly. "He rides the Peabodys' or the Brays' horses, or maybe Fred Fargo's horses."

"Oh——" Sandra said vaguely, buttering a bran muffin.

"It isn't that the Cavendishes couldn't," Miss Curtis recommenced presently. "It's just that they don't go in for that sort of display."

"You'd think men would ride their own horses," Sandra suggested, with an air of keeping an idle conversation moving. But, for some perverse cause she could not define, it was not idle.

"But he's the best," the other woman answered promptly. "They want him on the team."

"Mr. Cavendish is the best?"

"Oh, my, yes!" Miss Curtis took off her glasses; there was a faint red ridge across her high, bony nose. "He's one of the *nicest* men I have ever had anything to do with!" she confessed, looking into space, smiling reminiscently. "He's so considerate. It's a pleasure to work for him."

"Is his wife nice?" Sandra asked, in a dry voice.

"Oh, she's charming." Miss Curtis's enthusiasm was unabated. "They're lovely together. Last Christmas, you know, when she was in the hospital, she telephoned down to the office to ask me to remind him of Patsy's dollhouse. So he asked me if I would go up to the Emporium with him and pick it out. Well, we had more fun! He was like a boy that day. Well, then later she sent me such a darling note of thanks. I mean," said Gertrude Curtis, her face shining —"I mean how do fashionable people like that get *time* for these things? I mean I thought it was so gracious—so sweet of her! And then in May I was down at her place, you know."

"Visiting?"

"Gracious, no! It was at the tennis tournament for the Junior League, at the Brunwalds' place. He gave me my tickets; he had a lot. So that afternoon, strolling around— they had booths and ice cream, all that—my sister and I met him with his wife and this adorable little Patsy. She's a wonderful child, you know; plays the violin simply marvelously, they say. So then he told us their house was just next door and to come in and see where he lived. And we had tea; it was too delightful. When we left," the speaker concluded, her happy eyes still shining on space, "Mrs. Cavendish said to me, 'Now remember I expect you to keep him in order, Miss Curtis,' and I said, 'Oh, believe me, Mrs.

Cavendish, *nobody* has to keep Mr. Cavendish in order; he keeps *himself* in order!'"

She looked straight at Sandra as she said the words, with a noble and dignified expression; the younger girl with some difficulty kept the inner smile of which she was conscious from betraying her.

"She's simply mad about him," Sandra thought, "and she doesn't know it!"

And she reflected with a little bitterness upon the unfairness of the situation. After this daily association with one of the most fascinating of men, a man always perfectly groomed and dressed, a man familiar with all the plays, affairs of the nation, great cities of the world, a man who stood to her in the position of superior, how could poor Gertrude Curtis be expected to take interest in any other? The pleasant intimacy of their office relationship, her knowledge of the business, her concern for his success, his health, his happiness—these were so many barbs to fence Gertrude away from the normal love affair, the normal marriage and home that might have come to her otherwise. Sandra thought she could imagine exactly how good, plain Mr. Stevens, the cashier, or Ralph Miller, Gertrude's hotel-keeping brother-in-law, would seem to her after Carter Cavendish.

The whole thing fretted her, irritated her in a way she could not define. She disliked innocent Gertrude; she disliked the subject and the thought of Carter Cavendish, but she could seem to avoid neither. A misery of unrest possessed her.

It was November now; the popularity contest was a month in the background, and the Sunday upon which Sandra had discovered the picture of Carter Cavendish in the paper three weeks gone by. But still the western skies smiled on, and the shortening days were mild and blue. Sandra—her mother noted that she had grown thinner, grown graver, somehow —could wear her favorite suit of brown tweeds to the office, her favorite plain blouses, the snug brown hat. She had grown suddenly tired of the summer silks and the loose blue coat. It was pleasant to be tailored again, to step out freely in the exhilarating air, her brown bag tucked firmly under her arm, her brown fox skin loose about her shoulders.

Every girl in the office wore a fox or squirrel or rabbit skin this autumn; Sandra sometimes wondered where they got them. Hers had come from the effects of poor Yvonne Montgomery, when Yvonne, under her own name of Eda Roots, had died from self-administered poison in the upper front room at Mrs. Bevilaqua's. "Everything I have belongs to Flossy Trumbull!" Yvonne had gasped at the end, and of the poor estate the fox skin had reverted to Sandra. It was shabby even then; cleaning had not done much for it.

Her own brown-and-cream beauty set off by the tweeds, the fur, the brown hat, she was ready to go out to lunch one day, when a message came from the office of Mr. Carter Cavendish: Miss Curtis wanted to know if Miss Trumbull would step in?

Unsuspectingly, unthinkingly, Sandra went in, to find Gertrude Curtis important with authority, and Carter Cavendish at the main desk telephoning. A tall, square, lean young man, with sleek black hair rippled like wet feathers, he could have posed, with his straight nose, heavily molded chin and mouth, and deep eye sockets, for the head of some classic Greek boy in marble. But the skin of the living man was burned brown, was even peeling here and there, and there was no self-consciousness in the easy hint of a smile and nod that, without interrupting his conversation, he gave Sandra as she came in.

"Listen," he was saying, "you're all wet, Joe. Do you get me? You're all wet. Listen, it'll be a wash-out."

Miss Curtis waited until he had stopped and had stretched back in his chair to smile at both women. Then she somewhat fussily asked Miss Trumbull if she could take a certain envelope—the familiar, red fiber-paper envelope that carried bonds—to an address just up the street; the party was waiting, and Ken, the delivery man, was out. . . .

"Sure enough, it's Miss Trumbull," Carter said, now on his feet, fussing with the papers in the wire basket. He straightened up. "Been winning any more contests lately?" he asked.

"Once is enough," Sandra responded, outwardly easy, inwardly drowning, drowning under strange new thrilling waters.

"I told you what she did with it!" Gertrude Curtis exclaimed.

Sandra and Carter Cavendish looked squarely at each other. The girl made no protest, but he heard the quick click of the big white teeth and saw the warm color flash up under her clear skin.

Surprisingly, he saw that she was annoyed at the other woman; it amused him to ask carelessly:

"No; what did she do?"

"She gave it to Huchinson's wife—the janitor's wife," Gertrude Curtis answered, with a loyal apologetic glance at Sandra's hot cheeks.

Carter turned to the younger woman, but Sandra would not expand. She shrugged, smiled faintly with a barely moving mouth and strange long brown eyes, and taking the envelope from Miss Curtis, turned away.

"No," Carter said, almost sharply; "why should you do that?"

"I wanted to, I suppose," Sandra explained it, still smiling.

"You shouldn't have done that!" he protested.

Sandra merely widened her eyes again. In another moment, shaking and proud and thrilling, she was in the big elevator with the other office girls, she was going down to the street. But it was no earthly street that she walked that day, no ordinary sun that shone, no usual world that moved about her. She had met him, she had scored. Or if she had not scored, at least he had not entirely had his way.

The rest of the day was a blur. Electricity, champagne ran in Sandra's veins. She was only vaguely conscious of her return to the office, of the afternoon hours. Moments of ecstasy alternated with moods of dull despair, but both were so enthralling, so strangely different from anything that she had ever known before that Sandra clung to the new pain almost as to the new joy. She fell into a very stupor of daydreams, lying on her bed, when she went home, and was still deep in them when her mother came into the room in the darkness, at six o'clock. Flossy exclaimed in alarm when she realized that Sandra was lying there.

"For heaven's sake, Sandra! How you scared me!"

"I'm sorry. I must have fallen asleep."

But there was no sleep in the shining brown eyes, no drowsiness in the thrilling voice. Flossy looked at her daughter curiously when the lights were lighted. Sandra's rich chestnut hair was tumbled in a loose soft coil on her shoulders; her color was high. She gave an exultant mysterious laugh, sitting up, and bringing her feet to the floor.

"What about dinner, Flossy?" She glanced at the packages her mother carried. "Here?"

And suddenly a deep depression enveloped her, and she hated herself and her life, everybody and everything. The tawdry, disordered room, upon which the light streamed so mercilessly, the dirty area outside, the squalid street harshly lighted by cafés and tobacco stands, all seemed to overwhelm her like a sickening tide; the ukulele, the movie magazines, the grease seeping through one of the packages her mother had brought in were all a part of it. Their obscure, their undignified lives affronted her as she had never been affronted before. She sat tousled and blinking on the edge of the disreputable old white enamel and brass-trimmed bed, and felt her soul sick within her.

"Want to go to a picture to-night?" Floss asked.

"I want to die!" Alexandra wanted to exclaim. "I want to get out of this horrible place and live somewhere where there are clean sheets and servants and decency and flowers! I want to dress myself beautifully once, before I die, in lacy things and trailing things and pearls, and have some man take me to a wonderful place where the rooms are big and dim and scented and quiet. I want him to kiss me; I want something to stop this hunger that is gnawing me and making my heart beat so hard and my thoughts spin around and around this way!"

Her head in her hands, she sat silent, making no reply. Flossy dispossessed herself of her bundles, moved about the room, hung up her coat.

"I got cream cheese and ham," she said.

Still the girl sat motionless, her face buried, her softly tumbled bright hair falling over her hands, unable to speak. Flossy turned on the radio and a firm buoyant voice rang through the room.

"Friends, let's think happiness—let's say happiness—let's spread happiness to-night. Let this be happiness night. That's the way to do it! This is Wally White of the Buoyancy Boys talking . . ."

The heavy chenille cover of the table had been shoved back in thick dusty folds, pushing the lamp, the magazines, photographs, ash trays, boxes, and vases into a jumble. Flossy was drifting back and forth with butter and spoons, rolls, the sticky jar of marmalade with the spoon in it.

"We had that stuff called Bar-le-Duc to-day for lunch," she began. "I don't think so much of it. It's terribly expensive. Are you all right, Sandra?" she asked, suddenly, uneasy eyes on her daughter's face. "You certainly must of slept!"

"I'm fine," Sandra answered gallantly, dragging the words out over burning plowshares. "I'm starving!" she added. But after all she but nibbled the cheese and the rolls, her mother noted, and drank one cup of weak hot tea after another.

"You don't want to go to a picture!" Flossy predicted, in brave disappointment. But Alexandra, surprisingly, was all for the movie, and liked it so much that she sat through the first part of it again, listening to dreamy music, watching the lovers on the screen.

"That part of it where she was falling in love with her brother-in-law was good," Flossy said, walking home.

"Wasn't it?"

"But you'd think her sister would have thrown her out of the house, carrying on that way!"

"Perhaps she couldn't help it, Flossy."

"Anyone could."

A silence, while they moved along the littered black sidewalks under the night lights.

"Want a sandwich, Sandra?"

"Not for me. But if you'd like one——"

"No; I'm not hungry."

They were in their own room and undressing when Sandra said:

"A girl might not be friendly to a man, Flossy; she might not want even to see him. That would be in her own hands. But falling in love—falling in love——"

Her voice lingered on the words; she roused herself from thought.

"Wouldn't that be something different again?" she asked.

"You mean love at first sight?" the older woman demanded, flatly.

"Well, not exactly. She might have seen the man, met him—all that. Just as this girl did her brother-in-law. But she might never have had that—that special feeling——"

"She knew mighty well what was happening to her!" Flossy said virtuously, in the pause. "It wouldn't have happened if she hadn't let it happen."

"It wasn't—much fun—for her," Alexandra said slowly.

"Well, it was at the end, when his wife got killed," Flossy offered.

"Yes, it was at the end. But that was a picture. People don't get killed in real life."

Mrs. Trumbull had put out all the lights except the reading lamp above the bed. She had opened the window on the grimy court, and the dirty Nottingham curtains were moving to and fro in the cool autumn night wind.

The transom into the gloomy hall was opened, too; a current of air would move through the room all night.

"Listen, Sandra, you haven't got a crush on anyone, have you?" the mother demanded.

Sandra laughed quite naturally, as she jumped into bed.

"No, darling, positively not. I assure you," she said, and if there was a fine note of irony in her voice it was lost on her mother. "I assure you," Sandra repeated, "that I have not got a crush on anyone!"

She lay awake, on her back, her arms locked behind her head, and stared into the dim spaces of shadow and light that were the big room.

"No—I haven't got a crush on anyone," she thought. "This isn't a crush. . . . Why, you poor fool, you're beginning to—to like Carter Cavendish."

That was it. The conviction seized upon her with all the force of a finished fact. Alexandra was conscious of exasperation and amusement; she was also conscious of something like an odd little thrill of pleasure. That was it—and what a fool! Falling in love with the vice president——

"Sap!" she said, half-aloud.

"What say, darling?" Floss mumbled, rousing.

"Nothing." Alexandra lay wide-awake, thinking, oddly pleased with the situation. "You idiot," she reproached herself. "You poor fool—that's what it's all about—cutting out his picture, and going into spasms every time he comes out of his office. *That's* what it's all about. . . . And this," she told her soul solemnly, after a long, long while—"this is what it feels like, at last. This funny, tickly feeling in one's heart. Everything—so important. Everything—trembly. . . . Funny—to-day's changed everything."

It had to end there, of course. The day had been strange, important—but it was over. She had had an unexpected experience, emotionally, but there could be no more of it. The complete folly of nursing sentimental feelings for Carter Cavendish would put her in the Gertrude Curtis class —an unthinkable humiliation.

No, the thing was to get up the next morning, brisk and businesslike, and enjoy the usual session with scented soap and hairbrush and hot coffee, and read the paper, and start for the office, just as usual. Sandra tried to laugh at herself as she threaded the wet, awakening streets on her way to the office. At nine o'clock her neighborhood was still half asleep; the drug stores, the cigar stands were open, but the restaurants were being cleaned, the sidewalks washed, the little ticket offices of the theaters were barred and empty. Nothing was started for the day except Alexandra Trumbull in her brown tweeds, her brown hat, her worn shoes, her washable chamois gloves.

"Suppose I do love him?" she thought, walking along. "It won't hurt him and it won't kill me."

That was the attitude to take. A fierce "What-of-it?" would work the cure. And in the end this awakening to the thrill, the reality, of love would be of value. She thought that she could never go back to the old skeptical ignorance again; she felt old, wise. Love was the only truth in life; everything was different when one loved. That was living, that was learning, and she would welcome living and learning at any price.

But how her world had changed! It was as if clouded glass had been removed from between it and her eyes. Things stood out in clear outlines now, and the girl who was Alexandra Trumbull clearest of all.

She saw herself, a tall, indifferently content docile girl, moving through all the years between twelve and twenty, liking idleness, liking the comfortable squalor of the back bedroom, with a bag of candy and a book, liking the attentions of boys, whether expressed only by eloquent glances in the street or murmured over the bulwark of her mother's guardian form in the movies. She saw herself gradually introducing her own different standards here and there, as much to her own surprised amusement as that of her mother. Flossy had indulgently observed the finer personal habits, the little niceties of pronunciation affected by her child, without ever suspecting that Sandra's way was better than her own way. They were two completely different persons; Flossy had never criticized or attempted to influence anyone, least of all her daughter. Sandra, reading, studying, changing, had only done what was natural for her to do.

But now she saw the chasm that the years had channeled between her and her mother; she saw that not one thing in her life was right for the woman who loved Carter Cavendish.

She wanted to be perfect now, and live in some simple, perfect environment. A garden, an old butler, books, a frail old grandmother, a splendid judge or a doctor for a father, all these came into Sandra's twenty-one-year-old dream as she walked to the office on the day she knew first that she liked Carter Cavendish too well, that she must put him out of her head.

The office was just as usual; cool and wide in the early winter morning; radiators were clanking, but the day was clear and warm, windows were open everywhere. The girls were arriving and getting their desks in order; yesterday's letters, which old Mr. Runyon had given her late in the afternoon, lay in a neat pile on Sandra's desk; everything seemed reassuringly commonplace and normal.

Nothing to do but go straight ahead as if nothing had happened. As a matter of fact, nothing *had* happened. Little Myra Byrnes, looking somewhat less tearful than usual, came to balance on the edge of Sandra's flat-topped desk, and pass the time of day.

"I've got a word I don't understand here in my notes, Miss Trumbull."

"I probably don't know it, either."

"Well, I know it, as far as that goes. I mean, I've heard it. But I always thought it was a swear word," Myra Byrnes said, anxiously.

"A swear word!" Alexandra echoed, with her slow smile.

"Well, it's 'confounded,'" Myra explained. "Isn't that a swear word? It says 'this issue must not be confounded'—and that doesn't make sense to me."

"That could mean 'confused,' there," Alexandra explained.

"You mean my notes are confused?"

"No, I mean that the issue mustn't be confused with some other issue, d'you see?"

After awhile Myra saw.

"Are you English, Miss Trumbull?"

"Am I? No. Born right here in San Francisco."

"You talk as if you were English."

"My father was. But I hardly remember him."

"I think you're wonderful, you know!" Myra exclaimed, in a sudden shy rush.

Sandra smiled at her, amazed.

"You think *I* am?"

"Yes, I do!" Myra persisted.

"I don't know why," Sandra protested. But her sudden color showed that she was not displeased.

"You're so tall and you're so—lovely, so different from the rest of us!" Myra said ardently, in a quick, laughing, embarrassed rush. "You talk so different from the rest of us, and you're so kind; you're like someone just playing at being poor, at being a stenographer!"

"You little idiot!" Sandra said affectionately. But long after the impulsive little Irish girl had gone back to her own work, the memory of her tribute kept Sandra's heart warm. She worked on in a happy dream that had little to do with the office routine of Cavendish & Bartlett.

"Is Miss Curtis here, do you know?" The voice brought her out of her reverie with a shock. Her heart began to beat fast, she felt her throat close and her hands grow wet as she looked up to see Carter Cavendish pausing, with his hands full of papers, a few feet away from her desk.

Somehow she answered him, somehow told him that Miss Curtis was up in the office of Mr. Peter Cavendish; New York had been calling. Perhaps she did not entirely betray herself, perhaps he did not suspect anything wrong, but Sandra did not know. All the painstaking work of forgetting him, and more, had to be done over again. She was shaken to the innermost fibers of her being, her senses were moving about in a wild confusion, her hands were cold and her head feverish. Sandra sat with her forehead resting on her palms.

"Anything wrong, Miss Trumbull?"

This was the girl at the next desk.

"My head began suddenly to ache," Sandra said, smiling. She went to work again.

CHAPTER THREE

"LISTEN," said Betty Cavendish, with a warning glance at the auction players. "Don't talk too loud. Carter's home."

"Carter is?" pretty Mab Fulton asked, arching her clipped and molded eyebrows.

"Yes. My dear," explained Betty, dramatically, shuffling cards busily, with beautifully groomed hands whose slim tips were dyed with vermilion, "he was brought home this morning in a taxi!"

"Oh, for heaven's sake, Betty," protested stout Rose Bray, pushing back her chair.

"No, no, no; it's all right," the wife hastened to explain, arresting the game by keeping her hand laid on the dealt cards. "He was in a bump, and he didn't want it to get into the papers. He hurt his ankle, that's all. Riggs says he'll have to lay up for a few days."

"Hurt him?" asked lovely Helen Peabody, sympathetic eyes wide.

"No; he says it doesn't hurt him at all. We kept Riggs for lunch, and he and Carter were simply killing," Betty said, now studying her hand. "They told some stories—well! You can imagine. Now Carter's supposed to be resting. Partner, I'll start off with two hearts."

"How long will Carter have to be laid up?" Helen asked, in the next deal.

"Oh, only a few days. I hope only a few days," Betty

amended it, scoring, "for you know what a man is around the house! He wanted to keep Patsy home——"

"Maybe he'd like to cut into the game, Betty?"

"I asked him, scared to death that he would. But he's working."

"Poor old Cart in a smash!" Mab mused. "No bid."

"He was trying to get Pete and Fred Fargo to come over and play to-night."

"Where is he, Betty?"

"Fixed up in the library, there." Mrs. Cavendish jerked her pretty head in the direction of the adjoining room. "He had a lot of papers sent up here from the office, and he's working like mad."

"Whoever's dummy——" stout Mrs. Bray murmured—"whoever's dummy—Is it me? I pass—can go in and see him now and then."

"He likes to be let alone," his wife suggested. "Cart's queer, you know—cool about everything. You know what a fuss most men make about anything; he never does.—Three passes? I pass, too; let's have a goulash.—That time he was thrown off—no, you on top now, Helen, and then Mab, that's right!—that time he was thrown," she continued, now rapidly dealing by fives, "he wouldn't let me baby him or fuss over him."

"You're not much of a fusser or babyer, Betty," Mab Fulton reminded her.

"Oh, I'm a marvelous nurse!" Betty claimed animatedly. "I adore fussing round a sickroom."

"Carter's never been ill, has he?"

"Never but that once, and then he was in a hospital. No," said Betty, "I don't mind regular illness. But when it comes to a man's being round all the time, crabbed and critical—excuse me. When they haven't anything else to do, they grouch."

"Will Bray's got the divinest disposition I ever saw!" Rose Bray said, with the ready tears in her eyes. Rose had inherited the Brink millions; Will Bray had been the adored football player of his senior year; his wife still felt humbly surprised that the penniless stunning young sheik from Stockton had selected her for the honor of being his life partner.

"You couldn't baby Jud Fulton," Mrs. Fulton, who was divorced, observed idly.

"There was a man," she began again presently, for her decree was recent, and she was still in the defensive stage, "there was a man who hadn't one spark of affection or appreciation in him!"

The women who had been her bridesmaids ten years ago let this pass unchallenged, although more than one of them was fond of Jud Fulton and enjoyed his affectionate friendship in return.

"The ideal relationship between Mother and Dad spoiled me so," confessed Mab, taking off her eyeglasses, making sudden emotional appeal to the sympathy of her hearers, "that it was simply a revelation to me, the rough way the Fultons talked to each other! I was paralyzed. Why, nobody in our family ever—ever talked like that! We always made so much of each other———"

"It's your bid, Mab," Rose said.

"I know it is!" She settled her eyeglasses again. Mab was an assiduous embroiderer, and for reading and fine needlework and cards her eyes had to have help. "*You* remember the way he acted that day you were at the house last year, Betty?" Mrs. Fulton demanded suddenly, not quite done with the subject.

"I should say I do," Betty responded. "No bid."

"No bid?" Mrs. Fulton mused, studying her cards. "You —say—no—bid———"

"Hoenig!" Betty called suddenly.

"I always adore that butler's name," Mab Fulton murmured, as the man came in. "I'd love to call a servant 'Honey'!"

"Hoenig, did Mr. Cavendish speak to you about sending to the station when Paul goes to get Miss Patsy after her violin lesson?" the mistress of the house was demanding.

"Yes, madam."

"Paul knows that Miss Curtis is coming down from the office this afternoon on the four-o'clock?"

"Yes, madam."

"Well, will you please ask Mr. Cavendish if he's keeping Miss Curtis for dinner? It's four o'clock now, and if he does, tell Belle dinner for two.—I *have* to go to Mrs. Rogers'; Mr. Cavendish sent word he couldn't come——"

"I really don't see how you do all you do, Betty," Rose Bray said admiringly, when the man was gone.

"My dear, I like it! I'm really a tremendously domestic person," Betty Cavendish reminded them animatedly. "I simply adore to keep Carter and the house and Patsy and Mother and my Junior League work and the Rummage Sale all going like a three-ring circus."

"Well, you're marvelous," Rose persisted. "I have Miss Looly," she added, her eyes watering as she smiled. "I don't know what I'd do without her. She talks to the servants, she manages the children, she buys my clothes—underclothes, you know, things like that—she tells me whether I'll need two trunks or just one and a suitcase; she's just marvelous."

The others all knew about Miss Looly, who had a sinecure as Rose's housekeeper, confidante, and companion. The game went on.

"Who's Miss Curtis, Betty?" someone asked.

"My dear, she's that perfectly priceless person who has been Cart's secretary ever since time began. She adores him.

of course," Betty said, smiling, "and all she asks is that he'll let her slave along after hours and let him off for tennis and polo. She cries whenever she speaks of him."

"She's madly in love with him, of course?" Helen Peabody asked curiously.

"Well, in a perfectly safe, insulated sort of way, she is," Betty admitted carelessly. "She doesn't—*quite*—" the wife went on demurely, "tell me to be very, very tender with him, because he is so rare, but she very nearly does!"

The others were amused; there was a pause in the game.

"Does he like her?" somebody asked.

"Oh, my dear, you know Cart! All women go mad about his black hair and his stutter."

"He doesn't stutter!" protested Helen, with a shocked laugh.

"He does when he's very much interested," Betty said.

"Yes, I know what you mean," Rose contributed. "I remember once at a dance—oh, this was years ago, I was about seventeen, home from school in New York—and Carter asked me who sent me some flowers, and I remember he sort of stuttered, and I was thrilled to death!"

"Look here, Rose, you never told me you and Carter had had intimate love scenes before!"

"Oh, now, listen, Betty," Mrs. Bray stammered, delighted at the implication, and almost stuttering herself in her confusion, "this was years ago!"

"I'll keep an eye on you nevertheless," Mrs. Cavendish warned her guest.

"Is Miss Curtis pretty, Betty?"

"No-o-o!" There was utter indifference in the wife's voice. "No. She's nice-looking, spectacled, older than Cart. Quite a lady, but not thrilling, do you see? Not exciting."

"That's what he tells *you*," hinted Mab. "But they get an awful stranglehold on the men, these office wives. It's propinquity. It was his office nurse who got Fred Terry away from Leila, you know, and she was a *fright*. He just saw her every day and talked over his business with her and everything, until he thought she was the Venus de Milo."

"Propinquity's a terrible thing," Betty admitted. "Once Mother had a man come in to teach me riding," she began suddenly, "when I was about sixteen. I'd had curvature or spine infection or something, and I never had ridden. Well, this instructor was a Frenchman, a peasant, sweaty and red-faced, and with the brain of an infant, mind you, but he had that Frenchy eye, you know, sizing you up, saying 'Mademoiselle, you are onlee a woman, aftaire all, and I am a man!' I don't mean he said it—he looked it. Well, after about three days, when he helped me off, he'd give my knee——"

"Betty, shut up!" protested her hearers, laughing.

"I mean it. Or he'd jam himself up against my arm, and have to grab me to keep me from falling; I tell you we had a grand time, and it was all propinquity! Mother got onto it and she fired him and I felt terribly; really, I mean it. But about a year later I saw him at the Polo Club—I had a crush on Rob Wilson then—and I give you my word that the mere sight of Pierre all but turned my stomach!"

"Betty, you're a terror!" Rose reproached her fondly.

"You may be sure I'm going to watch Patsy," Mrs. Cavendish said seriously. "No fooling, propinquity's the limit!"

"And what would you do if Cart got a stenographer who wasn't safe and sanitary?" Mab asked, idly, over her cards.

"I don't know," said his wife. "I wouldn't mind a crush. It'd do him good. And anyway, I trust Cart."

"But just the same," interpolated the sentimental Mrs. Bray, "Cart's got that—that——"

"Look at her blush!" smiled Mrs. Peabody, as the speaker floundered.

"Well, I don't mean that he ever had a case on me," struggled on Mrs. Bray, laughing self-defensively. "But Cart has got—or at least *I* think he has, that—that thing you spoke of—that thing the French riding master had, that look—'you're a woman'——"

The others laughed. But Helen Peabody said seriously: "You're right, Rose. He *has*."

"Cart's divine with women," Mrs. Fulton said. "You always think he doesn't know you're alive. He's always dragging you round to tennis and golf matches when you'd much rather sit and talk. I think that's what Rose means; he gets you because he doesn't care whether he gets you or not."

"It's the truth," Betty Cavendish spoke up suddenly. "You girls think it's a joke, but Cart doesn't care much about women. They make a fuss over him; he doesn't see it. This poor girl in the office, she runs her legs off for him, and I have to remind him to send her a Christmas present!"

"You're awfully sensible about it, Betty," one of the other women said. "That's the way you hold him, by not being jealous."

"Oh, I'd be jealous fast enough if I had any reason to be!" the hostess assured them laughing. "Come on now, girls," she interrupted herself, briskly, "are we going to finish this rubber before tea, or aren't we? It was yours, Helen."

They were playing in the conservatory porch of the Cavendish home, an old-fashioned, comfortable country manor hidden away among the curving roads, the oaks and eucalyptus trees, the deep gardens of San Mateo's most aristocratic quarter. Potted begonias and palms lined the pleasant, warm apartment; a heavy rope rug was on the red tiles of the floor; Betty's magnificent macaw walked and muttered on his gay perch. Through the uncurtained windows that formed three of the walls of the room, the troubled winter sky, red with sunset, and the restlessly moving garden trees could be seen; a blanket of fog was moving slowly down over the range of the southern hills.

The fourth side of the room was merely a wide arch that opened upon one of the comfortable, handsomely furnished drawing rooms; all the rooms in the house were comfortable and richly decorated in the style of a bygone day. At the time of their wedding, eleven years ago, Carter Cavendish and his wife had moved into the place that had been his mother's and his grandmother's home. They had done little to change it since; it was not the sort of house that lent itself easily to change. There was an elegant spaciousness about the ceilings, a permanence about the marble fireplaces and heavy balustrades, that did not suggest alteration.

Betty sometimes said that in the event of the death of Carter's mother and grandmother, keeping house now in San Francisco, eighteen miles away, she, Betty, would have the old Cavendish place made French by the simple addition of plaster and green paint. But for old times' sake the mansion was perfection in the old ladies' eyes, and Betty good-naturedly let them think she liked it too. The senior Mrs. Cavendish paid the gardener; her mother, the aged Madame Hough, Carter's grandmother, paid for Patsy's violin lessons and her riding horse, paid Betty's chauffeur, had sent her her town car, and sent Carter at Christmas a check that took care of his duck club and polo expenses. The young Cavendishes considered the first article of their creed the advisability of never offending these important members of the family, and for the rest considered themselves, and were considered by their entire acquaintance, **as** extremely lucky.

Betty had always been lucky, she said. Hers was one of the forceful, confident natures that draw what they like from life. Everyone had conspired from the hour of her birth to confirm Betty in the opinion that she was beloved, amusing, delightful to have about, adequate and more than adequate to the demands of the varying rôles of daughter, friend, sweetheart, wife, neighbor, mother. Perhaps Betty's greatest good fortune lay in the fact that, unlike her circle, she was never bored; everyone who came near her was conscious immediately of her insatiable egotistical zest for life.

Now she had just finished a triumphant rubber, and was about to lead the auction players in to the fire, for tea, when there was an interruption. Patsy came home, and had to be encircled by her mother's arm and kissed on her little brown ear, even while she shyly greeted Mother's friends. Patsy was going upstairs to do her homework, and Anne was with her, but Anne didn't want to come in. And Miss Trumbull had come, Mother.

"Miss Trumbull?"

"From Dad's office, Mother."

"Oh? I thought it was Miss Curtis. Well, you run along, honey, and we'll have our tea. You and Anne can have cocoa or anything you ask Belle for. How was the violin?"

"Oh, he says I have been loafing lately." Patsy laughed joyously, and showed the space where a baby tooth had been.

"Oh, you mustn't do that," her mother smiled.

She turned to her companions.

"The infant's getting to be quite extraordinary with her music," she said in a lowered voice. "I want you all to hear her play some time." To the child she added:

"Well, run along, dear. I'll be up presently."

Patsy gave the group a general curtsey, and escaped, leaving a murmur of "Isn't she adorable?" behind her.

A moment later the four women were settling themselves about a luxuriously furnished tea table, beside the fire, when an unexpected voice spoke somewhat hesitantly from the doorway.

"Mrs. Cavendish?"

The others turned to see a tall girl standing in the glow of the early lamplight; a girl who looked all cream and gold and pale brown, in oatmeal-brown tweeds, brown hat, and trim brown pumps. Her pale brown hair, cream skin, and strange golden eyes repeated the note. Her costume was simplicity's self; she wore no rings, no earrings; an immaculate plain frill, falling away to show her rounded creamy throat was the only softening touch in blouse, suit, or hat. But there was a suggestion of something individual, something vital, in her appearance, of which all the others were conscious.

"I'm Miss Trumbull from the office," she said, expectantly, unsmiling. "They told me—your man told me—that Mr. Cavendish was in the library. But I don't find him there."

"Oh, yes," Betty said, getting to her feet. "He expected Miss Curtis," she added, a little confusedly. "The doctor wants him to keep quiet for a day or two—and I know he telephoned Miss Curtis——"

"She had gone home; we couldn't locate her," Sandra explained, with a glimpse of her big white teeth.

Before Mrs. Cavendish could speak again, Carter himself limped in and stood beside the girl in the doorway.

"Hoenig said you were here," he said. "I was telephoning the office this minute; I was afraid you'd missed your train. We'll go into the library."

He nodded easy greetings to his wife's guests. He and Sandra disappeared together, and Miss Fulton drew a deep breath.

"Do you know, Betty," she observed dryly, "I didn't note the eyeglasses and the age. If that girl is a day over twenty I'll eat——"

"That isn't Miss Curtis, you goose!" Betty Cavendish said with a laugh, as she poured tea. "That's just one of the office girls; what did she say the name was? I never happened to see her before."

"I'll bet you never happened to see her before!" agreed Mab, significantly.

"She's gorgeous," Helen Peabody said, simply.

"Has she got a perfectly safe, sanitary crush on Carter, too?" stout Rose Bray, already devouring caviar sandwiches, asked innocently.

"I don't know," Betty laughed. "I'll have to make it my business to find out."

CHAPTER FOUR

HALF AN HOUR LATER Betty put her head into the library door; Miss Trumbull was just going. She had several letters in her hand, and a leather briefcase under her arm.

"It seems a shame not to give you some dinner," Betty said, vaguely. She was annoyed by not knowing exactly what one did, under the circumstances. Immediately she added, "Cart, Pete's here, and Fred Fargo and Doc Riggs. They're all going to stay."

"Grand," Carter said, reaching for his cane, limping to the door with both women. "Paul's taking Miss Trumbull to the train. Is that all right by you?" he asked his wife.

"Oh, quite. But I'm afraid you'll not get into town until nearly seven, Miss Trumbull."

Sandra raised her gold-brown eyes. She looked steadily at the other woman, spoke out of a dream.

"That doesn't matter. My mother always waits for me anyway."

"If Miss Curtis's too busy I may have to ask you to come down again; we'll make it the morning and keep you to lunch," Carter said.

"You were only so fortunate not to have had a more serious accident!" Sandra observed politely.

She went down the steps and got into the car. All the way into San Francisco she sat close to the train window, one elbow on the sill, her cheek in her hand, her eyes fixed absently on the winter evening scenes slipping so rapidly by.

Houses and lights; little motorcars racing behind their own bright eyes up and down. Darkness, and the bulk of flying trees and fog-swathed hills. Alexandra did not change her position; she did not move; she was not conscious of thought. She breathed steadily, but a little hard. Her big white teeth lightly caught her lower lip; the flanges of her finely cut nostrils opened and shut. About her the unsensed world whirled in a cloud of star dust.

After awhile she was telling Flossy about it, over the table d'hôte at Roselli's. For her mother's benefit she described the beautiful gardens, so perfectly groomed at this unfriendly season, the sunset shining into the library, its big leather chairs, its sleepy fire; the ease, the service, the comfort of the Cavendish house.

"It makes all this—ghastly!" her thoughts added. She did not say it aloud. She played with her thick soup in its heavy plate, buttered her stiff crust of sour bread, rumpled her coarse, damp, gray-white napkin. Two friends, reporters from the *Examiner,* were dining at Roselli's; they came over to join Flossy and Sandra. Flossy was pleasantly cordial, but not effusive. Her daughter knew her thoughts: such fellers never had any money, everything had to be Dutch, and newspapermen were notoriously impecunious husbands. Still, she liked to talk with them about recent divorces and theatrical changes, and Sandra looked at them with her strange, gold-brown eyes, and smiled occasionally her slow, mysterious smile.

She was never very talkative. But to-night she was more silent than usual. Magic ran in her veins. The intoxicating sweetness of this afternoon's experience wrapped her in reverie. The big house, all order and sweetness and color of flowers, the silent library with its books and leather chairs, the coldness of sunset sky and winter branches outside, the softness of summer within, still held her. She still heard the voice of Carter Cavendish, still saw him, brown and lean and smiling, facing her across the table.

Passion consumed her like a fire; she did not know what it was; she had never felt it before. In previous casual affairs with this young man or that, Sandra had always been the loved rather than the loving; she had supposed it would always be that way. If she had thought of love at all it had been only as a deeper liking, a different feeling from her love for her mother, perhaps, but still only love—a controllable and enjoyable new emotion that should some day enlarge and enrich her life.

Impossible that she should recognize it in the feeling that was now absorbing her, soul, mind, and body. Sandra did not so recognize it; she would have been affronted and horrified at the thought.

She knew that she felt oddly awakened; felt as if she were seeing and feeling the things of earth for the first time, or in some entirely new and different fashion. And yet she experienced at the same time a curious lightness and giddiness, a delicious vertigo that seemed to be carrying her away from all anchorage. It was impossible to swallow food; food was suddenly only so much plaster and sawdust. It was impossible to take interest in what Kane O'Neill and Spike Whiffin were saying. But at the same time all this— the little Italian restaurant and the newspaper boys and Flossy—was all delightfully absorbing; Sandra's long hand, lying on the table, was fascinating, too, and Sandra's voice, when she occasionally used it, was full of cadences that enchanted her. She raised her eyes and saw herself in a flawed mirror that streaked her clear pure skin and her bright hair with spots of white. It made small difference; she was wonderful to-night.

Sometimes her thoughts followed the conversation for a few seconds; she was glad of that. It meant that she could presently rush back, in her thoughts, to the library and the soft lights and wide dim spaces of the old Cavendish home, rush back to the memory of a smiling brown-faced man seated on the other side of a wide, bare, leather-topped table, handling papers in strong brown hands, talking mere matters of business in a voice that would ring in Alexandra Trumbull's head for many an hour to come.

"Shall I ask Miss Curtis to telephone you to-morrow about that?" she had asked at one point.

"No; you look that up and telephone me, will you?" Carter had answered promptly, almost absently, as he studied a report. "She very likely hasn't got the data ready. She may have it, though, he had added upon consideration; "you might speak to her about it. I'll be in, in a day or two, anyway."

And he had glanced openly, innocently, across the table at the glowing face under the brown hat, the gold-brown eyes, the slow smile that showed Sandra's big white teeth, the loose soft frill of white silk that left the round column of her throat bare.

"Just one more obscure stenographer in love with her boss!" Sandra thought, walking to work the next day. "Carter Cavendish doesn't know I'm alive!" But even that consideration did not keep her heart from singing, her feet from touching the dirty wet morning sidewalks of Ellis Street with an almost dancing step, her eyes from finding the world miraculously beautiful and thrilling.

But not only was Carter Cavendish, as it happened, thoroughly aware that Sandra was alive; Betty was thinking of her, too. With a surprise only equal to what would have been Sandra's own, they had found themselves, after her first visit to the old San Mateo house, bringing her name more than once into their talks together.

On the surface all was well between the young Cavendishes. Their lives ran in an ordered, brilliant, conventional groove; a wide groove that included a beautiful home, servants, cars, country clubs, duck clubs, trips, dinners, tennis, golf, polo, theater—everything indeed that would have seemed to Betty Finchley desirable, when at twenty she had married the twenty-two-year-old Carter Cavendish eleven years ago.

They had enough money, they were both good-looking, they were popular. And Betty, in the fourth year of her marriage, had duly added to this full cup the requisite child; only one. That one was the engaging, black-curled gypsy of a Patsy. Carter adored her. Betty was not only an adoring but a capable mother. Her complete adequacy included teachers, friends, music, dentist, amusements for Patsy. The child had a gift for music; her mother assiduously cultivated it. Some day, Betty prophesied, Patsy would astonish more than San Mateo with her violin.

But when Patsy was about five, Betty had made a change in the fashion of her own life. The world never saw it; that small fraction of Betty's world that suspected it attached no particular significance to it. Betty, quite simply and finally, ceased to be her husband's wife.

She had inaugurated some changes in their own suite; enlarging a dressing room, putting on a sleeping porch where the old sewing room used to be, repainting, repapering, reupholstering. During these changes Betty had gone in to sleep with Patsy in the nursery, and Carter had had the big room that had been his and Peter's in their boyhood.

And after the changes were made, Betty had quite simply taken possession of the wide silk-covered, pillow-laden French bed that formed the central motive for the reconstructed room, and had asked Carter to stay where he was. Marriage, as marriage, was over for Betty.

The impulse that had carried her into wifehood, an emotion strangely mixed with pride in a good social and financial bargain, interest in trousseau and wedding presents, had been forgotten long ago. Whatever passion she had known in Carter's arms as his bride had not been deep; Betty had always been conscious of the need of becoming lights, becoming laces, becoming phrases, even in the most sacred hours of their love. Before they had been man and wife for a week, she had surprised him by tears over a missing lace stocking, by her insistence upon a trip to a beauty parlor. Carter had been too young to know exactly what he had missed; he had been very proud of the always lovely, always smart and smiling and social little wife.

But not many years had gone by before he had sensed the truth about her: Betty was incapable of true married love. Her only affectionate moments with him were when their group was about to admire the complete subjection of the big man to the saucy little woman. She never abandoned herself when they were alone; she chilled and angered him with a display of reluctance, of boredom, of annoyance; she bargained shrewdly, with herself for pay.

"If I'm terribly, terribly nice to you, can I have it," she would plead, for a new fur coat or a new car. And, so pleading, she would establish herself and her filmy laces in his arms and press against his cheek the kisses, and whisper into his ear the endearments for which he was always hungry.

"Ah, Betty, honey, you do love me?"

"Course I love you, silly!"

But at the first hint of love for love's sake only, he came to recognize a quick, suspicious look in her bright eyes. Betty had never loved anyone wholly, never would. She loved her pretty, dainty, clever self, she loved the body that was at the height of its beauty, loved it in dinner velvets, in silver slippers and fillets, loved it in bathing suits, in sports clothes and frail underwear; she loved her town suits, trim and tailored and smart, with the silvery fox fur slung across her shoulders.

To secure these good things, had they been jeopardized, she would have done anything. But comfortably married to Carter and admired by his friends, a favorite with his mother and grandmother, the mother of his beloved child, Betty was quite safe. Most of the women she knew had also taken her attitude, good-naturedly but firmly, in the fifth or sixth year of marriage, and, except for unusual circumstances they were true to their decision. Physically, they were all alike, starved into one mold of beauty, flat-breasted, carefully curled of hair, carefully rouged, painted, and clipped. Such energy as their sports, gymnasium work, and card games left them was for other men than their husbands. The bloom had left the legitimate relationship years before; they discussed their affairs, marital and otherwise, quite frankly, debating between bridge hands whether a divorce or another child would best accomplish the desired end of travel, more clothes, more allowance.

Betty was indeed better than most. She was always sweet to Carter; there was in her whole position a disarming kindness.

"You wouldn't want me if I didn't love you, Cart," was Betty's argument. She had long ago persuaded him that there was even something admirable in her stand; she told him and told everyone that she liked Carter. She said enthusiastically that he played square, and she adored that in a man. But at the slightest hint of tenderness she gently disengaged herself with a "Please, Cart, let's not be silly!"

Carter, as a younger man, had been angered, puzzled, hurt by turns. But now, for more than two years, he had accepted Betty's terms. He decided that love in its full power did not last long, and when it was gone there were other things. One made the most of those: business, duck-shooting, polo, theaters.

"In Europe," Betty had of late begun to hint, "you would quite naturally—find someone else."

"Find someone else!"

"Certainly, Cart. It would be taken for granted. They marry sensibly there and have families. And then both husband and wife do—well, as they like, and nobody makes the ridiculous blue-nosed fuss that we do here."

"I don't consider decency—fidelity—just blue-nosed fussing, somehow."

"Well, you certainly don't think that a man and a woman who marry at twenty are bound to spend the next thirty years pretending they feel something they *don't* feel, do you?"

"I don't know," he would sometimes say bewilderedly; "I suppose I thought that if a woman loved a man she liked to—oh, have him round her room, talking and laughing. It always seemed to me part of it."

"We had that, and we adored each other, and I had Patsy," Betty might summarize it sensibly. "And now we still like each other and the baby and our home—why sentimentalize about it? Let's be sensible and say honestly, 'that's that.' I hope I'm going to meet men I get crazy about, and I hope you'll get crushes on other women—what's the harm?"

At first it had hurt him terribly; when it stopped hurting, matters were worse than before. There was a deadness, an apathy about it now that was less endurable than pain. All the glamor of books and movies, all the love stories of the poets, simply—were not there. Love did not mean much to women, and when a woman ceased wanting a man, somehow he ceased caring, too.

He was the less concerned because this arrangement, or something similar, was the common fate of his group. All the "girls" were alike; no man had tenderness, devotion, delusion for his daily fare.

And Betty was clever and pretty, always beautifully dressed and animated and popular, always ready for bridge or a lunch at the club, or a dinner dance. His home was comfortable and hospitable, his gun had come from England, from the most expensive gunmaker in the world, his car was always a source of pride, and his daughter was a darling. Carter told himself that he could find no fault with his life.

Betty had for some time been saying that Patsy should be taken to Germany to go on with her violin work and learn German and French. All the mothers in Betty's circle had somewhat similar ambitions, and most of them planned to spend these years while the child was "getting her French" pleasantly established in Paris. But, reinforced by his magnificent mother and still more magnificent grandmother, Carter had managed so far to discourage that idea. He wanted his little girl at home, riding her pony and having her fun with the other kids, not isolated among a lot of prim schoolkeeping old maids in some foreign country. Betty had fretted and hinted and pleaded in vain.

On the night that Sandra had come down to San Mateo, when Betty returned from her late dinner party in her furry wrap and wilted orchids, she came into Carter's room. He was reading by his fire, the lame foot propped up on a chair.

"Fine, fine," he said to her perfunctory inquiries, closing his book and looking up at her. "Rigg's coming over to loosen the bandages after a party somewhere, and that's why I'm up."

He could see that Betty was tired, and annoyed about something. She was not listening; presently she burst forth into resentful speech.

"Cart," she began, "I know we decided not to discuss this again, but I *wish* you'd listen to reason. The girls have just been telling me that Rose *is* taking Barbara and Catherine in January, and Louise says she's going too, and taking Harriet."

"Going?"

"To Europe, Cart, of course!"

"Oh, is that so?" Cart asked idly. But his mouth hardened a little.

"Louise doesn't have to ask anyone, the lucky devil," Betty went on, discontentedly. "She's divorced, she can do as she likes! She's already taken the Hamilton apartment on the *Ile St. Louis*—it sounds too marvelous! As for Rose, she says Will lets her do just whatever she thinks best."

There was a pause. Then Carter said slowly,

"I know. But it seems like losing the kid, and you too."

"But it would only be for a year, Cart. And Patsy really needs someone who can go on with her violin work. Pellegrini is all very well, but he can't give her the groundwork she needs. And if it were for her good——"

"It doesn't seem to me it would be for her good. She might be terribly unhappy over there." His tone was determined; they had often been over this ground before.

"She wouldn't be! She'd adore it."

Betty dropped into a chair, frowning down at the fingers with which she traced lines on its square red-leather arm. Her small, finely featured face was jaded, her eyes mutinous.

Carter stretched out his hand to take her free hand, dangling over the chair arm; she jerked it petulantly away.

"No use for me, huh?" he asked, smiling a little.

"It isn't that; I'm tired," Betty answered shortly.

"Cart," she asked suddenly, "who's Miss Trumbull?"

For a minute his heavy dark brows went up in surprise. Then he laughed.

"One of the girls from the office."

"I never saw her there," Betty commented.

"She's been with us about a year or so, I guess."

"She's a beautiful creature," Betty commented thoughtfully. And in an absent tone she added, "Whoever marries *that* girl will have all the loving he wants! Cart," she continued, idly, "why didn't you marry some girl like that, a girl who would just live for one thing, to love and be loved?"

He was too genuinely surprised to show the amusement and the slight sense of shock her words stirred in him.

"Why on earth do you say that of Miss Trumbull?"

"Doesn't she strike *you* as that sort?" Betty asked innocently.

"What sort?"

"Oh, the loving sort," Betty answered ineloquently.

"Does she you?"

"Oh, heavens!" his wife exclaimed, almost impatiently. "Anyone can see it. She was just born to spoil some man, wait for him, feed him his supper, adore him. I mean," Betty added, "there are women—not many of them—but there *are* women who love men the way—well, the way men like to be loved!"

"You know the way men like to be loved then?" Carter asked with an edge to his voice.

" 'Mah baby don't want anything but me!' " Betty quoted, from a song of the moment.

Carter was regarding her steadily, an odd look in his narrowed eyes, a grim line touching his mouth.

"The idea being that while you and Patsy are in France I have an affair with Miss Trumbull?" he asked, slowly.

Betty giggled.

"I wouldn't mind your taking her to lunch," she offered.

"Well, I won't!" Carter said shortly.

"Well," Betty admitted, "I don't suppose you will!"

There was a silence. Then Carter said, disgustedly:

"My God, I don't know where you women think you get off, sometimes! I suppose you'd be tickled to death to have me fall for some other woman!"

"Well," Betty persisted, unabashed, "you can't say I'm jealous. She knows, of course, that you're married. But perhaps you could take her to lunch somewhere—I don't know. Only—she is certainly a gorgeous-looking person!"

She gathered her draperies together, passed his chair, and paused to put a butterfly kiss on the top of his dark hair as she went out. Carter caught at her hand and drew her down for a closer embrace. But with the light little laugh he knew so well she disengaged herself and was gone.

CHAPTER FIVE

IT WAS A WEEK LATER that Carter saw Alexandra Trumbull again. He was busy in his office, dividing his attention between a heap of letters and the constantly ringing telephone, when a familiar voice said vibrantly, "Mr. Runyon would like you to O. K. this, Mr. Cavendish," and he looked up to see her standing on the other side of the desk.

"Oh, hello, Miss Trumbull!" Carter said, surprised to feel a sudden odd confusion of his senses.

She answered something, of course, and he said something more himself. But her gold-brown eyes said much more than her words; there was friendliness in the tones of her voice, appeal in the beauty of her shining hair, her transparent skin, her white throat. Carter afterward could not quite remember what he said, or what she said. The light in her concerned smile, as she asked for the injured foot, had an element of spontaneity, of warmth, of eagerness in it. But for Betty's surprising observations Carter knew he might not have noted it, but Betty had commented upon this girl's responsive friendliness, and now he saw it.

He thought of the girl at intervals during the day, remembering her clear, flushed face, with the high cheekbones and strange eyes, and the disarming quality of her smile. He remembered her aside to Miss Curtis, "Don't worry about it, Gertrude. I'll make sure." The insignificant phrase took on importance; he neither knew nor cared what it meant, but he recalled it a hundred times, said in the clear-clipped English voice. . . .

Two days later, going through the almost empty office at one o'clock, he saw Sandra alone at her desk and stopped to speak to her.

"Aren't you back early?"

"I haven't had my lunch. I'm just going."

"Come and have lunch with me," he said, without preamble. The words surprised him no less than they did her. He saw doubt flicker in her eyes, and saw her color come up. "I shouldn't have asked her," Carter thought, "and she shouldn't come."

But she had risen to her feet.

"Thank you; I'd love to," she said.

"This is pleasant!" Carter observed, when they were seated in one of the Palace Hotel's big luncheon rooms. He had instinctively brought her to the place where he usually lunched; the conviction of having acted rather hastily and unwisely was strong upon him; he must avoid the appearance of anything clandestine or irregular. Here, among the familiar tables and lights, everything seemed normal again, reassuring. Their table was inconspicuously placed; they could hear the music, watch the crowd without being conscious of observing eyes. Sandra, he thought, was lovely in the mellow shadows of the little table lamp; there was a faint flush of excitement on her cheeks; her hair shone gold under her brown hat.

Carter wondered what she was thinking. Had he surprised her, or was she so entirely ignorant of convention that she considered this perfectly natural? At all events she was taking it simply. She observed that she was starving, and ordered quickly and definitely.

"Oh, and maybe they have the delicious chocolate cake?" she ended. "I had dinner here once, a year ago at least, and they had the most delicious chocolate cake!—Sort of squares," she explained to the waiter, "with cream inside."

The waiter nodded; wrote.

"My income," said Sandra, looking at her companion—"my income does not run to dinners at the Palace. But a man named Katz, a theater manager—brought Flossy—brought my mother and me here, to talk about something."

She had been rather silent as they walked the few blocks from the office; so silent that Carter had wondered if she were regretting their little adventure. He was enchanted with this change in her; she was happy and at ease now, at all events.

"The manager of what theater?" he asked, smiling.

"The old Columbia," she answered. "He was putting a company on the road in stock."

"You were—you are an actress?" Carter asked, surprised.

"No; but my mother was." Sandra looked up from her jellied soup. "You wouldn't know her name," she told him composedly, with her slow smile.

"Did he want you to try it?" Carter persisted, his interest engaged by this glimpse of a life he did not know.

"Well, now and then they do," she answered, the pleasant look for which he had found the word "affectionate" lighting her face.

"But you don't want to?"

"No, I don't like the stage," she said. "Not for me."

"You're very young to decide."

"Twenty-one. You should start younger than that for the stage," she said.

"I should think it would be the very thing you would like."

"No; not when you've seen as much of it as I have. I was brought up in greenrooms—back-stage."

"Would it have a better future?"

They were not quite comfortable yet: Carter felt constrained and he saw that her hands were nervous and her color high. He thought that when this experience was over it would be a long time before he showed Miss Trumbull any attention again. It had been done on an impulse; not a very wise one.

"Well, I don't know. It never," Sandra observed thoughtfully—"it never had much of a future for *her*."

"And your father, was he an actor too?"

"No; my father was an Englishman who came out here to Los Gatos. I think,"—Sandra smiled, speaking more naturally now, and with her direct look—"I think his family paid him a hundred pounds a quarter to keep out of sight. I *think* that was it. He had a ranch in Los Gatos, and my mother went down to San José, playing in a stock company, and that's how they met. After he died somebody came over from England and settled with Mother and cleared the ranch. She rents it now; it's a prune ranch. Flossy said—I call my mother Flossy because that's what all her friends do." She looked up, explaining, looked down again. "Flossy said," she added, "that from the look she got at my father's cousin *she* would have paid a hundred pounds a quarter to *get* away from them!"

It was the first touch of humor he had seen in her; Carter laughed joyfully.

"Is your name English?"

"Trumbull? Isn't it?" she asked, surprised.

"I meant your own name."

"Oh. Alexandra? Alexandra Mary Fox Trumbull," she supplied promptly.

"As British as the British lion," Carter said.

Walking back after lunch they talked of books. He discovered that she read a great deal. When they were going up in the big office building she said that she must go on up to the filing department, and left him with one grateful nod and smile for thanks and good-bye. He got off at his own office floor with a sense of having done something at once stupid and dangerous. Pleasant as it was to lunch with those gold-brown eyes opposite him, to note the roundness of the white throat and the little feathers of gold curling up against the hat brim, it was not wise or kind. Upon sober second thought Carter rather wondered about the whole performance.

He loaned her a book; she read it and brought it back with a fresh, simple, unaffected comment that seemed to him an indication of her own fresh, simple, unspoiled heart. She asked him if he liked Shakespeare.

Carter, with a little compunction, said he had not opened a volume of Shakespeare since college days.

"I like Portia," Sandra said. "My mother had me study that part in a dramatic school once. But I like Katherine in *The Taming of the Shrew* best."

Just before Christmas Miss Curtis was kept at home by a heavy cold for three days; Sandra took her place.

"Ask Miss—ah, Trumbull—to come in," Carter had said. "She knows about this particular thing."

So he had Sandra for his companion for several hours a day. His associates and friends who came and went would comment on her when she was not in the room.

"That's a beautiful girl, Cart."

"Yes, she's handsome, isn't she? And she's a nice girl too, Miss Trumbull."

He did not ask her to go to luncheon again, but at Christmas time he sent her a set of Conrad. Floss, seeing the girl stand thoughtfully and a little pale over the opened box, was slightly suspicious.

"What's that mean, Sandra?"

"I don't know," Sandra said.

"You don't suppose he sends every girl in the office a present?"

"I've been helping him since Miss Curtis was ill."

"And does he talk about books?"

"Well—yes."

It was a Sunday—Christmas Eve. Floss was going to a movie, but Sandra thought she would rather go out and walk first, joining her mother in the theater later.

"I'll be in the loges, down front, left-hand side," Floss said, as she always said.

"I'll find you."

Sandra walked out Ellis Street to the park. The day was sunless, silent, mysterious. Voices sounded odd and loud in the quiet streets. Trolley cars jangled by her; churchgoers streamed along the sidewalks. Christmas trees and wreaths showed behind plain bay windows; men with carts were selling mistletoe and potted poinsettia plants.

She had on the brown tweeds and brown fox-skin scarf; men looked at her; she did not see them. Now and then some man in a dark brown coat caught her eyes for a second—immediately she lost interest; it was not Carter, it was never Carter.

Her heart ached with a fierce, steady pain. Sandra felt as if she were alone in the strange, silent, Christmas world.

She thought of Carter in all the luxurious beauty of the old San Mateo home. His mother and his grandmother would be there this week-end, he had told her, for the festival and Patsy's tree. There would be fires, there would be hospitality there, fine voices, quiet service. Perhaps he would play tennis or golf to-day, and come home to a hot bath, a change to evening wear. . . . Carter in his dinner jacket, those big shoulders, that brown face in a formal setting. Sandra tried to see him.

He had sent her books. In all the rest of the Christmas rush he had found time to go to some shop and pick out the Conrads and put his card into them. What of it, what of it, what of it? It meant no more than that he liked the substitute clerk who had twice taken Miss Curtis's place.

"No more than that," she said half aloud, walking on and on and on. "No more than that!"

She could think of nothing else but Carter Cavendish.

"I must think of something else!" she told herself.

She began to think of him again.

"I *must* stop this!"

It was devouring her; it was like a fever. The quiet winter streets, the churchgoing persons flowed by her unseen; she did not hear the premature horns. Her head ached with the one thought that hammered—hammered—hammered there like the clapper in a bell.

She must get away from the office of Cavendish & Bartlett; that was obvious. But at the mere thought a sort of weakness and despair swept over her, and she felt her throat thicken and her knees grow shaky.

A sudden memory smote her and she stopped in the street.

"Oh, poor Gertrude Curtis; she feels like this. She's had it for years! And I laughed at her—I laughed at her. . . . But she's different," mused Alexandra, moving on; "she is proud because he's a Cavendish. She's satisfied. I'm not. He could be a beggar . . ."

Presently she turned back to grope in the darkness to the seat beside her mother in the movie theater. In a sort of stupor Sandra watched the love story on the screen; the man was Carter, the woman herself. They were married; they had a child. Her throat closed, her mouth filled with water, her hands were icy.

That night, when Floss had been fussing about their

cluttered apartment for some time, and Sandra was in bed pretending to read a Conrad novel, Floss sat down suddenly on the bed close to her daughter and touched her knee with a timid hand.

"Hello," Sandra said, smiling, still holding open the book of which she had hardly been able to read or sense a page. But she knew what was coming: her pulse missed a beat.

"Sandra," Floss began. Sandra knew that she knew. Her heart gave a strange twist and she felt frightened. She continued to smile at her mother, but the color drained out of her face.

"I've been wondering what's the matter with you," Flossy began again, and stopped.

Sandra swallowed, with a dry throat.

"The matter?" she echoed feebly.

"Sandra, you aren't falling in love with Mr. Cavendish?"

A silence. Then Sandra said lightly, with a hard note in her voice:

"No."

The mother interpreted this aright.

"You mean you have?"

Another pause.

"I suppose so."

"Why, but Baby—but Baby——" the older woman said, feeling her way. "What'll—what'll that get you?"

"Nothing," Sandra said steadily, clearing her throat.

"How long has this been going on?"

"Weeks. Except that there's nothing going on."

"He's making love to you?"

"No."

"He sent you books."

"Well——" Sandra said.

"Darling," Floss argued, "there isn't any happiness in this for you."

A bitter smile twisted the girl's mouth; she shut the book and put it on the table beside her bed.

"Is that so?" she asked, ironically. And as her mother did not answer she added, in a gentler tone, laying her hand apologetically on the older woman's hand, "I'm sorry, Floss But I'm not—exactly enjoying it, as it is."

"Then you ought to stop it, honey."

"I know."

"And are you going to?"

"You mean, get out of Cavendish & Bartlett's?"

"Well, don't you think?"

Sandra was silent a long minute. Then she said, simply: "It's all I have."

There was a forlornness, a weariness and helplessness in her aspect that silenced her mother. Floss looked at her daughter for a moment. Sandra's face was thinner and paler than it had been a few weeks ago; her eyes were set in delicate violet rings.

"Sandra," asked Floss, grammar forgot in her earnestness, "ain't he married?"

"Oh, of course."

"Don't he love his wife?"

"Devotedly, as far as I know."

"H'm!" Mrs. Trumbull muttered, nonplussed. "How old is he?" she asked, after a moment.

"Thirty-two or three."

"He's handsome, isn't he?"

"Yes. But it isn't that."

"Lissen," Flossy said in a troubled tone, after a pause in which she had studied her daughter's impassive face in vain for some light or encouragement, "you know that a man—a man like that isn't going to do you any good, Sandra?"

Sandra's serious face brightened with a laugh, and she once again affectionately touched her mother's hand.

"I've been to the movies, Floss!"

"Yes, I know," the older woman persisted uncomfortably.

"Darling," Sandra said dryly, "Carter Cavendish doesn't know I'm alive—not in the sense you mean."

"Doesn't?" echoed Floss, with a brightening face.

"No!"

"Then he isn't trying to make you do—anything you shouldn't, Sandra?"

"No," Sandra repeated. And with another rueful laugh she added, "That's the trouble!"

"You shouldn't say that," the older woman said, mildly.

"Oh, Lord, if you only knew the things I'm thinking and wishing and willing to do that I shouldn't!" Sandra half laughed, half sobbed into the spread fingers with which she covered her suddenly burning face.

CHAPTER SIX

THE DAYS began to go by, the lifeless dark winter days that began with artificial light in the dark back bedroom and moved on to a lighted office, and were ended with more lights everywhere: a green light in a round hood hanging over every desk in the long office, lights flashing in the wet rainy streets, lights dimly alive in the shadows of the back room and glaring boldly over the cheap tablecloth and soaped mirrors of Roselli's. Sandra felt a great need of darkness, solitude.

She would look at her mother thoughtfully when Floss was not aware of her scrutiny. But for her mother she could run away. Every fiber of her being thirsted for escape.

Early in the year Carter Cavendish had gone to New York for a flying visit of three weeks. There was a great blankness in the office; a great blankness everywhere. Rain fell; there were foggy days when mists circled and smoked mysteriously among the tall business buildings of Montgomery Street; there was lightly falling, warm spring rain again.

"Why am I sitting at this dull, unimportant desk, doing this perfectly unnecessary work?" Sandra would ask herself as the long afternoons droned by. "Why isn't there any leisure or beauty or dignity in my life? What does a person like Betty Cavendish do, that she should have it all?"

One day Mrs. Cavendish came into the office. She was beautifully groomed as always, a damp rich curve of dark hair set immovably upon the careful peaches and cream of her cheek, her little hat drawn down smartly, her furs, her suit, her gloves perfection. She asked confidently for "Frank Bartlett," and stared, while she waited, directly at Sandra without the faintest flicker of recognition in her amiably smiling face.

"I'll see if Mr. Francis Bartlett is in," Miss Graves said formally. But there was no reproof in her eyes when the wife of the first vice president asked to see the second. Mrs. Cavendish could call Mr. Bartlett "Frank" if she liked.

Mr. Francis Bartlett came out instantly, of course, all smiles. Mrs. Cavendish clung laughing and small and engaging upon his arm as they went back to his office.

"What kind of mischief have you been getting yourself into, Betty, while Cart's been away?" Sandra heard him ask, indulgently.

"Oh, I've been awful!" laughed Mrs. Cavendish, just before the door closed.

After that Sandra could not work at all. She presently heard Miss Graves say to the boy: "Run in, Mike, and tell Mr. Bartlett that the car is waiting for Mrs. Cavendish."

The back bedroom seemed very dark and gloomy indeed that night. After the long rainy spell Sandra was conscious of the smell of plaster and woolen upholstery and dust.

"The car is waiting for Mrs. Cavendish." The words kept Sandra tossing and restless all through the dark hours. She pictured all that went with them: the young mistress gracious with her servants, the mother interested in her beautiful little girl. Jealousy devoured her. She writhed at the thought of this other woman who could claim before the world the honor of being Mrs. Carter Cavendish.

On the next Sunday, an exquisite flashing spring day of heat and color and blue skies, she walked far out into the more open, residence section of Sacramento and Clay and

Octavia Streets, house hunting. Golden Gate and Eddy were nearer, but there there were too many motor showrooms, too many small hotels and boarding houses. But when she finally did find clean, sunshiny apartments, the rents were alarming. She and Floss would pay no rent for their one room as long as Mrs. Bevilaqua used their furniture. Out here rents began at eighty and ran easily into the hundreds.

Over on sunshiny California Street, far downtown and just above the templed roofs of Chinatown, there were indeed beautiful Spanish apartments of one big room each. This might have been near enough to her old neighborhood to satisfy Floss; it had a magnificent view of the Bay and the waterfront; it was furnished in soft creamy plaster, with Spanish grills and black iron fixtures to carry out the Castilian note. But here the rent was an even hundred.

Sandra went home in the house hunter's mood of exhaustion and discouragement. That night, desperate almost to bitterness, she discussed suburban cottages with her mother.

"I'd die," Floss said simply, looking up over her soup spoon.

"But, Mother,"—the word was coming into use of late—"it is really terrible, living like this, putting our coffee cups down on the edge of the couch, and keeping potatoes in the bathroom."

"I'd die anywheres else," Floss predicted simply. "I've been right here for fifteen years. All my friends are here. I don't have to make any effort to see them. . . . You know, once, when you were about two," she presently added, as Sandra, frowning faintly, continued to look down at the tablecloth she was marking with her unused spoon, and did not speak—"once when you were about two your father and I took a little place in Thousand Oaks. It was a friend of his's house," Flossy, who never let a matter of grammar annoy her, went on. "It was an awfully cute place—breakfast porch, all that. And view! There was nothing but view, whichever way you looked. Well, your father went off duck hunting with some friends for a few days—that's what he *said,* anyway," Flossy with remembered feeling interrupted herself to interpolate ironically, "and I was there alone with you. My goodness, I thought I'd lose my mind! By eight o'clock at night you'd have thought it was a cemetery. Quiet —it was something awful! Just your voice and my voice and black streets with trees waving over them and a light shining here and there. It almost broke my heart. It wasn't long after that we moved here, and it was heaven to me to run downstairs again and see all the lights and hear the theater racket."

"I know," Sandra admitted in a voice of pain.

"You see, when I came here I rented the whole house," Floss went on. "Then afterward I was glad enough to get this room for nothing and have Mrs. Bevilaqua take it over. All I had then was my rent from the prune ranch. I used to check coats and hats at the Elks' and the Shriners' parties —and glad enough to have it to do! Then I took a job with the telegraph office right down here——"

"I remember, darling."

"My whole life's been right here."

"I know."

"And if you got married, Sandra, this'd be the place I wanted to be! You can have all the sun porches and back yards you want," ended Floss with a shudder. "Give me the crowd!"

Sandra laughed and stretched out an affectionate hand. Her lashes were misted; the laughter might as easily have been tears. But Floss neither saw nor suspected that.

"Sandra, you've got the sweetest disposition of any human being, man or woman, I ever knew!" her mother said.

The girl made no answer beyond a vague smile. She was hardly listening. True to a race instinct she could not have defined, of whose very existence indeed she was ignorant, she was changing in these days. Carter Cavendish might never know it, but for his sake her voice was gentler, and the smile in her eyes sweeter. For his sake Sandra chose her words carefully, groomed her hands, her hair, with painstaking care. It was as if she prepared herself by fasting and vigil, in soul, mind, and body, like some young knight of old, for accolade.

On the wettest of late January afternoons, when the green lamps of the office had been lighted all day long and sheets of rain slashed at the high windows and ran in gray gutters through the streets, Carter came back. Sandra heard his voice at the door that led to the elevator hall; he came through the office with Mr. Bartlett, returning a smiling greeting here and there; then the door of his office closed behind both men. Sandra had not dared to look up. She worked on busily, blindly, with a fast-beating heart.

At five o'clock he reappeared, and she heard him say to someone, in his characteristic half-laughing manner, "I've not seen them yet. But I've a present for Patsy; couldn't return without that!"

She looked up; he was looking straight at her. The brown face, the square shoulders, the look about his firm, hard mouth; her eyes could drink them in again. He half smiled, as if there were some little secret joke between them. Then he disappeared and Sandra sat on in a daze, not conscious of what was going on about her, her senses washing back and forth idly in a sea of vague dreams.

Half an hour later, when she was certain he had gone home, she carried a sheaf of papers into his office and laid them on his desk. Miss Curtis was there, just going. The two girls talked together.

"Seems so good to have Mr. Cavendish back!" Gertrude Curtis said.

"Doesn't it?"

"He's so marvelous," the older woman said. "He put over a wonderful deal while he was in New York. Both Mr. Bartlett and Mr. Peter are perfectly delighted with him. They well may be!"

"It's like a different place when he's here!"

"Isn't it?"

Miss Curtis went away and Sandra returned to her desk in the now deserted office. It was after half-past five o'clock. Mike, the boy, was emptying the wire wastebaskets; Huchinson, the janitor, was talking to some peddler or agent, down at the other end of the long room.

She sat down, her fair hair caught in the cone of gold light that poured down directly above it, the purity of her flawless skin and the delicate violet shadows about her eyes enhanced by the artificial light. She had only to put some papers in a drawer, lock the little center drawer, where she kept her fountain pen and other personal treasures, and go home, go home to remember that one moment when Carter had looked straight at her with so kindly, so significant an expression of understanding in his dark eyes. He was home again!

There was a stir at the door; someone coming in. It was Carter. He wore the big loose Raglan coat with which she was familiar, his hat was in his hand, the rain had spattered his fresh, hard brown face and dark, scalloped hair.

"I forgot my——" he began, and stopped.

Sandra had gotten to her feet; she stood looking at him, under the light, her fingertips braced against the big blotter on her desk.

Carter came to the other side of the desk and their eyes drew together. The end of his sentence was lost; he stood still, his lips parted a little, his breath coming short.

"I thought you might be here, alone."

Sandra said nothing; her eyes were fixed steadily on his.

Carter was standing on the other side of the desk; his face was red, he laughed a little as he spoke.

"It just suddenly occurred to me that you might be here, alone."

"The others," she said vaguely, "have gone."

Carter laughed again, foolishly and excitedly.

"Did you miss me?" he asked.

"Oh, yes, Mr. Cavendish."

She had to clear her throat to say it, and it sounded odd and flat. Carter Cavendish alone with her in the office, asking her if she had missed him. Her senses revolved slowly—everything revolved. . . .

"Could you come with me now and have a cup of tea?"

"No, I couldn't."

Sandra laughed a little, too; they were looking at each other strangely, smiling and yet nervous. There was a pause.

"Have to go straight home?"

"Well—I ought to. . . ."

Another silence. Her eyes were dark gold in her white face; the light above her head turned her loose soft waves of hair to dark gold, too.

Carter drew back a little; swallowed.

"But I *must* talk to you," he said, laughing confusedly.

"I think I had better go home," Sandra said.

She went over to the coat hanger and put on her brown raincoat. She drew her small brown hat snugly down over her hair. When she turned back Carter was still standing where he had been, watching her. They walked out to the elevators together.

Downstairs at the big street door they could see that the darkness outside was slit by the silver needles of the rain. Lights were shining against it; the black street was filled with reflections and blots of light.

Carter put his hand under her elbow; the touch of his fingers robbed Sandra of any power to speak.

"Which way do you go, Miss Trumbull?"

"I—I—this way," she said, with an effort.

He delayed her in the doorway.

"You look—*awfully*—well," he said.

To this Sandra found nothing to say. The home-going world was wheeling about them in the dark night; she was conscious of none of it. She saw nothing but the tall man in the spattered raincoat, who was watching her with so strange an expression in his smiling eyes.

"I often thought of you," Carter added.

"Oh, did you?" Sandra heard her own unnatural voice ask inanely.

"Yep. Did you know that?"

There was a pause. Then almost without her own volition she said slowly:

"I think I did."

And then for a long time they stood looking at each other.

"You did?" Carter asked presently, in a changed tone.

"I think so."

He laughed awkwardly, boyishly.

"You don't seem very happy about it."

"About what?" she asked, with a look.

Carter's expression changed again; sobered.

"The point is," he said, "how to get you home, in this rain."

"Oh, I walk!" the girl said quickly.

"My car is right here in the garage."

"Oh, no, I like to walk! I always walk. It isn't far."

"It's raining."

"Very lightly, though. I like it!"

"But it's raining."

"I like the rain. This hat—everything I have on has been rained on before."

"Is it far?"

"No. A few blocks. I always walk it. I like to."

"The East," he said, "is buried in snow."

"I can imagine."

"Do you like it?"

Her eyebrows went up in interrogation.

"Snow."

"I've never seen it."

"Never seen snow?"

"Never."

"But you've seen it in the Sierras—at Yosemite?"

"No. I've never been there."

His eyes were smiling at some pleasant and exciting thought.

"How you'd love New York!"

"I imagine so. I often think of it."

"Some day——" Carter began, and stopped abruptly. Sandra's face grew rosy, and she laughed in embarrassment. Neither spoke for a moment, and then the man went on: "Well, do I see you to-morrow?"

"Oh, yes!"

"I may have to be down early—that is, about nine," he began inconsequentially. Sandra looked at him respectfully; there seemed to be nothing to say to this. "You won't," he persisted, feeling the absurdity of the conversation, trying to extricate himself, "let me take you home?"

"Oh, no, I like the walk!"

"Then I'll see you to-morrow?"

"To-morrow."

They looked at each other smiling. Then Sandra nodded, and she and her umbrella vanished into the early winter dark and the glancing silver raindrops. Carter stood for a full minute, for another minute, motionless where she had left him.

CHAPTER SEVEN

SANDRA, walking home, through the lessening rainfall, was only vaguely conscious of her surroundings. The warm wet blackness of the night was fairyland; the colored lights of Market Street might have been a brilliant oriental bazaar. Florists' windows were bright blurs of rich color, street lights reflected themselves into long crossed and intercrossed strings of diamonds in the black pavements.

She felt strangely excited; strangely cool. As yet she was not thinking, merely feeling, but it was a delicious, satisfying feeling; it carried her along on wings. It was good to be young, strong, to be walking lightly, swiftly through the friendly streets of downtown San Francisco to-night. Sandra felt that she could have danced, could have shouted from the deeps of exultation that were in her, could have sung her way home.

And all the while it was merely feeling, no thinking yet. Her thoughts, her recollection of this afternoon she was carrying with her as a miser might carry a hidden bag of gold, as a pirate might carry a case of sparkling jewels, shimmering pearls. Presently she would take them out, one by one: the enchanted words, the touch of her coat sleeve that had reduced her to trembling helplessness, the friendly, eager smile, and above all the stupefying moment when he had come back to stand in the doorway, rain-spattered, puzzled, all a man and yet all boy, too.

The evening was a dream. Her mother was in bed when

she arrived home, suffering aftermath from an extracted tooth. The room looked frowsy; its atmosphere was heavy and close; rain was slopping and spattering dismally into the cemented area between the tall buildings at the back. But to Alexandra the world was heaven to-night.

She telephoned for a near-by doctor, and when he came made so deep an impression upon him with her fresh beauty and earnest sympathy that he went to unusual pains to alleviate Mrs. Trumbull's suffering, and promised to look in later to be sure that she had had relief. Of this Sandra was only vaguely conscious; when he had gone she went about the dreary room straightening it as best she could, looking anxiously now and then at the tumbled head plunged into the sodden pillow.

By eight o'clock Floss was talkative and comfortable, sitting up in bed; Sandra could send downstairs for two large bowls of onion soup, and toast stale French bread in the tiny kitchen. Through the opened window fresh wet air came in; by the simple process of stuffing them out of sight Sandra had disposed of some of the smaller articles that usually cluttered the room, and Floss could not say enough concerning her own restored spirits and her appreciation of Sandra's goodness.

"When's Mr. Cavendish get back, Sandra?"

"He got back to-day." The words brought it all to her heart in a glorious rush.

"Oh, zat so?" Flossy asked, watching her daughter. But no flicker of smile or color betrayed Sandra.

She slept hardly at all that night, and rejoiced in lying awake; it was refreshing, thrilling to lie awake and think of Carter. Toward dawn sleep came, but she was walking to the office duly at ten minutes before nine. Yesterday had been dark and rainy; now the sun was shining and the world was all flash and sparkle, washed fresh and new.

Yesterday Sandra had carried a heavy heart; she had felt all the bitterness of impotent and futile suffering, hating herself and her job.

To-day everything was different, and as she went up in the elevator she felt that she would not have changed places with anyone in the world. The office glittered and trembled with the light that never was on land or sea.

She was talking to Marg'ret Maguire when she heard Carter come in. Marg'ret, with a puzzling letter in her hand, had drawn a chair to Sandra's side, and Sandra had wheeled about so that her profile was to the door where Carter must enter. She did not see him, yet she knew to the deeps of her being who had come in, felt the thrill run to her toes and tingle in the roots of her hair. She went on talking to Marg'ret.

"I wonder if you could telephone our man—it's Mr. Leonard, I think—telephone our man in Portland—good-morning, Mr. Cavendish!—and ask him to see Mr. Younger?"

"Good-morning, Miss Trumbull! Good-morning, Miss Maguire."

"He's handsome, isn't he?" Marg'ret asked in a whisper when he was gone.

Sandra's face was April.

"It seems to me, Miss Maguire, that if I were going to be a Little Sister of the Poor I wouldn't care whether a married man was good-looking or not!"

"Oh, you go to grass!" the prospective religious said, departing in high good humor.

Sandra squared her chair again, recommenced her own work. Her hands were trembling a little, and her throat felt dry, but despite the humming in her head she worked on, not letting herself think what might happen next.

At half-past twelve, going out for her lunch, Miss Curtis stopped at her desk.

"Miss Trumbull, could you go into Mr. Carter's office before you go out?"

Sandra looked up composedly, nodded. A minute later, feeling as if it were all a dream, she was alone with Carter Cavendish in his own office.

Her heart gave a great plunge when she saw him; he was standing with his back half turned to the door, a tall, square, black-headed young man in a dark blue suit.

He turned round and nodded at her without smiling. There was a round-backed chair beside the desk. He indicated it.

"Will you sit down?" he said. Sandra, without moving her dark gold eyes from his, took it; he sat down in his own chair. He was a little pale, his expression serious.

"First," he said, locking his big hands before him, looking at them rather than at her—"first, I want to say that I am very sorry for what happened last night. There is no possible explanation of it. There is—no—apology that I can offer you," he stammered on, beginning to plunge in his set speech, "—that—that—— In short—I'm very sorry. It was a rotten thing to do!"

Sandra had linked her own hands; she was looking at him quietly with wide-open eyes. She cleared her throat.

"That's all right," she answered simply.

"I wish," Carter said, once again assuming the air of the office manager interviewing one of the girls, as he moved an inkwell and glanced unseeing at some letter—"I wish you would act as if it had not happened."

"I will!" Sandra promised earnestly.

"And it would make me very happy if you would go right along here," Carter pursued, speaking always in the same careful and formal way—"it would make me very happy if you would go right along here as if nothing had happened."

He paused, not looking at her, reading instead a penciled memorandum on his desk and crumpling it before he dropped it in the wastebasket.

"I never thought of doing anything else," Sandra confessed in a faintly surprised voice.

"You never——?" He seemed relieved. He looked at her now, folding his arms. "Then I hope," he said—"I hope—and after this we need not speak of it again—I hope you will forgive me for being so—well, for everything!"

"Certainly," Sandra answered, politely. "Mr. Cavendish," she added, with her earnest, starry look, speaking slowly, feeling for words, "I knew you would say something—like this. I knew that we—you and I—couldn't be friends!" She looked down at her linked fingers, looked up again. "I would rather have only this," she said, in a whisper, as if she were thinking aloud—"I would rather have only this," Sandra repeated, "than—than anything else I have ever had!"

"Only what?" Carter asked in a low voice, watching her steadily.

"This——" she repeated, with a long look.

"Thank you, Miss Trumbull," Carter said in the same low voice. He was smiling, but his eyes glistened.

Glowing, she looked at him; the golden eyes were lambent now, her long, dark, upcurving lashes misty. The brown velvet office dress she wore was cut away at the throat; there was a line of creamy embroidery across the full, swelling whiteness of her breast. There was about her round neck, her warm, firm hands, not small hands, her height and bigness, a certain generosity and appeal that were irresistible. In the unwonted heat of the day her fine gold-brown hair had flattened itself into damp little spirals against her low white forehead; her face was unusually pale, and the dark shadows about her eyes made them seem bigger than ever.

"You are very beautiful, my dear," Carter said involuntarily. He put his hand out; she did not move hers as he touched it; she sat very still, looking down. "I am sorry," he said, trying to laugh, "that we can't be friends."

As she did not speak he added, "It seems to me it would be a great privilege to be your friend. . . . I'd like you," he said, in a dead silence—"I'd like you to tell me your troubles, and to tell you mine. I'd like to help you out of anything—that worried you. I know you haven't any father or brother——"

"No," she admitted, as he paused, "I haven't anyone but my mother."

"I wish I were your big brother," Carter finished.

"And in ways I am older than my mother," Sandra presently said. "I know—for instance—I'm not like most girls about things—about, well, men. I'm not—ignorant, you know," she finished, looking up. "I mean—" and Sandra smiled—"I mean I'm not ignorant! I know what's right—and what's wrong."

Carter looked up, smiling, too. The interview was ended.

"Will you lunch with me, now and then, and let us be friends?" he asked suddenly. For a minute he sat silent; amazed at his own words.

"Is there any good reason why you should not lunch with me now and then?" he repeated presently, still to his own complete surprise as Sandra did not answer but sat looking at him with bright, thoughtful eyes. "Can't a man and a woman have a friendship, a mere friendship, just as any two men or any two women might have? Why am I saying this to Miss Trumbull?" he thought.

"Come," he added, as she still hesitated. "We like each other very much, don't we? Can't we be friends? Look here, if it makes you feel any better I'll tell Mrs. Cavendish about it every time we lunch together! Maybe sometimes she'll come, too."

"I don't know what to say, Mr. Cavendish," Sandra said, awkwardly, flushed and troubled.

"But I don't mean to-day. You don't have to decide now!" he said, with steady determination. None of this was premeditated, but he could not seem to stop now. Everything was completely unimportant except that they two should be friends. He spoke naturally, good-naturedly. "Some day next week, or the week after, I'll stop at your desk going out and take you along," he said. "Good heavens, there needn't be anything secretive or underhanded about it! I know women love secrecy!" Carter could even add, with a smile.

"I don't suppose there need be," Sandra agreed. It was all safely far in the future anyway.

Suddenly all the constraint, all the self-consciousness that had hung so heavy between them seemed to have vanished. Carter smiled at the girl, and she responded with her own disarming slow smile.

"We're friends, then?" the man demanded.

"Friends," she echoed.

"And you'll lunch with me some day?"

"I'd love to!"

"Good!" he said, with a brisk, satisfied air of closing the interview. He stood up, and Sandra rose to her feet, too, and went out. Carter sat thinking, frowning, for a long time after she was gone.

She lunched alone, thinking, smiling absently. Much later in the day Gertrude Curtis stopped at her desk to ask her delicately if everything was "all right."

"Mr. Cavendish looked so queer when he asked you to come in, Sandra. It wasn't a call down?"

"Oh, no; it was all right," Sandra answered mildly.

Gertrude was present when Carter next spoke directly to

Sandra. It was a week later; Sandra had been sent for, and had come into his office to find him deep in business, Miss Curtis murmuring at the telephone, Mike waiting for telegrams.

"Oh, yes; Miss Trumbull," Carter said, with a casual nod. "Will you sit down? Miss Trumbull," he began suddenly, when he was free, "Miss Curtis and I have been discussing for the past few days the need of someone else in here to help out. We've been rather rushed lately, and Miss Curtis feels she needs an assistant. Isn't that it, Miss Curtis?"

He turned to his secretary deferentially, and Miss Curtis from her desk in the corner said brightly, "Well, it would be very nice, I'm sure, Mr. Cavendish."

"I don't know how long we'll need you, but we can try it for a while," Carter continued, not the faintest significance in his eye as he fell easily into the managerial tone. "I thought I'd speak to Mr. Runyon and have Miss Maguire take on some of your work in the main office. We need you more in here, I fancy, than they do out there. Miss Curtis can easily explain the work to you."

"Oh, she doesn't need any help; she can catch on in no time," Gertrude Curtis, at whom he glanced for encouragement, said generously.

"Well, now, what do you think, Miss Trumbull? Would you try it?"

"Why, of course," Sandra said, the office going round her.

"That's that, then!" Carter said, with a nod of dismissal.

"My dear, you'll love him!" Gertrude Curtis said, very chummy over a cafeteria lunch with Sandra an hour later. "You'll have your desk where mine is now, and he wants me to take that lovely sunny corner where Mr. Peter's desk used to be. Isn't he lovely, in his manner I mean? He always acts as if anything you did was a favor. I told him I was afraid I'd always be looking out of the window over in that corner, and he was so darling! He said, 'I'll take a chance on you, after eight years!' As for his wife," Miss Curtis went on—"but you've met her?"

"That day last autumn when I went down to their house," Sandra reminded her, beginning on her grapenut pudding. The beat of her heart was shaking her whole body.

"The day Anna's baby was so sick. I had to go to Alameda, Sandra, I *had* to," the older woman said earnestly.

"But I loved it!" Sandra protested, wide-eyed.

"Don't you think she's perfectly adorable?"

"Mrs. Cavendish?"

"Yes. Don't you think she's adorable?"

"She seemed lovely."

"She came in with Patsy the other day—they were going to meet his mother at the train. She was so cute! She told me to remind Mr. Cavendish that he had a date with two pretty girls. Did you see them?"

"I saw them go through the office, yes."

"And, Sandra, don't worry about a raise. That's the way they do. They'll let you go on for a couple of months, and then just tell you they're going to give you more, whatever it is."

"I'm not worried," Sandra said.

She worked very hard in her new position; she made herself everything that tiresome old Mr. Runyon and Frank Bartlett talked about in their "efficiency assemblies." She was quiet, accurate, willing, pleasant. And while she murmured with Gertrude and answered her desk telephone and clicked at her machine, she was aware of Carter's presence only a few feet away. This was happiness; this was enough.

About a week after the change Carter chose a moment when they were alone in the office to smile across at her and ask:

"How's it going?"

Sandra's desk had a flat top; she faced across it the wide room that was shaded to-day against the too bright spring sun. She looked up smiling.

"Oh, fine."

"Miss Curtis put you onto everything?"

"Just about."

"She told me," Carter said, opening a drawer and looking into it before slipping in a paper—"she told me—she was all broken up about it yesterday—that she had a criticism of you and hated to make it."

Sandra's clear skin flushed sensitively.

"What was it?"

"She didn't tell me. But she was joking, I could see that."

The girl's color returned to its normal cool tones and she smiled her slow illuminating smile.

"Oh, I know. I know! It was——That was funny," Sandra interrupted herself to say musingly, and fell silent.

"What was it?" Carter demanded, amused.

"She said," Sandra began, after a second's hesitation, "that you, and Mr. Peter, too, always liked bright and—bright and cheerful people in your offices, and that I mustn't be *too* businesslike!"

"She didn't say that?" Carter demanded, his dark handsome face breaking into a laugh.

"She did."

"Priceless!" he said.

"It seemed that way to me," Sandra said.

Nothing more. The girl resumed her work; she heard Carter's voice at the telephone a minute later. But the little moment that excluded Gertrude Curtis from their councils had established a subtle, deeper understanding between them, and kept Sandra's heart warm all day.

Three days later he said to her,

"Mrs. Cavendish has just broken a luncheon date with me, and I told her that I was going to ask the prettiest girl in the office to go out with me. How about it?"

"I don't think that's true. There are lots of prettier girls in this office," Sandra objected. But five minutes later they walked out through the main office quite openly together. There was no one to see them anyway; it was the luncheon hour.

"How about Jules'?" Carter asked.

"Jules' sounds nice."

"You mean to say you've not been there? Come on, then, we'll go to Jules'!" Carter decided.

They walked to a parking station a block away, and Sandra established herself for the first time beside him on the low, heavily padded seat of his handsome brown roadster. Everything was pleasant, unalarming, to-day; their second meal together was infinitely more enjoyable than the first had been.

They talked like friends; once or twice she made him laugh, and once he brought the happy color to her face with the mere pronunciation of her name. All through the busy afternoon hours in the office there was nothing for Sandra to remember with regret, only happiness and satisfaction. Her heart was singing in the new bewildering richness of knowing that she had a friend. "What harm was there in that?" she asked herself. "Good heavens! We aren't living in the Victorian era!"

CHAPTER EIGHT

THEN FOR BOTH came enchanted weeks, when the early spring broke over the western city and the Bay was blue and the sky blue and the eastern range of mountains only a silhouette of deeper blue. Sandra's new suit was blue, too, and her hat with its wisp of brown and gold feather blue. Her plain blouse had the white frill she loved; her chamois gloves were washed every night now, and always immaculate.

The beautiful blue leather bag she carried was Carter's first gift, except for occasional violets or books. One day when they were lunching he had reached across the table and had taken away from her the shabby old brown purse that she had carried for three years. Under her surprised, smiling eyes he had emptied the old bag of handkerchief, letters, money, beauty case. Then he had opened a package he carried to throw aside wrappings, box, tissue paper, and reveal the dark shining blue beauty of a Russia bag with a black metal monogram.

"Oh, listen——" Sandra had protested.

"It was cheap, honestly. It's nothing!" Carter had hastened to say reassuringly. He had jumbled the old bag in with the other rubbish, had the waiter carry it away. When he had handed her the new bag with his boyish, eager look, he had found her studying him thoughtfully, both elbows on the table, her chin on her hands.

"How did we get this far?" she had demanded simply.

He had laughed, but immediately his face had grown sober, as hers was. He had leaned forward.

"I don't know, dear," he had answered honestly. "It seemed to come of itself. It seems—inevitable."

Sandra had looked down at the new bag, caressed it with her fine, sensitive hand.

"It's beautiful," she had said slowly, reluctantly.

"It's nothing," Carter had protested. "Why, good heavens," he had said, "can't I give you a little present without all this fuss? Just forget it."

"I can't forget what it stands for," Sandra had said in a low tone.

And suddenly they had been in a new mood; his guard down for a memorable moment, Sandra's citadel undefended.

"You mean," Carter had asked, in a low voice that matched her own—"you mean how we feel about each other?"

"I think I mean that."

"I know," he had said. A silence had deepened and spread between them. Sandra's eyes had been lowered again to her blue bag; her hand had still rested upon it. For weeks now her exquisite face had been the only thing he saw in the world, her voice the only voice he heard. And when she had raised the dark gold eyes he had known that he read in them the helpless, the consuming love that such a woman knows only once in all her life.

"I might have seen this coming," he had said, in deep self-reproach.

"I did, I think," she had answered, very low.

"You knew it, even in the beginning?"

Sandra had been silent for a minute, thinking, her face troubled, her finely etched dark brows faintly drawn together.

"I can't remember," she had said confusedly, looking up.

"It's all so——I don't know. I can't remember how it started."

"You're not sorry that we—found each other?"

"What else can I be?" she had demanded. "My life—my life is so strange now. Everything's—wrong."

"Sandra, I don't make it harder?"

"I don't know."

"But my darling, we mustn't let it make us sorry!" he had pleaded.

"I don't know," she had repeated.

"It is the thing I value most in my life, Sandra. Nothing can take it away now."

"Yes," she had said. "It is the best thing in my life, too."

"Then can't we just—be happy about it?"

Sandra had laughed an unhappy little laugh. She had put her elbows on the table and framed her face in her hands.

"I don't see how we can, exactly."

"Why not?"

"Probably," she had mused, looking at him thoughtfully—"probably because we know we never should have commenced it."

"What did commence it?"

"That's exactly it!" And she had given him her anxious smile. "I can't seem to remember."

"Sandra, I'm never going to let you be sorry about it!"

"Oh, Carter," she had said, with the first hint of impatience she had ever shown him, "don't talk like a—like a *man*. You know, and I know, we had no business to begin all this—the presents, the lunches, the feeling—the feeling we have! It might get too strong for us, and then what could we do?"

"It is too strong for me now," he had said quietly, after a moment.

The fire had died out of her suddenly. There had been a pause.

"It is too strong for me, too," she had repeated, in the same expressionless tone that he had used, after a moment.

"Even at Christmas I couldn't—get out," Carter had said.

"I know."

"And it's March now, Sandra."

"I know it is."

She had become thoughtful, glancing away, frowning slightly, biting her lip.

"When could we have stopped it, Carter?"

"I don't know, dear."

"Have you thought what's—what's going to happen?"

"I can't think ahead."

"No," she had said, "and I can't seem to think ahead either."

"But you mustn't feel sad about it," he had pleaded, his heart touched with pity and love for her youth and bewilderment and simplicity.

"No, I know." Her mood had changed, and she had been friendly and confident again; it was as if she had given herself a shake; warned herself to be sensible. "I'm just going to enjoy it," she had said bravely, "and be glad of it! Why shouldn't I like you and why shouldn't you like me? It's all so silly, our worrying about what other people say we may or mayn't do!"

"Well, now you're talking!" he had exclaimed, in great satisfaction.

"Why, a few months ago, Carter, I would have thought just one of these lunches, just one of these talks, was heaven!"

"A few months ago I didn't know that there was anyone like you in the world," he had countered.

After that they had often lunched at the Palace Hotel, their favorite place. They always had their old inconspicuous table; not only did Carter nod to an acquaintance now and then, but he would cheerfully introduce Sandra when some man came over to draw a chair up for a minute or to stand talking.

She had grown to be less afraid of these encounters. If Carter did not dread them, why should she? She had no social position to lose; he risked everything.

They talked inexhaustibly. They leaned on the table and murmured; they stopped, walking in the street, to face about and smile at each other; they had everything in the world to say. Sandra used to ask herself sometimes, when she was away from him, if it could be true; was it only a dream that she and Carter Cavendish were friends, that he called her "Sandra," and sat opposite her through so many enchanted noon hours, his elbow on the table, the cigarette smoking in his fine brown hand, his earnest eyes on her face?

Sometimes she thought confusedly to herself: "Lunching with a married man, not once but two or three times a week, letting him tell you he likes you. Lunching with the boss . . ."

But these phrases seemed to make no particular sense now; they had no significance. Carter was Carter, and she was Sandra, and they could no more keep apart than the river can keep from the sea. Theories of morality seemed only theories, and morality itself mere words.

"You mustn't do this; you mustn't do that!" Persons who were not concerned were very glib to say that a working girl ought not to lunch with a rich young man; they would have had Sandra lunch with Gertrude Curtis in the Maple Leaf Cafeteria and Carter go alone to his club.

They would have thrown these exquisite, these priceless minutes away, just because a girl "ought not" lunch with a married man!

Didn't a lot depend on the girl and the man? Sandra would ask herself fiercely. She, Alexandra Trumbull, was no fledgling; she had known what happened to Mamie Batts. She had accompanied poor Mamie to the Emergency Hospital on the awful night when Mamie took poison, and Mamie in her dying agonies had told little wide-eyed Sandra what it was all about. She was not going to be "led astray."

Lunching with an intelligent, stimulating, admiring man was not being led astray.

"This is a great day in our annals," Carter said, on the day when first they talked of themselves as having come to care for one another.

"Why, specially?"

"Because it is only to-day that you and I have faced things," he explained.

"We knew," she answered artlessly.

"We knew? Of course we did."

"Does it make any difference?"

"No, I don't suppose so. But—yes, in a way it makes a difference. It—frightens me a little."

"Of what?" she asked, golden light welling and sinking in the brown eyes she fixed expectantly on him.

"It frightens me to think you like me, Sandra," he answered humbly.

"My liking you—isn't so much," Sandra murmured, looking down.

"It frightens me to think I might have missed it," Carter went on in the quiet voice he sometimes used on these phrases that thrilled her so when she first heard them, and that went into her treasure chest to be eternally kept sacred.

"And it—well, I hate to think of what I would like to do for you, dear, and how little I am able to do! I'd like to—— No use talking about it!" he interrupted himself to say.

"But why should you do anything for me?" she demanded.

"Because I want to."

"But I don't want you to do anything for me."

"I know you don't. You're not like most girls in that," Carter said.

"All your other girls?" she asked good-naturedly, smiling over her salad. Sandra was too happy to be jealous.

"Why, what a little cat you are! Yes, all my other girls, if you like. But I only had girls before I was married, and I was married at twenty-two, so you can't get far with that."

"You never liked a girl since?"

"I never liked any girl at all the way I like you. And like," Carter said, analyzing it, "like is the word for it. I like you tremendously! I'd like to dress you up in furs and jewels and things. I'd like to have you shut away in some beautiful little cottage, with a garden, waiting for me, belonging to me!"

They walked down Post Street after luncheon and looked into the shop windows, at the beautiful brown slim furs and at old-fashioned exquisite jewelry, pearls set in black enamel and gold, emeralds and diamonds flashing together.

"Sultans, I can understand them now," Carter observed. "They loved to see their wives in rich silks, covered with jewels."

"Only they weren't their wives, Mr. Cavendish."

"Well, their what-d'you-call-'ems, then."

"You called me a cat. I'd rather be a cat than a what-d'you-call-'em."

"Oh, shucks! It was a different generation and a different civilization," argued Carter.

"Very," Sandra agreed.

"Would you let me buy you that?"

"Which one?"

"The golden brown one to go with your eyes."

"But why should you buy me a fox skin? No, I'll not let you buy me that."

He did not press the point.

"I don't feel guilty about this," Sandra told him, walking on, "but I would feel guilty if I let you give me things."

"I don't see that we have done anything to feel guilty about," Carter said. "We are friends, that's all. There's no law against our being friends."

But she was more honest than he about it.

"There's an unwritten law."

"Against a man taking a girl to lunch?"

"A married man."

"Well, perhaps," he admitted, after a moment's thought; "I suppose there is. I suppose there is. This thing ought to stop here. I'll be hanged," Carter added, in the aggrieved, youthful fashion that so often amused her—"I'll be hanged if I see why, though. We don't harm anyone, and we make ourselves happy. But of course I know what you mean—Betty would object, and your mother would object——"

"It seems so funny," she commented innocently in the pause, "for *they* don't want to lunch with us!"

"It's all very well to talk of stopping it, Sandra," he began again as they walked along. "But it would take out of my life everything that counts now. That sounds silly. That must seem awfully silly to you because you know that I play golf on Saturdays and Sundays and go to the club afternoons for bridge, and all that. But even when I'm not with you I'm thinking about my—my friend, and of how good it's going to be to get back to the office in the morning and see Miss Trumbull in her brown suit——"

"Blue," Sandra corrected, as he paused.

"Blue, you darling. And I love it, too. But seriously, I come into town every morning thinking, Sandra, of that moment when I'll open the office door."

"I think of it, too."

"I always imagine," Carter went on, "exactly how you'll look. Sunshine at the windows and the shades drawn down, and Miss Curtis telephoning, and you with letters before you, looking toward the door across your desk——"

"Yes, I know," she said.

That night, lying in bed with her hands locked behind her head, Sandra told her mother all about it. Flossy, with her henna-dyed hair and her general easiness and lenience toward the world, her liking for little dinners and "gentlemen friends," was firm, and fearful, Alexandra knew, where moral law was concerned. Not always temperate about eating and drinking, laughing and crying, the little cabaret star of yesterday had every reason to be satisfied with her own personal record, and was proud of it. She might word her theories inelegantly, but they were sound.

"It don't do a girl any good to be talked about," Floss might say simply, and she had believed it to the extent of never getting herself talked about. Sandra's father, she would sometimes tell the girl, in that mood of emotional self-pity that occasionally followed too good a dinner, was the only man in the world who had ever laid a fingertip on her.

Sandra knew that this was true only in the important sense her mother intended it to be understood. Many of her men as well as women friends kissed Flossy when they met; sometimes Flossy would lock her plump little hand in that of her nearest male neighbor and sit so, talking affectionately, intimately, for half-hours at a time. But all this meant nothing to Flossy, and Alexandra knew it.

"Floss," said her daughter, stretched in bed, staring up at the discolored dismal ceiling of their big room, "there's something on my mind."

"You don't have to tell me," Flossy murmured, her knee crooked, her fingers tenderly exploring a bare, plump foot.

Sandra's eyes moved to her obliquely.

"How do you mean?"

Flossy tested the foot by a tentative pressure on the floor.

"I've known what was the matter with you for a long time," she observed.

Alexandra swallowed, with a dry throat, and looked up at the ceiling again.

"It's Carter Cavendish, isn't it?" Flossy asked.

"Yep," Sandra answered briefly. The mere name sent a hundred electric vibrations through her body.

After a silence, in which Flossy continued her undressing and disappeared into the bathroom for ablutions, Sandra asked:

"How'd you know, Mother?"

"I saw the way you were eating, and you haven't heard half I said since Christmas," the older woman answered, dispassionately. "I guess there isn't any question you've *got* it," she finished, with a long sigh.

She came over to sit on the foot of the bed, looking patiently, expectantly, at her daughter. So seen, she was not an impressive figure; her henna-dyed hair, gray at the roots, bunched severely back, her plump, lined face smeared with the cream she was gently rubbing into her skin. But for the first time in her life Alexandra was afraid of her mother.

"I suppose," she began with a certain sinking at her heart—"I suppose you think I'm a fool?"

"You *know* you're a fool," Flossy answered simply.

This was like a slap in the face, and Sandra lay still, recovering from it.

"Why?" she asked presently in a hard, hurt voice.

Flossy, wiping her face on a mud-colored, soft old towel, made no answer.

"Of course, if you feel that you can't trust me, Mother——" Sandra presently began, resentfully and proudly.

Again the older woman had recourse to a silence far more effective than words; she did not look at her daughter, but having finished with the cold cream began to manicure herself carefully with a pair of scissors.

"What do you do, go to lunch with him?" she asked, after awhile.

Only her desperate need of counsel could have kept Sandra's voice patient. The question seemed to coarsen it all so, cheapen it so!

"Sometimes."

"He gave you your blue bag, didn't he?"

The flimsy lie about having seen it at a sale died forever; Sandra indicated "yes" with a faint motion of her head.

"You oughtn't to have taken it," Floss told her firmly. "It cost a lot of money—it cost fifty dollars if it cost a cent."

"It didn't!"

"Well, go try to buy one like it. Go to Shreve's to-morrow and ask them."

"How do you know it came from Shreve's?"

"It's as good a place as any other. That came from one of the expensive places."

"Then you think," began Alexandra, in a young tone that trembled a little—"you think that in this day and generation, with all the petting and necking and everything else that's going on, anyone cares if a girl and a man walk over to the Palace Hotel now and then and lunch together? Or if he gives her a handbag."

"You bet your life *she'd* care!" her mother answered promptly. The emphasis indicated Carter's wife.

"I don't care if she cares!" Alexandra blazed in sudden fury. "What's it to me if she cares! I don't matter to her."

"I know it," Floss retorted promptly; "nor to him either."

"I wish I hadn't told you!" the girl muttered resentfully.

"You didn't tell me, Sandra. I've known it all along. I was just about ready to give you a good talking to."

Sandra lay silent. Her lower lip was slightly bitten; she was looking up at the ceiling again through narrowed lids.

"You want to talk about it, don't you?" Flossy said sympathetically. Through all her indignation and shame Sandra found a moment to wonder at her mother's shrewdness.

"Just tell me what's wrong about it, Mother!"

"He's married, Sandra."

"Well—but good heavens, aren't married men supposed to eat?"

"Not with their stenographers, they're not."

Sandra sat up in bed, her shining hair tumbled in a loose mass about her ears. In her pale face her eyes blazed darkly.

"Mother, doesn't that idea seem simple idiocy to you?"

"No," her mother answered, after thought. "His wife has a right to get good and sore if she catches him at anything like that."

Again the coarseness of putting her affair on this footing smote Sandra to silence. Presently she said:

"So you think it's wrong?"

"'Tain't a question so much of its being wrong, Sandra; it ain't safe, and you know it. It ain't safe to have lunch with a man who's got a good healthy wife, and take presents from him. You know what it leads to. It's just one step after another."

Sandra had fallen into somber thought.

"It means I give up the finest friendship I ever had," she said after a while in a dead voice, as if she were thinking aloud.

"You and Carter Cavendish can't be friends, Sandra."

"But we *are*."

"Then that's his fault, and he has a good right to be ashamed of himself! Why, Sandra, he isn't in love with you; he doesn't *have* to be, as long as you know he's married and will take the chances you do!"

"What chances am I taking?" Sandra demanded, with a fair imitation of a scornful laugh.

"You're taking the chance of getting to care for him more than you want to, Sandra."

Sandra locked her hands about her knees and put her head down on them. She rocked a little to and fro.

"Suppose—it's that way—now, Floss?" she asked, in a humbler, lower voice, looking up. Their eyes met in a long silence.

"Well, I suppose so," the mother conceded, with a philosophical sigh. "Honey," she went on, as usual ungrammatical in earnestness, "you ain't the first."

"No, I suppose not," Sandra agreed bitterly.

"But, Floss," she burst out, after a minute, her voice hard with pain, "we like each other so much! We don't hold hands, Floss—honestly! He's never kissed me. He never would. But we have such fun, talking, laughing; we have such happy times together. He's the vice president in the office; he's the boss. But off with me alone he's so different, like a boy, and like a man who wants to take care of the—the woman he likes, too."

"You say 'off with you alone'," Floss demanded. "What else have you done except lunch with him?"

"*Honestly*, Floss——" Sandra said, at the end of her patience.

"Well, then," her mother said, the anxious keenness of her look abating, "then you have time to get out."

"You mean give up my job?"

"Guess it means that."

"Not see him again?"

"There isn't," Flossy said, after a second's hesitation and in a reluctant voice, "any other way. . . . Now I'll tell you, Sandra," she presently added, as the girl, staring darkly into space, was silent. "I don't care how honorable Carter Cavendish is, he can't marry you. He's got a wife and child. That's flat, isn't it? Well, now, if you let this thing go on he's going to want you more and more. That's men. They don't want to stop short of getting her into their arms when they like a woman. You know that, Sandra? And meanwhile you lose some fine feller that you *could* marry!"

Sandra, whose tousled head had been down again, looked up over her knees, but did not speak. Her mother's words set her pulses on fire. In his arms—in the arms of the man who loved her . . .

"It's a game that don't pay," Flossy added.

"Oh, it's a game that doesn't pay!" the girl in the bed said on a great desperate sigh.

Immediately she shook the subject off and fell to reading. But much later, as her mother turned restlessly beside her, Sandra said:

"My mind's made up, Floss. It's all over. I'll wait for that fine, upstanding, noble man to come along and marry me. I'll—be good."

A moment later she turned off the light. She made no sound, but her mother knew that she was crying.

Next day she told Carter, and he listened with an attentive, kind face. They were alone in the office, both standing at one of the big windows looking out into streets made soft and mysterious in a warm spring fog.

"You are quite right," Carter agreed, seriously. "We had to come to this. You are quite right!"

"Yes; we had to come to it," she said, ruin and desolation spreading in her soul.

"But you don't think, Alexandra, that this is the end?"

"It has to be the end."

"For a while perhaps. But not for long. Why, you didn't think I could let you go, did you?" Carter asked, his resolution taking form as he spoke. "You didn't think I could let you calmly walk out of my life? Sandra, you know I love you, don't you? You know I love you with the best, the very best, that's in me. I can't give you up! I *won't* give you up! Do you think I'll let you go?"

Suddenly, suddenly, the affair took on a wholly new aspect. Carter had not seen this coming: he could not stop now.

She glanced at him. He made no attempt to touch her. He was not even smiling. But she felt that she had never known him, never loved him, until then! She felt the world turning round beneath her feet.

"What else?" she managed to stammer.

"A good deal." He said no more, and they looked out of the window together. The warm spring morning was cloudless; ferryboats were moving to and fro on the Bay like swans; the mountains were lost in a soft haze. Masts were crowded along the piers; whistles pierced the blue air with mellow notes. "You and I'll sail out that Gate some day, Sandra," Carter said, "and have adventures."

She stood immovable; when he glanced at her obliquely he saw the bewilderment of her face.

What he could do, what was the next step, he could not

think. But he felt confusedly that she was the one reality in his world. Nothing mattered but Sandra.

"For the moment," he presently said—"for the moment let things go on as they are. This week—damn it, there's the convention coming. I'll have to give all my thought and time to that—you know how important it is. You're going to Del Monte on Thursday?"

"I was, but now I don't know——" she faltered, with a forlorn little laugh.

"Oh, you mustn't throw us down—you mustn't throw *me* down, now!" Carter protested, in quick alarm. "Why, I'm *depending* upon you. I thought it was all arranged. Miss Curtis told me it was. Afterward—afterward we'll have to think——"

"Yes, I know; Miss Curtis spoke to me about it a few days ago. She said you needed someone down there to help you with the golf tournament."

"It isn't only that. There'll be a hundred ways in which I'll need you. I've agreed to help Bill Stevenson run the golf tournament; that's a terrific undertaking in itself, and then there'll be some tennis matches, I presume, and swimming—you haven't an idea what a mob and a mess it will be, with all those delegates and their wives. I couldn't get along without someone." He was all youthful alarm. Sandra laughed. "Don't you want to go?" he demanded.

"I *did* want to," Sandra admitted; "I was wild about it. But now—last night I decided I'd tell you I couldn't."

"Couldn't!"

"Carter—on account of—it will only make it harder——"

"Oh, no, it won't! We'll hardly see each other. Honestly."

"But Mother—Mother thinks——"

"But you can let that wait. Two or three days more won't do either of us any harm. I want you to go. *Please*. It's all settled! We've got to go through with it now. In the first place, I'm particularly anxious to run my end of the show without a hitch. Joe Tillman and Leon Voorhees have charge of the convention; that's up to them. Peter and I are not concerned, but Bill Stevenson *is* chairman of the tournament committee, and I promised him I'd furnish him some clerical help. I've been counting on you. I hoped you'd go down Thursday and stay down until Sunday afternoon or perhaps come back Monday morning. That would give me a chance———" He stopped. She was silent, frowning faintly.

"Sandra, I've *got* to talk to you. Not with everyone at the Palace looking on, but alone. I'll go down on Friday, and we'll manage it somehow or other. You'll love it, Sandra; you'll have a wonderful time!"

"I'd love it, of course. It isn't that."

"We'd be under the same roof at night for the first time," Carter rushed on. "So would about twelve hundred other people," he interjected, with a laugh. "But that would help, too. In such a mob, with everybody rushing about all the time, playing golf and tennis and everything else, we ought to manage one talk."

Her pulses responded thrillingly. It sounded marvelous; it was inconceivable that she must give this up. She couldn't.

"And after we've had our talk," Carter continued, "you can decide whether you want to quit here or not. It will be entirely up to you; I promise I'll not try to influence you. But let's have these few days at Del Monte first. Do that much for me, at least. I may be selfish, I may be asking more than I ought, but I've been looking forward to this so. You wouldn't find the actual racket hard, would you?" he broke off to ask. "It's just straight bookkeeping."

"Hard? No; not hard. But you see, Carter, I'd made up my mind. I talked to my mother about it last night, and I told her I'd leave here immediately; I promised her I'd resign."

He looked his disappointment, frowning, his eyes full of protest.

"Couldn't we have this experience at Del Monte first?" he pleaded. He was suddenly youthful, impatient. "Listen!" he said. "I see as clearly as you do that this situation can't continue. We can't go on meeting in restaurants this way; it isn't fair to you, to either of us. I've been thinking. There must be some other way out. But that can all wait— one week, can't it?"

Her heart rose on a great wave of hope. Some other way out! Perhaps she would not have to exile herself from his company, turn away into the utter solitude and blankness of a world without him. He had been dissatisfied, too, troubled over the situation, and his powers, his resources were infinitely greater than her own. She didn't want to question him; she wanted to believe him. He said there must be some other way out!

"You see, Sandra, *I've* got to go to Del Monte," Carter was saying; "and I need you there very badly, honest I do. Miss Curtis ought to stay here in the office. There'll be a lot of things turn up while this convention's on. I can't spare her; I told Peter so when he suggested it. He said—I didn't! —'Why not have Miss Trumbull?'"

"Yes, I know; Miss Curtis told me he spoke of me."

"I won't be in the hotel much," Carter hurried on; "I'm going to be in one of the cottages, I believe, with Peter and Joe Hamilton and probably Fred Fargo, or Sam Kirby of New York. You'll be in the hotel somewhere." He smiled, and the smile brought the color to her face and set the blood pounding in her heart. "You'll be safe," he finished with a reassuring nod. "Nobody's going to watch us!"

"I'd like so much to go——" Alexandra said, impulsively.

"Then come along. I *have* to talk to you; there's a lot we've got to say to each other. Besides, Sandra, I need you. I couldn't do my job down there, and see all the men I have to, without you to help me.

"Mrs. Cavendish—Betty—" he broke off suddenly to add, "isn't going to be in the hotel at all. She hates conventions. She's to come down for the week-end and visit at Pebble Beach with one of her friends. She may come over to watch the golf, but she'll probably be playing bridge the whole time. Patsy's there already, staying with Mrs. Bray and her children. Of course it'll be three days of pretty strenuous work for you," he reminded her, excitedly, and hesitated, waiting for her reassurance.

"It'll be three days in heaven," Alexandra said involuntarily.

"And after that—the deluge," he said.

"After that the deluge."

"Good. You'll come then?"

"Oh, Carter—I shouldn't!"

"I need you."

Her eyes were smiling.

"You say you do."

"But I do—darling."

"I'll come," she presently said almost inaudibly, not looking at him.

Carter was businesslike. "Take the three-o'clock on Thursday. I'll wire Chandler to expect you. I'll motor down on Friday and look you up right away."

Her eyes were starry, her breath coming irregularly between half-parted lips, her face radiant. She did not speak.

CHAPTER NINE

THE TRAIN stopped among trees. It was the most exquisite hour of a shining June afternoon. The happy excitement that had possessed her at intervals all day and for many days returned again to Sandra's heart as she took her big suitcase and the little suitcase, and descended into afternoon garden beauty and the penetrating sweetness of scented pine and eucalyptus and pepper trees. An omnibus was waiting; the hotel was but a few hundred yards away. This was Del Monte.

The world was drenched and running over with beauty. Beauty of spreading levels of emerald lawn with long mellow shadows beginning to fall across it. Beauty of over-arching enormous oaks that stretched their mammoth branches low against the roses and high against the sky, beauty of massed bright banks of blazing flowers: blue delphinium, creamy showers of banksia roses, rioting salmon-colored roses, nasturtiums twisting and curling among the pale green discs of their leaves, low beds of verbena and stock and sturdy mignonette. Alexandra Trumbull felt her breath snatched away over and over again by the sheer loveliness and peace and bigness of it all. After Ellis Street, after the office, this was devastating.

Crossing the deep cool Spanish foyer, she followed a bellboy along the corridors and up the curving halls that united the old buildings to the new, and was presently installed in a room that had three slightly dormered windows on one side, looking out into the tops of trees, and pleasant, comfortable old-fashioned furniture. An adjoining bath had evidently been painted and papered and curtained many times, and undoubtedly dated back to the hotel's very beginnings half a century before, but afternoon sunshine slanted into it: the towels were enormous and white—it was all her own, like the big room and the little old wooden balcony up in the tree-tops. Alexandra fell in love with her quarters at first sight.

The effect of the whole was enchanting. When the boy was gone she had hard work to keep her feet from dancing, as she explored her kingdom. The big hotel downstairs— between guests arriving, guests departing, golfers coming in, dirty and tousled, some with bags of clubs hanging from their shoulders, riders, smart in boots and breeches, going out, telegrams being called, nurses shepherding boisterous children—had been boiling with confusion. But up here in the tree-tops all was exquisite fragrance and peace.

"Miss Trumbull?" the man at the desk had inquired.

"Miss Trumbull, from Cavendish & Bartlett. Mr. Cavendish's secretary."

"Ah, yes, Miss Trumbull; we've been expecting you. We're going to give you a desk over there next the Travel Bureau, and there'll be a telephone connection put in by to-morrow morning. You have a typewriter, and you can get any of the bellboys to bring you anything you want. We've put you up on the top floor, Miss Trumbull, at the back. We're pretty crowded, you know, but I think you'll find the room all right. We often put a child and a nurse up there. Do you think you'll mind that? It's comfortable."

"I think I'd like it!" Sandra had said, surprised, her gold-brown eyes wide.

"Well, now, you'll let me know if everything isn't all right," the clerk had said, suddenly won; "we may have some late cancellations, and in that case I'll see you're moved."

So here she was in the big room where a nurse and a child often were put, and she knew even in these first few minutes that she would accept no change, no matter what cancellations were made. No, this was hers for three wonderful days and three nights. It promised to have a share in the happiest adventure of her life.

Her suitcases were unpacked with the care that meant that every detail was a joy. She hung her dresses neatly on hangers; the old brown lace with the gold rose, the two plain rajah silks for hot mornings, the old blue taffeta and the new delicious evening dress she could not wait to wear. It was a plain enough dress, as befitted a secretary, but it was soft, silky, flowery, dimly colored in brick and brown and hints of gold; even to herself Alexandra looked taller, looked unwontedly well in it.

A great dressmaker, on far-away Fifty-seventh Street, had designed it especially for one woman, and that woman not Alexandra. Helen Romayne had worn it in a play, and after a few weeks had sold it to Mollie O'Mara, who had a "used frock" shop in Turk Street. And there Flossy and Sandra had found it yesterday for twenty dollars, as they found many of their clothes. It had the great Eva Metstein's own name in it, and the date was but five months back. Sandra knew there would be no prettier, smarter frock than this even at Del Monte. That a popular actress had used it first affected it not at all in her eyes.

Her new pajamas, her plain black Japanese robe devoid of trimming except for the little silver embroidered medallion on the sleeve, her white rabbit slippers, her boxes of powder and cream, all found their places. Alexandra set her typewriter and her fountain pen neatly on the little table desk; she put her book beside the bed beneath the night light. And all the time, as she went to and fro, it was hard to keep her happy feet from dancing.

At five, in the white plain tennis dress and the white hat, with white buckskin shoes, she walked downstairs, hardly able even now to believe that this was not a dream. But the sunset light on the gardens was real, the scent of the flowers was real, the smooth lawns were deliciously firm beneath her feet.

She walked to the pool where some youngsters were splashing and swimming, and thought with a daring little lift at her heart that she might come down before breakfast, if to-morrow were as warm as today, and swim herself. She had learned to swim years ago at the Sutro Baths and the Lurline Baths, as a girl with the high school crowd.

Beyond, under the oaks, the rolling highway went from the hotel grounds past the long shadows on the golf links to the cemetery, and up the little rise to the Mission whose bell tower was pierced by arched openings that showed the ancient bells. Shadows were blue upon its weather-beaten adobe walls.

To the right lay the fishing harbor of old Monterey, with the fleet in; gulls were careening madly over the shining flats and reflecting their white wings in the low shallow slide of the tide. Nearer was the new town and the modern note of movie houses, cafeterias, souvenir shops filled with abalone pearl pins and painted slices of redwood. But even here there were wonderful bits of plaster wall hiding away deep gardens a century old, and glimpses of balconies and shutters against banana and mimosa trees and blue-flowered passion vines.

Sandra wandered back to the hotel; it was after half-past six o'clock now and the dining room was opened. She had thought she might have to change for dinner, but evidently everything was very informal to-night; she could slip in quietly in her plain white and experience all the thrill of listening to music, watching the crowd, and enjoying a delightful dinner, quite unobserved.

The music made her think of Carter, and once again it seemed like a dream that this man, of all the men in the world, had given her his friendship. The past—those months so short a time ago when all this had been sealed from her eyes—seemed dim and unimportant now; of the future she would not think.

It was useless to remind herself that Carter was a married man, with obligations befitting wealth and position and domestic responsibility. It was futile to say to herself the words that nice girls did not fall in love with married men, especially when those married men were their employers. Alexandra herself was a nice girl, a scrupulously proud and fine girl, and she was in love with a married man who was her employer.

As for Carter, with his fineness, his friendliness, his puzzled small-boy anxiousness to play fair, his occasional flash of a passion that frightened her with its depth and its earnestness, he was not to be trapped by any petty general rules of morality or convention. What he and Alexandra Trumbull decided to do would be their own affair, and no one else's.

Fortified by these reflections and by the deeper, more emotional happiness that the mere thought of him brought her, she slept deep, and went down to breakfast at eight the next day in glorious spirits.

And now she discovered for the first time that the duties of a secretary "in the field" were no sinecure. The delegates to the convention were arriving in droves by train and motor car. The entries for the golf tournament had to be listed, handicaps recorded, the time and order of play-offs— as furnished her by the tournament committee—noted.

There were also tennis and swimming matches, and a bridge tournament in which the wives were to participate.

Eagerly she plunged into it. Her face grew flushed and her hair tumbled; she laughed cheerfully as she scratched names, added fresh ones, copied new pairings of contenders, turning constantly from typewriter to telephone and back again. Bellboys came and went, perspiring porters pushed hand trucks laden with luggage, guests were being paged, golfers, slated for immediate participation in the morning round, vainly sought. Sandra loved the excitement, loved being in the thick of it all. She had quite forgotten everything but the problems of the moment when she heard Carter's voice, and looked up to see him smiling at her.

"How goes it?" he asked.

Their eyes held one another's.

"Fine."

"Can you handle it?"

"Oh, heavens, yes!"

"You look happy," he said.

"I am."

"Treating you all right?"

"Oh, perfectly—marvelously. I'm having a wonderful time."

"It doesn't look marvelous to me," Carter commented simply.

It did not matter what they said; these were moments of magic.

"This is the worst of it," she told him. "Mr. Stevenson told me that after two o'clock there wouldn't be any more until about five."

"Good," he said. "It's nearly eleven now. Will you go to lunch with me at two o'clock?"

"The dining room closes at half-past one!" she reminded him, with round eyes.

"Oh, is that so? Well, will you go to lunch with me at two?"

"Yes!" she agreed, with a laugh.

"I'm in Cottage Two, by the way," he said. "They've given us a lot of room—my brother and Joe Hamilton, and this man Sam Kirby of New York. I'm going over there now to unpack and clean up and all that, and then I've got to do some telephoning. But two o'clock?"

"Two o'clock," she said.

When the hour came she put herself entirely into his hands, asking no questions; it was wonderful to let him take the full responsibility. He had parked his car down the drive toward the Roman Plunge; there it stood, twinkling brown, under the big trees. Sandra got in and settled herself and was happy.

"Are you starving?" he asked. "Or would you like to see Cypress Point and Pebble Beach and Carmel? They're all strung along in a row."

"I'd rather eat," Sandra said firmly. Carter laughed.

"Come on, then, we'll eat!"

The girl asked no questions; indeed she hardly spoke at all, as he climbed the Carmel grade and descended to turn the car south and drive along a winding dirt road that followed the line of the cliff.

They went through a toll gate and out upon a wild point crowned with tangled pine and oak trees. Below them the sea foamed angrily over the sharp points of rocks; gulls wheeled and piped in the fine mist that rose from the splintered breakers. But the sun shone warmly and peacefully on the short tufty grass just above, and the face of the cliff was set closely with symmetrical little plants like the stars and daisies and tiny berries of a Botticelli foreground.

Carter put a leather luncheon case on the furze beside an ivory-smooth polished fallen log, and Sandra unpacked chicken and sandwiches, and poured coffee from the thermos bottle into the fascinating little white enamel cups. Not much was said as they feasted, but their eyes kept meeting, with a felicity, an understanding needing no words.

"You are the most wonderful woman in the world. You are the most beautiful woman in the world. There is no one like you," Carter said, when they had finished.

"This is lovely!" Sandra murmured more than once, on a long deep sigh.

"I wish we had brought Patsy!" he presently exclaimed. And she liked that; she liked the idea that he would have been glad to have his little girl with her.

They stayed on the cliff until after three. It was all enchanted; it was too perfect. Carter told her that it was the happiest hour of his life.

"Just to be with someone I can talk to," he told her; "just to be here with you, and quiet . . ."

He spoke of his boyhood, and Sandra made him laugh with stories of her own small days: her mother's theatrical experiences, her babyhood in the wings and greenrooms of theatres.

"And yet you didn't want to be an actress?"

"Never. Mother always said that I ought to fall in love," Sandra confessed, smiling. "She said an actress didn't know anything about acting it until she fell in love."

"And do you suppose you ever will, Miss Trumbull?"

"I'm sure I don't know, Mr. Cavendish."

"Don't we have fun!" he exclaimed, after a while.

"Ah, indeed, don't we have fun!"

At half-past three she said she must go back, and he that he must go, too. But they hated to move from their comfortable seats on the rough stiff furze, with the big log at their backs, the afternoon sun beating warmly down upon them, the sleepy sea rolling in to splinter into mist in the channels and rocks below their feet.

"Sandra, one thing——" Carter said, when they were standing. His tone brought her heart almost to a stop; she looked at him expectantly, without a word.

"Did you know this, my dear," he said, putting his hands on her shoulders, but holding her only lightly, "did you know that two years ago I asked Mrs. Cavendish to give me a divorce?"

Sandra's eyes widened. Still she did not speak.

"After Patsy was about five," he said, "she left me in no doubt that she had ceased to care about me. D'you get me, Sandra?"

"Surely," Sandra answered slowly, with a dry throat.

"I wanted you to know."

"But—she wouldn't, Carter?"

"She wouldn't give me Patsy. And Patsy——" He smiled, but Sandra knew his heart was not smiling. "Patsy's an awfully good little sport. I couldn't throw her down," he said. "You see, Pat's different from other children; she's musical, she's gifted. I don't quite understand her—she's a queer kid—I know she needs me. No," he finished wistfully, "I couldn't throw Patsy down."

"Is Mrs. Cavendish as fond of her as you are?"

"Well, yes; but in a different way. Betty's strong for the violin and goes in for riding and diets and teeth. All I do is spoil the kid! Now, mind you, we don't fight, Betty and I," he said, as they turned toward the car. "But it's just civility, friendly enough, if you happen to have lukewarm milk running in your veins."

The glance he gave his companion suggested to Sandra that it was not lukewarm milk that ran in his veins at all events, and the excited happy thrill sprang up in her heart again.

"That was all I had to say," he added. "Except this: I am going to ask her again."

They stopped walking, and somehow she managed to raise her eyes to his.

"What about Patsy?" she whispered.

"She may feel differently about Patsy now," Carter said. "In any case, she wants to take Patsy to Europe for a few years. She wants her to study the violin."

He opened the door of her side of the roadster and Sandra got in. Carter slammed it shut and stood there leaning on the car, his face close to her own, his big brown hand covering one of hers as she rested it on the top of the door.

"Listen," he began, steadily, unemotionally, "I don't know how we started into this. I can't remember! I remember thinking that pretty Miss Trumbull was—— But Lord," he broke off with his boyish smile, "it doesn't seem possible that that was *you*.

"However it began," he recommenced, "it's everything I have in life now. I have to have you, Sandra. I have to have your love. I have to have you being kind to me for all the rest—the rest of the years there are! It was a sort of joke once, a sort of daring—taking a pretty girl to lunch, giving her flowers. It's no joke now!"

"It's no joke now," Sandra echoed, faintly. "Carter," she added, arresting him with a faint movement of her fingers in his, "I've been feeling so badly about it. Not at first; then it all seemed fair. I had nothing then! But now, when I have so much, I've felt so ashamed. I did what I knew was wrong. But it seems now," she went on, with her face flushed and earnest—"it seems as if it were some other girl who had done that, a cheaper girl—a—coarser girl——"

"I feel like that myself," he agreed, instead of protesting against her burst of self-blame. "I feel as if we had started in one way and were—were coming out another," he ended ineloquently.

She laughed ruefully, happily, in a sort of shamed relief. "You feel it too?"

"Feel it! Why, Sandra, everything's different. You and I," Carter expanded it—"you and I, sitting on the grass here and talking and laughing like a couple of kids, are we anything like the man and woman who went to lunch last November? You can't hold us responsible for what *they* did."

"But if—doing that—flirting, putting it on, taking a chance, whatever we did do," she argued, with her faint anxious frown—"if that brought us to this—to the real thing—*then* was it wrong?"

For a full minute they looked at each other, the man smiling, Alexandra's face gradually losing its sober look.

"I was so unhappy, Carter. I was afraid nothing good would ever come to me; I was ready to steal, if I couldn't get it honestly. But now, now I'm only afraid that it *is* coming, and that I won't be ready for it!"

"It's made that difference in me, too," he answered. "I don't know just how it's all going to come about, or whether it can come about. It's all up in the air. But—well, I want it to be right now; I want it to be honest."

Her gold-brown eyes were filled with eagerness. Her fine, nervous young hand clung tightly to his own.

"So that if the start was wrong, Carter, the rest will be different, the rest will all be right?" she asked, like a confident child.

"The start wasn't wrong," he said. "It was just that we—seemed to see it all differently then. And Sandra," he reminded her, "we haven't won the day yet. It's all in the future. Betty may not let me go."

"But she doesn't love you, Carter!"

"No, she doesn't love me. But you've got to remember that to our crowd ours is just—well, one more marriage. Home and cars and maids and furniture and kid; all that makes a sort of—sort of——"

He floundered, smiling at her, shrugging his shoulders.

"I know," Alexandra said reluctantly, slowly.

"It sounds so easy to bust all that up," Carter went on. "But it's—it's a rotten job. My mother and my grandmother'll raise hell," he added simply.

"They love your wife?" the girl asked quickly, with a little stab of jealousy.

"They love the whole—racket," he answered.

Despair chilled her. She looked down at their linked hands, looked up with shadows playing in the golden depths of her troubled eyes.

"Then—what?" she whispered.

"Exactly—then what?" he echoed. "That's just what I'm going to find out. I'm going to talk it over with Pete. I'm going to see if Betty's changed her mind in two years."

"Tell your brother?" Sandra echoed fearfully.

"Oh, you don't have to be afraid of Pete. He's a wonder. Did you know that Pete was Betty's beau before she ever thought of me?"

"No!"

"Yep. Pete was cracked about her when I came back from college. I was twenty-two and he about twenty-eight. He went off around the world. I never knew why."

"He told you afterward?"

"No; she did. They've been great pals since, but I guess it hit the poor old fellow pretty hard. Pete'll see all this clearer than I do," Carter predicted.

"Carter, I never thought of all this—your brother and divorce and Patsy. It'll all come out right, won't it?"

"It'll all come out right," he assured her. "We must just

sit tight. Meanwhile," Carter went on, smiling down at the flushed face so near to his—"meanwhile, I'm not going even to kiss my girl!"

The thick dark lashes that fringed her eyes were lifted; over her sober face a hint of her own illuminating smile flitted.

"I love you, Carter!" she wanted to say, but the words would not come. Instead her eyes filled with tears.

Driving back to the hotel a few minutes later she said:

"I never will forget that place or that picnic. I feel as if I were older, as if I were someone else."

"Don't be anyone else," Carter said.

"Older and better," Alexandra explained. "What was that place?"

"Point Lobos."

"Point Lobos. I'll always remember it."

"I hope to take you to all sorts of places—Paris and Honolulu, some day."

"It would be fun enough to go right on working in the office together," she suggested wistfully, "and having lunch at the Palace and having the right to go home together at night. I wouldn't care if it was three rooms in McAllister Street!"

"Until I have my talk with Pete and Betty," he began in a businesslike tone, "what d'you think of stopping the lunches?"

"Positively!" she agreed quickly. "And you know," she went on, after a moment, "I must—I *must* give up my job. I don't feel right, going on. Flossy thinks I ought to stop, and I *know* I should."

"I suppose so," he said slowly.

"I can always get a stenographer's position with the Standard Oil."

"Taking dictation from somebody else?"

"Well, Carter—I *must.*"

"I suppose so," he repeated.

"Alexandra," Carter said when they were rolling back through the dunes and cottages of Carmel and through scattered, fish-scented Monterey and past the golf links, "we've come a long way to-day."

"I feel as if we had!" she agreed, her face radiant. She went upstairs along the winding corridors and the ramps of the hallways on winged feet.

CHAPTER TEN

THE ENCHANTED June-time life at the big hotel went on; it was one blur of ecstatic happiness to the quiet secretary who discharged her duties in connection with the tournament so scrupulously, and drifted about when not on duty with so radiant a face.

On Saturday she watched the golf, morning and afternoon. Never before had Sandra seen a game, and the first of these had the unspeakable thrill of including Carter among the players. He lost to his opponent in the second round, and was free at five to drive her about Cypress Point and show her the new country club and the magnificent homes, Spanish, Italian, Byzantine, Colonial English, that were built over the rocks and the surf along the shore.

They had been asked to tea at one of the most fascinating of these. Betty Cavendish and her hostess had been among the two or three hundred spectators who had strolled after the golf players, and in the afternoon Sandra had met them and Carter with them.

There had been a pleasant exchange of greetings.

"Miss Trumbull!" Betty had said cordially. "Mr. Cavendish told me you were here! Are you having any fun? Is the hotel awful with this crowd?"

And Betty's friend, fat, soft Mrs. Bray, who had been picking her way along gingerly, hot and uncomfortable in a beautiful frock and four-inch spindle heels, had said in indifferent kindliness:

"Why don't you go and get Miss—Miss—this afternoon, Carter, and bring her over for tea? It must be horrible in that hotel bedlam! I'd like to show you my dogs, Miss—Miss——"

"I think you'd really enjoy it," Carter told Sandra, discussing it later, as they drove through the pine forest after leaving the Point. "The Brays' place is well worth seeing. She was a Brink, you know, and the old Senator had scads . . ."

So Sandra went to tea on the beautiful terrace of the Bray house, and could watch Betty and Peter and others of Carter's intimate set while she sat in a great Filipino chair with a curved high back like a fan, and sipped her orange pekoe. Behind her the setting sun flamed across the Pacific; before her were the arches of the terrace cloister, the awnings and rugs and basket chairs that made the place ideal for lounging, gossiping, bridge, the before-dinner cocktails, the tea hour—in short, for all of the out-of-door life of the household.

More interesting, painfully interesting, to Alexandra was the sudden entrance upon the scene of little Patsy Cavendish with Barbara Bray. Patsy had been riding and was in rumpled linen with leather boots and cap. She was eight years old; small for her age. Delicately built, slender, her soft dark hair in a cloud on her neck, her small brown face earnest and sensitive, there was something fairylike, unearthly about her. She had Carter's dark skin and flashing smile; Sandra saw how instantly she found him, how she clung shyly to his side. Patsy seemed quite different from the other children, older in her gravity, in the anxious expression of her little face, younger in the babyishness that sought out a protector immediately and held fast to him.

"Say how-do-you-do to Miss Trumbull, darling."

Patsy smiled shyly up at Sandra. The Bray girl, thirteen,

clumsy, her skin hot and broken, her big hands fumbling everything they touched, was also introduced. Barbara fell over everything, stuffed sandwiches into her mouth, licked greasy fingers.

"Hear you got licked, Uncle Cart?"

"Licked is right," Carter said. "I can't play in that gang of cutthroats."

"Rotten luck!" Barbara exclaimed, loudly.

"Barbara!" fat Rose Bray pleaded.

"Oh, I know I ought to say 'How extremely unfortunate, my dear Uncle Carter!'" the child rattled off glibly. She laughed, stopped laughing suddenly, turned a fiery red and, seizing Patsy, made her escape, overturning a light wicker magazine stand as she went.

"I ask myself every night," Will Bray said, "why I don't brain that girl!"

"She's simply terrible," Rose lamented, "and I can't do a thing with her, and neither can Fräulein."

"Siff monff Swifferlan——" Mrs. Fulton began, and interrupted herself long enough to swallow the mouthful of chocolate cake that had been impeding her speech. "Six months in Switzerland would be the makings of her, Rose," she said.

"Oh, don't tell *me* that!" Rose exclaimed, significantly.

"Believe me, I'm going to get Patsy over there this year," Betty Cavendish said.

Sandra did not look at Carter; her eyes moved only as far as his brown hands, casually leafing a magazine. She saw the fingers stop moving; move again. Her heart followed suit.

"Cart," his wife said, "remember we're having dinner on the *Yellowtail*, with Batesey. Seven-thirty, and only eight of us, so do for heaven's sake be on time!"

"Oh, Lord, I promised to meet the tournament committee at the Lodge!" Carter exclaimed, on his feet. "I told Bill Stevenson I'd meet him there at six o'clock sharp."

"I'll drive Miss Trumbull back," Peter Cavendish offered.

"Oh, I think I can make it in time!" Carter protested.

"Carter, it's quarter to six now! It's a good half hour to the hotel."

"I'll go with you," Alexandra said to Peter Cavendish.

His was a big car; she got into her usual seat beside the driver, and on the short run talked to him in her friendliest, her simplest manner. Upon this man's decision the happiness of her life might hang.

He was as like his brother as a big clumsy good-natured dog might be like a prize-winning specimen of the same breed. Where Carter was brown and hard-muscled, tall and athletic, Peter was slightly stooped, his big untidy leonine head bent a little sideways, a generally good-natured and sleepy expression replacing his brother's alertness and keenness. In the office, little more was known of him than that he loved music, never missed a concert, played good golf and superlative auction bridge, and that no one had ever found him ill-tempered or ruffled. Alexandra had gathered in addition that he and Carter loved each other deeply.

"Gettin' any fun out of this thing?" he asked her.

"Oh, the best time I ever had in my life!"

"Like Del Monte?"

"It's wonderful." Alexandra laughed. "I never saw it or any of this part of the country before," she added.

"Zat so?" He was plainly amazed. "I don't know where I got the idea you were a San Franciscan," he said.

"I am."

"Oh!"

"And that," she went on, to save him any embarrassment his too hasty conclusion might be giving him, "that makes it all the more wonderful!"

He gave her a friendly, approving side glance that brought her heart into her mouth, it reminded her so poignantly of Carter.

"Thank you!" she said at the hotel entrance.

"Quite welcome, I'm sure! By the way," Peter asked, in kindly interest, "you're having dinner here to-night. Going to look in on the dance?"

"I was thinking I might. It might be fun."

"Friends here? Someone to dance with?"

"Oh, yes—enough to dance if I want to. Thank you!"

"I'm playing bridge with three crooks," Peter explained. "But I could speak to Chandler here——?"

"Oh, Mr. Chandler and I are good friends. And I met some of the officers from the Presidio, too," Sandra hastened to say, smiling. "But thank you very much!"

That night she wore the Metstein creation. Coming downstairs at half-past seven she saw Joe Bullard, who had once worked for Cavendish & Bartlett, standing in the wide hallway, and they went to dinner together. Joe, a golf fanatic, had managed to squeeze himself into the hotel for the Saturday game, and was delighted to find Miss Trumbull there, and free, and so surprisingly—as he told her simply—"easy on the eyes."

"Joe, what happened to your red-headed girl?"

"Oh, Anna? Oh, gee, yes, Anna, she's okay," Joe answered, vaguely aware that everyone was looking at his companion as they walked into the dining room. Sandra seemed completely unaware of it.

But in every fiber of her being she was keenly, exultantly conscious of her gown and herself in it. She knew the effect of the dim flowery ruffles of brown and brick and gold against her smooth shoulders and round throat and the curve of her breast. She knew what her hair did to her head to-night, drawn sharply away from her temples, massed in little waves and curly ends on her neck. The loveliness of her gown was no more evident to her senses than her own youth and beauty.

"But how about you, Miss Trumbull? Aren't you going to get married?"

"Oh, some time! Maybe."

She encouraged him to talk about his Anna, because while he talked she could think of Carter and of the thrilling events of the day and of yesterday. Joe was still telling her artlessly about his affairs and his plans when, after dinner, they went out to look at the night. Alexandra stood staring up at the soft dark blue of the sky, the throbbing stars, the floating disc of light that was the moon. Barheaded, barearmed, the ruffles of the flowery gown falling about her, a strange sense of power and joy seemed to flood her being; she had never felt like this before; it was like being reborn. The feeling was enchanting, yet there was fear and bewilderment in it too.

"Dance?" Joe Bullard asked.

"Oh, are they dancing?"

"Sure. There's a dance here every Saturday night."

She and Joe went back into the hotel and walked through the big arches and halls, among the scattered dancers and spectators, to the ballroom. Not many couples were dancing, the music was perfect, the floor smooth; Sandra, thinking of Carter, danced with Joe.

Just before the second dance Carter joined them; Sandra had never seen him in evening dress before. Everything seemed to become dreamy and unreal; she could not speak— there was no need for words. Joe faded away into space as she surrendered herself to Carter's arms; the music seemed to carry her away from everything she had ever known before—her mother, her dull life between the dark back bedroom on Ellis Street and the office, away even from herself.

When the music stopped they stepped out into the sweet dark night, and Sandra looked up at the stars again, and the pale scarf of the Milky Way, and the moon that floated above the clustered tops of the great oaks.

"My girl can dance!" Carter said.

She turned to smile at him, and he could see her eyes glitter in the dark.

"I thought you were dining on someone's yacht."

"I was. But they had two tables afterwards without me, and I told Bates I was tired, and came home."

He jerked his head toward the cottages whose lights gleamed red between the bushes and tree trunks of the dark garden.

"Peter and the others are having a poker game; I'm going to sit in later on," Carter explained. "I asked Pete to lunch with me on Monday," he added, significantly.

"To talk?"

"Yep."

A delicious shudder ran through her; this man and his brother were to talk of her.

"Does he know?"

"Sure, I think he knows."

"It seemed to me when he brought me home this afternoon that he must know."

"He knows this," Carter said, looking up at the sky, "that I asked Betty two years ago—more than two years ago—to give me a divorce."

There was a silence. And in the silence she felt his fingers touch hers, grip them, hold them tight. Sandra began to tremble.

"She said she'd give me a divorce when my grandmother died. She knows Gran will leave Pats a lot of money."

"But she isn't just waiting——" Sandra turned her head, and her eyes glittered on his in the darkness. "She didn't say that!" she protested.

"Give you my word."

"But—to stay married for *that!*"

"Oh, she doesn't make any bones about it. That's the reason."

"But yet—knowing that you liked somebody else, Carter, wouldn't that make a difference?"

"It'd make this difference—that she wouldn't do it at all then," Carter answered. "That," he added bitterly, "is marriage. You like a girl when you're a kid just out of college, and she gets a stranglehold on you for life."

"That's not fair," Alexandra said slowly.

The garden below them was like a breathing presence in the night. Soft lights bloomed among the trees and sent pools of silver down on the walks where lovers wandered in darkness and in moonshine. A warm breeze rustled high up in the tree-tops and was gone.

"Some night," Carter said.

"The most beautiful night I ever saw," Sandra agreed.

"Did you ever think how simple it would be if marriages outlawed at—say five years?"

To this she made no answer. But after awhile she asked:

"Do you think—you do think, don't you?—that all this—our affair, I mean—can be worked out without hurting anybody? You think that—that Mrs. Cavendish won't mind it much?"

"I don't see why she should mind it at all."

"Because she knows," Sandra pursued it reasonably—"she *knows* you aren't happy—I mean that you and she aren't—doesn't she?"

"Unfortunately," Carter said, in a hesitating voice, "that may not do the trick. Betty, if she suspected that you were in it—a good many women—might feel, 'Well, if he wants to marry somebody else, I'll be hanged if I let go of him!'"

"But that's—that's being a dog in the manger!" Sandra protested. Carter laughed, and as she turned to him eyes that shone in the warm starlight he put both arms about her and held her lightly by the shoulders.

"I don't care!" he whispered.

She laced her bare arms against his, bracing her shoulders and drawing back as far as she could.

"I'm not going to hurt you!" Carter said. "But as long—as long as I have you I can't worry about anything! Betty may raise hell; I don't care!"

"No, and I don't care!" she breathed, infected with his own mood.

"Because, whatever happens, we have each other."

"We have each other."

"And that's the miracle. This time last year you were just one of the girls in the office."

"This time last year you were just one of the vice presidents of the firm."

"And this time next year," he said, "we'll—well, no, we'll not be married! But the day'll be set."

"Married!" the girl echoed in a whisper. "I hate," she added suddenly, in a hurt tone—"I hate to feel that you and I have to wait, to wait for anyone else. It seems our affair, just us, you and me."

"It'll pass."

"I'll be glad when it *is* past."

"It's done all the time, you know."

She had seated herself and her spreading ruffles in a deep porch chair. Carter had drawn a smaller chair beside it and was squared about, almost facing her.

"You mean divorces?"

"Sure. Nobody thinks anything about them any more."

"I don't believe," Sandra murmured, her hand locked tight in his—"I don't believe there's a woman in the world who doesn't mind—deep in her soul."

"Mind—being divorced?"

"Or liking a man before he is divorced; all of it. Your wife and you and me, we're all in it. And it's all horrid."

"Before you know it, it'll all be straightened out. Betty'll go to Reno or Paris; Paris, probably—that's where she wants to go. And you and I'll see each other all the time, and have little dinners and Sundays; it won't seem long. We'll have Pats half the year."

"It might have been better," she said gloomily, her eyes near his own in the dark of the wide porch—"it might have been happier for us all if you and I had never met each other."

"That's a silly way to talk!"

The girl laughed penitently.

"I know it. But it—it seems——" She interrupted herself abruptly. "It has to be that way!"

"So we might as well be sensible about it."

"We might as well be sensible."

"Because look, honey, there's no use saying what might have happened—if I'd never married, or if Betty died."

"I know, Carter. I know!"

"I mean, we have to take it the way it is, dear."

"Well, of course."

"And in a couple of years we'll be just one more married couple. We'll have a place down here somewhere for summers; nobody'll pay any attention to us!"

"That's what we have to think about."

"Exactly!"

"I suppose," Alexandra said—"I suppose this is going on all the time, only we don't know it!"

"Of course it is," he said, eagerly reassuring.

"Perhaps," she confessed, looking down now at the big, hard hand that held hers so closely—"perhaps what I'm really afraid of, Carter, is that, somewhere in all the delays and confusion and everything, we'll—we'll lose each other."

She heard him laugh.

"That's what's worrying you?"

"Kind of," she answered youthfully.

"Why, you darling, if we had to wait seven years, it wouldn't make any difference to me!" he said.

"That's what I want you to say, Carter. But that's what I can't believe."

"Well, you're going to hear me say it over and over and over."

"I seem," she said slowly, looking down at the thumb she moved idly against his brown hand—"I seem to—give so little and take so much!"

He looked at her, stretched back in the low chair, her ruffled gown spreading about her. The moonshine was in her eyes, and against the dim lights that penetrated through the hotel windows her head was aureoled in its own stately beauty; the soft gloom showed the outlines of her bare shoulders and the ivory smoothness of her throat. Against Carter's hand her own hand was quick and warm.

"You give me you," Carter said. "You give me ten years—twenty years—thirty years of having the woman I love best in the world beside me! I've never had that, Alexandra. I've never had companionship—just comfortable, affectionate companionship. I want it so! Every man wants it. I want a lovely, kind, friendly person around me; that's all."

"That's everything!"

"That's everything."

"We only have to wait a little while to have everything."

"So let's be sports about it."

Alexandra laughed.

"All right. I'll be a sport."

"Good girl," he said.

"And now I'm going upstairs. And to-morrow I probably won't see you at all. This man—the man I was dancing with when you came in—is driving up at ten o'clock, and he'll take me home. The trains will be terrible, with everyone going away."

"I wish I could drive you up," he said. "I can't. I'm playing a foursome with Pete and the two other chaps in the cottage."

"I know you are. Your brother told me so."

"Isn't he a good old guy, Pete?"

"He's lovely to me now," she agreed, with a faint significance on the last word. "But I imagine he'll feel terribly about your getting a divorce."

"Why should he care?"

"Oh, I don't know. I think he adores you, Carter."

"Well, then," Carter argued mildly, "he ought to be glad to have me get a beautiful wife."

"He said he was devoted to Betty—to Mrs. Cavendish."

"He used to be crazy about her. I don't know whether he is or not, now. Well," Carter went on, musing and amused, "maybe they'll fix up something. I never thought of that!"

"I think that would be terrible!" Alexandra protested.

"What'd be terrible about it?"

"Oh, for a person to be married to a man and then marry his brother!"

"It's been done. You know what the Potts and the Arkers did?"

"But Carter,"—she did not hear his question—"you and your brother would always be friends?"

"Sure. Why not?"

"But then if he was married to your first wife, how *could* you be friends?"

"But I don't have to fight with Betty just because we were divorced! As a matter of fact," Carter added, "that would probably be a situation she'd love. She's very dramatic."

"It would be ghastly."

"Well, don't you worry, honey, there isn't much danger. Peter probably wouldn't marry her or anyone under chloroform! But Betty's very casual about marriages—half her friends are divorced, and she always stands by 'em and defends 'em. In this Arker case she fought on both sides——"

"What was that?" Alexandra asked, as he stopped to laugh.

"Oh, they were in Paris, the Fletcher Potts and the Arkers—and they all got very friendly, and it turned out that both the women had had half a mind to get divorces while they were over there. But they got playing round together, and things sort of smoothed out and they went to races and down to Biarritz and everywhere together, and finally they decided to get divorced and all marry again the other way."

"Carter!"

"Certainly they did; why shouldn't they? And the Potts took a place near Nice after they were married—that is, Phyllis Arker and Fletcher did—and they asked the others down and they had a swell time. It was all in the paper."

"Well, honestly, I think that is about the most disgusting thing I *ever* heard!"

"That's what my mother thought. But I don't know," Carter went on tolerantly—"I don't know what's so disgusting about it. They're really awfully nice people; you'll like them. And if they were tired to death of each other——"

Alexandra felt suddenly tired and depressed. The road before her seemed ugly and sordid. She felt a wave of resentment; it was not right that she, Alexandra Trumbull, should be put, in spite of herself, in the class of such women as Mrs. Pott and Mrs. Arker. She rose and told him that she was tired; she was going upstairs.

Carter had never seen her in this mood before; it made him at once anxious and amused.

"What is it, darling? You're tired?"

"No," she said perversely, walking rapidly ahead of him toward the lighted hallway. Tears glittered in her eyes.

"Sandra—dearest——" His hand stopped her; she half turned. "Why, what is it, you poor little muggins!" Carter exclaimed, tenderly.

"Oh, nothing——"

"Ah, but tell me, dear!" He would not let her jerk away.

"Oh, just that I hate it all to be so horrid," she said morosely.

"It won't be horrid," Carter assured her seriously. "And at the end, we'll have each other. Can you imagine our letting things go on, and *not* having each other?"

A reluctant smile tugged at her mouth; she gave him a fleeting look at her eyes.

"No-o-o."

"Well, then, darling? And I'm doing it all—you've only to wait!"

Sandra was softened; her eyes showed penitent in the gloom.

"I'm sorry I'm so peevish."

"You peevish!" Carter echoed with a joyous laugh. They went in together.

CHAPTER ELEVEN

THE ORCHESTRA was playing a dreamy slow waltz as they reached the ballroom. Sandra put up her bare arm, and Carter's arm came tightly about her—the most wonderful feeling in the world. She was swept off her feet, out into the wide ocean of enchantment and ecstasy. She could hear him humming the words of the song as they danced:

> *"This waltz . . . is the kiss waltz*
> *Telling us both what to do . . ."*

It was breathlessly, briefly, that she said good-night to him in the big hallway by the elevators a few minutes later.

"I'm going to take you up to your room," Carter said.

"I'd rather you didn't."

"Please let me!"

"Please don't."

The world was all melody and excitement and the beauty of big darkened halls and softly swaying distant music, and she was twenty-one and wearing her first formal evening gown.

"Then come out on the porch for just one more minute!"

"Truly, truly no, I won't."

The elevator was waiting now and she stepped into it and he with her. Alexandra said nothing as she got out on the top floor and they walked down the long corridor together in a throbbing silence. Turning up the big ramp he said:

"I want to see you to-morrow. What time are you going?"

"About ten, I think. It's a long run, you know. It's more than a hundred miles. Mr. Bullard is stopping for his girl and her brother in Santa Cruz, and we're to lunch there."

"Oh, he has a girl, has he?"

"Oh, my, yes!"

"Good for him!" Carter exclaimed cordially, and Alexandra laughed. "What's her brother like?" he asked.

"Whose brother?"

"This man's girl's brother?"

"Oh, I've met him. He's fascinating!"

"Zat so?" Carter asked dryly, and Sandra laughed again. "He's fourteen," she said.

"You ought to get kissed!" the man warned her, and set her pulses hammering once more. They had almost reached her door now, at the far end of the long hall, and she began to wonder uncomfortably if he would want to come in, and if she could refuse him if he did. He had a way of making her feel very inexperienced, very young, alternately afraid of him and ashamed of herself for being afraid.

Another girl was saying good-night to a man at an opened doorway across the hall. It reassured Sandra to see them. After all, it was not very late, it was not yet midnight.

Carter neither asked to come in nor seemed to be thinking about it. He unlocked her door for her and detained her a minute for a farewell word. She was even conscious of a little sense of flatness that she had been so fearful where there was nothing to fear.

"What time do you breakfast?"

"About half-past eight, I suppose."

"I'll be over."

"I hate to go," Sandra lamented. "It's been so beautiful, so wonderful!"

"You'll have more visits here."

"But none like this one."

"Well, we'll have breakfast anyway," he said.

"Don't forget your twelve-o'clock date!"

She had said it carelessly. But his surprised glance made her instantly serious.

"What twelve-o'clock date?"

"Why—why, Carter, you got that message!"

"I got no message."

"The message from the office this evening?"

"Not a word."

"Oh, gracious!" she exclaimed, once more the secretary. "Why, I telephoned your cottage and nobody answered, and then I remembered you'd said you were to meet Mr. Stevenson and the tournament committee at Pebble Beach Lodge. I called him and he said you'd just left, so then I telephoned Mrs. Cavendish at Mrs. Bray's; I talked to her myself, and she said she'd surely tell you. I don't think it was so awfully important," Sandra hastened to add; "it was Mr. Pocock in New York. He called the office in San Francisco, and they called me here; they got me right after I got back from Mrs. Bray's about six-thirty. They told me they'd call you again at twelve to-morrow, our time. I told the operator downstairs you'd be at your cottage waiting for the call."

"Sure," Carter agreed. "What's it all about?"

"It's a transfer—as nearly as I could get it—a transfer for a big block of stock. Mr. Pocock wouldn't act without personally discussing it."

"Why didn't he call earlier than twelve if he was in such a hurry? That's late by their time. That's four o'clock."

"Perhaps he was going down to the office Sunday afternoon"

Her door was open, and Carter could see the big dim orderly room within, the window curtains moving lazily in night air, the lamp lighted above the two fat white pillows. Sandra's pajamas had been laid on the bed.

Suddenly while they stood there the telephone rang sharply.

Alexandra glanced at him, surprised, as she moved toward the instrument.

"Could it be your brother? No, he wouldn't know you were here."

Carter, in the room now, touched her arm.

"I wouldn't answer that!" he warned her in an undertone.

"Wouldn't answer it?" Her honest eyes were so amazed that he laughed in a little shame and confusion. "It might be my mother."

"It might. Oh, listen," Carter exclaimed, with a complete change of tone. "It's the New York call. *That's* what they meant, 'twelve o'clock your time!' Pocock always calls at night."

"Oh, *that's* what it is. Of course—— Hello?" Sandra said at the mouthpiece. "It *is* New York," she said in an aside to Carter, "trying to locate you. All right," she said to the operator, "put that call through as soon as it's ready.

"It must be important," she observed surprisedly, as she hung up the receiver and turned to Carter; "she said they had been trying all evening, and that they were coming on again in five minutes."

"It's not important at all," Carter predicted. "It's Pocock. He blows up at the least chance. He's probably the biggest ass in the business. This is a sweet time for him to be calling anyone."

They stood staring irresolutely at each other. Sandra had thrown her light wrap on the bed; she sat down in a winged old chintz-covered chair; the soft light set off the colors in the spreading ruffled gown and shone on her tumbled hair and her bare shoulders and the gold-brown eyes that looked dark in the unusual paleness of her face.

"You're beautiful, Alexandra," Carter told her.

"I must be—tired to death and with my hair all tousled!"

"You are actually the most beautiful person I ever saw."

She smiled at him, wearily, happily.

"It'll take me days—weeks—to think out all of the—the *joy*—of these few days, Carter. It's dizzied me; it's been almost too much."

He was seated sideways on a small chair, his arms locked across the back, his eyes studying the girl in the chintz-covered armchair.

"It dizzied me all right."

"It doesn't seem as if we had any right to so much—fun."

"I don't know where you get the idea," Carter observed, "that there is something wrong in having a good time."

"The people you go with," she mused, staring at him as if she were studying him as a specimen, "just about live for pleasure, don't they, Carter?"

"If they have the dough," he conceded simply.

"It's bridge, polo, tennis, golf," she went on. "They talk about going to New York for clothes, and going to Biarritz and Nice, and putting the children into school in Switzerland. They do just what they want to, don't they?"

"Why not?"

"Well, of course 'why not?'" Sandra agreed. "But the people I know," she added, after a moment, "do things because they have to, because they must. They live in places they hate on account of rent; they can't buy their children shoes and things; they have no tennis courts."

"No, but they have lots of other things."

"The law of compensation."

"Sure, the law of compensation. It's this everlasting whatnot that old guy what's-his-name is always talking about."

"Einstein!" Alexandra interpreted it, laughing.

"All right, laugh at me."

He looked at the silent telephone, looked at his wrist watch.

"I'll give Pocock half a minute more," he said, "and then I'll beat it. And if he should call—— Or no," Carter interrupted himself, starting up, "why didn't I think of that before? I'll tell the operator to put the call through to the cottage."

His hand was on the instrument when there was a sharp knock at the door. Alexandra's heart, for some reason she had neither time nor power to define, stood still. Her mouth grew dry; she looked at Carter in terror. The expression in his eyes chilled her.

"What's that?"

"I don't know," he said in an undertone. He was standing with his eyes on the door, his brow knitted, his evening overcoat on his arm. With a faint motion of his head he indicated she was to open it.

Sandra, bewildered, frightened she knew not why, went to the door. Two men and a woman, a middle-aged woman with a cold, stupid face, the alpaca dress of a housekeeper, and uncovered gray hair, were standing in the hall. The face of one of the men was vaguely familiar, but Sandra could not place it.

Nightmare followed. Like one trapped in a dream, unable to move, awaken, or escape, Sandra could only stand by and let the events that followed take their course.

The three late callers walked in and past her immediately, without waiting for explanation or invitation. The last of them, the man whose face she knew, closed the door. There was about the trio a sort of dreadful detachment; they seemed not to see Sandra at all and to pay but scant attention even to Carter.

"Mr. Cavendish was waiting for a telephone call from New York," Sandra began. But even as she spoke a wave of pride, a bitter sense of the flatness and futility of her words stopped her. She felt the blood burn in her face.

No one took any notice of the words except that one of the men gave her an abstracted glance.

"We might have thought of this," Carter said to Sandra in an undertone. "What's the big idea?" he asked the men.

"Sorry, Mr. Cavendish," the man Sandra did not recognize said respectfully. He moved his coat lapel.

"House detective, eh?" Carter asked in a measured voice with a touch of iron in it.

"No, sir. Haversham's."

"I see."

"May I ask your name?" the man said to Alexandra.

"This young lady's name has nothing to do with it," Carter broke in sharply.

"It's not important." The other turned to the woman and asked, indicating Sandra, "You'd know her if you saw her again?"

"Yes, sir," the woman answered.

Sandra, in her flowery ruffles, had backed against the bed, her eyes blazing in an ashen face. She stood holding the bedpost, her free hand pressed against her heart.

"Carter——" she whispered with a gesture.

Carter seemed to come out of a bad dream. He looked at her, nodded. His voice, when he spoke, had quite its normal, crisp ring.

"I think we needn't continue this," he said. "We've annoyed this young lady quite enough."

The detective was not listening.

"Identify this young woman?" The question was to the second man.

"Yes, sir. She was at Mrs. Bray's for tea this afternoon, sir," the man answered, studying Sandra at leisure. "I saw her then, sir."

In the middle of the nightmare Alexandra suddenly placed him. The butler who had offered her caviar and paté sandwiches this afternoon—such endless æons ago!—on the sunset terrace of the Brays' home at Pebble Beach. Happy, at ease, watching the pageant about her—only those few hours back. And now——

"You've got what you came after," Carter said brusquely to the detective. "I think we'd all better get out of here. I'd like to talk to you a minute."

"But let me explain——" Alexandra began with white lips. Carter smiled at her.

"They don't want explanations, my dear. They wouldn't be interested in them. This is Betty's work. I think I can fix things. You mustn't let yourself be frightened or concerned. Whatever happens, I'll see your name doesn't come into it; in any case, I'll see you early to-morrow."

He opened the door, nodded to the visitors. No one of them glanced at Sandra as they filed out. Carter went last, sending her just one reassuring half nod as he closed the door.

Alexandra sank down, sitting on the bed, her cold hand still gripping the wooden knob of its foot, her eyes staring vaguely into space. Now and then she swallowed with a dry throat. She felt tired, cold.

Some rioters emerged into the garden below somewhere, were vocal in the black night. Car engines started with buzzing and roaring; then there was silence again.

How long this lasted Sandra never knew; she was entirely unconscious of time and only vaguely aware of her surroundings.

After a long time she went to the telephone. She had to clear her throat twice before the operator could hear her.

"Could I have the chief operator, please?"

It had to be repeated. Then the girl said:

"There is only one operator on after eleven."

"Oh. Then perhaps you would know. Was there a New York call on this wire this evening?"

"No, ma'am," the girl said unhesitatingly.

"There was a call—about half an hour—an hour ago——"

Good God, that she had been sitting serene and happy and pleasantly weary in this very spot with Carter only a short hour ago!

"No, ma'am. That was a local call from the hotel."

"They told me," Alexandra persisted, feeling that she was going to faint—"they told me—it was New York—calling."

"You mean the party that got you at twelve?" the telephone girl exclaimed, outraged at this infringement of her sacred rights.

"Yes," Sandra answered, wearily. "It doesn't matter. It doesn't matter. Thank you," she said.

She hung up the receiver and went back to sit again on the bed. The world would go on and she had to go on with it. She could not stay here forever in this room that had staged the most terrible moment of her life; it would be morning after a while, and daylight. She must somehow go on into it, facing what she had to face, hearing the voices, conscious of the eyes.

"Oh, you fool—you fool—you fool!" she said out loud in a tired, dispassionate voice. "You—*utter*—fool."

The moments went on; she was hardly conscious of them. Her mind moved fitfully, now arrested by some trivial, unimportant thing, now clearly and swiftly recreating every detail of that moment when someone had knocked at her door, when her Cinderella dream of moonshine and waltzing and love had turned to pumpkins, mice, hideous glaring daylight.

"What now?" she wondered. What would happen now? Would she be a marked and disgraced woman when she emerged from this room to-morrow morning? Would the hotel take action? Would the papers get it? Betty—Betty had planned this. How long?

Well, only a few hours. It must have come to her as an inspiration; perhaps fat Mrs. Bray had thought of it. When Sandra had telephoned about the New York call perhaps Betty had thought, "She just wants to get hold of him!"

It sickened her to think of them talking about it, and of herself walking into the trap. The coarseness of it, the ugliness of it! In what words had Betty consulted the Bray butler? Had she and the others come to the hotel?

Not for one instant did Sandra credit Betty with any motive as honest as jealousy. Betty neither knew nor cared what the feeling was between Carter and "one of the girls from the office." No; she had seen a chance to be mischievous, and she had seized it.

Sandra pressed cold fingers to her blazing cheeks.

"She can't think—it's too ridiculous. . . . It would be easy to prove that we were waiting for a New York call. . . . But of course she doesn't really think anything at all. And it doesn't matter anyway. What matters is that I—I was caught like some poor little sixteen-year-old fool . . . I hate her. I hate that woman! . . . That butler—that horrible smirking—*animal!* . . . They can't make any real —case of this. A divorce—a 'co-respondent!' It's all too ridiculous!"

After a while, spasmodically, mechanically, she began to

undress. But her face was still blazing and her throat dry; there was a blankness, a futility about doing anything at all now. She had an impulse to dress again, go out and try to walk off the desperate fever of her thoughts.

She laughed a little bitterly as she locked her door instead and got into bed. Locking the door—*now*. The words of her book moved in meaningless circles under her eyes, the dreadful story that she was living completely obliterated them. As for sleep, she knew it was impossible. Never in her life had she felt more feverishly, hopelessly wide-awake.

After a while she put out the light and lay on her back, her arms locked under her head, her wide-open eyes staring at the dark bulk of the ceiling above her. The moon was setting now, and there was a blackness over the earth in the early hours of the summer Sunday morning.

Alexandra lay without moving hour after hour. Now and then she sighed.

All the circumstances of her life moved about her slowly like a panorama. The background was the back room of the frowsy, dirty house in Ellis Street; her limited little kindhearted, simple mother, who was yet so honest, so immovably "straight," the chief figure.

The child of this retired variety actress and a ne'er-do-well English younger son, Sandra had yet felt in herself from very babyhood impulses and ideals that had come from neither. She had known in high school days that to her mother's energy and her common sense she might well hope to unite something her mother never had had—the fineness, the intelligence, the ambition of her father's people.

All down in the dust now, those hopes and dreams and blind impulses toward goodness and improvement and cultivation! All over.

Anger would interrupt her musing.

"Oh, good heavens, in this day and generation, can't a

man step into a woman's room to take a telephone message without this kind of dirtiness!"

And then, with a sickening slow rising like some ugly tide, the memories would begin to return: the knock at the door, the private detective with his impassive, businesslike manner, the odious housekeeper and the butler from Mrs. Bray's sunset-flooded, awninged terrace above the Pacific.

"Identify this young woman?"

She would have a few moments of a sort of vertigo, when it all seemed to suffocate her, to rise and overwhelm her. Then everything would quiet down again and Alexandra would tell herself that rather than face any actual scandal she must give Carter up forever—she who had never had him, she would reflect contemptuously, and go away, anywhere, and somehow live through the next few years, and some day forget.

If it were only over—the flight back to town and her mother to-morrow, the horrible explanation and adjustment, whatever it must be, the good-byes at the office, the escape into blessed obscurity and work. Work—that must be her cure. . . .

The quiet hours of the black summer night wore away. She heard the clanking of milk tins far below her windows, the subdued burring of a motor engine, the early gay singing of birds. Morning was painting her big windows gray; it was the first day in her twenty-one years that found Sandra unwilling to see the light. Oh, to go back to yesterday and have this morning sweet and safe, like all the others! To wipe out those five brief minutes last night, to have them over, not to have to think about them!

She spoke in the soft gloom of her room, that room that had seemed so delightful only a few days ago and that was like a death cell to her now.

"You fool! You utter *fool!*"

CHAPTER TWELVE

IN THE COOL WET DAWN she got up and bathed and dressed herself carefully, pulling the white hat down snugly over the bright chestnut of her hair, wearing one of the plain white dresses, the white shoes, the tan net stockings.

Then she packed everything—the book Carter had bought her in Carmel yesterday, the flowery gown in which she had danced last night, the toy golf sticks that had been souvenirs at last night's dinner and which she had thought little Gemma Bevilaqua might like.

Her heart seemed to be slowly bleeding to death; she tried not to think.

It was still very early. Sandra went quietly downstairs and out into the gardens. The clocks were striking seven as she crossed the big empty office hall. Chinese boys were cleaning the floor, the big doors were all open, a yawning clerk was at the desk.

The blood flew to her face as he addressed her, but what he had to say was all amiable surprise and admiration for the young lady who was astir so early.

Sandra went on into the wet freshness of the morning air. Birds were still circling and singing; lawn sprinklers whirred, flinging fans of diamonds into the soft, opal morning. The air was still cool, but it held a promise of warmth to come; under the oaks the shadows were deep and wet, but light had found the pool and turned it into a great emerald.

Gradually, as she walked, healing and peace came to the girl's tortured spirit. She crossed a strip of bay beach, where the tide lipped idly on clinking pebbles and the air was scented with fish. Here gulls flapped and settled, printing little crisscrossed tracks on wet sands. The town's one crooked street was asleep, but the bells of the old Mission were ringing, and Sandra pushed open the swinging black door of the church and timidly entered the narrow building.

At this early hour the worshipers were of the humbler type; Sandra saw Mexican faces, Spanish faces, worn old Irish faces in the heavy candle-lighted dusk within. She heard Latin words; they had no meaning for her, but she rose and knelt with the rest.

She walked back slowly, thinking. The dining room was open and she could go in and breakfast. Other early risers, governesses with beautifully frocked, high-voiced children, were there; sunshine was everywhere and flashed on the silver and glass as the trays went to and fro. Sandra drank her hot coffee gratefully, played with toast.

Suddenly her heart stood still; a page was standing beside her with a note; she knew that handwriting. Trembling, the room going about her in a circle, she tore it open.

"Don't worry," Carter had written, without preamble, "everything is fixed. Hell of a night talking to Pete. For good reasons better not try to see you to-day. To-morrow in office."

It was signed merely "C. C."

The blood came back to Sandra's heart in a rush. The room settled down to normal. Life was life again, not a nightmare. She could smile at her waitress.

"I think I will. I think I'll have some scrambled, please."

The maid, who had seen the note delivered, smiled sympathetically. Suddenly everything everywhere was smiling.

Oh, the relief of it! The divine and heavenly reaction.

She opened her bag, took out the letter, read it again. Everything was fixed. She was not to worry. She put her elbows on the table and buried her face in her hands.

"Oh, my God, if I once get out of this! If only nothing happens, if only everything really *is* fixed!"

Everything was changed now; everything, if not restored to the happiness of yesterday, was at least no longer immediately threatening and fearful. She could breathe again; she could attempt to think.

But she was glad, just the same, to leave an hour later the hotel to which she had come with such a happy, carefree heart only three days ago. Joe Bullard found her a quiet companion on the long run. Sandra looked at the glittering ocean, at the rolling low foothills that were already turning brown; she met Joe's occasional sidewise glance with her own slow smile, but she had little to say. In Santa Cruz they stopped for Joe's chattering girl: Sandra was glad to take the obscurity and silence of the back seat.

Her mother was discovered to be fortunately absorbed in the demands of a sick old actress on the top floor when Sandra got home. Sandra could satisfy both with enthusiastic accounts of what was safe to report, and plead a sun headache as an excuse for retiring early.

But going to the office the next morning was hard work. After a second restless night, Sandra felt exhausted, nervous, jumpy. Every time the office door opened her heart stood still. Ten o'clock came, eleven o'clock, and there was no Carter.

At half-past eleven there was a message for her. Mr. Peter Cavendish would like to see her in his office.

Sandra was badly frightened. Her knees shook under her as she went through the main office and up in the elevator to Peter's office.

In this shady, spacious place of paneled walls and rich

dark carpeting the heavy wooden jalousies had been dropped against the hot summer sunlight. Peter was alone; he nodded to Sandra, indicating a chair with a movement of his big leonine head, and Sandra sat down and waited with such composure as she could command for the ordeal. After disposing of a letter or two, shutting a drawer, he picked up his desk telephone and spoke through it, his eyes on Alexandra.

"Please don't call me until I call you, Miss Willis," he said. "Miss Trumbull," Peter began, "good-morning." He opened another drawer, looked into it, closed it again, and looked up. The girl perceived that he was as nervous as she was. "About what—what happened—down at Del Monte," Peter recommenced. "My brother, Mr.—ah, Carter, thought perhaps that you and I could have a little talk——"

"*What* happened?" Alexandra challenged him nervously as he paused.

"Well," he conceded, with a tolerant shrug and a half smile, "you're right. Nothing happened; it was much ado about nothing. At the same time——" He stopped.

"It *was* nothing," Alexandra persisted, two nervous red spots burning in her cheeks. "I had danced with Mr. Cavendish——"

"Yes, yes, yes," Peter interrupted, moving a desk weight.

"I had danced with Mr. Cavendish," the girl repeated, brushing this aside, "and he walked with me to my room. When we got there the telephone operator told me there was a New York call for him, and I suggested he wait for it."

She had rehearsed all this through the hours of the endless night; polished and simplified what she must say. But somehow, now that her chance to say it had come, it did not seem convincing.

"You see," Peter said mildly, not looking at her as he

straightened his pens and pencils, "You see, that call was for twelve o'clock noon, yesterday."

"I know it!" His tone stung the color into her face. "But it seemed to me it might easily have been a mistake," she explained, eagerly. "When the telephone rang the first thing I thought of was they had meant twelve o'clock midnight."

"That would have meant that they were talking from New York at four in the morning," he offered mildly, always in the kindly, soothing tone of a man who fears a scene with a woman.

"I didn't know it was coming from an office," Sandra defended herself stubbornly; "Mr. Pocock might have been telephoning from his home!"

"There wasn't any telephone call at all from New York that night," Peter said.

"I know it, but there *was* one in the late afternoon! The second one of course was faked. . . . They deliberately faked it!" Sandra repeated with bitterness.

"Betty—Mrs. Cavendish denies that," Peter said, made uneasy by her vehemence.

"She's telling an untruth then," Sandra exclaimed hotly. "She'd planned to trick Carter before any of us went to Del Monte. How did it happen a Haversham man—a detective—was there all ready to carry out her orders? She'd hired the detective agency in advance to spy upon her husband!"

She had not meant to say it; she had determined, long before this, to keep her temper at any cost. But now it was said, and Sandra could see that she had displeased her hearer. Color came into his cheeks.

"She—unfortunately, had reason," he offered simply. "Let's—let's take this—reasonably."

"What reason?"

"Reason to believe that her husband, Carter, was spending a good deal of time in the company of another woman—

lunching with her, growing to be fond of her," Peter summarized it, uncomfortable, but with determination.

"Isn't a married man supposed to lunch with a friend if he chooses?" Sandra demanded, sulkily. She wished that she had not come in here, to be interrogated, humiliated, at all.

It sounded like poor Mamie Batts, dying in the Emergency Hospital, talking about her "friend." All Mamie's defenses hadn't saved her and her baby. All Sandra's were not making her feel proud of herself, honest, justifiable, now.

"I suppose, if he is married, the wife might feel she could object."

A silence. What a trap they had her in, and what a fool they were making her feel!

"It seems," Peter began again—"although neither my mother nor I realized it," he digressed to say—Sandra had a second in which to wonder resentfully what his mother had to do with it—"we never realized," Peter went on, "that there was any real trouble between them. But Carter tells me that he asked his wife to give him a divorce some time ago. He didn't, naturally, mention your name, but she says that she knew from his manner that there was somebody else."

"He asked her two years ago, before he ever heard of me," Sandra added bitterly. She saw him flush slightly again.

"Mrs. Cavendish is prostrated," Peter observed.

"Your mother?"

"Betty."

"At what? She doesn't love him," Sandra wanted to add indignantly. But she controlled herself, and instead said impulsively, like a penitent child, "I'm sorry. You can imagine," she stumbled on, tears in her eyes, her prearranged rehearsed words forgotten and her manner the simpler and more impressive for it—"you can imagine what a difficult position I'm placed in. I do—I do care terribly for Mr.

Cavendish—I can't deny that. He's different from anyone I ever knew—I couldn't help caring——"

Tears stopped her. She put up her head, swallowing, and let them run on her cheeks. Peter pushed his big soft handkerchief across to her.

"There's nobody like Cart, of course," he agreed, clearing his throat.

After that it was easier, although she had a bad twinge when he happened to say that the "one important thing was of course to protect Betty and Patsy."

Betty had been "wonderful." She had even said, yesterday afternoon, when Peter had driven her home from Del Monte, talking all the way, that she was sorry she had spied on Carter; Rose Bray had suggested it and she, Betty, had acted on impulse. That this impulse must have followed a complete confidence in Rose and a conspiracy between the two women to trap Carter evidently had not occurred to Peter.

"Frankly," Peter said, "I am going to tell you that we still hope, my mother, my grandmother, and I—I spent last night with them here in town—to reconcile them. It wouldn't be honest not to tell you that. Betty is a—splendid woman, and she is devoted to Cart. She sometimes may have a little flirtation here and there, as he does, but fundamentally—fundamentally——

"However. This was what I wanted to see you about this morning, Miss Trumbull. Carter went down to see—his wife this morning. He and I spent last night with my mother here in town. And he asked me to see you and tell you not to worry. He hopes to see you himself to-night or to-morrow.

"Mrs. Cavendish," Peter added in a dead silence as if that inflexible honesty of his were driving him to the unwilling statement, "Mrs. Cavendsih—Betty—feels now that she wants—that she won't—in short, that no reconciliation will be possible."

"Wants a divorce?"

He was uncomfortable, his face as well as hers red.

"I am afraid so." He smiled ruefully. "You see I'm quite honest with you," he said. "I say I'm afraid so. I'd be very glad if they could patch it up, for everybody's sake."

"Except mine!" Alexandra thought bitterly. But she did not say it aloud. Aloud she said, "If Mrs. Cavendish didn't want to give Carter a divorce two years ago, why should she take such trouble to do all this—to get evidence—now?"

"I don't know," he answered. But she suspected that he was holding something back, and it occurred to her suddenly that under these circumstances Betty could make any terms she liked: Paris, money, the custody of the child.

She sat staring down at his desk, scowling faintly.

"I'm very sorry, of course," she admitted reluctantly.

"It's most unfortunate!" he agreed, also staring down at his blotter. "I feel—my mother feels—completely upset about it."

"Mrs. Cavendish," Sandra began—"Mrs. Cavendish may use my name in this matter, of course. But I know—and that's all that matters!—that the circumstances were—well, were not what they seemed to be. And she," she added, with an upward glance—"she knows that, too."

"She wouldn't think of using your name," said Peter with a touch of quick, arrogant assurance that reminded her for a second of Carter.

"She couldn't, honestly," Sandra countered. "She has no reason to bring me into it. She has nothing against *me*."

"No," he agreed hesitantly. "And I don't think she'll— well, make any trouble. She hates—we all hate anything like newspaper notoriety."

"Newspapers!" Sandra whispered, dropping back into her chair again. She had half risen as if to terminate the interview; now she sat staring at him in blank dismay.

"A reporter was here this morning."

"But they don't—they can't connect *me* with it?"

"In case they did, in case they came to you," he said, "I'd simply—know nothing about anything."

"Good heavens!" Sandra whispered, looking into space.

"Eventually we'll give them some story. But meanwhile——"

He paused and shrugged. But Sandra was not paying any attention to him.

"We couldn't have it in the newspapers," she said.

After a moment's thought she leaned forward on the desk and spoke simply.

"Mr. Cavendish, you must see how silly this whole trumped-up story is—how unfair it is! Why, what has happened? Nothing. *Nothing!* Surely—surely Mrs. Cavendish would take her own husband's word for that if she wouldn't take mine?"

"Women," Peter answered hesitatingly—"women—well, they act queerly sometimes."

"Carter and I are friends," Sandra said. "I admit that. But it would be unjust—it would be untrue——" She stopped, baffled.

"I hope," he said, in the manner of a man who is troubled and reluctant—"I hope that it won't be necessary for anyone to—to *admit* anything. You mustn't think that we don't see your—your side of it, too."

"What *is* my side to it?" Sandra asked. *"I'm* not in it."

"But you *are* in it, you know," he insisted.

"Not unless Mrs. Cavendish makes statements that aren't true," Sandra persisted, hating her own voice.

"She won't make any statement that isn't true," Peter said.

His tone rather than his words gave Alexandra's rising anger pause. There had been no telephone call from New York to Del Monte late Saturday night. A private detective, accompanied by Mrs. Bray's butler and a hotel housekeeper, had discovered Mr. Carter Cavendish in Miss Alexandra Trumbull's room at midnight.

Her face burned. She was indeed caught.

"It's so *ridiculous*," she said, trying to speak lightly.

"It's too bad. It's all too bad," Peter agreed. "But I think it will clear up," he added more brightly. "I think you needn't be afraid of any—developments. Betty is a peppery little soul. But she is a splendid sport really. She'll come round all right. It was only—unfortunate, the way it all came about. And I think," he concluded, with a kindly impersonal smile—"I think the only thing for us to do is just—sit tight and keep it as quiet as we can."

"Which means that she can say anything she likes!" Sandra burst forth, to her instant regret. For once more he did not accept her challenge; she perceived that his one object after all was to soothe her, to quiet her down, to keep the Cavendish family safe from anything like a scandal.

The maddening part of it, the insufferable thing, was that her only course was to fall in with their plans. With the facts what they were, there was small chance of her defending herself.

"I don't seem to have any choice," she said, rising. "I have told Miss Curtis that I am giving up my position."

"You have?"

"I told her it was on account of my mother's health. Mother," Alexandra said, holding her voice steady, "isn't well."

"I'm sorry." Peter was on his feet, too; they faced each other across the flat desk.

"We will probably go away," the girl said, formulating the plan as she talked. "If that," she added—"if that makes any difference to Mrs. Cavendish, I wish you would tell her so. I haven't," Sandra went on—"I haven't taken her husband away from her, and I'm not running away. But if my saying that I don't intend to see him again will make any difference, you are at liberty to tell her so."

"It's too bad," Peter protested, in his own peculiarly gentle way, "they've always been so happy together."

Alexandra threw her head up proudly, opened her lips to speak, was silent. There was no use. There was no use.

"Well," she presently said, with a hard little edge to the voice that had so many haunting and tender cadences in it, "I won't complicate the situation any more. And I do thank you for—talking to me about it, Mr. Cavendish," she said, tears suddenly filling her eyes as she tried to smile. "I'll say good-bye to you now. I'm sorry for—all this. I may not see Carter again, but I'll write him what I've told you and how I feel."

"It would be very generous for you to do that," Peter said.

"It wouldn't be generous at all," Alexandra said, ungraciously.

"You can see," Peter argued, "that if we could patch it up, for the sake of the little girl and all——"

"I can see that."

"I don't mean," Peter exclaimed, in an obvious relief that Alexandra in another mood might even have found amusing, "that there was any *harm* in it, d'you see? But for the sake of my mother and the little girl and all of us, it *is* unfortunate! And if Betty *would* forgive him——"

From the bottom of her heart Sandra hated this man.

Fussy, nervous, trying to save only the Cavendish honor, the Cavendish privacy, she thought scornfully. She was trapped, baffled by it all, again.

"I won't see him again," she said.

Peter became serious.

"Thank you very much," he answered simply.

"The whole thing seems ridiculous to me." Young and tall and with a certain reluctant youthful awkwardness in her manner that had its own odd charm, she continued to face him with a puzzled and mutinous brow. "My—getting out," she persisted, "seems to make it look as if I had something to hide—as if I were ashamed——"

"No, no; I assure you it doesn't!" Peter exclaimed in the pause. She perceived that he was anxious to terminate the interview in all kindness and harmony, eager to be able to report to the others that Miss Trumbull had acted with great consideration and good sense. "After all, for a little while anyway," Peter added, kindly, "isn't that the wisest thing to do?"

"For the Cavendishes," she muttered, under her breath.

"For——? I didn't hear you."

"For the Cavendishes, yes," Sandra repeated, looking up.

"For you, too."

She pondered it, scowling.

"I suppose so."

The time had come to terminate this interview, for her to go. But still she stood on, staring somberly before her, biting her lip.

"It's so easy for you, Mr. Cavendish, to decide that Carter and I oughtn't to see each other again. It's so easy for her."

She was silent, and Peter said, somewhat vaguely and inconsequentially:

"I've never married, you know. But"—he cleared his throat—"I suppose it is!" he said.

"She doesn't love him," Sandra argued, always unwillingly, always in the same reluctant and rebellious manner, as if she were driven to speak, "And he and I—he and I——"

"I know," Peter put in sympathetically.

"And now," Sandra pursued, "I have to go away. I have to get out. I'm to blame."

"No, I wouldn't say 'to blame.' It's all——" Peter smiled brightly. "It's all unfortunate," he substituted.

She lingered, despising herself, unable to go until she had in some way restored or partially restored her injured self-esteem.

"Will you tell—Carter I am writing to him?"

"Indeed I will, Miss Trumbull! And you and I," Peter said cordially, imperceptibly—or so she fancied—edging her toward the door as he spoke—"you and I will talk this over again!"

"I do appreciate your sending for me—your talking to me," she persisted, in a sort of sullen gratitude, still lingering. "And until Carter feels that there's no use in trying to—to smooth it all over, I will do nothing."

"My mother and I will really appreciate that," Peter told her, gratefully. "She feels very badly about it."

"Then good-bye," Sandra said.

There was an interruption; the door knob rattled. Carter brusquely entered.

At the mere sight of him, groomed and composed, Alexandra felt half the weight that was resting there slip from her heart. He came over to her smiling, locked a big arm about her shoulders, and grinned across at his brother with all his characteristic little-boy openness and naturalness.

"Hello, Pete! Hello, dear," he added, in an undertone

for Sandra, with a keen look. "What have you and Pete been chewing the rag about? Lucky to find you," he went on to the girl, without waiting for an answer. "I asked Miss Curtis where you were, and she said that you were either here or at lunch. We'll go to lunch in a minute. I've just left Betty, Pete," he said to his brother.

Peter Cavendish looked almost ludicrously dashed at the sudden change in the atmosphere. The gently reproachful, monitory position he had taken toward Alexandra, and her sullen, apologetic, resentful attitude vanished like mist. Carter was exactly himself, bracing, eager, and confident. Peter knew that the careful, painful work of the last half-hour had been thrown away. For Alexandra the sun had suddenly burst forth in glory; Carter was beside her again, and nothing else was of any importance.

"Betty is going to see Reggy Pry to-day or to-morrow," Carter told his brother. "I've telephoned Jones. Isn't this," he went on, smiling at Alexandra, "the darnedest break? Jones," he explained, "is our lawyer."

"Listen, Cart," Peter protested in a troubled tone, and Sandra could have laughed at the dismay in his face, "you don't want to move too fast in all this."

"I'm not moving fast," Carter answered, almost cheerfully, but with a rueful tone in his voice too. "It's Betty that's putting the skids under me!"

"There's Mother to think of, you know," Peter argued unhappily, trying to draw him aside, speaking in an undertone. "And Patsy and—everything."

"And my girl!" Carter added, with an oblique glance for Sandra that sent the happy blood racing through her veins. And as Peter sat down heavily as one beaten, Carter leaned over to murmur to him rapidly for a few seconds, without releasing Sandra's fingers from his own.

"Now then, Sandra," he said, straightening up, "we'll

go and have lunch. You get your hat and I'll speak to Miss Curtis, and we'll meet—well, maybe we'd better meet downstairs. This thing may break any minute, and it's just as well not to get the office talking. Isn't she lovely, Pete? I'd forgotten how lovely she is!"

CHAPTER THIRTEEN

FIVE MINUTES LATER they were in the sunny street, together, walking toward the garage, and the world was once more singing and shining for Alexandra.

"Carter, it's been like some frightful dream!"

"Well, I knew it must be. But I couldn't get in touch with you until I'd sort of had it out with Mother and Betty and found out just how rotten they were going to act."

"Were they—rotten?" Alexandra asked timidly, as the roadster threaded the downtown traffic and turned westward toward the Park.

"No, they were both sports, everything considered. I think Betty knew she had done a stinking, dirty trick," Carter said, in a tone much milder than his words.

"Your brother feels terribly about it."

"Pete?" Carter laughed. "Oh, you mustn't mind Pete," he reassured her easily. "He's a sentimental old guy. He takes the family seriously. He adores Betty and Patsy, and he thinks everyone ought to love everyone else and that things ought to go on the way they are. This has been a terrible jolt to him; he evidently hoped Betty and I had given up the divorce idea, although I haven't made any secret about it."

"Does she feel furious?"

"Well, she was pretty much the injured, virtuous wife, with my mother just now. No," Carter went on, as sheer mortification kept Alexandra silent—"no, Betty doesn't really feel mad. She's wanted this for years, really. . . . You know Pete thinks you're grand, Sandra," he presently said, as Alexandra made no comment on this. "He was standing up for you last night."

"He *must* think I'm grand!"

"Well, he does."

"I don't see how you can say that, Carter."

"I want to tell you that that old boy feels as badly for you as he does for anyone. 'Why,' he said to my mother last night, 'Miss Trumbull is one of our finest young ladies— a very beautiful girl, an aristocratic-looking girl. To drag her into anything like this, to let Betty use her name——' "

"He sounded all for her this morning," Alexandra said, in a somewhat mollified voice, in the silence.

"He's all for everyone but me!" Carter explained it with a laugh.

They were seated at a little window table in a famous beach restaurant now; the hum of a dozen small dining rooms, through arches and doorways, was on Sandra's right; on her left the window gave upon the long strand, with its twinkling line of parked cars, and on the softly heaving blue ocean beyond. The early summer day was exquisite beyond earthly understanding; Sandra felt its unsensed and escaping beauty flowing about her like a healing ether.

"What are you laughing at?"

"I can't help laughing, Carter, although God knows I don't feel much like laughing. I was thinking how indignantly I promised Mr. Cavendish, your brother, not to see you again, and then walked off in three minutes to lunch with you!"

"Oh, you mustn't mind Pete!"

"I don't mind anything now."

"Pete's all up in the air," Carter said, leniently. "He got his worst jolt from Betty. She telephoned him this morning and asked him very calmly where I wanted my clothes sent. Pete nearly dropped dead. All through breakfast he kept saying, 'It happens to other people, but I never thought of it as happening to us!' "

The waiter interrupted; when he had gone with the order Carter said:

"Now that it's happened I feel like a kid. I'm going to move into town; I'll be with Mother and Pete for a while, and then I may go down to the Los Angeles office for October and November. Betty will be off to Nevada in a few weeks to establish her residence there, and then in six months she'll file her complaint for divorce on the ground of desertion. I'll write her I don't intend to live with her any more—and that's all there'll be to it!"

"Desertion! Then what was the object in trying to prove—in that performance Saturday night?"

"Oh, Lord, she never meant to prove infidelity."

"But then—why——?"

"To get what she wanted. To get alimony, for one thing—I've agreed to pay her two thousand a month—and to get the custody of Patsy. She would have divorced me years ago if she could have gotten all that," Carter answered carelessly. "She was laying for me, and she—well, she made her point."

"Her husband, her little girl's father——" Sandra said, stupefied.

"Oh, well—that's the way they are, you know."

"They?"

"All the girls. Alimony's a damn' serious thing, these days," Carter conceded.

"Oh, Carter, don't talk like that!"

"Well, it is. Betty—in the midst of a regular jumble of talk, of course—we weren't talking very calmly—but she'd put in things about the grand piano her mother loaned her—*that* was hers—and the payments on the road work, and the club membership—you'd be surprised at what she'd thought out. Even two cases of gin——"

"Carter, *no*."

"Yes, I tell you. I didn't realize she knew about half of it."

"She was all ready," Sandra mused slowly.

"Oh, sure she was!"

"But *I'm* the home breaker."

"'What did I ever do to her?' Betty kept saying. 'What did she have against me?'"

Sandra's face was scarlet.

"Carter, she didn't say that?"

"Indeed she did. 'I was always perfectly kind to her,' she told my grandmother. The old girl gave me a look."

"Your brother said that you and Betty had always been perfectly happy," Sandra said, trying to smile.

"Pete's all right. But it's funny to hear the women. My mother has it, of course, that it's all 'flattery.' Men will do anything if women flatter them enough."

It was unpalatable; Sandra winced. She felt almost angry at him for retailing it. She went back to Betty.

"If I had ever loved a man—if I had borne him a child—I can't see myself discussing pianos and gin and club memberships," she said in distaste. "I don't think I could even talk about alimony."

"Of course you couldn't, but then, you're you. This morning," Carter said, busy with his fruit cocktail—"this morning my mother and grandmother and I went down to the St. Francis—Betty's mother lives there—and we all talked about it. Betty had been crying, and she wore a dark little suit, and no rouge—playing the part. The three old ladies sort of sat around her in a circle. I was the pariah, get me? I was the outcast. Betty'd look over at Grandma and say, 'I might have been able to do something to prevent it, but

I never *dreamed* it, I never knew there *were* women like that!'"

"Never knew that there were women like me?"

"That was the idea."

"Ha!" Sandra murmured, and looked out of the window with narrowed eyes.

"I think Mother was kind of onto it; Mother's no fool. But Grandma took it all down, hook, line, and sinker. The looks she'd give me! Finally she said to Mrs. Finchley—Betty's mother—'I don't know why a dishonest husband isn't a dishonest agent!' The point being," Carter elucidated with a grin, "that I handle all the old lady's affairs.

"No, the real rub," he went on more soberly, as Sandra refused him an answering smile—"the real rub is that I give up the kid. Betty wanted to take her to Paris for her French and her violin work anyway," he added, with a philosophical smile, "so it comes out about the same. That's where she scores, and it's the only place she scores, and Gwin Jones—he's coming up from Los Angeles this week to handle my side of it—told me once that there was some clause you could put in, in case of a woman's remarriage——"

"You think she might marry again?" Alexandra asked as he paused.

"No," he answered definitely, going on with his meal, "she'll not remarry. Why should she remarry? She gets something from her mother, two thousand a month from me, and an allowance for Patsy. That's enough for her to take care of some titled fellow over there who'll go round and dance with her. A lot of her friends are working it that way; why shouldn't Betty?"

"It's a lovely world!" Sandra observed, looking out of the window again.

"It's a swell world! *She,*" Carter recommenced forcefully

—"she 'didn't know there were women like' that in the world. But she can have you chased up to your room by a detective and a butler when she wants money!"

"It makes me sick."

"It makes *me* sick. However," Carter said, with a sudden change of manner and topic, "let's not think about it! You're beautiful. You're so beautiful in that hat that every man in the room has been looking at you and trying to catch your eye. You're beautiful and you're good and you're kind as an angel. Do you realize what it means to a man when his girl is kind to him? You're the kindest person I ever knew."

"But Betty didn't know there were women like me!"

"And that's no lie, either. The biggest thought she ever had would be little for you."

"She must have had a protected life."

"Betty?"

"Most people know that there are women like me."

"Why, that got you, didn't it?"

The reaction of the too exciting days was suddenly overwhelming her. Sandra felt suddenly tired and cold and angry.

"Isn't it the sort of thing that would 'get' most women?"

"Aw, come, honey," he pleaded. "I've been arguing with women all day!"

Alexandra's face did not brighten, but there was a little penitence in her voice as she said:

"I feel disagreeable."

"I adore you!" Carter said.

"I've put myself in such a rotten position," she complained, "and I have nobody to blame but myself."

"It's going to be the best thing that ever happened!" Carter said with conviction. "Be nice to me, darling. Let's not talk any more about horrible things. Let's just eat and look at each other——"

"I didn't know there were women like her," Alexandra said, with an accent on the last word.

"Oh, forget it!" he said. "We have to plan," he added, as she refused to brighten. "We have to plan. Everything's happened all at once. We have to think it out."

"It doesn't seem to me there is anything to think out."

"Peter thinks I ought to go down to Los Angeles for a few months. We were going to send someone down. Now that it's happened," Carter said—"now that it's *happened*, I have the greatest sense of relief! And I'll bet even money that Betty has, too. I've always dreaded the idea—the newspapers and what-not. But I feel like a kid to-day!"

"How much did—that event of Saturday night really influence her, do you suppose?"

"Oh, that was just a fluke! That was a peg to hang it on," he answered confidently; "that was all she wanted."

"It makes it nice for me," Alexandra commented somberly.

"You don't come into it at all actually. Betty asks for a divorce on the grounds of desertion and I don't contest. The terms are settled already. . . . By this time next week," he went on, as Alexandra continued her luncheon without comment, "you'll be used to the idea, you'll begin to think of all the happiness that's ahead. You and I belonging to each other——"

"It sound wonderful," she admitted, looking up at last with her own smile. Leaning on the table, Carter fell into eager talk. The dining rooms were slowly emptied, shades were drawn and tables reset for the tea hour; sunshine lowered and mellowed in the west.

But still the man and the girl sat on, talking, talking, talking, and when finally they came out to the roadster again Alexandra was happy, dreamily happy in a summer world of dreams. Their plans had taken a long leap forward to-day; the future, if not clear, was clearing.

He took her home to-day for the first time, climbed the dark and odorous stairs of the Bevilaqua establishment, and met Flossy.

Flossy was in bed, extremely apologetic to Carter for her appearance and the appearance of the room, and cold toward Sandra, who had brought this unexpected visitation upon her.

But to Alexandra the mere detail of her mother's unpreparedness seemed of small consequence. All through the endless and exhausting day she had been smartingly aware of the hideous discrepancies between her own life and the lives of such persons as Carter, Betty, their group. It was for this late afternoon hour, when she was destined to see him in all his easy perfection of manner and clothing and grooming, actually sitting beside her mother's bed, to bring it home to her with insufferable pain.

Betty's mother living at the Hotel St. Francis; Carter's mother and grandmother majestically going down there to discuss the new turn of affairs in the family; these rich, powerful, arrogant women had nothing in common with the daughter of Flossy Belleau, the one-time darling of the cafés and night clubs.

Alexandra, during this day, had remembered the beauty and smoothness of life in the San Mateo home where she had gone as a substitute for Miss Curtis on a day less than a year ago. The gardens, flawless in ordered beauty; the big rooms handsomely furnished in all the elegance of yesterday; the trained low voices of the servants; the flowers and books and crystal and silver; the pleasant leisurely talk of games and trips—all these had marked sharply the difference between her and the man she loved.

Now he knew it, too. Now he must see it, too, with sensibilities keener than her own. Now he was here—here where even in a nightmare dream she could not have pictured him!

For Sandra had always seen herself and her mother in some other environment when this meeting took place.

Now the shipwreck that had precipitated so many of their problems upon them had brought this about, too. Carter was sitting in the collapsed old Morris rocker, the late afternoon light was straggling drearily in through long, dirty window curtains, and Floss, in a welter of drab baby pillows and tumbled blankets, was explaining to the caller the nature of her malady.

But Alexandra made no apologies, even when she and Carter were alone in the hallway at the head of the gaslighted stairs, and he was going away.

"Couldn't come out for another half-hour? Just to run out to the Park and back?"

"I think I had better stay with my mother. She's uncomfortable, I can see it. I want to find out how she really is."

Carter went away, and Sandra turned back to plunge into care of the invalid with heart and soul. She would not think. She would not think. It was all confusion and shame and pain; it was all resentment—resentment that she should be so continually forced into a position utterly unnatural and false.

This was at five o'clock. At six flowers came; roses for Floss, with a message from Carter. And wet, sweet, long-stemmed white violets for Sandra, with a note. She kissed the note when she had finished reading it, and read it again, and put it away with a few treasured documents in her desk, only to find it and read it once more.

"My darling," it read. "I think if I didn't love you before I would have loved you to-day, realizing what you might have been and how wonderful you are! What a day this has been—and what a lunch hour—hours, rather, they were! God bless you, sweetheart. I liked the courageous mother so much. I hope she liked me. Some day she has to."

It was signed "C." He had gone to his club to write it, and then taken it down to the florist himself. He had her mother's name correctly, "Mrs. Rodney Trumbull." Flossy appreciated that only a little less than her daughter, though Alexandra gave no sign.

He had done all this although he was as tired as she after the terrific ordeals of this revolutionary week-end. It was only Monday night now; on Saturday, two short days past, she had trailed happily about after the golf players and had had tea on the terrace at Mrs. Bray's. . . . .

She talked little of him this evening. But her senses were inundated with the thought of him; she moved and spoke in a dream of memory and happiness and hope.

"Sandra, you've grown up more in the last few months than in all your life before."

"D'you think so, Floss? I seem to myself to have only begun."

"You said that just like your father would of. He talked like an actor."

"Growing up is a queer thing," Sandra mused aloud. "Things happen, and they push you out of your old ways of doing and thinking. You look back and wonder how you could have done this or that."

She fell silent, remembering the office on a winter day and herself going in to ask Mr. Carter Cavendish to sign a paper. It was like thinking of another girl. The emotional crises through which she had passed since then, the developing and broadening experiences, were making it impossible for her to understand how that girl could have acted as she had acted: gone to luncheon with a man she believed happily married, accepted his compliments and attentions!

"Floss," she said out of deep thought, "isn't it funny when you do things that change your life—for the better——"

She floundered.

"And yet that were bad things to do," she pursued, trying to express it clearly.

"Take a girl like myself," Alexandra presently added, as Floss, utterly content in the freshly made bed and plumped pillows, and with a cup of smoking tea on her tray, made no answer except by a sympathetic look. "I did things six months ago I couldn't possibly do now. And yet those very things brought me to—where I am now."

"Landed Cavendish, you mean?" Flossy asked, with simplicity.

Alexandra laughed protestingly and reddened.

"Well, not quite that!" the girl said.

"Well, I don't mean quite that, either. I just mean—all that's happened."

"It wouldn't have seemed anything to me to have a man getting a divorce to marry me a year ago," Alexandra began.

"Lissen," Floss said sagely. "No woman ever took a man away from any other woman. She's lost him long before you came along."

"Oh, she had! He says so," Alexandra agreed eagerly. "It was only a question of the little girl, and his mother, and Mrs. Cavendish's mother——"

She fell silent, thinking, and Flossy said, "Well, you see!" in a triumphant tone.

CHAPTER FOURTEEN

TWO WEEKS LATER, by special invitation, she went to call on Carter's grandmother. Carter himself was in the south; they were exchanging daily letters. Betty with her child and maid and chauffeur were to drive up in the big car to Reno. It would be simpler and quicker that way, Betty had decided, and the sooner it was over the sooner she and Patsy could be off to France.

These had been hard and humiliating days for Sandra. She had felt a bitter envy of Betty, who, having had Carter, and possessing his child, was now planning a confident, happy future in some European capital. No matter what happened, Betty seemed always to be the winner.

Starving for news of Carter, even though she heard from him every day, hungry for proof that she still was important to him, Alexandra had opened one morning the formal note that asked her to come and see his grandmother at a specified time "to discuss something of importance to us both." It was signed "Ella Houghton Hough." Sandra, already writing a description of the interview to Carter in her thoughts, answered in her smartest, simplest style, on very heavy white paper with very black ink, that she would be glad to comply.

The town house in which the two elderly women lived had been the Hough town mansion a generation ago; it was a heavy, handsome old wooden house, bay-windowed, with lawns and palms about it. At the narrow old round-topped windows there were spotless curtains, the big entrance hall was silent and shadowy, deep in rugs, flanked by high-backed chairs that looked like thrones. Sandra had never been in quite such a place before; it made her feel nervous and depressed at once. Carter's world again, not hers.

There were big, dark rooms on all sides, glimpses of a library with bronzes and leather chairs and books, glimpses of social rooms all French furniture and dim pink and dark blue carpets and mirrors, glimpses of the imposing stairway, palms, statues, oil portraits. A colored window, halfway up the stairs, threw an almost cathedral radiance into the hall. Great masses of formally arranged flowers were everywhere.

The butler showed Alexandra immediately up these enormous stairs, and a maid, meeting her halfway, escorted her across an upper hall and into a luxurious sitting room whose comfortable chairs, pillows, photographs, magazines, and flowers all struck a note of pleasantness and informality.

Accompanied by a maid, old Mrs. Hough—she was eighty—at once limped in. Tall, with piercing eyes, rouged cheeks, and imposing white wig and a man's voice, she made Alexandra think, as the girl later wrote to Carter, of an elderly Marie Antoinette.

"How d'ye do?" she said, touching Alexandra's hand before they both sat down, Sandra in an armchair that enhanced her beauty like the background of an old painting, Mrs. Hough on a couch where the elderly maid fussed with pillows and coverings to establish her comfortably.

"Did you hurt your foot?" Alexandra asked.

"No, my dear, I'm lame," the other woman said fretfully, whimsically. "And I'm old and cranky, and they only put up with me because I've got money!

"Bah!" she added, smiling a rather terrifying smile at the bewildered Alexandra. "That's what it is to be old!"

And studying her caller with eyes as sharp as those of an old eagle, she went on:

"Why, you're pretty—the child's very pretty!"

Alexandra was conscious of hating her deeply, completely. This shrewd old lady, under the calculated bluffness of her manner, under her deliberate rudeness, was really as nervous as she was herself. She wondered why on earth she had come. But old Mrs. Hough was an important figure in Carter's world and there had seemed to be small purpose in ignoring an overture from his family that might be friendly.

"My dear," old Mrs. Hough began without preamble, "you've done a very terrible thing, do you know that? You've taken a man away from the woman who loved him and from the beautiful little girl who needs her father. Every child needs a father," she added angrily; "and Carter Cavendish was a devoted father until you came along. Now what's your idea, what are you after?"

The onslaught came with so sudden and so violent a shock that Sandra felt physically shaken. She trembled and her hands grew cold. Her mouth was dry.

"I don't think we can discuss this," she said, getting to her feet. But she felt dizzy, and put out a hand to steady herself on the back of her chair.

"Oh, yes, we can discuss it!" Mrs. Hough answered.

"But there seems——" Sandra managed a pale ghost of her usual smile. "Nothing to say," she ended.

"I'm only telling you the truth," the other woman said. "If you had married him I'd feel just the same way about any other woman who came along and broke up *your* home!"

"I didn't break up her home," Sandra protested, against her own better judgment. She wished desperately that she was out of this room, out of this house, that somebody else would come in. She was afraid of the orderly, big, empty establishment, with its palms and its rugs and its servants, and she was afraid of this terrible old woman.

"What'd you think you'd get—money?" Mrs. Hough demanded. "My grandson has no money. He has his salary and a few thousands! Peter has something, but Carter hasn't. Carter wasn't born until after my husband died; my husband left his money to Peter. *My* money is going to the child, and to Peter, if this kind of thing is going on. Carter won't have anything."

Alexandra felt inexpressibly shocked and somehow ashamed for the old eagle-faced woman in the white wig.

"You don't have to talk to me like this," she said mildly.

"How do you mean I don't have to talk to you like this?"

"I mean that whatever's been done is done, without my having had anything to do with it."

"Of course you've done it. Betty says so; Carter admits it. What was Peter standing up for you for if you had nothing to do with it?"

"I mean that the trouble between—Carter and his wife," Sandra pursued it, feeling for words, red-faced, but facing her accuser steadily, "has nothing to do with what he does or doesn't do after they're divorced!"

Mrs. Hough assimilated this in an angry silence for a few minutes; it was as if she chewed upon it like a cud, her sharp old eyes meanwhile moving suspiciously up and down over Sandra's face and figure.

"Isn't this sort of thing—pretty common?" Sandra asked.

"Divorce, you mean?"

"Well."

"Yes," the old woman said discontentedly, "it's too common. Only this morning," she went on, "the Bishop was here. He said that he thought it was the evil of the day."

"Carter and I," Alexandra said slowly, "aren't happy about it."

"I shouldn't think you would be!" Mrs. Hough exclaimed promptly, with an air of scoring. But the dreamy expression of Alexandra's face did not change.

"You would have had them go on for all the rest of their lives, not loving one another, Mrs. Hough?"

"Nonsense! Of course they would have loved each other—might have had more children. They're young, they've friends, a home——"

"But they don't love each other."

"He told you that, I suppose?"

Sandra made no answer.

"I'd like to congratulate my grandson upon his loyalty to his wife," the old woman said, tartly.

As if she had not heard her, Alexandra continued to regard her absently, thoughtfully. When she began to speak it was very simply, as if she were not personally involved in the matter.

"I wouldn't have come to-day, Mrs. Hough, if I had known that you were going to—talk like this. It's too late for that. Mrs. Cavendish will get her divorce, no matter what you say or I do. I'm sorry you feel so badly about it. We had hoped not to hurt anyone, just to go along as quietly as we could, minding our own affairs."

"It doesn't hurt an eight-year-old child, I suppose, to have her father deserting her mother?"

"I shouldn't have come," Alexandra murmured, rising, looking away. There was a silence, during which Mrs. Hough watched Sandra suspiciously, shrewdly. Suddenly she spoke.

"Now, look here, my dear, I'm prepared to make it worth your while to give up the whole thing. I know that makes you angry—well, I'll pay for that, too." Old Mrs. Hough clutched at her skirt desperately as Sandra, on her way to the door, passed near her. "Come," she said, "you tell me what you have in mind, and I'll put something more on for what I've said, and because you were so obliging as to come see me."

"Why, you're just silly!" Sandra said, trembling. "I thought perhaps you wanted to help us out in some way; you're his grandmother, after all. I thought you were interested. Please let go of my dress——"

"You thought I was going to say I was glad, 'bless you, my children,' is that it?"

"I don't know what I thought!" Sandra said, frightened and frantic. "Please let go of my dress!"

"You don't think that a pretty face is going to hold Carter Cavendish? He'll tire of you as he has of others."

"Oh, stop!" Sandra gasped, beside herself.

There was an interruption. A slender pretty woman who looked about forty-five, but who was in reality more than ten years older, swept into the room, flew to the couch, sustained the old woman with an embracing arm, and stared perplexedly at the caller. This was of course Carter's mother, correctly hatted, impeccably gowned, her gloves white, her bag matching her shoes, a slim sable skin on her shoulders.

"What's the trouble, Mother?" she demanded.

"That's Carter's precious—Miss Trumbull!" old Mrs. Hough cawed rather than said.

"I see it is," Mrs. Cavendish said, coldly. Having somewhat restored her mother to calm, she straightened up without for one instant relaxing her look at Sandra. "I am sorry you thought it necessary to come and see my mother," she observed.

"She wrote to ask me!" Sandra returned, struggling to contain herself.

"Mother did?" Mrs. Cavendish exclaimed, jarred out of her dignity by surprise. A glance at her mother confirmed

Sandra's words, and she forgot Alexandra completely as she asked, sharply, "What possessed you to do that?"

"I wanted to see her, Evelyn," the old woman said, placatingly, almost whiningly.

"Why, you know you shouldn't have done that, Mother!" Evelyn Cavendish reproached her. "I'm sorry," she said briefly to Sandra. "My mother sees almost nobody, and of course the first thing I thought—— Don't go," she interrupted herself to say. "Sit here and have a cup of tea with us. I've wanted to meet you, of course. You must forgive Mother." She smiled, and stretched a finely groomed hand out to ring a bell. "You know, I'm not the normal mother, Miss Trumbull," she said, with the brisk egotism of her type. "I'm quite unnatural. I like my children to be happy! Isn't that outrageous? Do sit down."

"Oh, my God, is there no loyalty left in the world?" asked the old woman loudly of the air.

"Don't talk of loyalty; I can be loyal to Carter, I suppose?" Mrs. Cavendish demanded, without any particular feeling. "We don't have to be fools, Mother." Her friendliness, her easiness, were as balm to Sandra's sore heart. She sat down.

"I shall be glad when my Maker takes me away from the falseness of this world!" Mrs. Hough soliloquized.

"You will not, you know, Mother," Mrs. Cavendish retorted dispassionately, as she poured a cup of very weak tea, sugaring and creaming it carefully. "Jenny, give that to Mrs. Hough, and put that red stool under her feet," she digressed to say. "You know very well you will not, Mother," she repeated. "So don't talk that way."

Alexandra paid to the conscious humor of the other's manner the tribute of a desperate little laugh, and had to busy herself resolutely with her own cup to keep from following it with tears. Old Mrs. Hough appeared much less formidable now that her vigorous daughter was here, and in Mrs. Cavendish Alexandra saw much of Carter and much that she could like.

"I don't mean to say," Mrs. Cavendish presently said, in a calmer tone, after having given Sandra a glance of sympathetic approval for the laugh—"I don't mean to say I'm not extremely sorry about Betty and Cart. Of course I'm sorry. But do let's act like intelligent people, and not like medieval what-nots! Betty," Evelyn added in an aside to Sandra—"Betty wasn't his wife for years, and we all know it!"

"We know nothing of the kind is nothing sacred?" Mrs. Hough demanded without punctuation.

But Sandra was no longer intimidated by her; she could ignore her in the half hour that followed. It was astonishing and confusing to find herself liking Mrs. Cavendish, to be conscious of winning her. Sandra sat forward a little in her chair, stirring her tea, looking at Carter's mother with her golden brown eyes.

"If this girl loves him," Evelyn Cavendish thought, watching her, "if this simple and beautiful girl really likes him, how can you blame him, after Betty? A man is a man, after all, and a woman is a woman."

She walked downstairs with Sandra, completing her conquest of Sandra's susceptible heart.

"You mustn't mind my mother."

"I don't. And I'm grateful to *you*."

"Grateful to me, my dear child! For what?"

"For being nice to me."

"You understand, of course—we've not been talking of Carter—we couldn't, naturally, with Mother there—but you understand, of course, that there'll be no end of delays. Betty may change her mind even now."

"Oh, yes," Sandra said, suddenly flushed, "I understand."

"I mean it's just one of those things——" the other woman said. "It's Carter's affair, after all."

She evidently was washing her hands of any responsibility. But it was done in a kindly, well-meant sort of way, and Sandra could understand it.

"I don't think—anyone thought it would ever come out like this," the girl said, explanatory, apologetic.

"I suppose not. And you mustn't mind my mother. She feels terribly on account of little Patricia."

"It seems so unfair to take her away from him completely," Sandra said, slowly.

"Betty, you mean? Well, she may not."

"She seems to be putting all the blame for everything on Carter."

"Betty?" Mrs. Cavendish said again. "She naturally would."

"I don't think," Sandra said, "that Carter would have done that to *her*."

Carter's mother looked at the girl strangely, with a surprised and sympathetic expression deepening in her eyes.

"I think perhaps you are the sort of woman he needs," she said, almost involuntarily, but with her characteristic brisk air of settling everything.

Tears of pleasure rushed into Sandra's eyes.

"I hope I am," she said.

"And you and I will see each other again."

"Surely, Mrs. Cavendish."

"Good-bye, then."

"Good-bye," Sandra said, hoping some of the gratitude she felt got into her voice, for she could not express it.

"She is really very beautiful, and she has manners," Evelyn Cavendish thought, going upstairs. "She's quite beautiful; she's mad about him. He has something; they all feel it. That girl never was mixed up in any ugly hotel scrape.

Why, she's only a child. What did he say she was—twenty-two? She looks about seventeen, in spite of being so tall and full-built. Mother," Evelyn said aloud, entering the upstairs sitting room where old Mrs. Hough was drowsing in lamplight, "if Carter came up here with a gun looking for you it'd just about serve you right. He's mad about this girl. What earthly good would it do for you to fight with her?"

"D'ye like her, Evvy?" the old woman asked, unabashed.

"I actually do. She's quite different from what I thought. Betty said she was something-or-other—aggressive, I think it was. But this girl is nothing but—well, love. It'd be perfectly ridiculous if it all worked out for the best," Mrs. Cavendish said. "A nice meddler you'd feel then!"

"There isn't much 'best' to his losing Patsy!"

"He may not lose Patsy. Betty was angry when she said that. Anyway," predicted Carter's mother, "this one will have a houseful of them for him. And at least it's something that she's gentle and loving and that I can actually like her."

Alexandra knew nothing of this conversation. But she felt light-hearted, excited, hopeful, as she walked home without noticing the streets and the crossings through which she went, and began excitedly to think that evening, for the first time, of what marriage to Carter might mean.

"Just the same, I'd rather he had never been married," she said to her mother, telling her all about it. "To have him a bachelor like Peter, I'd manage on forty a week and take a flat in Fulton Street!"

"I was getting eighty-five a week, only I wasn't working, when I married your father," Flossy said, reminiscently. "He didn't have anything but what his family sent him—a hundred pounds a quarter—and he always borrowed on that!"

"He must have been a great comfort to you."

"He was good-looking," Flossy recalled, with a dreamy smile.

"That helped, of course."

"I'll tell you what he looked like. He looked like one of those collar advertisements. I used to tell him his face looked like he had just washed it—always."

"A hundred a quarter. They must have been somebody, Flossy, to send a son that much. Why, that'd be two thousand a year!"

"Well, it wasn't enough for him. Money went through his hands like nobody's business."

"But he must have been *some*body. His people, I mean."

"He had a name you've never heard the like of," the widow observed simply.

"My father?"

"His name was Rodney Howard St. George Trumbull."

It set Alexandra off into a dream. She had pored over the pages of *Little Lord Fauntleroy* as a little girl; she played some such part now. Equal to Carter, more than the equal of his outrageous old grandmother . . .

"You ought to see the Hough house, Mother. Servants, flowers—it's like being in a church."

"I can't abide servants," Flossy observed contentedly. "They give me the creeps. As for nurses and hospitals," she added, not without significance, "I'd kill myself before I'd go into a hospital. I honest would, Sandra. I'd kill myself."

The change of tense did not escape the girl, as her mother fell silent.

"We won't talk about hospitals and nurses until you've seen Dr. Schmidt and the specialist," she said.

CHAPTER FIFTEEN

LIFE SEEMED TO BE MOVING in great disconnected jumps. Alexandra Trumbull, in her neat office clothes and the sable that had belonged to poor Eda Roots, was no longer employed by the firm of Cavendish & Bartlett. Carter Cavendish, one of the young vice presidents of the firm, was no longer merely the distant and respected name of a fortunate young man married to a beautiful woman and father of a fascinating child; he had become "Carter," and his personal history was henceforth to be closely intertwined with Sandra's own. The dreams, the dissatisfactions and discontent of office days, the association with the kindly girls who had elected Miss Trumbull as the most popular member of the staff, had drifted into the far background.

The stolen, happy irresponsible lunches with Carter were things of the past, too, and the mood in which she had packed her bag for that week-end visit to Del Monte.

There had been an iridescent glory about them that to-day's certainties lacked. There had been a—something about that lunch at Jules', about that particular day when Carter had given her the blue bag, that would never return. They belonged to the uncertain beginnings, to the excitements of discovery.

It was all settled now. Betty was in Reno; Carter had remained in southern California. Carter and Sandra were engaged.

And Flossy was not going to get well. Whether she knew

it or not, Alexandra could not ascertain. If she did know it the truth had added itself to her mother's consciousness gently, dreamily; Flossy was not afraid. Life was ending kindly for the little cabaret singer of yesterday, and in the softening and ripening and spiritualizing of her mother's nature in these last quiet months Alexandra was able to see the woman that, more fortunately placed, Flossy might have been.

In the foggy coldness of July it had chanced that Flossy's little prune ranch in Santa Clara County had lost its tenant; it had been Alexandra's suggestion that she and her mother go down there to see for themselves the possibilities of the place. Sandra had never seen it before.

Hence, in exquisite hot summertime, they had taken possession of the four-roomed ranch shack, the outbuildings and the languishing garden, the redwoods and madrones and oaks.

And here another phase of Sandra's life had begun, a phase so completely disconnected from anything that had preceded it that sometimes she felt she had been reborn into a different world.

The ranch house was nothing; it was made of mere boxes with windows in them, set down on rough earth under prune trees. There was a small rusty wood stove in the kitchen, and an "air-tight" in the room that was used for dining and reading and general living. There was no bathroom. The whole place smelled of bacon fat and apples and pipes when Sandra and her mother first opened the door; there were grease stains imposed upon grease stains on the uncovered pine of the kitchen floor; the exposed rafters were smoked; ashes had drifted from the cold stove.

But just outside the door a majestic oak stretched sprawling great arms against the top of the hill, and fifty feet away there was a grove of glorious redwoods that to Sandra was like a palace of her own. On three sides below the shabby place the hills moved away in manifold great shoulders, clothed in chaparral and manzanita, and standing in the kitchen door Sandra and her mother could look in the fourth direction down upon the level stretches of the Santa Clara valley, the acres and acres of fruit trees that carpeted it like a floor.

The air up here in the high mountains was always sweet and vital, even at the burning heat of noonday; the nights were crystal, and sang with chilly, fragrant, moon-drenched sweetness. Flossy spoke over and over again of the odors that swam all about: the burned odor of the mountain growths, the odor of redwood gum and wood fires, the odor of coffee drifting under the trees.

She and Sandra put on old cottons and bound up their hair for tremendous activities with brooms and buckets of soapy water. They swept, rearranged, they lighted rubbish fires upon which half the furnishings of the place went up in clean and scented smoke. Flossy laughed, she ran to and fro like a girl, she ate prodigiously.

"Ain't it wonderful to be a woman, Sandra, and be at home?"

"Well, it is!" Sandra agreed, laughing.

"Your father wanted me to do this when you were a little girl, Sandra, but I couldn't see it. I told him it'd be like being buried alive."

"It would have been hard on you, Floss, when he started drinking again."

"Started? He was one that never stopped!"

And they would laugh joyously together in this new world of effort and novelty and achievement.

There was a triumph about this sort of thing. Alexandra told herself that it was ridiculous, but she was conscious of it all day long just the same. Just to manage a bath was a triumph over buckets and slowly heating water, and the day she first washed her hair at the ranch was one never to be forgotten.

To get Rondani, the nearest neighbor, to bring a pot of white paint up the hill, and personally to render one of the dark bedrooms dazzling and habitable, was sheer thrill. To see the rubbish disappear, and the colors of the wood emerge from old coats of dirt, to get the fire going in the mornings, and have experimental corn bread turn out to be eatable, was enough to keep both women chattering and happy for hours.

There had been an Airedale dog on the place when they came; they were to keep Nelly only until they could find a good home for her. But long before there had been any possibility of sending the dog away Flossy had grown deeply attached to the pathetic, gentle, emaciated animal, and when the third of the anemic litter was born only to die, both Alexandra and her mother genuinely grieved. The other two puppies and the mother became the darlings of the place; there were quail for which Flossy watched eagerly, too; the trees flashed and sang with bird life; rabbits crept out at dusk to attack Sandra's protected geraniums and stock.

When she and her mother had been almost two weeks at the ranch the new prospective tenant drove up from San José to see it. He impressed neither of them favorably, and it was when he had gone without making any definite offer that Flossy said:

"What'd we live on if we stayed here ourselves awhile, Sandra?"

"Mrs. Bevilaqua could rent our room for forty. She said she'd give you twenty-five of that."

"We couldn't eat," Flossy mused.

"Well, there's something in the bank, Mother."

"But I always understood that what you had in the bank was your capital."

"Even so."

"But ought you spend your capital?" the older woman asked anxiously.

"Well, what'd Fonseca live on when he was here? He paid you forty a month."

"That's right, too."

"The prunes!" Sandra exclaimed, enlightened. "We have ten acres of prunes. I'll talk to Rondani to-night."

"Your crop'll bring you about eight hundred this year," Rondani, upon being interviewed, told her.

"But, Mr. Rondani, Fonseca paid Mother five hundred, And they had five children!"

"Sure they did. But they had chickens, and all the fruit, and she'd come over and milk my mother's cows for four quarts of milk a day. He had a good truck patch. Fonseca didn't spend much money. His boy used to hire out some, too."

"The economic problem is different," Alexandra wrote to Carter. "A family of seven, recently our loyal tenantry, used to get in cash income something like three hundred a year. They had a motor car—to be sure as unlike our roadster of heavenly memories as Mario Fonseca is unlike you—but they did have one. And by the way, I improve in driving, and yesterday went gingerly down to the village and back for the first time, praying loudly all the time of course. Several trees got out of their way to lunge at me, but I missed them and came back 'in wunna swetta,' as Mrs. Rondani put it delicately, but without other mishap.

"My mother is amazingly well," she could presently write him, "and the happiest, busiest ranch woman in Santa Clara County. Between the dogs, who really are too adorable, and cooking, for which she seems to have a genius, and gardening—we have to drag all the water we use from a well conveniently placed over the county line—she is a different creature. She looks thin, but she's happy.

"As for me, I never have a dull moment. I read Shakespeare and Stevenson and Dickens—my father's books had been in storage in the barn here for years, and I find glimpses of him in them here and there. And the last thing of all, at night, when the puppies are in their box in the kitchen, and the fire is out, and we have our hot water bottles, and utter peace has descended upon the world, I read your last letters again, and sometimes I read them all."

She wrote to him every day, and had a daily reply. And for proof that besides that he was constantly thinking of her there were endless presents, little and big. Perfume, books, frail filmy handkerchiefs with her own dashing signature cunningly embroidered upon them, gloves, stockings were only a few. There were also trifles; the sketch someone had made of Carter on the back of a dinner menu; a snapshot of Carter playing golf with Harold Lloyd; the souvenir from a movie-theater opening. His ingenuity in finding little things with which to amuse her and please her was inexhaustible.

The crisp sweet autumn days came on, and the crop ripened and was sold, and Sandra and Flossy entered upon experiments with apple butter and canned corn. Plenty still reigned at the ranch; there were pumpkins now, and grapes, and the yellow September tomatoes. Night shut in earlier, and the dews were cold on the garden when Sandra and her mother looked out from the breakfast table at nine o'clock in the morning. But still the days were clear and hot and cloudless, the redwoods pouring out their balsamic sweetness, the skies soft and hazy and blue.

"Sandra, I want you to promise me something," her mother said one day.

"Go ahead."

"If I should get any sicker than I am, promise me you'll never put me into a hospital."

"You haven't got that pain this morning?"

"I feel grand. But I know that Carter'll want you the minute he's free, and then you'll begin to worry about me. I don't want to leave. I'm going to get someone to stay with me here," Flossy added. "I think Kate Sudden would jump at the chance, and her and I always hit it off."

"I suppose so," Sandra agreed, giving no hint of the quiver of sheer delight that ran through her whole body at the thought her mother had expressed. Carter would want her—in his arms, in his heart—when he was free.

"But leave me here, Sandra, and come and see me when you can!" her mother pleaded. Sandra smiled at her through suddenly misted lashes.

"Why, you idiot, you're crying!"

"I am not," said Flossy. "But I know I'll die if you let those doctors get me into a hospital!"

"I promise, darling."

Only a few days after this particular conversation Alexandra heard the booming of a powerful motor engine coming up the hill, and saw the flash of spokes in the autumn sunlight under the oaks, and the familiar tall figure at the wheel. Carter was all in brown, brown suit, brown coat, brown cap on his black hair, his skin was brown, his brown eyes shining with excitement. Alexandra, dropping her trowel, was instantly in his arms; her own warm cheek pressed against his cold, firm one, their hearts beating together.

She wore an old blue cotton gown, an old blue sweater, her usually colorless fair skin was flushed with exercise and sunshine, her chestnut hair flattened in little rings and fishtails on her wet forehead. Surprise and joy had shattered her usual self-control; she clung to him and laughed and repeated his name in a very ecstasy of happiness.

"My God, but you are lovely!" Carter said, holding tightly the firmness and softness and sweetness of her and kissing the tumbled beautiful bright hair.

"I'm filthy!"

"You're gorgeous. You simply—but let me look at you!"

He stepped back, his hands still linked in hers, and held her at arms' length, and feasted his eyes on her.

"Carter—you didn't let me know——"

"You're so wonderful! You're the most beautiful woman in the world!"

They said all the foolish incoherent words over and over, not knowing or caring what they said. The autumn sun was beating down serenely upon the mountain-top ranch; the air was like mellow wine. Good odors of earth and piny redwoods were rich upon the warm still world; there was a smell of ripe apples.

And it was one of the heavenly days; they were together again after three endless months. Every moment of this day was exquisite to both of them. Alexandra thought that if she had never loved Carter before she must have loved him when she saw his manner with her mother and with Mrs. Sudden, who were both completely captivated.

Sandra took him into the kitchen and showed him the new blue and white checked curtains and spice boxes and linoleum. He had given them the linoleum, she reminded him.

"Oh, shucks, forget it!" Carter protested at this, laughing and flushing.

Everything had to be right to-day. There were big firm tomatoes for a salad, there were chives, and the last of the tarragon vinegar. And there was a lot of yesterday's chicken, melted down into the creamy gravy, and browned to a crisp top in the oven. There was French bread and there was an apple pudding, and there were artichokes.

The meal was one of those miracles that goes together easily, prettily, that holds a group of congenial folk long at the table.

"Do you girls live like this every day, for heaven's sake?"

The women all laughed delightedly.

"These are Monday left-overs," Sandra told him.

She poured his coffee, remembering how he liked it, and the look he gave her as he took it brimmed with just what her heart had needed all this long time. They were lunching on a level out under the oak; the glowing day shone and sparkled all about them. The prune trees were bare of all but a few yellowed leaves now, but the madrones wore scarlet berries and the rich foliage of the redwoods was unchanged.

"It's Paradise!" Carter said.

After lunch he and Sandra walked out the old wood road that was almost obliterated after a half-century of neglect, running about the great shoulder of the hill like a shelf. They sat down on the edge of it in the dry, brown, slippery grass, and dangled their legs over the precipitate canyon below. In the thinned, hot, crystal air a buzzard hung motionless; quail drummed out of sight in the underbrush far below.

Just to be together again, to hear each other's voices, was such complete, such breath-taking excitement for both that it was hard to find words big enough, important enough, for this perfect hour.

"I didn't say anything to your mother about it, but what brought me up from Los Angeles was my grandmother's death—you know that?"

"Mrs. Hough!"

"Yep. Funeral yesterday."

After a while she said, "Did she disinherit you, Carter?"

"No, that was all bluff. She's fixed the kid up in great shape."

"Patsy?"

"Patsy. And she left me a pot of money, too. If Betty had been onto it," Carter observed mildly, "she never would have let go of me."

"They're still in Reno?"

"Yes, but they'll light out for Europe as soon as she gets her decree. In January, that is. My grandmother's estate ought to be cleared up by that time. Pete and I are guardians of Patsy, which makes it nice."

"Did you see Betty?"

"No, no; she didn't come down."

They fell to talking of themselves, of the man and woman who so deeply loved each other, who were to be married in a few months more. All the old enchantment of the lunch hours came back for Sandra as she heard his voice again, his abrupt, confident answers to the problems she had hardly dared face even in her thoughts. Life was so refreshingly simple to Carter; he could solve anything in that quick, definite way of his, with his brows drawn together in the hint of a frown and the hint of a smile twitching at his strong mouth.

Plans, plans—they were really planning at last! It was intoxicating to her after the lonely months. To see Carter look serious for a second, and then suddenly smile, to appreciate his concern for her, the tenderness with which he had worked out every detail, was to float into a happiness deeper than any she had ever known.

"And you have plenty of money, dear?"

"Plenty!"

"I want to put a cook in here, Sandra; some sort of servant."

"After we're married, maybe."

"Well—— You're really going to stay here?"

"We love it."

"I don't wonder you love it."

After a while they walked back to the cabin, their hands linked.

"I've been waiting three months for this day, Sandra."

"I've thought of it every hour of every one of those days."

"Hasn't it seemed as if there were no end to them?"

"Well, I don't know. In one way this has been the happiest time of my life."

"You look it!" he said. The girl was glowing; her eyes shone like stars under the soft disorder of her hair. The old blue cotton dress she wore showed the superb fullness of her figure, the firm lift of her young breasts. The country months had warmed her smooth throat and her cheeks to a clear brown, her fine nervous hand gripping his own, brown too.

"You're gorgeous!" he told her.

Her golden eyes, in which the golden afternoon was reflected, met his with a smile.

"All yours!" she answered simply.

"Don't talk like that," Carter warned her in a low tone. The girl laughed.

"The one fear of my life," he presently said, "is that you'll stop loving me."

"I think that's the one thing you needn't be afraid about. I'm only afraid I love you too much, Carter. I—I break the First Commandment whenever I look at you."

"I'm not sure which it is!"

"I wasn't sure myself until Mother, Mrs. Sudden, and I happened to get arguing about them. 'Thou shalt not have strange gods before me. Thou shalt not adore them nor serve them.' "

"You *are* God to me," he countered, "or you're religion or spirituality, or whatever it is. An hour with you is heaven to me, and what it's going to be like——"

He stopped speaking; they walked over rustling yellow leaves in silence.

"What it's going to be like to have you always with me, across the breakfast table, and going to shows, and loafing about on Sunday mornings," he presently concluded, "I don't dare think."

"No, and I don't dare think!" she said, in a low voice.

"You're growing up, Alexandra," he said. "You seemed lovely enough, God knows, in the old office days. But you're marvelous now."

"I'm twenty-two," she admitted with her own odd smile breaking slowly over her face.

He went away at six, in the dark, and suddenly with that night winter seemed to reach the ranch; frosts, early sunsets, binding cold. Winter reached her heart, too, and wrenched it and chilled it. Mrs. Sudden, a tearful, stout, emotional woman, stayed on, and instead of a cook a trained nurse came, and hard days began for everyone.

Everyone, except perhaps Flossy, who was perfectly happy every morning when Rondani brought up the paper, and her coffee was ready, and when she had exacted from Sandra, Mrs. Sudden, and Miss Costello a fresh promise that "those doctors" should not inveigle her into a hospital.

Her bed was comfortably established in the sitting room now, and the door between it and the kitchen kept open. The air-tight stove burned redly early morning, late afternoon, night; the dogs lay on the floor beside it, their sleepy eyes on the glow. In the middle of the day the sun still shone warmly, and doors and windows could be opened wide and the wet sweetness of garden and woods pour through the little house.

The doctor came every day; there was little for him to do, but Flossy liked him. Magazines, flowers, pillows, great fat satiny comforters, potted chicken, jellied apricots, and caviar came from Los Angeles.

Alexandra forgot her pride; there were hundreds to her account in the village bank now, and she drew upon them recklessly. She cooked, she laughed, she resolutely climbed the winter hills and came back with glowing cheeks and great branches of toyon berries. These days belonged to Flossy; nothing should cloud them.

When the early, bitter dark shut in, Sandra moved to and fro, between the lighted kitchen and the dim rich lights of the poor little sitting room, always conversational, teasing, gracious. She and Flossy's nurse, Helen Costello, were warmly friendly; they had endless talks in the long evenings. Helen loved poetry, knew something of it; Sandra drank it in thirstily. Mrs. Sudden was with them most of the time. Now and then she went into town, to return with theatrical magazines and all the gossip of the old neighborhood. Carter drove up from Los Angeles twice, to spend only two or three hours with them.

It was a grave, a hard, a not all-sad time. Alexandra was exulting over the successful roasting of her first turkey when he stopped in, on his way down from a Thanksgiving visit to his mother in late November.

"Admit it was delicious, Flossy!"

"It was honestly the best turkey I ever tasted!" Flossy said in her hoarse, loving whisper. "I've got some daughter!" she added to Carter over Sandra's shoulder as Sandra straightened and raised her tenderly.

"Every time I see her she looks to me like a new girl," Carter commented.

"Oh, listen to them, Helen!" Sandra appealed.

"And this isn't showing off for your benefit, either, Mr. Cavendish," Helen told him.

"Somehow I didn't think it was!" And Carter smiled at Alexandra the quietly sure, the confident smile that thrilled her from the roots of her hair to the tips of her toes.

They were not flattering her; deep in her heart she knew it. She felt the growth, the refining, the deepening that was going on in mind and soul and body. And it was all for him, all for him, all for him!

CHAPTER SIXTEEN

ALEXANDRA MARY TRUMBULL and Carter Hough Cavendish were quietly married in San José on the afternoon of a late February day. Alexandra had had a few days of complete collapse after her mother's funeral, and even on her wedding day, six weeks later, was paler and thinner than she had been during the happy summer, and showed delicate lines of umber about her beautiful eyes.

She wore dark blue, with a blouse that was nearer cream than white, a dark blue hat, with dashing line that was infinitely becoming to the sweep of bright hair and the golden brown eyes, and the new sable scarf. Her gloves, her shining pumps, her clocked transparent stockings were new, the pigskin bag initialed "A. T. C." was new. She had some color in her cheeks when Carter came to the rambling, shabby Costello homestead to get her; he could not keep his eyes off her in his delight at her beauty.

"Sandra, you look so lovely in color again after the black!"

"Oh, I couldn't be married in black," Sandra explained, in a deep, faintly hoarse voice that had a new and touching note in it. "Mrs. Costello says that means 'wish you were back.'"

"You're not going to wish you were back, darling!"

"I know it."

"You could marry that one in rags an' tatters, an' get the

best of the bargain!" Mrs. Costello said for herself, firmly, with a jerk of her gray head to indicate Sandra.

"That's to make up for the way she bullied you last night, Sandra," Helen said, kissing her mother's broad, lined forehead.

"I never bullied anyone in this world!"

"You did! Didn't she, Tom?"

"She's a crook and a liar, Mom is," Tom Costello, wishing in his soul that Alexandra Trumbull had never come to live at their house or that he, Thomas Aloysius Costello, had never been born, answered out of the anguish of his spirit.

"Well, look at that now!" the mother said.

"You know you bullied me," Sandra reproached the older woman, her arms about Mrs. Costello's broad shoulders, her lovely face against the smiling old wrinkled face. "You said that Carter and I would be no more married than the ducks and the drakes themselves!"

There was a shout of laughter, in the midst of which the matron's outraged protests were lost.

"All I said to thim," she presently explained to Carter, "was that anny religion that let ye commit a sin was no religion at all!"

"Yes, that was all she said!" Helen admitted, in another burst of their wild laughter.

"Whatever you said or did to my girl it's agreed with her," Carter told the old woman, with his easy, winning manner, "and we're grateful, aren't we, Alexandra?"

"Always!" she answered, in a shaken voice.

Flossy had died on Christmas Eve, late in the dark, cold, mountain night. There had been a deep frost over the world when Helen and Sandra had stepped out onto the cabin porch on Christmas morning; the air had been singing like a taut wire. Wet leaves had been packed under the delicate silver filigree; spider webs had flashed with jewels.

Mrs. Sudden, after the strain, its abrupt ending, and the sobering whispering hours that had followed it, had sobbed herself to sleep. There had been a terrible silence everywhere when Flossy's whispers, her hard breathing, could be heard no more. No labored thanks for the cup of coffee this morning, no sunken bright eyes following the antics of the dogs, no witch-claw catching at Sandra's warm, round wrist to draw her attention to the dear adoring smile, the inaudible words of love.

That was all over. She had found in Floss a new mother this year; she was alone now. There was only the silence, deepened by the purring of wood in the stove, the snap of a frostbitten branch in the woods.

She, Alexandra, had not broken at all until after the funeral, and then there had been no luxury of grief. There had been but a few quiet days, lying on the couch in the very center of the Costellos' household confusion, listening, smiling, reading, trying to live again.

Helen's brother Tom had fallen painfully, deeply in love with the guest; Helen's married sister had brought Margaret and the baby over every day to see Aunt Sandra; Helen herself had been a miracle of real sisterly love, sympathetic, amusing, devoted.

But the mother had done most of all toward the cure. Sandra had never known that there were such women, so good, so kind and capable and generous and brave. Annie Costello had borne eight children and "bu'rid" two. She had never been beautiful, although there was a spiritual grace in her face that to her children, and to all children, was beauty. She had always been poor and hard-working and humble, and she had always loved her life and thanked God for it.

She made beds and fixed flowers with her big capable hands; she baked pies and cooked chickens and peeled potatoes. She considered three new dish towels a treasure, and to have all the children at home and good and well for Sunday breakfast a weekly triumph. When she was not talking or laughing she was apt to be crying, asleep, or at her prayers.

Sandra, drowsing by a fire, would hear the neighbors' voices in the kitchen, the queries, the complaints; would hear the deep true voice of her hostess, advising them. There was nothing Mrs. Costello couldn't cure or help or solve.

Peter attended his brother at the wedding; Helen stood next to Alexandra. Peter seemed kindly, but confused and nervous, to Sandra; he disappeared immediately after the little ceremony and the registering of names; there was a little subdued laughter and kissing. The wedding had been set for four o'clock; it was not half-past four when Sandra came out into a sober, clouding afternoon on her husband's arm, and got into her old seat in the roadster; the deep, padded, sloped seat beside the driver. Carter, driving slowly, clamped his free right arm about her shoulders.

"Well, it's all come true, honey. Here we are! Betty and Patsy get off next Monday, Mother goes off to New York in three weeks; everything serene."

"It's all like a dream."

"Do you know where we're going to-night?"

She sounded a negative.

"Don't you care, Mrs. Cavendish?"

The dreamy, comfortable little note was repeated.

"We're going to the Fairmont. And to-morrow at eleven we sail for Honolulu."

"I rather thought that. I mean you said so once, Carter."

The spring day was shining and blue; the sky high and crossed by drawn fleeces of cloud. Grass was growing everywhere; acacia trees bursting into yellow bloom and apple trees painting pink and white shadows against the new green. The roads were wide and clear, washed and packed smooth by long rains; the roadster purred along comfortably. Sounds came clearly from far away; children's voices, the crowing of cocks.

"Worth while, Sandra."

"Carter, the lives that never have even an hour of this!"

"And we have it all—all the time there is."

Their rooms at the hotel were enormous, with a green iron balcony toward the east, over the Bay that was radiant now in sunset. They had a great stone fireplace, Italian chairs of black wood, candlesticks and plates and glass bowls from Trapani. Carter stood on the balcony with his arm about her, and showed her the *Malolo,* waiting to take them off to the Hawaiian Isles to-morrow.

"It's too cold to have dinner out here, but we'll have our first breakfast here to-morrow, Alex."

The faint possessive pressure of his arm about her reminded her that she was to be made a wife before that, and she turned to him eyes grave in their steady beauty, and said in sudden youth and fear and helplessness.

"Be kind to me, Carter. Always—always love me!"

"You darling!" he whispered, under his breath.

Then they went in, and Carter rang for a man, and there was talk of dinner. Sandra went into the bedroom where lights were lighted, and saw boxes, boxes, boxes, little and big, piled on one of the beds.

"Things I got you for the trip!" Carter told her.

Dazed, reproachful, she laid aside the blue hat and the fur, and like an awed, serious Christmas child, began to open the boxes one by one.

Everything was white or black; a heavy Japanese jacket of lustrous black lined with white; an exquisite filmy tea gown of creamy white, with panels of sheer white embroidery, and foam of delicate white laces. A white bag, enchantingly frivolous; a black bag, handsome and heavy. White slippers fluffy with feathers; black slippers with great flashing buckles; a white jersey suit, a jersey suit of knowing black-and-white. Next to the last box held a great white fox skin; the last box of all a soft belted white topcoat.

"Mother sent you the fur, and Pete sent you the coat," Carter said.

"Oh, Carter, they didn't!" She was in ecstasies; she was beautiful, glowing, sparkling, after the fatigues and excitements of the day, trying on the little white hat, flinging the fur about her shoulders, belting the big loose coat about her. "Oh, this is such *fun!*" she breathed.

He caught her, to kiss the soft crushed hair at her temples and the lips she so instantly raised.

"Want to put on something fluffy and comfortable for dinner?"

"Are we going to dine up here?"

"Why not?"

"Oh, lovely! It seems so strange," she murmured, at the window, looking out at the dusky city and bay and the first lights—"it seems so strange to have it right for us to be here—nobody's business any more."

"It seems awfully sweet," he murmured against her hair.

There was a tap at the door; the waiter to lay dinner. It was almost seven o'clock.

"He brought up a paper, but the press hasn't got us yet," Carter said, giving her the newspaper. "They can have it to-morrow, if they like! We'll be far at sea."

He had turned back to the other room; she took the paper in her hand, looked down at a headline.

"Child Hurt in Crash," she read. "Daughter of Carter Cavendish Taken to Hospital——"

Alexandra stood looking at the words for a long time without moving. She was still transfixed when Carter came in with a telegram in his hand. He snatched at his hat and coat. Sandra caught up the slip of yellow paper and read the typewritten lines:

"Patsy hurt. Have taken her to Dante Hospital. Is asking for you. Come at once."

It was signed "Betty."

CHAPTER SEVENTEEN

FROM THE BEGINNING she had hoped for the time that must come, sooner or later, when she and Carter would be just one more married pair in the world, not discussed or criticized or watched, happy in their love and their life together and neither knowing nor caring about anything beyond.

Alexandra had been married a year—married more than a year—before she began dimly to perceive that that time never was coming. In the entirely new life in which she found herself there was no room for that peaceful, detached, ideally devoted home of which she had dreamed and for which she had planned.

Everything moved at a fearfully accelerated pace now; everybody shifted about, traveled, rushed hither and thither; there was no time for leisure, for talk, for lazy mornings at home and quiet evenings by the fire. Carter and his wife were caught in the whirlpool and must revolve about in it or sink.

At first it had rather amused and excited Sandra to follow the novel new course of her life. Nothing had been as she had anticipated it. Her honeymoon had been a month delayed because of Patsy's accident; it had been mid-March before she and Carter had sailed for Honolulu. Patsy meanwhile had gone off to Europe with her mother. That had been a hard month, one she hated to remember, but Sandra had told herself it "didn't count"; it was the last payment Carter would make on the old debt.

Then had come the heaven of their trip, their four unclouded weeks of tropical sunshine and beaches, white clothes, moonlight, marine band playing under palm trees. Carter had been all pride; she herself all adoring devotion; the brief days had flown by like hours.

Then back to San Francisco's smartest hotel for a few weeks, and then to San Mateo; Carter's mother added to the party now. They were reopening the home that had been Betty's, sending books away, packing garments, deluging the Rummage Sale with odds and ends. "High Hill" was to be rented; Alexandra had mildly expressed herself as preferring not to live there.

Even remaining there a few weeks had not been pleasant. The house had been haunted by Betty, which was bad enough, and by Patsy, which was worse. An oil painting of the child was over the dining-room mantel; an exquisite chalk drawing of her in the room that had been Betty's. Mrs. Cavendish had taken Betty's room, and Sandra and Carter the suite that had been his. One day Alexandra had asked the old housekeeper which room had been Miss Patsy's.

This door had been closed, but the old woman had opened it readily enough, and Sandra had walked in to study with a strangely leaden heart the gay walls papered with Mother Goose characters, the little-girl checked gingham curtains, the white tables and low chairs of babyhood, and the abandoned doll's house. Everything had been in order, dusted, bright, but she had felt as if it were a chamber of death.

The elder Mrs. Cavendish, in mourning for her mother, had lived very quietly, but Sandra had never spoken of her own mother's death, and had joined Carter in everything without protest. They had gone to early summer dances at the club and to bridge dinners. Sandra could not play bridge with this group of women who played all day long and every day for very high stakes, but Carter loved a good game at night, and, even when Sandra believed that they had a free evening, would come home from the office to announce that Pete and Joe and Thorny or Fred were coming to dinner. "They wanted me to cook up something, and I thought we'd rather be here."

Sandra presided with a charming dignity at these dinners, and looked like a young duchess at the head of her table, but the talk of the men was all of sports—polo, tennis, baseball; she was often bored by it all. They made bets on football games, squabbled about batting averages, argued about ponies, and generally came back to guns. All these men belonged to duck clubs, and Carter's mother warned Sandra that as soon as the season opened she would be a "duck widow."

Peter was always her friend, and would come and talk to her when he was dummy and ask her what she had been doing all day; all the men were nice to her; but at about ten o'clock she would grow sleepy and go smilingly away. Sometimes Carter did not come upstairs until two or three.

Alexandra would lie awake for awhile, staring into the warm gloom of the room, through whose windows moonlight and tree shadows made their way. About her would be the rampart of the big, imposing, old-fashioned mansion, its gardens and stables and garages and hothouses. Downstairs, sipping his highball without taking his eyes from his cards, was her husband, rich, handsome, and devoted. The touch of the bell beside her bed would bring a servant; her signature on one of those pink checks over on the desk could command a good deal of money now.

She could order the car to-morrow morning and be driven into town and shop for anything she liked: frocks, hats, Paris underthings. Then she could go into Carter's office, smiling on all sides as she passed the girls at the desks, gracious to Miss Curtis, who had been ill, poor girl, welcomed by Carter with a shout of pleasure.

Perhaps he could go to lunch with her; perhaps he would have "a feller I can't shake." If he did go to lunch it would be for a briefer time than they had wasted in the old days not two years ago. Natural enough, she would tell herself, for of course he was coming home to her anyway at night.

Once, on a Wednesday, she had suggested a matinee, rather to his surprise.

"I'll tell you why I can't, honey," he had said. "I don't want anything to interfere with the foursome at Lakeside on Saturday, and if I'm away too much . . ."

So she must amuse herself alone during the afternoon.

The women of Carter's set had been surprisingly nice to her. Once Alexandra had thought that it would not matter whether they were nice or not. But now she was very thankful for their friendliness.

Friendliness; it was hardly more. They did not speak her language, nor she theirs. Their talk was largely gossip and often scandal, and Alexandra did not know its significance. She knew herself to be a complete outsider and feared it would always be so. Her old life must not be mentioned here; she felt still too confused to make any capital of the new.

Any allusions to the old lodging house in Ellis Street, her theatrical mother, even to that half-year on the ranch, would have embarrassed and shocked and annoyed the new friends. They had some rather odd family histories themselves, if the records of the pioneers were to be closely studied, but these they ignored. All of them claimed birth and lineage, claimed familiarity if not kinship with the great and the rich. Fluttering about, faultlessly dressed and groomed, chattering in French or Italian if neither French nor Italian visitors were present, easy with references to Grandpa's stable of Kentucky hunters, or Grandma's adorable place in Paris, they lived in a world of make-believe.

A very few assumed from the first the pose of loyalty to dear Betty Cavendish who had had "such a rotten deal." But most of them chose rather to be nice to Carter's wife; Carter was an important figure in the social and sporting world.

She could smile at them at club lunches and golf meets; they waved at her, came over to speak to her. Sometimes she hoped that an intimacy would develop here or there, but it never did. Gentle Mrs. Peabody was the nicest of all, but the Peabodys were not often at home. They went to New York, to Hawaii, to Tahoe, to Agua Caliente and Pasadena, to Santa Barbara and Palm Beach, they went away on friends' yachts or in their private cars.

When the old Cavendish house was rented, Sandra and Carter took the Cutler house, a bright, modern, much-bathroomed place of the English pattern, timbers and plaster without, paneled walls within. Also they decided to build on Carter's lot at Pebble Beach, and this Sandra thought for a few months of the year at least would be "home."

The fast-flying months were not without their exquisite hours; she loved him so dearly, he seemed a very miracle of force and cleverness and charm to her. But they had their pricks, too, from the first day.

Even that wedding day had been clouded, that perfect day that had worn away to dusk in the great hotel with the light fading along the level surface of the Bay and the waterfront, and the soft lights blooming in the great Italian suite, blooming upon Sundra's flushed happy face and tumbled hair, and upon the new white coat, the fur, the laces and silks and embroideries that were tossed about and piled on one another.

Upon this scene had come the newspaper and the telegram

that told Carter that his little girl was seriously hurt and needed him. He had gone at once to the hospital, of course; he had telephoned Alexandra an hour later. He and his mother were there, he had said; she had known that Betty, the child's mother, must be there, too.

Fracture and concussion; they would know more about it to-morrow.

Alone at ten o'clock on her wedding night, Sandra had finished the disposition of all her effects carefully. She had opened the steamer trunk and packed the new possessions within; she had unpacked some of the dresses she would need in town, if she and Carter were delayed. Her suitcase empty, she had attacked his, placed his toilet requisites in the big bathroom, his brushes and her picture and Patsy's picture on his bureau.

Then she had undressed and wrapped herself warmly, and gone out to the green balcony above the Bay, to study the green moonlight and the threading specks of gold that were ferryboats moving against the dark green water, and the blazing distant bracelet that was Berkeley and Oakland. The night had been warm and soft; the sky a bright blue-green flooded with silver light.

Carter had come home at about five the next morning, exhausted. He had wakened for a bath, a late breakfast with Sandra, at eleven. She had asked him all the questions she dared.

They didn't know anything yet; nobody knew. Patsy's leg was broken and her face had been cut; these were the least of it. Betty had collapsed and was in bed herself in an adjoining room, under a nurse's care.

Alexandra did not belong there with them—the mother, the father, the child; she knew it. He did not urge her to come. Late in the afternoon he had taken her driving; she had eagerly, lovingly agreed with his hesitating, his regretful suggestion that they must wait. They would sail on the first steamer after the child was really well.

So the first three weeks of her marriage had been strange, quiet weeks. Sandra had gone to movies, ordered little meals that should appeal to Carter when he came in tired. Most of her time had been spent in the beautiful Italian suite, where she read and idled all day.

One afternoon she had gone to see Patsy, small and pathetic and friendly, with her bandaged head. Patsy evidently had understood the situation, for she had said gayly, "If Gran and you and Mother were all here there'd be three Mrs. Cavendishes in one room, wouldn't there?"

But the visit had been rather flat, and Sandra had been sorry afterward that she had gone. She did not fit in.

The older Mrs. Cavendish sometimes had come to dine with Alexandra and Carter, and once or twice had taken Sandra to lunch. Sandra had tried to be dignified, composed, philosophical, but she had been under a hard strain. It had been like emerging into daylight again after an endless night to find herself actually on the big clean deck of the liner at last sailing for Hawaii.

Then, upon their return, had come the confused impressions of the San Francisco hotel, Carter bringing her violets and handkerchiefs and old earrings and necklaces every night, dressing for parties in a glittering room, stopping to kiss each other. Then the San Mateo house to which she had been sent from the office two years ago, and which never seemed home to her, and never could. And afterward the Cutler house—a week in Santa Barbara for the tennis— visits, Tahoe visits, visits to lodges up on the Russian and Rogue rivers, visits to Pebble Beach.

Always the same thing: the porches, awnings, glint of water, the servants carrying suitcases, the host all agog over tennis scores or race-boat records. Always the luxurious guest room, twin beds, drawn shades, bathroom with fat towels embroidered in color, the copies of *The Spur* and *Punch* and *Vanity Fair* on the reading tables. Always porches, telephones, radio—everything. And Carter always tearing open his luggage, snatching out white things, shouting to some man below on the lawn, "Be with you in half a jiffy, old boy!" before they had been ten minutes in their room.

Alexandra could proceed more slowly, straightening the disorder he left behind him, changing her own gown, using the beautiful stationery with the tiny telephone and map and wireless signals engraved upon it, to acknowledge flowers, to decline some invitation or accept one.

Then she would go down slowly, secretly shy, outwardly her usual serene self, to find four women playing bridge somewhere, a tall girl idling with a young man, somebody wheeling a smart open car on the gravel, more awnings, more flowers, more discreet servants, more cocktails. She could watch the bridge or the tennis, or wander along the lake or beach or in the woods, or find a book. Now and then an old person was playing solitaire somewhere and was grateful for a companion and advice as to play.

Carter loved her and was proud of her; why wasn't that enough? Why was she so tortured with the need to be more to him, nearer to him? She wanted to be his very life; she found herself just one element in it.

He would come home on Saturday, Sunday afternoons, flushed and perspiring from tennis or golf, his brown throat showing where the thin wet white shirt fell away, his brown face lighted by his flashing smile.

"Kiss ze papa. Look at my wife, Peter, isn't she easy to look at? Listen, darling-and-beautiful—by the way, the earrings are grand, aren't they?—I'm going to take a shower and see if I can catch up some sleep; don't bother, don't come up!"

But she would go up to turn down his bed, folding up the fat comforters, drawing shades, exclaiming in fond wifely fashion at his carelessly abandoned clothes, his hopeless disorderliness.

In five minutes he would be deeply asleep, his black hair emerging in a rich wave above the delicately tinted green or apricot or peach-colored sheet. She was forgotten.

But when he awakened he liked to see her stirring about, her tall, beautiful figure as much revealed as hidden by the frail lacy draperies of her dressing gown, her cloud of chestnut hair tumbled on her shoulders. Brushing the short curls and waves vigorously, she would expostulate with him.

"Dinner is at eight, Carter."

"Oh, help! Oh, death, I'm tired. Oh, darling, that clock isn't right!" There would be earthquake among the bedclothes; he would be snoring again.

"It's slow, if anything. It's quarter to eight."

"Oh, Alexandra, if you love me—give me five minutes more . . ."

In the car, half an hour later, he would be at his handsomest. It would be impossible to believe then that this groomed and polished gentleman in irreproachable evening wear was one and the same with the disheveled, protesting boy who hated to be waked up for dinner. Alexandra was conscious of a special adoration for him when he was formally dressed; but then there was no moment when she did not adore him. He was always handsome, splendidly strong and hard and eager and energetic, so vitally engaged in living his own fascinating life that he needed no one to help him live it. Everyone liked Carter, and without being spoiled he knew it. Every club welcomed him, every man was his friend, every discussion invited his opinion, every golf team or polo team or tennis tournament needed him, and no woman who ever met him failed to take note of him and remember him.

When there were distinguished visitors at the club, strangers from Washington or Boston or England, Alexandra never failed to notice the impression Carter made on them early in their stay. The handsome, hard, happy young fellow with the tennis racket in his hand, his shirt open at the throat, his big teeth flashing in his brown face, always could take a few seconds out of his own all-important affairs to welcome newcomers, to ask concernedly about their plans —how about guest cards at the club? How about—see here, Sandra, can't we show 'em the Skyline and Stanford, if that's what they're so keen about? How about Monday? How about Tuesday?

When the day came he was invariably unable to share the expedition, but Sandra always went, entirely winning the visitors with her gracious young beauty. Sometimes she knew that between the first meeting and the second they had been told her history, perhaps ungenerously.

Not that anyone disliked her especially, but a retouched ugly story was always more interesting, was better dinner-table conversation than a dull, true one.

"That Mrs. Cavendish is the second wife, you know. She was his secretary. His first wife and the little girl are in France; it all but broke Betty Cavendish's heart. She and Carter had been married eleven years. We all felt terribly! But Alexandra Cavendish is really awfully sweet . . ."

That was the way they put it. She knew it without resentment. After all, that was the way they saw it, and their opinions were not important. What was important was the frightening, strengthening fear in her heart that Carter really did not need a wife at all. She began to feel pangs of jealousy of him, always so well and strong and brown and competent and resourceful.

Jealousy. Jealousy. Not only of what the other women thought of him, but of him, himself. Sleeping so deep, eating, drinking, living with such zest, incessantly in demand, incessantly occupied and interested.

Her mind seethed with plans; sometimes she felt as if her imagination were a tangible creature, running about in her confused head, seeking a solution, trying to find some way in which she could be busy and absorbed and popular, too.

Not with bridge and tennis and golf, she knew. The others had had a long start along these lines. Not by frocks and grooming; they all had those, too. Not by the dinners she served, not by the correct pronunciation of French words, not by a liking for music or books. Not by anything she could do.

She could only be as sweet and make herself as attractive and interested and pretty as possible, and wait until time found her her own activities and her own groove.

Alexandra, dressing, laughing, answering the telephone, would sometimes think it would have been quite easy if she had been the first rather than the second Mrs. Cavendish. Betty still had the right of way.

Betty had had her life, first. Betty had been driven into town by Paul, the chauffeur; Betty had gone about among these hospitable homes, playing bridge, sitting at dinner tables, displaying New York frocks and Paris hats.

Worse, Betty had been Carter's wife. She had shared his room, brushed her loosened hair in the same sacred intimacy that Sandra knew. Perhaps she had sometimes come across the big room, as Sandra did, to establish herself half on his knee, half on the broad arm of his chair, to put a soft fragrant arm about his neck, to lay her cheek against the rippling black satin of his hair.

Betty had given him a child, too. That was why the thought of another child, which had been a very earthquake of emotions—joy, fear, incredulity, amazement—to Alexandra, had found him just his usual cheerful, detached, kindly self.

"How d'you feel about it, honey?"

"Oh, I'm glad!" Sandra had said, smiling with watering eyes. It took nothing at all these days, she had reflected, to bring tears to her eyes. "But of course it's not much fun feeling—so rotten," she had added, quite against her own will. She had not meant to strike this note.

"Oh, you'll get over that!" he had said, not unsympathetically, but in all kindly reassurance. "Betty felt like that for the first few months; everyone does."

It was unreasonable, it was ridiculous, to let a few careless words like these overbalance the sum total of her marvelous good fortune: "the chorus girl's dream," as she had called it to Carter. But she could not help it. Any mention of Betty set her teeth on edge, and made her forget that she, Sandra, had been picked out of the office rank and file to marry a rich and handsome and popular man, to have gowns and servants and motorcars, and position. All this overnight, as it were, at the wave of the fairy godmother's wand. More than had ever befallen any real flesh-and-blood girl before.

But it was not enough. No, not to be Mrs. Carter Cavendish, not to be mother, one of these days, of the Cavendish baby. Her heart was still hungry, she was lonely, she was baffled by a constant sense of having missed somehow the heart of everything, the true sweetness of everything.

She knew herself jealous, but Carter had no spark of jealousy in his being. He liked to see other men admiring her; he showed an enhanced appreciation of her because she found favor in other eyes.

"How d'you suppose I ever got a girl like that to look at me, Jim?" he would ask some casual guest with relish, when Sandra came over to the card table to put the cigarettes where everyone could reach them, and lay a hand—simply because she could not pass him without touching him—on her husband's shoulder.

Upstairs, later, perhaps Carter would say: "Do me a favor, Baby. Put on the Mary Queen of Scots thing for dinner——"

"The velvet, Idiot?"

"The green velvet."

"I always feel 'bought and paid for,'" she would think, "when I walk into some place, all pearls and velvet! They all say it—they know . . ."

But she could not tell him this. No, if he liked to be proud of her, openly boastful, openly triumphant—then it was part of her new life to give him the opportunity.

CHAPTER EIGHTEEN

IN THE FIRST MONTHS of her marriage, like a little girl playing lady, she had loved to dress up, to put on the handsome clothes and the old-fashioned rich jewelry of pearls, black enamel, red gold. But after a while that had come to have its sting, too. It was too visibly the price of her; or in her nervous imagination she made it so. The penniless nobody who had married a rich man would take her toll of furs and jewels and laces, of course. The buyer would want his world to see his bargain.

One hour with her mother might have straightened it all out; but that hour could never come now. One healing, laughing, busy hour down on the ranch would have worked the miracle, if she might have put on one of the old blue cottons, seized the broom or dish towel once more, opened small-paned farmhouse windows to sunshine and scented wet autumn airs. It had been a strange, keen, happy time, that ranch interval, with Rondani bringing Carter's letters up the hill every morning, and the little Airedales wagging and frolicking everywhere. A time of love and service, of expectancy and hope—Sandra looked back at it with heartache.

After Christmas she and Carter lived more quietly. They were still in the comfortable Cutler house in Burlingame: Sandra was amusing herself with plans for the Pebble Beach house, which was to be built as soon as the rains stopped. It was to be a "Norman farmhouse," the architect said, although just why a Norman farmhouse should have been set down on a western American coast in among colonial, Spanish, Mexican, Byzantine, Hopi Indian, French, Tudor English, and Italian houses he did not make clear. Sandra had discovered in herself a real gift for the designing of rooms and for ingenious devices and details, and Thomas Jefferson Jones not only asked her quite simply for suggestions about her own and about other houses, but praised her to Carter, which was balm to her soul.

As the time of the baby's arrival drew near, Carter was increasingly tender and considerate, too. She loved to hear him at the telephone explaining:

"Mrs. Cavendish and I are taking it easy just now, you know. Ask us again after Easter."

One day a telephone call from some enthusiastic unknown woman upset her for a while. The voice supposed itself to be addressing the first Mrs. Cavendish.

"Betty darling, this is Louise! Just in this morning, all the way from China. When will I see you?"

Often letters intended for Betty came to her; often her days brought some small pinprick that had to be borne and forgotten. In a book she might find an inscription."Carter from his Betsy," or "Daddy from Patsy. Merry Christmas." Betty's pictures had been eliminated, but Patsy's were everywhere. In her own home and in other houses Alexandra was constantly coming across snapshots—glimpses of yachting trips, tennis and golf groups, with Betty always smart and smiling in the foreground, somewhere near Carter. Carter himself had often spoken of a possible trip to Europe in the autumn, a prospect that would have seemed dazzling to Alexandra a few years ago, but that now was clouded by his casual, "to have a look at the kid."

Patsy wrote to her father once a month; references to "Mummy" were frequent, but Sandra never was mentioned. Patsy was living in Paris now, taking lessons only in French and on her "voilin," and she was going to play an étude at a children's concert. Her letters ended with loving rings and crosses and daisies, indicating "hugs and kisses." Carter was always made proud and happy, was always deeply touched by these little epistles; he would show them shamefacedly to Alexandra, and eventually leave them with his mother to display to anyone and everyone else.

"The only thing I can do, Carter, is to have a boy; that's the one thing life hasn't done for you!"

"I'd rather have a girl, myself. They're awfully sweet. Pats from the hour she was born had something—*something* . . ."

Alexandra and Carter and Peter were idling about after lunch on a rainy April Sunday at home when the summons came. It was a fortnight early, and Sandra was somewhat surprised, and conscious of a flutter of fear, as she and the two men hurried into town. But they were all ready, all confident enough, and Peter's anxious "I *know* it'll be all right!" to his brother, as they helped Sandra's bulkiness from the car at the hospital's Spanish doorway, set her laughing. "You don't know *anything*, Pete!" she said.

It was a long time before she wanted to laugh again. On Monday in mid-morning her daughter was born, and Sandra with the terrible prescience of the new-born mother knew from the beginning that something was wrong. Carter was too deliberately cheerful, the nurse too gently congratulatory upon Sandra's own young health and strength.

"You look beautiful, sweetheart. They can't lick *you*, can they?" Carter said when it was all over and she was sweet and fresh again, and resting.

"Is she sweet, Carter?"

"Well, the nurses were fussing with her, honey."

"We're all so proud of you, Mrs. Cavendish," the nurse

said. "You've had a hard time, and you've been **wonderful**."

"Am I not to see my baby?"

"Well, they're busy with her now, dear."

"Busy with her! Isn't she——" Her eyes moved in swift, sick apprehension from face to face; the doctor was here now, the two nurses; Carter was kneeling beside her, holding her limp hand.

"I think you're a brave enough woman to hear a piece of hard news, Mrs. Cavendish," the doctor said.

Three days later Alexandra, patting his hand, smiling through lashes that had been drenched and dried, drenched and dried over and over again, told Carter that as soon as she was strong, as soon as she was well and at home again, she would stop crying.

"It's just that I'm so rottenly weak, Cart," she faltered. "And I lie here thinking of that room—all pink and white—and the little dresses——" She stopped, suffocating.

"Mother came down and packed everything up."

"She's awfully kind."

"Maybe you'll have 'em all out again next year, Sandy. I know how that sounds to you now, sweetheart, but you'll feel differently when you're up and around again."

She lay listening, raised her wet lashes to smile at him, trembled into tears again.

"I'm such a—c-c-contemptible b-b-baby!"

"That's all part of it."

"Cart, do you suppose my having said I didn't want a girl, I wanted a boy——"

"Now listen, if you're going to be a damn' fool——"

"No, I'm not, I'm not!" She made herself laugh, caught at his hand, kept him from rising. "Now I've stopped," she said.

But a few moments later she touched the soaked silk at her full breast.

"They aren't letting me drink anything, Cart, except a little black coffee in the morning—and look at me! So much of it, and it was for my little girl."

He knelt down, put his big comforting arms about her.

"You poor little thing!"

Sandra locked her arms about his neck and hid her face, and cried to her heart's content.

That summer they began to build the Norman farmhouse, living meanwhile at Peter's rambling bachelor establishment seven miles farther down the coast. Sandra entered resolutely with heart and soul into the social activities about her; it was a world of cocktails, card games, beauty parlors, tennis, yachting, polo, golf. Carter had to stay in the city at least four nights a week, Sandra sometimes accompanying him, sometimes remaining at the Peter Cavendish ranch. The week-ends were one flash of excitement and amusement; the season rushed by as usual on wings.

Peter had a comfortable, ugly, too modern and yet not sufficiently modern white house, acres of meadow, a half-mile of rocky coast, plenty of ocean view, barns, oaks, windmills, eucalyptus, fences, and gnarled apple trees. Alexandra adored the place, and was mistress there, pouring the men's coffee, directing the Chinese servants, arranging Peter's books and pipes to suit herself.

Peter was like a fatter, softer, more genial, lazy, and older version of Carter; the brothers loved each other dearly, and Peter told Alexandra that when Carter was not actually with him he always drank an evening toast to his brother's portrait in the dining room, and greeted the photograph on his dresser with a "Good-morning, kid!"

In fact, it took little encouragement from her to launch Peter into a disquisition upon his brother's perfections, and as that was always her own favorite subject, too, they discussed him for hours together. She could not play golf or tennis or bridge in Peter's class, but she could constitute herself with a sympathetic listener, and she made an art of it.

Peter was loyalty itself to Betty; he had for her the admiration felt by an unmarried older brother for a young sister-in-law. Betty had been an important figure in his life: as a bride when he stood beside Carter as best man, as a member of the family of Cavendish to be remembered at birthdays and Christmas times, and finally as giving Peter the closest glimpse he had ever had of a new baby's eventful days and the honor of being Patsy's uncle. Even Carter was not prouder of the little girl than was Uncle Peter. He had been amazed, reverential, breathless by turns before the miracle of Patsy's being and his own relationship to her. That class of costly bauble known to saleswomen as "uncle toys," and usually in Christmas windows, had been sent to Patsy from Peter: life-sized mechanical goats, French waitresses with trays of glasses and bottles, Punchinellos worked by electricity.

But now out of a gentle and somewhat lonely heart he began to love Alexandra, too. She saw tears in his eyes when he first spoke to her awkwardly, briefly, in her hospital room, of the lost little daughter, and loved him for them. She made him laugh as Betty had never made him laugh; her interest in his garden and dogs and horses delighted him. They became confidential and affectionate friends, so that Alexandra fell into the pleasant family habit of consulting Peter about his plans for the day at the breakfast table quite as interestedly as she did Carter. If Carter were to play polo or in some special golf or tennis match, or if he wanted to go off for a day or two with some yachting or hunting group, Sandra and Peter arranged their own plans accordingly.

"We could ask the Baxters and the Whites and your mother, Pete, and take them along with us if we go to Senator Gregg's luncheon Sunday."

"Well, listen, if I get steaks and what-not, will you cook 'em?"

"Will I?" She loved the open-air grill that was built on a level of the cliff, loved to help him cook there; Peter was a famous cook and a recognized epicure. His friends were not surprised at being offered choice morsels of beefsteak, or asked to sample hot doughnuts at all hours.

"You should have married Pete," Carter said once. "You and he would have hit it off like nobody's business!"

"Meaning that we don't, you and I?"

"Meaning that as long as I was round Pete never would have had a look in!"

"Oh, I don't know." Sandra had been with them at breakfast, lovely in white, with sunshine glinting on her shining hair and catching a thousand points of light from the silver and glass on the table. "You see, *you* asked me," she reminded Carter, "and Pete didn't. I had to take the one that asked me, didn't I?"

"Well, I would have—my gracious, I never even dreamed ——" Peter had begun in confusion, and Sandra and Carter had laughed delightedly as they always did when Fate offered them a chance to get "a rise" out of Peter.

In late September Carter took her to New York for three bewildering weeks. Alexandra, in her smart new suit, with sables, and a topcoat, and a pigskin handbag, met him at the office on the exciting afternoon when they were to leave, and the old office staff saw her come in, fortunate, beloved, established. Sandra could imagine old clerks saying to the new girls: "She was Miss Trumbull; she used to have that desk."

It made her feel deeply proud, happy; it was good to be pointed out and envied and watched while she smiled and talked with Gertrude Curtis and Peter just as if she were completely unconscious of the stir she was creating. An hour like this was all that Sandra Trumbull might have believed it to be years ago.

The trip was perfect, too—or if not quite perfect, almost so. Its only flaw was in the little episode of old Mrs. Trout, and she did not matter. Old Mrs. Trout was on the train taking a granddaughter to Vassar. Carter and Sandra met them when they were walking up and down on the platform at Cheyenne, getting a breath of fresh air while the train waited for right of way.

Carter spoke to the old lady, and Alexandra beside him smiled at her, and at the smart, proud-looking young girl. But Mrs. Trout did not answer the smile nor extend her withered old aristocratic hand when Sandra was introduced.

Instead a hard ugly flush came into her raddled face and she said sharply:

"I don't think I'll shake hands with your wife, Carter! You know I think you treated Betty very badly—very badly. I really do! I might as well say it! I know that sort of thing is goin' on all the time, but that doesn't excuse it in my opinion. Gracie tells me that Betty almost broke her heart . . ."

Carter and Alexandra walked on, the man parting from the vituperative old woman with merely a bored nod. Afterward he told Alexandra what he thought of old Mrs. Trout, and Alexandra, whose comment upon the conversation had been merely a wide-eyed "Whew!" laughed generously and said that she didn't care what old battle-axes like that thought anyway. But they both did care; they both felt snaken and shocked by the little encounter, Sandra choosing to ignore it after the first few minutes, and Carter breaking out several times in the next few days with a disgusted, "Well, what do you know about old Jane Trout!"

Then they were in New York, and Alexandra was breathless with enthusiasm for everything they saw and did. The autumn coloring all along the last thousand miles of roadbed delighted her, the little villages on river banks touched some chord of memory and love "older than I am," she told Carter. "I've been here before; I've seen all this before!"

They walked in the October sparkle of the Avenue, and Sandra had more presents, more bags and silk stockings and rings. They went to brilliant shows and wandered back to their hotel under soft thick stars, through the fascinating streets; streets wheeling with Northern Lights of color, or sober and dark between old redstone-fronted houses. When Carter was busy in the mornings, Sandra liked to climb on the top of a green omnibus and ride and ride, tirelessly, through the hurrying, jumbled, miraculous new world. Out —out—out through the Park and along the river and up to the new bridge, or down—down—down to the Square where the sun shone on old brick homes that had been standing in Lincoln's day, and so on and on, walking through the crowded thick quarters of the ghetto and perhaps out again into the height and airiness of Brooklyn Bridge. It was all fascinating to her; the wooden Indians, surviving relics of an earlier day, outside cigar stores, the chestnut venders and hurdy-gurdies unknown to San Francisco, the shops crowded into basements or carried in carts along the curbs, were all the subjects of animated reports to Carter at night.

They went to the Long Island country clubs; but that was not quite so much fun. To see Carter in polo clothes again, his wide grin white in his Indian-brown face, the usual group of friendly men and interested women about him, reminded her to be jealous once more, to want to carry him off somewhere where she could have him to herself. He was happy, at home in this atmosphere, eager in his talk about ponies and scores; she was much the outsider still.

On the last day of their stay they went to lunch with Gus and Mima Fitzpatrick at the Ritz. The Fitzpatricks had just come back from Paris. And that was horrid.

Gus started the lunch off badly to begin with by being completely bowled over by the charm and beauty of the second Mrs. Cavendish. He had not seen Sandra before, and being an artless, transparent sort of fellow, he could not disguise his feeling.

"By George, Cart, you can pick 'em!" exclaimed this simple creature. "Looka that hat, Mima. Why don't you ask Mrs. Cavendish where she got that hat, and get one like it! It's a peach of a hat."

"Isn't he marvelous?" Mima Fitzpatrick drawled. "I've two exactly like it, and he can't stand them."

"I'm crazy about your suit, Mrs. Cavendish."

"It's new," Sandra said, with a look from gold-brown eyes.

"Say, why can't you and Cart have dinner with us this evening, and take in a show?"

"We have a date, Gus," Mrs. Fitzpatrick said, as one who chips icicles off a tombstone.

"Oh, and we're leaving at five for California," Sandra added, in her soft, protesting voice.

"We'll see you out there next month," Gus reminded her.

"Month after," Mima amended it. And immediately, turning to Carter, she said: "Cart, have you heard Patsy play?"

"Patsy?"

"We saw a lot of her and Betty in Deauville."

"You mean the violin?"

"Cart, how long is it since you've heard that child play?"

"Oh—year. More than a year."

"Well, my dear, she's perfectly marvelous. Everyone's talking about her. Schroeder—you know he's the new teacher they're all flocking to, an Austrian, and quite extraordinary—says she could play in concert now if Betty'd let her. I assure you she's perfectly marvelous!"

"Patsy!"

"Not eleven yet, if you please."

"You don't mean it!"

"*Mean* it! I tell you she's going to be a sensation!"

"I don't believe Mother knows that," Carter said, pleased.

"My dear, nobody knows it! It's all come out of a clear sky. This child was plugging away with Schroeder—he comes to Deauville for two days every week—and Betty told me he asked her, quite casually, if Patsy could play in a benefit concert for the soldiers or sailors or whatever it was. Well, my dear, she was a *furore*. She played the same programme for some of us, later. She was *the* loveliest thing I ever saw in my life. Betty said she walked out as cool as an old hand, her little violin under her arm, bowing this way and that—Gus, wasn't she remarkable?"

" 'Dorable," Gus agreed.

"Applause! Well, they just went crazy about her, that was all. They just went ga-ga," Mrs. Fitzpatrick went on.

She was a big, rangy woman, this Mrs. Fitzpatrick, Alexandra thought, watching her, with a face like a horse's face, long teeth like old piano keys making themselves grooves in her thick lower lip. Her eyes bulged, her voice was coarse, her hat stood too high on her head, she wore too many jewels. Alexandra did not like her at all.

Mrs. Fitzpatrick doubled up a lettuce leaf on her fork and put it into her mouth, saying juicily at the same time:

"Betty says Cotta wanted to give her a contract!"

"Betty wouldn't do that!" Carter said quickly and anxiously.

"She says not yet."

"Good gracious, that'd be a terrible mistake!" Carter protested.

"You saw her picture in this month's *Stirrup*, Cart?"

"Whose?"

"Patsy's.

"In the *Stirrup*?"

"Certainly. It was out yesterday, I think."

"Is that so?" Carter asked, excited. He signaled the waiter.

The lunch went on, the talk went on. Presently the heavy, thick, smooth pages of the *Stirrup* were opened before them, and there Patsy was; Patricia Cavendish, in the center of a page of print under the heading "Music and Art."

"My God, isn't she lovely!" Carter said, under his breath.

The Patsy of the picture stood squarely on her feet, a little girl of eleven; her dark hair was in a mane on her shoulders, her hands locked before her. On a table beside her was the violin with its bow; a shadowy grand piano, a shadowy arch, filled the background.

Patsy wore a plain frock, socks, childish-looking patent leathers with low heels. There was an earnest, winning expression on the small brown face with the broad brow and big mouth, the face that was so like Carter's own.

"I tell you, people are crazy about her!" Mima Fitzpatrick repeated.

"They well may be!" Sandra said generously.

Carter did not speak. With his fine brown hand he opened his little flat gunmetal penknife and cut out the page containing the illustration and the article. He folded it and put it in his pocket, and for the rest of the day, even when they were on the train moving smoothly northward through the busy streets of the biggest city, even when they were dining, looking out at the Hudson and the factory chimneys of Poughkeepsie, Sandra saw he was abstracted, thoughtful. Her own heart sank—sank.

"Wouldn't you know it'd be Betty's luck to have a child like that!" Carter burst out, after a silence, late that night.

They were in the club car waiting for their drawing room to be made ready for the night. They had not been speaking of Patsy.

"You mean Patsy?"

"Yep. Think of the fun of running her, her little triumphs and all that."

She tried to keep voice and pulses steady, tried to sound merely interested and friendly.

"Responsibility, too, Carter."

"Well, that's just it, you see. Betty's a rotten person to manage anything like that. She'd let the kid kill herself to get publicity!"

"Oh, no, she wouldn't! Betty's lucky—nothing'll happen to Patsy! It—it was my baby who died," Sandra said, trembling. Carter gave her a quick look; reached for a magazine. It was some days later, they were at home again, when the storm broke.

"Cart, please—please don't rub it in *quite* so much!"

He was astonished.

"Rub what in?"

"Oh, Patsy. You tell everyone about her, you talk of nothing else."

She was shaking with terror. "We're fighting, we're fighting," her thoughts said in a sort of sick amazement. It was so common to fight. She and Carter were looking coldly, angrily at each other.

"I suppose you think it's an everyday happening for a kid of eleven to be making herself—by gosh, that's what she is, famous!"

"Famous!"

"That's what it is."

"It's a remarkable thing, of course," Sandra began, in a voice she tried to make sound steady and natural, "but it's perfect nonsense to say——

"Stop this—you'll be sorry!" she said, in her soul. But she could not stop.

Suddenly, when it was all at its height, she weakened and said:

"I'm sorry, Cart. I haven't meant half of this. I suppose I'm just jealous. Jealous of Betty and jealous of Patsy. I'm awfully sorry! It's terrible to have you and me talking to each other like this!"

He could not follow suit immediately. He said sharply, sulkily:

"Well, I should say you *are* jealous!"

But as she maintained her silence in the pause, only looking away from him with troubled beautiful eyes dark in her pale face, he softened, and the making up of their first real quarrel was exquisite to both. Alexandra, trailing turquoise draperies, came over to sit on the arm of his low chair, and Carter tightened a big steadying arm about her. Her soft cloud of hair was loose, and fell in a cloud on his shoulder as she laid her arm about his neck and her cheek against his.

"Are you jealous what-d'ye-call-it?"

"I'm horrible." The words were dreamily murmured into his ear, her voice was repentent, weary, content.

"Are you a harridan? Am I hag-ridden?"

"You are. I am."

"Don't you want me to love my little girl?"

"Oh, yes, Cart, of course."

"Then why are you so crabbed?"

"I don't know. But listen, Carter. Suppose——" She sat up to put it to him more clearly, the golden-brown eyes shone upon him in a frame of soft hair. "Suppose I had been married before," Alexandra began. "And suppose I had a phenomenal little boy, call him a golf player. Suppose he was taking cups and getting his picture into the papers and everyone was talking of him, wouldn't *you* be jealous?"

"My darling, when you and I are alone together like this and when you are so beautiful and soft and loving, the mere thought that any other man had had you in his arms and had been kissing your exquisitely lovely shoulder—like this——"

"But Carter, would you be jealous?"

"Jealous? I'd have to go kill him, that's all!"

"Well, sometimes I think I must go kill Betty!" she murmured, satisfied, and mumbling the words with her face down in his neck again.

"Betty! Betty and I have no more in common than—than you and she have."

"But she'll get you back through Patsy, Carter."

"Get me back!"

"You know she will."

"Why, you're just a half-wit, aren't you, darling? Just a case of arrested development?"

"I love you so, Cart," she whispered. "I'm *crazy* about you!"

"Ah, you're awfully sweet," he said, surprised, his voice losing its laughing note and becoming tender and touched all at once. "If you're going to be as sweet as all this about it let's—let's fight a lot!"

But her face was still serious and her voice weary.

"No, no," she said, tightening her arms about his neck and the pressure of her cheek against his own, "let's never fight again!"

CHAPTER NINETEEN

THE WINTER that followed was happier than its predecessor, although that had been Alexandra's first as Carter Cavendish's wife, that had been her honeymoon, her bride year. But now, with every passing month, she felt surer of herself, she felt Carter's group more friendly. And then there was Peter now, genuinely her brother, champion, companion, friend.

But a strange baffled sense of not being awake, not being alive, persisted. Alexandra had been conscious of this feeling ever since her marriage; she had not been able to analyze it last year; she could define it now. It was not always with her; sometimes weeks would go without more than momentary recurrences of it. Sometimes for whole days it fretted her like some small persistent fly buzzing about her face, like some stupid little pain at the base of her brain. In vain she might struggle to forget it, ignore it; like the thrumming of a stupid tune it repeated and repeated itself until she felt as if her mind itself were affected.

It was simply that she did not seem to *belong*. She did not belong to the comfortable house in Burlingame, with its chauffeur and Chinese servants, its telephones, flowers, chairs and tables. She did not belong among all these superficial, social men and women, these golf and polo players, dancers, eaters and drinkers, who knew one another so well, so easily. She was not really Carter's wife; nobody felt her so. They had not started out in the freshness of young love together, solving problems, growing closer and closer through common need. No, she had been his employee; that strangely powerful thing called love, making his one thought to possess her and her own one need to surrender to him, had had no background; she sometimes felt afraid that it had had no roots. Or perhaps it was simpler to explain it that even at best Carter did not need her; he only desired her. His business, his amusement, his servants and car and home ran quite smoothly without any effort Alexandra could make or anything she could suggest.

"It isn't marriage," she would think, puzzled. But then there was not much real marriage in the whole group; Mab with a lover of whose existence Jud Fulton was perfectly aware, Elinor divorced, Rose Bray with her millions and her handsome idle partner who was incapable of doing a day's work of any sort. Helen Peabody, nursing Harry through the after-effects of a war injury, came nearest of them all to that service and mutual dependence of which every woman dreamed when she dreamed of marriage.

And whatever her own problem was it was for her to solve it and not complain, and worry as little as possible. Forcing herself to philosophy she would find things going better, only perhaps to be suddenly plunged into the depths again by some casual word or glance that seemed to shatter the illusion that she was really and truly Carter's wife, that she belonged in this environment.

His birthday came only a few days before Christmas; she had hoped long before that to be able to tell him of the beginning of happiness once more, that there would be another baby in April or June or late summer.

The months went by; that hope never came. Sandra tried not to fret about it; fretting would defeat it. But the thought was with her day and night just the same; there was always a little bitterness there, bitterness when she remembered that

Carter had already known the joy of holding his first-born in his arms, and when she thought of Betty, to whom motherhood had come as a matter of course.

A full week before the birthday, on a clear soft December afternoon, she and Carter were in San Francisco. They had spent Saturday night with his mother; they had all gone to the theater together. Now, on the following afternoon, Carter and Sandra were on their way home to Burlingame in the car when they suddenly remembered an engagement, a large and formal tea that was being given by friends whose feelings ought not be hurt.

"Carter, the Underhills!"

"Oh, my God, is that to-day?"

"The fourteenth. That's today."

"It can't be!"

"It *is*."

"Oh, Lord," Carter moaned, "d'you suppose we ought to look in there?"

"They mightn't miss us—there is to be music; they've probably asked everyone!"

In the end they stopped at the imposing Pacific Avenue house, a big brick house set on a hilltop with a wide sweep of view. Cars were parked for blocks about, furred women and men in formal afternoon dress were ascending and descending the wide, garden-framed steps.

The afternoon was dark and quiet, with a gray sky and a steely sullen bay, but inside the house there was summer weather. The color of flowers, the scent of them, other delicate odors of tea and perfume and furs, soft lights, soft voices, persons coming in, persons going out; it was just like every other tea. No earthly need to have come: no one would remember it. Alexandra and Carter, working their way down the receiving line in a little babel of chatter and laughter, found themselves presently in the big library beyond the reception rooms and exchanged the swift, hopeful glance that meant, "Let's get out!"

Beyond the library there was a ballroom, darkened now, with strains of music coming from it. Sandra touched Carter's arm, her lovely, laughing face close to his. She spoke guardedly.

"How about going across the back of the music room—there's a side door—we can escape!"

"Done!" Carter murmured in the same manner.

They slipped through parted heavy curtains into the ballroom. It was quite dark; there was a sense of many persons there, all silent. At the end of the room there was a stage, raised a few feet from the floor, empty, lighted, with palms and one great jar of enormous chrysanthemums for its only furnishing.

Carter and Sandra had entered a door at the side of the big room; they were not far from the stage. In the half-minute that they stood there, glancing curiously toward it, a little girl came out into the soft great circle of light, a violin beneath her arm.

She stood squarely, firmly, in shining low-heeled slippers; a mane of dark straight hair fell to her shoulders. Her gown was of black taffeta, cut slim and close and tight; the awkward, exquisite grace of little girlhood was part of her. She looked down toward someone at the piano, nodded, an anxious smile lighted the brownness of her thin, serious little face. Immediately the strains of the violin began.

"Adorable!" Alexandra breathed. "Who is it?"

Carter gripped her hand; she felt his wet.

"God, it's Patsy!"

Sandra felt her own hand grow cold and her mouth dry. She did not speak again. The big, dark, fur-scented room was very still.

When the lights were suddenly up and the room began to buzz with appreciation, she could look at Carter. He seemed to have forgotten their plan for immediate escape; he was thinking; brows drawn and lip bitten.

"Did you know they were here?" he asked in his abrupt way.

"I heard they were coming," she answered, as he continued to frown and did not speak.

"Ha!" he breathed on a deep breath; then suddenly: "Isn't she wonderful!"

"Wonderful!"

"She's—she's marvelous," he said.

There was an interruption. The child, who had come down the three steps from the door beside the stage, and was surrounded by admirers, had caught sight of Carter.

"Daddy!" she called out, happily, eagerly. She flashed through the group, was in Carter's arms, her own thin little arms about him. "Oh, Daddy," she said in loving, excited reproach, "I didn't know you were here! Mummy said she thought you were in Los Angeles!"

"Hello, my little sweetheart," Carter said in a low tone, smoothing the hair from her high, pale forehead, his eyes for no one else. "Where'd you learn to play so beautifully? You must have done a lot of practising."

"I've wanted you so often, Dad. *Why* didn't you ever—*ever* come to Paris?"

"I've been too busy, Pats. Men can't go to Paris, you know, as ladies do."

Was everybody enjoying the scene? Sandra suspected it, but she dared not look round to see. She could only remain still, watching father and daughter with a sympathetic fixed smile on her face. She was conscious of an appreciative silence among the groups of men and women about her.

She saw Betty come up; Patsy was still clinging to her father's arm; Carter had to free his hand from the child's tight grasp to extend it to his first wife. Obviously Betty had not recognized the man to whom her daughter was speaking until this instant; her small, pretty face turned red.

"Oh, hello, Carter!" she said airily.

"It's Dad!" Patsy protested, wide-eyed.

"I know. But when you whisk away from me that way I never know where you are!"

Betty was obviously nervous; she covered it with a laugh. There was unmistakably an audience now. Alexandra was conscious in every fiber of her being of eagerly watching eyes, eagerly listening ears. "I wish you'd be more considerate, darling!" Betty said irritably. She looked at Carter.

"Well, what do you think of her?"

"She's—lovely," Carter answered, with a fond, downward look at the eager child in his arm. "But you're too thin, Pats," he said, making talk in the silence.

"I'll get fat now. Is my pony down at Uncle Peter's, Daddy?"

"You won't have much time to ride a pony," Betty told her quickly.

"But I can ride a *little*, Mummy?"

"When'd you get here, Betty?"

"Only this morning. I telephoned Alice Underhill; she said she was giving a musical this afternoon; I suggested she let Patsy play."

"The child looks thin."

"She's all right. I wish to goodness I looked thin!" Betty said.

"You've changed," Carter told her, smiling. She looked strange, Sandra thought; she was too powdered, her lips too red, her dark hair curled into two iron fish-hooks against her cheeks; her eyebrows had been picked into two thin arched penciled lines. She was changed in manner, too, rapid and affected in speech, her body twisting sinuously, her words tinged with a French accent. Her gown was long, winding, theatrical; she wore a chain of great amber beads, and amber pears pulled down the lobes of her ears.

"You know my wife, Betty," Carter said, drawing Sandra forward. "You know Alexandra?"

Half their world witnessed the scene; saw Betty draw back, head up, like a snake. Alexandra did not smile; her golden brown eyes were fixed on Betty's own.

It was Betty's opportunity; she had been waiting for it for two years.

"Excuse me," she said clearly. "I'd rather not know Mrs. Cavendish!" She spoiled the effect with a nervous titter.

"You were magnificent!" Carter told Alexandra a few minutes later when they were driving home.

"It was difficult."

"You looked simply magnificent, like the Goddess of Liberty looking down at some fly crawling up her."

"Well, when anyone does anything as—as raw as that, it seems to—well, reflect more on her than on the other person!" Alexandra formulated it, slowly.

"Exactly! She made a fool of herself."

"I suppose a hundred dinner tables will enjoy all that this evening."

"Sure."

"She had been saving that up, Carter, rehearsing it."

"Oh, sure!"

"Cheap," Sandra murmured, dispassionately.

The winter scene slipped by the car windows; there was Sunday leisure along the roads, men were raking leaves in the little gardens down the Peninsula, brush fires smoked into the twilight. Christmas was already in the air.

"You were gorgeous," Carter said, out of deep thought. "I've been proud of you before; I never saw you so gorgeous!"

"You make me idiotically happy when you say that, Cart."

"It's true. I was proud of you. You faced her down, and she knew it, too, don't you worry!"

They fell to marveling at the child; her sweet, gawky, little-girl charm, her astonishing performance on the violin.

"Because it was good, wasn't it, Alex?"

She loved the name; no one else used it. She was beginning to feel strangely happy somehow.

"It was wonderful."

"Isn't she cute?"

"Adorable."

"She's always been cute."

"I know." There was suddenly a knife in her heart. Her own baby would have been cute, too, eleven months old.

"Would you mind if we had her down for a visit?"

"Patsy? Good heavens, Carter, I'd love it!"

"I knew you would." He leaned toward her gratefully, put his arm about her. "Do you know you're a lovely woman, Alex?" he asked. "You're so dignified—you're one hundred thousand times more dignified than Betty Finchley ever dared to dream of being!"

"Is it good to be dignified?"

"You bet your life it's good."

"I'd rather be popular, and let someone else be dignified."

"You're damn' popular with me to-night!"

She turned, smiled into his eyes. She wanted to say from a too full heart, "Betty, superficial and cold and grasping, can keep her child—and what a child! My child has been lying in her lonely little grave for nearly a year."

But Sandra was growing up. He needed her to-night, and she would not fail him. She said:

"It makes me so happy when you love me, Carter. It's all I ask."

She made herself look her best for the informal Sunday supper; the new gown had come home, a trailing creation of gold and silver and black and violet brocade; there were amethysts set in old pearls and black enamel in her ears; a chain of them was about the smooth young column of her throat. At dinner she gave Carter's mother and Peter so sympathetic, so enthusiastic an account of the little girl and her violin that it brought a look of pride and pleasure to Carter's eyes. The older Mrs. Cavendish was indignant.

"Will you kindly tell me why Betty brings that child home without letting any one of us know about it? I think it's the most outrageous thing I ever heard!"

"Betty wants something," Carter predicted.

"Wants what?"

"I don't know. But she's got a reason. She hates California."

"I shouldn't wonder if it had something to do with Grandmother's estate," Peter suggested, mildly.

"Why do you say that?"

"I've an idea—Carter's had hints——"

Mrs. Cavendish looked from face to face, spoke sharply.

"What earthly claim can Betty make? Why——"

She fell silent, not encouraged by their patient glances.

"It's Patsy," Carter said briefly and was silent. They were all silent. "If it wasn't for Patsy she could go roll her hoop!"

"How does she look?" his mother presently asked Sandra.

"Thin. She has a dear little face, but she looks—well, thin."

"She might well look thin," Mrs. Cavendish fretted, "with

Betty dragging her all over the country giving concerts! I don't think a child that age has any business on the stage!"

"She just appears at amateur affairs, charity things, Mrs. Cavendish."

"It doesn't make any difference. I don't think, and I never *have* thought, that Betty was a fit person to bring up a child. She's too nervous and high-strung herself. I never thought —you remember this, Peter—that Carter should have given the complete control of the child to Betty; no, I didn't, Carter, and you know it perfectly well!"

Carter made no defense: he was unusually silent, he was not like himself this evening.

Later, when they had gone upstairs, to the room that was so restful, so luxurious, so peaceful and warm and welcoming on this winter night, Alexandra found in him a husband she had never seen before. She herself felt in a strange mood, excited, a little fearful, a little wondering. To have the element of Betty and Patsy back in her life was disturbing, stirring. But there was a challenge in it, too; a stimulus that she knew now she had been unconsciously awaiting. The issue was joined at last; she could fight now.

Her hours of doubt, loneliness, and alienation could not be made worse; they might, when this crisis passed, be found to be better.

It was different with Carter. He had been confident, bold, sure of himself all the way along; now he was shaken.

When she was in her pajamas with a coat of gold Chinese silk wrapped about her, she took a comfortable lounge chair by the fire and began to look over her letters; she had been for two days in town; correspondence and magazines had accumulated.

Meanwhile Carter ranged about the place restlessly, disappearing into the dressing room, returning, standing irresolute beside the hearth, stopping short with one shoe off and one on to stare at the fire, his body sunk into a chair, knees crossed, narrowed eyes on space.

He was suffering; she had never seen him suffer before. Her heart went out to him in a wave of pity and love that made her forget the personal jealousy that had gnawed so long at her heart. And it was good to forget it.

When Carter spoke to-night she knew that it was not to her he spoke; he was merely thinking aloud.

"Betty isn't mean; it isn't that. It's just that she doesn't understand the kid, never did. . . . Thin, poor little monkey, she's awfully thin. . . . I wonder if I could possibly persuade Betty to leave her here with us for a while?"

Sandra had not spoken. Now she said:

"We could fatten her up."

"Oh, we'd have her in great shape in no time!"

He continued his restless moving about and she glanced at her magazine.

"She seemed so much my little girl to-day. . . . Cute. Running through them all to get to me!"

He flung himself into a chair before the drowsing fire, his brows knitted.

"A woman like Betty never should have a child."

"Patsy," Sandra said timidly, "is your child, Carter. She's your image!"

"Poor little kids, they're so helpless! She seemed to me——" He cleared his throat, began again: "She seemed to be turning to me for help," he said in a voice full of reluctance and pain, "and I can't do anything for her!"

"Perhaps she's happy, Cart."

"No. She wants to stay in California. She whispered it to me as if she were afraid of saying it aloud."

"Dearest, you imagine that."

"Oh, no, I don't. Oh, no, I don't. No child likes to be exploited."

"Probably Betty isn't exploiting her. She's just showing her off a little—and no wonder!"

"Betty says her master—she called him Schneider or Schofield or something——"

"Schroeder. He's an Austrian, a Hungarian, I think your mother said."

"Well, he says that Pats can give concert performances next year."

"Carter, she shouldn't."

"From what Betty said they want her to give three in London next May and one at Vienna."

"Well—if she gets rested here and puts on a little weight——" Sandra began in a dubious voice.

"Ah, they'll kill her, they'll kill her!" he said. He plunged his head into his hands. "Damn it all—my little girl, who thinks her daddy can do anything for her! You ought to have felt her hand. Sandra, it was—feverish. 'Let me go with you, Dad,' she whispered."

"She was excited, Carter; she'd just been playing."

"It wasn't all that! She pulled me down against her; the hot little face and her hair tangled against my ear the way it used to be. And she said, 'Take me with you, Dad! Let me go with you!' . . . And I couldn't," he muttered.

Alexandra went over to him, knelt beside him, put her young arms about him. He was broken at last, suffering, filled with misgivings and fears; he was hers at this moment as he had never been before. With an exquisite reassurance she drew his dark head against her heart, comforted him.

"Help me, Sandra! I can't let her be taken away again."

"We'll keep her, darling; we'll find some way."

"We'll go away, just you and I and Patsy. We'll let everything else go—Mother, Pete, business, everything."

"There'll be some way, Carter."

"You're so kind to me," he said, clinging to her like a despairing child. "You're so good to me, Sandra!"

"I want to be good to you, Carter," she murmured, with her lips against his hair. Out of his agony and her own there suddenly bloomed for her the deepest, the fiercest joy she had ever known.

CHAPTER TWENTY

BETTY was enthusiastically entertained on all sides for the first few weeks after her return. Alexandra had to reconcile herself to the idea; steel herself to see Betty's name in the morning paper's society columns without wincing. Mab and Rose and Elinor rallied to Betty, of course, and wherever she went Sandra heard glowing reports of Mrs. Finchley Cavendish.

But before the first month of the new year had run its course there was a change. Betty, rumor began to hint, was not the same. She had grown away from her old group, or they had grown away from her. She could say nothing kind about California, or of American ways of doing and thinking; she wanted to go back to Paris, and back she was going as soon as the rather mysterious "business" that had brought her home was finished.

Burlingame did not approve of the way she treated her child; she had grown sharp and nervous in her attitude toward Patsy. The senior Mrs. Cavendish expressed herself as uneasy about the child's health; everyone began to say that cold, overcast, grimy Paris was no place for a little Western girl. And it was but a step from all this to a sudden access of sympathy for Carter and affection for Alexandra. Sandra found herself presently carried forward on a delightful wave of popularity.

Rose, for example, who besides the Burlingame mansion and the Pebble Beach place kept a luxurious suite at the

St. Francis Hotel, asked Alexandra to come and stay with her for the night of the Junior League Follies. Carter was duck hunting; half a dozen of the women were going to dine and go to the review together, afterward spending the night at the hotel.

This was a great occasion, it meant Alexandra's prettiest clothes, it meant a few hours of that intimacy and nonsense and chatter from which she had been excluded a year ago, and for which she had hungered.

She was in Rose's hotel rooms, sitting on the floor on a big satin pillow on the afternoon in question, looking over a score of proofs of pictures of the Bray children, when Betty chanced to come in. It was twilight and tea time, most of the women were in informal dress, lounging about before the time came when they must dress for the evening's festivity.

Betty was visibly taken aback to find Alexandra comfortably established in the very center of the group, her head bare, her rich shining hair rumpled, her eyes narrowed upon the outspread proofs. The friendly atmosphere about her had caused Sandra to unfold like a flower; she had kept them all laughing for half an hour; they were still laughing when Betty came in.

The two women acknowledged each other's presence only by a faint motion of heads, then Sandra, quite sobered now, returned to her self-appointed task, and Betty sat down on a couch between Helen Peabody and Louise Gwin.

"You girls all look happy. What's up?"

"It's the Junior League show to-night, you know."

"Of course it is. I'd forgotten we all used to stay here and go together. Nobody's said a word to me about it. Do you all go still?"

"Usually," someone admitted with a nervous laugh.

There was an awkward second of silence; then Sandra said:

"I like these two, Rose. They're perfect of both."

Rose instantly affected a great interest in the proofs.

"Oh, not that one!"

"This one, then."

"If you don't take the one that shows Barb's curls I'll never speak to you again," Elinor said.

Sandra put one elbow on Rose's knee without leaving her pillow on the floor; her voice was quiet, natural, her hand steady. But the room was moving round her in long slow circles.

One of the other women spoke, and Sandra said easily, "Oh, no, Mab!"

"Mab!" They were all intimate enough, Betty thought scornfully. But she was shaken herself. She rushed into conversation, saying just what she had not meant to say.

"It's so funny, finding you girls all here exactly the way you used to be! Nothing changes in California. Same old things, year after year."

Rose did not like this. After all, the British ambassador and a great Italian tenor had both been her guests this year, and she had flown to Los Angeles.

"I mean," Betty floundered on, determined to carry the conversation with a rush, to show them all how little the presence of Carter's new wife disturbed her—"I mean, you do such—well, they seem to me to be such—queer things out here. Polo and golf, and everyone talking about tennis and the Junior League! In Paris all the men talk books, plays, and music, and it's all so tremendously thrilling. I mean we have a leisure class there, and here you simply haven't! It *does* make a difference—a class that have been—has been gentlemen for—well, for generations!

"I mean, if a man's father and grandfather have been

in the hotel business there, why, he stays in it. And he's very happy, he's just as well off. But here you don't know what anyone's grandfather was—a saloon-keeper or a miner —nobody cares!"

A sulphurous silence followed this speech; then Rose, Elinor, Mab began talking scornfully, indignantly, all at once. They protested that they couldn't see Betty's point *at all*. Why, American men . . . Why, European men . . . Why, everyone *knew* . . .

Alexandra said nothing, but she looked at Betty curiously, almost amusedly, and Betty laughed nervously under the look, and flushed. Sandra wasn't taking the trouble to argue. Getting up from her cushion, she went over to the tea table.

"Half a cup, Helen?"

"Not a drop."

"Sandwich?"

"Sandra," Rose, trembling with indignation after delivering a last broadside to Betty, said with a great air of calm, "want to fill my cup?"

"You—take—two——" Sandra mused aloud. She carried the cup to Rose. "Won't it be too bad if it rains for the show to-night?" she said, casually.

The other women welcomed the change of topic and seized her cue of calm indifference almost hysterically. Betty said, "I'm sorry if I've made you all mad, but I can't help feeling the way I do about Europe. I suppose you think I'm perfectly terrible to want to live there!"

Nobody took up this challenge; the other women were murmuring with studied zest about the entertainment and the weather. It chanced therefore to fall to Sandra to look Betty squarely, bewilderedly, in the eye and ask surprisedly, "Who? *Me?*"

The absurdity of this striking the entire company, there was a gale of laughter, during which Betty withdrew. All, through the evening the little conversation was hilariously recalled. And from that moment Betty's popularity was on the wane.

It waned steadily; Alexandra felt herself gaining ground. In the happiness of increasing friendliness and diversion all about her, she fairly bloomed. It even became "fun" to encounter Betty here and there, always to be the younger, the more dignified, the prettier of the two. With the sympathy of her group, the affection of Carter's mother, who could not forgive Betty her exploitation of Patsy, and with Carter beside her to champion her through any awkward moment, Alexandra would have been quite happy, if it had not been for Patsy herself.

There was no "fun," no happiness in Patsy's nearness for Carter. He loved his little girl; Patsy adored him. The tragedy of their relationship, their helplessness under the power of the woman who was Patsy's mother and had been Carter's wife, and the shadow of their impending separation were always before Alexandra's eyes.

At first Betty would not have any meeting at all between Alexandra and Patsy. No, Patsy should not have anything to do with "that woman." But this only lasted while it was impressive; as Betty began to lose power and Sandra to gain it, Betty saw fit without explanation to change this attitude.

In the first place it was lonely for the child at the hotel. Patsy grew quiet, languid, in the long afternoons when she was left alone. Betty, who had confidently if secretly expected to leave Patsy with Carter's mother, had been somewhat discomforted to discover that the city house was rented, and that the older Mrs. Cavendish was dividing her time between a hotel and Carter's home down the Peninsula.

The convenience of being entirely rid of responsibility for Patsy was in the end too much for Betty; she began only a few days after her arrival to imply to intimates that she did not intend to keep the child away from her grandmother. It had perhaps occurred to her that her purpose in coming to California might easily be frustrated by any antagonism of the Cavendish family. And finally there was talk of a marvelous party presently to be given down in Los Angeles to which Betty would be asked and to which she would certainly go.

So in mid-January she indicated that Patsy could pay Grandma a visit, and as Grandma happened to be at Daddy's house in Burlingame, to Daddy's house Patsy went. And when Grandma went back to town, she remained.

Sandra's manner with a small girl was exactly what it was with everyone: anxious to please, anxious to be of use, affectionate. She did not regard Patsy as a child; she treated her exactly like another human being, and Patsy adored her before she had been her house guest for two days.

Sandra not only let Patsy dawdle at the shop windows of San Mateo, but she enjoyed the dawdling herself. She not only sympathized with Patsy on the day when the puppy came up the drive, but she held the puppy gently by his poor scraggy head while Patsy ran for a rope and some milk. Sandra conspired with Patsy; they had secrets. They looked at each other significantly across the dinner table.

"If I play bridge," Carter would say, "what'll you girls do?"

His wife and daughter would giggle; perhaps Patsy would cram her small thin hand over her mouth for fear of betraying herself. Sometimes she had to get up and go round the table and hurl herself upon Sandra, kissing her, bursting with affection and excitement, whispering close at her ear.

They went to five-and-ten-cent stores together and bought frying pans and enamel cups. They made candy; they rode horseback. Patsy in her pajamas came to find "Aunt Sandra" every morning, and Sandra had to go in and kiss Patsy good-night in bed the very last thing before going down to dinner. Sometimes they talked then, talked so long that Carter had to come find his wife. In the car Patsy always shouted "Dibs on Aunt Sandra!" which meant that she was to sit next to Sandra. And when seated there she would say, eagerly, "Talk!"

Alexandra had made no conscious effort to accomplish this little conquest, but she did not appreciate it the less for that. She would have said a few months ago that to win the affection of Carter's little girl was quite out of the range of imagination or possibility. But she came to value Patsy's love as she did nothing else in life except Carter's. Patsy was Betty's child, yet she was presently a bond of fresh happiness and devotion between Carter and Alexandra; Sandra was never so bright and so amusing as when she was retailing for his benefit the ridiculous adventures of their day, with Patsy ecstatically supplying details all along the way. Carter, coming into the house now, summoned both of them with a shout, and they rushed for his arms and dragged him into his chair by the fire in an easy relationship that contained all the gayety of genuine mother and daughter.

In February for a hot spring week they went down to Peter's ranch house, and here all four of them enjoyed an interval memorable for its happiness. Sandra had supposed that she never again could be as happy as this; it was the happiness of the long-ago visit to Del Monte, the happiness of the Honolulu honeymoon.

Peter's house was old-fashioned, plain, but it was delightfully comfortable, and the freedom, the quiet, the freshness of the garden, the oak-dotted meadows and the eternal beauty of the sea enraptured Sandra, and seemed to awaken unsuspected gypsy qualities in Patsy, who kept up a continual chant of content all through her crowded days, and went to sleep after supper before the fire in her father's arms.

"Carter, are we dead and in heaven?"

"I don't know, Alex. I swear I think we are! I've never been like this. If I could have you girls and old Pete," Carter said, "I'll be hanged if I wouldn't live along here forever."

The weather was perfection—hot, clear, sweet-scented with new grass, lilacs, and fruit blossoms through the daytime, chill, silent, and dewy at night. Sandra and Carter had the big front bedroom upstairs; Patsy the smaller adjoining room. Peter's quarters were on the ground floor. Sandra, dressing in the morning, would look down to see Peter walking among the dewy flowers, standing in talk with a gardener or farmhand. They all breakfasted together, Carter and Peter going into town only once, on the Tuesday, and returning with their mother on Thursday afternoon.

For the rest, they were all together. They dawdled over breakfast, loitered about the farm in the spring sunshine, lunched in the warmth of the leafless arbor, where great pottery jars were tumbled on their sides, where the grill was still littered with winter leaves and mold, and white cherry blossoms floated down on the green, green grass that grew between the flags.

Sometimes Peter and Carter went over to Pebble Beach five miles away to play golf, and Sandra and Patsy went too and scrambled along the beach while the men had their game. One day they took their lunch down to their own beach, and picnicked in white sand just above the tangled tide line where cocoanut shells, dried seaweed, and driftwood lay in long curves. And one night Patsy played for them in the evening gloom of the old-fashioned parlor.

A dinner guest who had come over to make a fourth at bridge happened to be a pianist, and Patsy, who had been enjoying a blissful vacation from practice, got out her violin, straightened her little figure beside the piano, and began that expert sounding for the keynote that is so much a matter of course for the fiddler and so strangely impressive to the mere listener.

The movements of her brown little hands, the borrowed handkerchief she tucked into her neck, the first swift confident strains of sound—these all seemed to show Alexandra a new Patsy, a personality that had little to do with the eager, joyous, almost hysterically responsive little companion who scrambled and slipped on the rocks beside her on their afternoon walks, gave her good-night kisses flavored with scented hot soapsuds and tousled sunburned hair and flannel pajamas, and came sweet and sleepy into her bed each morning to be cuddled for a while as a start for the day. The sacred responsibility that her genius imposed upon them all impressed Alexandra afresh whenever she saw Patsy with her violin.

During this happy week the child bloomed and flourished like a weed, putting on weight and height with every passing minute, and Alexandra blossomed too into a laughing, joyous, confident beauty that she had not known for many months.

"If we could only have her forever, Carter!"

"Don't speak about it."

"It wouldn't mean her giving up her music; in fact, I don't believe anything would ever stop that. But the anxiousness, the cramming—that's so cruel for such a baby!"

"You're pretty sure they work her too hard?"

"I think so. This Austrian, Schroeder, I suppose he has European ideas about—well, *'kultur,'* " Alexandra said.

"I suppose he has, damn him!"

"They think nothing of asking a child to practise seven hours a day."

"She's never done that?"

"No. But she practises four and sometimes five, and I believe it's to be more."

"She's got a swell mother."

"Betty?"

"Yes. She's got a swell mother that would let her do that."

"The notoriety, the celebrity is what Betty likes."

"Patsy loves music."

"Yes, she loves music."

"You mean they're kind of rubbing it in?"

"Well, yes. A child could love music, and yet not want to work so hard at it day and night."

"Think she's afraid of Betty?"

"Afraid?"

"Yep. Think Betty bullies her?"

"I don't know that you could say that, Cart. But she wants to please Betty. She told me that sometimes when she had a specially hard piece to learn she stayed with the Schroeders and that they had a little boy, and that her maestro beat him sometimes. It didn't sound very—happy."

A long silence. Then Sandra said:

"Is there any way in which you could keep her, Carter?"

"I was thinking. Of course I've been thinking of nothing else."

"Could you delay Betty's business here?"

"You know what she's after, of course?"

"Peter told me. Or perhaps you told me."

"It won't take a week, once we agree about it. She wants my grandmother's legacy to be made over to Patsy with herself for sole guardian. And she wants a sum outright herself."

"Too much?"

"It isn't that. But my mother's afraid she wants to marry again and hand it over to some titled French moron."

"Couldn't you find out, Carter? It might mean that we got Patsy."

"You're so sweet," he told her, watching the eager face and the shining eyes.

"I'm so sick over the whole thing," she amended sorrowfully.

"Betty denies the marriage idea, of course."

"Betty told Rose," Alexandra told him after a while, "that she never would love any other man but you."

"That's funny."

"That's what she told Rose."

"That's very funny." She saw that it made him angry.

"Rose told me. She said she could have burst right out laughing."

"Betty said she'd never care for anyone but me?"

"That's what Rose said."

"When was this?"

"A while back. Just after they came home."

"That gives me a pain," Carter said.

"Patsy's just eleven. . . . It's a long pull before she comes of age . . ." Alexandra mused.

The dreadful hour rushed upon them; they had two days more at the ranch, one more whole day, they were going away to-morrow. Toward the end Patsy counted the meals: "I'll have lunch, Aunt Sandra, and dinner and then breakfast! And I'll surely be back for another visit before we go away, won't I?"

"Surely, darling. Dad and I are going back to the Burlingame house, too, you know. We'll be right near you."

"And can you and I go to movies and everything?"

"Every time Mummy'll let you!"

The child was very silent all through the last evening. She clung to them all, going from Peter's knees to her father's, and from them to Sandra's arms. There was no talk of bedtime to-night; she stayed with them until the clock struck eleven, when they all went to bed. Sandra had superintended the packing of Patsy's trunk: middies, brief pleated skirts, stubbed little shoes, music, violin. Their happy time was over.

"You want mush to-mollow mo'ning?" the old Chinese cook asked Sandra at breakfast.

"No; no mush. Miss Patsy not here to-morrow."

"You go back Yullup with Mama?" Hong asked the child.

"Oh, no!" Patsy said jealously. "I'm coming down here again first for a long visit. Aren't I, Dad?"

"You certainly are——" He had to pause. "If your Dad can manage it!" Carter qualified it.

"But you *can,* Dad?"

"I'm going to try, Patsy."

"Anyway we've had *one* beautiful time!" Sandra put in, heartsick.

"Dad can manage anything!" Patsy said confidently.

At the end it was Sandra to whom she clung, and they were Sandra's tears that mingled with her own on the little brown cheek.

"I don't want to go 'way!" sobbed Patsy, suddenly all baby.

"But we're all going to-morrow, sweetheart, and it'll be all lonely down here! I'll telephone you as soon as I get in," Sandra soothed her, smiling through her own wet lashes.

"Promise!"

"I do promise, darling."

Patsy got in the front seat beside Carter, her camel's-hair coat belted snugly about her, her brown hat drawn down over her brown little tear-streaked face.

"Tell Aunt Sandra you won't cry any more, honey."

"Honest I won't!"

"That's my darling."

The car wheeled, twinkled under the oaks, was gone. Alexandra stood watching it out of sight; she was not conscious of thought, of pain. Only the world seemed to have stopped; there was nothing ahead. The spring morning had suddenly clouded, the sky was gray and the sea sullen. A cool wind rippled through the air, and some long-dead leaves swept down to the wet, packed earth. Gulls were wheeling and piping; a cowbell clanked somewhere. The effect was all of silence, of emptiness and blankness; the wind ruffled the full plumage of a lilac tree, and fruit blossoms came down across the orchard in a storm.

"You like fire?" Hong asked.

Alexandra started and turned.

"Yes, light me a fire, Hong. I'm cold," she said.

She went into the parlor. On the couch by the fireplace three paper dolls were ranged; beside them there was a little red cap. Sandra put the dolls carefully in a desk drawer; wilted and worthless as they were, they might be treasures to Patsy.

The fire was beginning to snap and crackle now; she stood looking down at it. The red cap was pressed by the tense, nervous fingers of both hands against her heart; she felt as if blood were oozing against it.

CHAPTER TWENTY-ONE

SOME DAYS LATER, back in the Burlingame house, Carter told her that the question of the settlement with Betty was at a deadlock.

"She wants sole guardianship of Pats."

"Hasn't she got that?"

"She has the custody; that's all. Pete and I and Reggie Pry are her guardians now."

"Don't give in, Carter."

"I'm not going to. But she says she's going back to Europe early in March anyway."

"With the alimony arrangement just what it is?"

"She says so."

"And you can't stop that?"

"I can't stop that. I've told Gwin Jones," Carter added, "that I'll make any arrangement, I'll settle *any* sum on her, if she'll give me the kid for half the year."

"But she won't?"

"Nope."

Alexandra mused with knitted brows.

"I feel so responsible, Cart."

"You!" he said. And then, in the tone she loved, "You darling!"

"Well, it's too late to go back. No use regretting anything now, Carter," she presently said. "We have to go on from here."

"Yep. We have to go on from here. . . . It's the kid," he

began again presently, out of a silence. "It's not what I think, or Betty does. But to take it out on a kid! ... There must be some way out of it!" he said resolutely.

Alexandra presently fancied she perceived a way. She said nothing to him about it; it was but a desperate chance after all, and what it involved was so much that she dared not think out the consequences. That would have been to have her heart fail her entirely.

She telephoned Betty. And on an afternoon a day or two later, when Betty's mother, Mrs. Finchley, had Patsy and three other small girls at the circus, she went to see Carter's first wife.

It was an ordeal for which she braced herself with a constant interior reminder, "She can't kill you. It'll all be over by five o'clock!"

But even that did not keep her from trembling and feeling cold and sick when the time came.

The two women talked in a hotel room that was embellished with flowers and with the hundred small possessions Betty could not be without; a gold folding clock, photographs, ash trays, toilet trifles in enamel and glass, perfume bottles, jewels, books, magazines. Betty was in a silk and lace tea gown; she sat, or rather was curled, on the bed, in a nest of pillows. Her attitude was proud, scornful, amused, and occasionally a little pouting and pathetic.

Alexandra, who was very pale and serious, had a winged chair facing the bed, her back to the light.

"You are very kind to give me a few minutes, Mrs. Cavendish."

"Well, I think I am!" Betty said, with a flippant little sputter of laughter. "For you know I think I have been very badly treated through this whole thing!" she added, sharply.

To this Alexandra found nothing to say. She saw that

the note of the interview was to be painfully frank, that Betty indeed was enjoying this unexpected opportunity to speak her mind to that particular actor in the drama whom she held to be most at fault.

"You told Mrs. Bray," Alexandra began without preamble, "that you had always cared for Carter—that you aren't angry—with him."

"And Rose Bray repeated it to you! I must say I have a fine lot of friends here at home!" Betty, seizing an opportunity to score, however irrelevantly, put in neatly.

"Perhaps she thought you wouldn't mind."

Betty, comfortable in pillows, looked across at Alexandra with mischievous eyes.

"Mind?"

"My knowing——" Sandra supplied, floundering a little.

"Knowing what?"

"We'll get nowhere, this way," Sandra thought. Aloud she said: "That you still had a kindly feeling for—for Carter, I suppose. That you felt no resentment toward him, anyway——"

"But you knew that. You knew," Betty said in the pause, with great simplicity, "that I loved my husband. Everyone —everyone knew that!"

To this Alexandra seemed to find nothing to say. Hard red color burned in her cheeks.

"Everyone," Betty presently added, as an afterthought, "except Carter himself. Now—*now,* all of a sudden," she went on, with growing warmth—"now he wants to manage Patsy's affairs—now he's very much concerned about her and about me. Well——" She half smiled, looking through narrowed eyelids into space. "A little late!" she observed dryly.

"Carter would love to have Patsy here, part of the time," Sandra said simply, after a pause.

"Oh, would he!" Betty answered, with a little trembling laugh of anger. "Really? You don't say!"

As Sandra could make no answer to this, she presently went on:

"You can tell him that it will probably be three years before Patsy is back in California again. If Carter Cavendish sent you here to discuss what really—if you'll excuse my saying so—isn't *your* affair," Betty pursued, flatly, "you may go back and tell him I said that!"

It was very hard. It was very hard to speak patiently, reasonably. Betty was like a rude, triumphant, excited child. Her pretense of indifference and scorn had vanished now; she was breathing hard, and her cheeks were red.

"Carter doesn't know I'm here," Sandra said mildly.

"Oh, come!"

"No, I didn't tell him. It was because of something Rose said that I came."

"You can hardly—*hardly*, expect me to believe that."

"Why am I here at all?" Sandra thought. "Why am I letting this woman insult me and humiliate me this way?" She thought of Patsy, eager, affectionate, confident little Patsy. "Carter told me," she said aloud, with what dignity she could command, "that the discussion between you had reached a sort of—a sort of—deadlock."

"I wonder," Betty responded, in a sweet, remote voice, "if you will allow me to say that what concerns my child is my business, after all? It's very charming of you to take such an interest in Patricia, but when all's said and *done*——"

She smiled, shrugged, studied a row of vermilion fingernails thoughtfully, with pursed lips.

"I know," Sandra admitted. "You're quite right. But just the same I feel that there is something I might do—or there might be—about this question of Patsy's guardianship."

Betty regarded her with a hostile smile.

"I would be very much interested to know what you think it is. Cart's grandmother," she went on, drawn into discussion in spite of herself, "left the child a fortune. Carter—when he met you—couldn't throw Patsy over fast enough—he didn't care what became of her then. I was given the custody of the child, but presumably . . . Presumably," she resumed, after a pause, during which she had inspected the other hand carefully, "I'm not intelligent enough to take on the custody of the money! Carter was quite content when it was only Patricia. But now it's the Hough money, and that's different."

"That isn't fair!" Sandra was stung into saying indignantly.

Betty raised an eyebrow; laughed lightly.

"Why don't you make Carter do his own fighting?"

"Mrs. Cavendish," Sandra recommenced, after a silence, "Carter loves Patsy dearly, and he is very unhappy about all this. It's made me—desperately unhappy, too. Perhaps he didn't understand, at the time of the divorce, how he would feel—to-day, about Patsy——"

The unsympathetic, triumphant bright eyes were watching her smilingly. Betty had the whip hand, and she knew it.

"My dear Mrs. Cavendish, isn't all this just a trifle *late?* You didn't see all this coming when you took a man away from his wife and baby, did you? You didn't care about anything, then, except to get Carter. Well, you got him. Now don't come whining to me about a daddy's feeling for his dear little girl. Patsy and I go back to Europe next month no matter what the Cavendishes do—and Patsy'll have to get over her homesickness, because her maestro wants her to work for three years in Europe, where he can watch her. You can tell Carter Cavendish that there's no money in the world, and no law in the world, that will give him one instant's control of Patsy, and my compliments with it!"

It was so spitefully said, so coarsely said, that Sandra had to gather her self-control afresh.

"What you said to Rose made me want to talk to you," she began again, with difficulty.

"I can't conceive why," Betty interpolated, spiritedly.

"I came to ask you," Alexandra said steadily, "if—if it would make a difference to you if Carter were free?"

"I don't in the least understand you," Betty answered, watching her warily.

Sandra had known it would be hard; she had not dreamed how hard this arrogant, haughty little woman among the pillows could make it.

"I mean—if Carter were not married to me, would you—forgive him?" she made herself ask.

Betty stared at her for a long minute; then she burst into loud and not very merry laughter.

"Oh, I think that's funny!" she exclaimed, and laughed again. "Did Carter ask you to ask me that?" she demanded.

"I told you that Carter doesn't know that I'm here."

"You don't know how funny I think that is."

Alexandra said nothing. After a minute, warming, Betty added:

"You mean that you think I'd take him back *now?*"

"If I were out of it," Sandra supplied with a dry mouth.

The other woman gave her a long, scrutinizing look.

"I think you have your nerve to come and ask me that!" she said.

"Perhaps I have. It occurred to me," Sandra offered simply, "that I—I complicated the situation—that it would be—easier for Carter and for you if I were not here."

Betty, an unconvinced look on her face, considered this.

"You've never thought that before, I suppose?" she asked.

"You never thought," she repeated in the silence, "all

these years—you never thought that you were complicating the situation, before?"

"I don't think I—saw it, Mrs. Cavendish, three years ago, as I see it now."

"You came down to my house—a clerk from my husband's office," Betty said with deadly readiness. "I was kind to you, asked you to stay to dinner. I remember it as if it had been yesterday! And you began your work of getting him away from me—getting my husband away from me, taking my child's father away from her. . . . And now you come to me and calmly suggest that I take him back. You've had your years with him—you've tired of him, I suppose—perhaps you're after some other woman's husband by now."

The words rattled about Sandra like some deadly hail, like a rain of bullets. She felt physically bruised, sick, frightened by them. The sharp-voiced woman on the bed, with the steely, narrowed eyes, was like a gun firing, firing with a deafening, deadly sureness.

"If Carter Cavendish were as free as air," Betty finished angrily—"if he and I were alone on a desert island, I wouldn't even let him put a fingertip on me again!"

"I didn't know——" Sandra said, and was still. The air cleared: cooled.

"Now that Patsy's famous," Betty went on, in a slightly modulated voice and manner, "now that everyone wants to see her and hear her—— I'm sorry to get so excited, but it makes me mad," she added, and now there was almost an apology in her tone—"it makes me mad to have Carter talk now about wanting her. He gave her up fast enough when she was only an ordinary child! Now, now he wants me to act as if nothing had happened; everything must be as it was before! It's not fair; it's utterly unfair. I wouldn't think of it!"

"I don't know that *he* would do it," Alexandra suggested,

always in the same weary, quiet voice, with a touch of puzzlement in it.

"You don't know he would!"

"No. We've never talked about it. It seemed to me that if —*if* Rose was right in saying that you had always cared for Carter, and since—*since* I seem to be the one——"

She stopped, floundering. All this had accomplished nothing at all.

"I'd like to know why you came to tell me this?" Betty presently asked.

"Because I am so sorry, I suppose," Alexandra answered, with a little difficulty, but without hesitation. "So sorry to have been the cause—to be the cause——"

Betty was studying her again, with bright, hard, curious eyes.

"You knew that three years ago."

"I seemed to be—younger three years ago."

"You weren't so young but that you knew you were breaking—up—my home!" Betty accused her.

"I never meant that," Sandra murmured, as if she thought aloud. "I thought——But no matter!"

"I've been generous," Betty went on. "I've let Carter have Patsy for visits. I've tried to be fair. But I don't get much reward for it. Carter and his mother block me in everything I try to do; they as good as say that I'm a bad mother to Patsy. They want to take her away from me!"

"If I were out of it," Alexandra repeated, "could you— might you and Carter—for Patsy's sake, I mean——"

"You don't know how funny that sounds to me," Betty said, puzzled and suspicious, after a long, curious stare. "You mean that you'd actually get a divorce and give Carter up?"

"I mean that I think it is a terrible thing to take a child's father away from her," Sandra answered, suddenly very white in the fading light of the room.

"Children get over anything!" Betty countered carelessly. She got down from the bed with the air of terminating the interview, and walked with Sandra toward the door. "Patsy," she added suddenly, as if gaining a sudden courage from the dusk of the room and the fact that the chance to say anything to Sandra would not long be hers—"Patsy is better off with me, with her own mother, than with a father who could treat me as he did! Don't forget," she added sharply, but in a guarded tone, for they were in the very doorway now—"don't forget that the reason Carter finally gave me a divorce was because he wanted to shield you—*you!* Don't forget that they found you in his room down at Del Monte at one o'clock at night! It was to save *your* reputation, it was so that everyone in the world wouldn't know *you* for the kind of woman you are, that he said—at last, at *last!*—that he'd give up Patsy, that he'd let me have my own way about the divorce. Why, he came to me—I was right here in this hotel with my mother, and he came to me and said—I remember the words—'Betty, my cards are on the table. Make your own terms!'"

Sandra felt the solid floor rock beneath her feet. Everything seemed to be moving about her, rising up to strike her. She steadied herself with a hand on the door.

"Carter wouldn't have *you* dragged down into it!" Betty said, fiercely and swiftly. "I said, 'Then that means that Patsy's *mine,* mine forever!' and he said, 'Anything!' Rose and Mab and the others can make as much fuss about *you* as they like, but I know *that.* And if it weren't for the money her great-grandmother left her, the money they won't let me administer for my child's musical education, I'd never have brought her back here at all! I didn't have to bring her back!"

"That isn't true!" Sandra whispered. She was supporting herself weakly against the door; her eyes blazed darkly in a white face.

Betty was puzzled.

"What's not true?"

"That—that—that—no," Sandra stammered, incoherently. "No, your divorce had nothing to do with me!"

"Why, don't you *know* it did?" Betty asked, genuinely surprised.

"It didn't!"

"It was because Carter wanted to protect you, wouldn't have anything said against you——"

"I don't believe it! My name wasn't mentioned."

"No, your name wasn't mentioned, because I threatened if he didn't give me my divorce and my terms and my child I'd name you as co-respondent and sue him on the grounds of infidelity!"

"Oh, my God, my God, my God," Alexandra whispered.

Whether Betty said good-bye and shut the door then, or whether she simply walked away, walked weakly and uncertainly into vague dark spaces somewhere—halls, elevators, corridors—Sandra never knew.

"That was it!" something kept saying dully in her heart. "That was it! He gave up Patsy to protect me! It's on *my* account that Patsy has no father to take care of her now!"

After a while she was in the street, dazed, stunned as if by a physical blow.

"So that was it," she said aloud, standing still, "that was it. . . . He never told me."

There was a tea shop near the hotel; she walked in, sat down, ordered tea. But when it came she had not even the strength to pour it; it cooled in the pot. After a while she pushed the toast and the cup aside, picked up the slip and looked at it dazedly. Forty cents. Forty cents.

"Forty cents!" she said aloud in the taxi, driving home. They were staying for a few days with Carter's mother at her apartment in the Mark Hopkins Hotel in town; Alexandra looked up at the hotel strangely. What was she doing, going in here? Mrs. Cavendish's maid encountered her as she entered her mother-in-law's suite.

"Mrs. Cavendish would like to see you, Mrs. Cavendish."

Alexandra went to her room. Carter's mother was resting beside the fire.

"Hello, dear child, what kept you so late?"

"I—I went to a movie with—with Mab."

"Sandra dear, will you do the honors to-night? Carter's having dinner brought up from downstairs. Those two Englishmen are coming—you know, General Brooks, a delightful soul, and Sir George Wylie. I wanted to slip over to Mrs. Butler's and have a quiet little game. She needs a fourth, and I thought perhaps you would take my place here."

"Glad to."

Sandra relaxed into a chair; the other woman observed that she looked tired.

"Tea, dear?"

"No, thanks. But I believe I'll have a sleep and a hot bath before dinner, if Carter's having men here."

"I'm to have my darling Patsy all day to-morrow."

"I know."

"You don't know, Sandra, when they plan to go?"

"Soon, now."

"Carter will mind this parting much more than the first one."

"She's grown so companionable. She gives him so much more than she could three years ago."

"Betty has been behaving so badly," Carter's mother complained.

"My mother," the older Mrs. Cavendish continued as Sandra did not speak—"my mother was to name Betty a trustee for Patsy's fortune. But after the divorce she changed her will. That seems to be what is angering Betty, and then the question of more alimony, of course . . ."

She rambled on comfortably. Sandra answered perfunctorily, mechanically. After a while she found herself in her own room, lying on a couch in the dusk, thinking. She was asleep when Carter came in.

Awakening, and lying among her pillows watching him, she thought he had never seemed so wonderful, so infinitely dear. He looked tired, thoughtful, his manner was more than ordinarily sweet.

"Alex, it's good to get home to anyone like you, and peace and quiet."

"Was to-day a hard day?"

"Nope. But I feel kind of—I'm all right, I guess."

There was a small fire burning in the tiny grate of their hotel bedroom. He drew up a chair before it, and she came over to establish herself at his knee.

Carter leaned back to snap off the lamp, and Sandra rested her rumpled head against his knee, and felt, as she loved to feel it, his hand lying on her shoulder, drawing her close to him. The room was full of dusky shadows, full of peace.

"Funny how it goes, Alex. If anything worries me or if I get tired——"

He passed his hand over his forehead, smiled down at her.

"Why, then I want you, and need you, and love you, more than ever," he finished.

"You're being worried, Carter?"

"Oh, it's about the kid."

Her heart ached fiercely; she could not speak.

"Why couldn't it be that you and I and Pats and Peter could always be together, Sandra, as we were down at Pete's place last week? It'd be so easy! She was so happy——"

"I never was so happy in my life as I was then," Sandra said.

"No, and I never was. You know, Sandy," Carter went on, thinking aloud, "I'm changing. And what's changing me, what *has* changed me, is loving you. I was trying to think it out to-day. I was remembering those days when I used to say to myself all morning, 'I'll take Miss Trumbull to lunch——'"

"Ah, don't!"

"Remember the day we went out to the beach for lunch?"

"And the day you gave me my blue bag?"

Man and wife now, shut away from the world in this sacred intimacy of dusk and firelight, they linked hands, and the glance she gave him glittered with tears.

"Alex, here's what I was thinking. We were only kids then, really. We didn't know anything! I wanted you to be mine—to show off. You seemed to me so beautiful—— Well, I don't mean," Carter went on, with a boyish awkward laugh—"I don't mean that you don't seem beautiful to me now. But I never thought then of the gentleness, the goodness, the sweetness of being with you all the time. You're so darned sweet, Alex. It makes a man's life so—different— when he's got a sweet woman in it. . . . I'm different. Pete sees it—everyone sees it."

She raised her face and he bent his, and they kissed each other.

"You were so game about losing your own baby," Carter presently said. "I didn't realize then what it meant to you— my God, it must have nearly killed you! And then when Pats came home, you were so good to my kid. She adores you. I suppose she loves her mother, too. But Betty doesn't understand kids; she says so herself. Last week, when I was bringing Pats home from the country, she said to me in that sort of confidential way she has, you know, that 'you-and-I-understand-and-we'll-fix-it' sort of way——"

"I know!" Alexandra said, a knife in her heart.

"She said, 'Dad, suppose we let Mummy go back to Paris, because she loves it, and I'll stay with you and Aunt Sandra for a while?' "

"Ah, wouldn't she love it!"

"You see, I have the feeling," Carter began, trying to express it—"I have the feeling that I sort of dragged myself by the back hair out of the mess—— I mean I got away from fighting with Betty and thinking of nothing but the club and so on. And I feel as if it was kind of up to me—up to us—to get the kid out, too! To take her away from the practice and the scolding and the nervous strain, and spoil her."

"I love you to say it's up to *us*."

"Well, you're the real reason. You're what's waked me up, if I am waked up," Carter told her, humbly. "You're what's taught me a little sense, if I've got any!"

"You didn't talk to me this way even when we first loved each other, even when we were first married."

"I didn't love you this way even when we were first married!"

She caught his hand tightly against her cheek, turned to the fire.

"Ah, that's *something!*" she whispered.

"Alex, if we could only get the kid out, then somehow I'd feel that everything was going to be all right, that we—well, that we'd worked it out."

"I know."

"If we could only have her for four months a year, Alex.

By God, it doesn't seem right that a kid's mother should have all the say. Sometimes a father loves his children more than their mother does. It's—it's the limit," Carter went on, with his boyish forceful ineloquence—"it's the limit if a man who loves his little girl and a little girl who loves her dad can't ever—ever be together! It's not natural!"

"No," she agreed, "it's not natural."

"You know that Betty didn't love me. She hadn't lived with me for four years—more than that—before the divorce."

"I know."

"Then I met you, and you *are* loving and gentle and sweet. Was I to go on with a marriage that was absolutely a farce, that had no love in it and no happiness in it—was I to find some woman outside, some mistress—to keep from going crazy?"

"No——" she agreed hesitatingly, with another upward glance.

"There's no sense to that, Alex?"

"No-o-o."

"That would mean that I sacrificed my life for the kid."

"The thing for us to do now," she said, thoughtfully, "is to see that Patsy doesn't sacrifice her life for *us*."

"It almost amounts to that," he said, struck.

"We can't——" Sandra began slowly. "I don't see how we can let Betty take her away next month. It would be like deserting her, failing her."

Carter did not speak for some time. Then he leaned forward to say, with another kiss against the soft warm sweetness of her temple:

"Alex, how I love you!"

A moment later the time of idyll was over. Alexandra glanced at the clock. Five minutes to seven, and dinner in little more than half an hour! She and Carter must be about their dressing.

Before the time was up she walked into the room where the two Englishmen were waiting. It was to be an informal evening; her beginner's bridge was courageously offered to fill the fourth player's place until Peter could join them later. Sandra had put on an old gown, a New York gown beloved because it was comfortable and becoming, and because, she said, she always had "fun" in it. It was of ivory chiffon velvet, with only straps across her ivory shoulders, the beautiful line of her back was bared, the folds of the silky fabric no smoother than the firm full curve of her breast.

Her shining hair was brushed smoothly back from her forehead; there was an innocent, a touching candor in her wide-open brown eyes, a gentleness and sweetness in the wide line of her mouth as she came forward, holding out her hand, smiling at her husband's guests.

Later the older man, General Brooks, asked her if she knew Violet Anstruther—Lady Anstruther, who had been Vi Trumbull.

"No," Sandra told him, shaking her head slowly. She wondered how he chanced to know that her name had been Trumbull.

"You're not London-born, Mrs. Cavendish?"

"No, I'm a San Franciscan."

"By George, I thought you were an Englishwoman!" he said. She knew he meant it for a compliment, and that he liked her; certainly she liked him.

But that this casual exchange of pleasantries held the nucleus of a great change in her own life, that Betty's fate and Patsy's, Carter's, that the lives of them all were to be affected by this kindly, charming English voice, she could not dream then. She only knew that some race instinct, deeper than her own consciousness, older than herself, drew her to these charming visitors, and that their friendliness to her, Carter's new tenderness, his talk with her before dinner, the closeness into which their common anxiety about Patsy was drawing them, were filling her heart with a new happiness, sweeter, realer, deeper than the happiness of a few years ago. General Brooks was just spending a holiday in America? Well, not quite. He was getting notes together for a little study of divorce. He and Sandra talked of divorces, in all the different states. "America has every variety!" she told him, with a rueful little laugh.

Later, when the men were still playing, and when she herself was tucked up in bed, the events of the day passed dreamily in review before her eyes, and she faced them seriously, bravely, albeit with an occasional flutter of her heart.

She thought of the child, and that when men and women had done a child an injustice they must move heaven and earth to right the wrong. The child was helpless; it was for them to act.

Alexandra could find for the situation only the phrases she and Carter had used so often:

"There must be some way out." . . . "We can't go back." . . . "We must go on from here."

CHAPTER TWENTY-TWO

"AUNT SANDRA, I'm going to tell you a secret!" Patsy said.

They were playing with Patsy's stone bricks in the upstairs sitting room of the Burlingame house. Rain was falling heavily on a March Saturday, and Alexandra and Patsy had been in gales of laughter over the difficulties of getting from the hotel in the rain. Two of Patsy's friends were coming to dinner; they were all going afterward to see the Harold Lloyd film in San Mateo.

To Patsy at eleven this was enough and more than enough to know about the future. Eleven rarely concerns itself with to-morrows; she was happy. But just before it was time to put on the velvet dress and get ready for Doris and Jean, she arrested the brown hand that was steering sheep and cows through long brick paddocks and fences, and said with all a child's mysterious solemnity:

"Aunt Sandra, I want to tell you a secret."

"Go ahead, sweetheart."

"But you mustn't tell anyone!"

"No, I know. It's a secret!"

"Even Dad."

"No, not even Dad. I won't."

"Well," Patsy continued, "it's this: I don't want to go back to Paris with Mummy."

A secret! It was no secret to the aching heart that heard her.

"You don't, darling?"

"No. Because I'd rather stay here with you and Dad and Uncle Peter."

"You'll come back and visit us, you know."

"Yes, but when?"

"When? Well, we'll have to decide that with Daddy.—— This old fellow," Alexandra diverged, touching a squarely planted, stubborn-looking little leather bull, "could get out through the fence here if he got mad enough."

"Oh, I'll build up that fence!—— But you see, Aunt Sandra," Patsy pursued, her hands busy, "if I'm giving concerts I'll have to go to Vienna and Berlin and everywhere, and I *can't* come back!"

"Is it fun," Sandra questioned, cheerfully taking the pleasanter side, "to play before those big audiences, and have them applaud such a little girl?"

"Well, you see I never have yet, Aunt Sandra; I've never done any concert work. I've only played in people's houses. Herr Schroeder"—the sophisticated effect of the name from such a little girl impressed Alexandra once more with that odd, other side of Patsy, the side that was so far away from childhood, so precious, so needful of love and protection—"Herr Schroeder wants me to play three times in London and once in Vienna before the season's over," Patsy went on, "and then he wants to book about eight summer concerts."

"And does it make you nervous, Baby?"

"Well, it never *has*. But of course it might, Aunt Sandra, if I was afraid I couldn't remember some of the music, and I knew," the child explained seriously, "that Herr Schroeder was listening right there on the stage——"

"Is he ever unkind to you, Patsy?"

"Who, Herr Schroeder? Oh, no, never; he kisses me. He says I am his *'Wunderkind.'* But he whipped Hans, you know, until Hans was just—well, not shouting any more.

not shouting *'Bitte, bitte, Väterchen!'* but just sort of whining, whining like a puppy, sort of. And Herr Schroeder held his hands so tight, Hans' wrist was all red the next day. But Hans is quite big—he's thirteen."

"What——" She had to clear her throat. "What had Hans done, Patsy?"

"Wouldn't practise."

"I see."

"Hans says he's going to be a sailor."

"But you practise?"

"Well, 'most always. And if I don't Herr Schroeder always just laughs and says, 'I hope I do not get a telephone message from that big rocking horse that he has broken his leg!'"

She laughed deliciously, heartily, and Alexandra made her own face smile.

"Have you a rocking horse?"

"Oh, everything. Only—only of course they won't let me ride a real horse as I do down at Uncle Pete's. Mummy," Patsy remembered—"Mummy was wild when she knew I'd been riding."

"But why, darling? You ride so well."

"Yes, but you see, Aunt Sandra, if I broke an arm or hurt my hand or sprained a wrist, I couldn't go on with my violin playing any more!"

"Ah, of course!"

"Then I'd have to give up my work," Patsy reminded her, in her precocious little responsible fashion, "and that would mean that Herr Schroeder would have to go back to teaching."

The full significance of the last words stunned Alexandra into silence. Patsy was once again a cattle farmer before Sandra could say:

"Will Herr Schroeder travel with you, Patsy?"

"He wants to if it all goes right. That is for three years, about; he wants an American tour, too. Then he says—work, no concerts, until I am eighteen. He says child players always must do that. Mummy was telling me all about it last night, what fun it would be. She said all the little girls would envy me, and all that. And she said I could have anything I wanted. So I said right away that I would much rather stay here and have Jean and Doris down at the ranch for visits and have my own pony and not do any concert work until I was quite big."

"But she wouldn't promise to let you do that?"

"No, she said that that was the one thing she couldn't let me do."

"You see, your mother is very proud of you, Patsy."

"I suppose she is. But I wish," Patsy said quaintly—"I wish she would be proud of me at home!

"All the ladies crowd round me," she explained, "and my hair gets all mussy and I feel tired. And they say, 'Won't you let her play that *allegretto* movement again, Herr Professor?' and then they want to kiss me and make me write my name on their programmes."

"Not much fun for a little girl, really." Sandra was thinking aloud; she spoke absently. "Your mother likes Herr Schroeder, doesn't she?"

"Oh, well, Aunt Sandra,"—the child's face was full of an indulgent amusement—"if she's going to *marry* him——"

Sandra's mouth was dry.

"Oh, is she going to marry him?"

"Well, yes," Patsy answered moderately.

"Oh, I see!"

"You always like a person when you marry them," pronounced Patsy.

"Of course you do. But you said he had a little boy? Isn't there a little boy? What about his mother?"

"Frau Schroeder, yes. But she's going to get a divorce. And Hans—Hans is thirteen. But he's very little; he's not quite as tall as I am. And his head is very round; they shave it. I don't like boys to have their heads shaved, do you?"

"I think it makes them look ugly."

"He looks ugly. Herr Schroeder wanted him to be a pianist. But he can't seem to be a very good pianist," Patsy explained simply. "Herr Schroeder wanted him to accompany me, but Hans just can't do it, and Hans says he is going to run away to sea when he's fourteen. Hans used to cry and I would give him my chocolate."

She gave the last word the German pronunciation. Alexandra, looking down at the upturned, confident, sensitive little face, felt her heart wrung and twisted with pain.

"So that's sort of why I don't want to go back, Aunt Sandra. And if you tell Daddy don't tell him anything about Mother and Herr Schroeder, because she said she wanted to tell him herself!" Patsy interrupted herself to remind her hearer anxiously. "But you tell him to 'range it so that I stay here. I don't like Paris."

She got up from her blocks and fitted her small thin body snugly into Sandra's arms, and Sandra rested her face against the dark little head and hugged Patsy close and stared blindly, blankly into space.

All through the whispering and giggling of the three little girls at dinner, all through the movie, when Patsy was happy between Jean and Doris, and when Carter next to her in the dark held her hand, as he loved to do, in his own, Sandra was thinking.

And later, when the laughing and racing and flying of pillows and slamming of doors was over, and when the three little girls were asleep and Carter was asleep, she sat on by the fire, thinking, facing the situation squarely.

"There must be some way out. We've done this, and we have to go on from here. But—there must be some way out."

This tender, eager, sensitive child was flesh of Betty's flesh and bone of her bone. But she was Carter's child, too. He had held her in his arms when, rolled in blankets, and sputtering and waving small weak arms, the nurse had first shown him his daughter. She was his as much as she was Betty's; to fail Patsy now would be to fail life. To let Betty take her away to that world she hated—a world of harsh foreign voices, strange foreign streets and hotels, queer hours, queer alternations of blame and flattery, fatigues and responsibilities far beyond her years—would be to hurt her irreparably, perhaps to kill her. Alexandra could visualize a thin, nervous, awkward Patsy at fourteen, reaching that time when her stepfather had decided that it must be "work, no concerts, until I am eighteen."

Terrible years those, that would transform the little spoiled, pampered prodigy into the young musician. No fun, no Jean and Doris and giggling and movies and horseback. Just practice and practice, auditions and masters.

Thrilling enough for Mummy and "Schroeder." Not so good for the little chief actor in the piece.

Carter and Alexandra had contributed to the ruin of this little life. Innocently on Sandra's part. Or if not quite innocently in every way, at least she had never foreseen this: Betty's ambition, the cupidity and vanity of a far-away unknown Austrian music master, the helplessness of herself and Carter and the elder Mrs. Cavendish, of everyone who loved Patsy.

Carter, handsome, nonchalant, and gay, hitherto completely equal to any emergency, was checkmated here. Sandra had seen him grow gray over it in these last few weeks; grow sober and quiet and anxious. He was powerless against this complacent, determined little woman who held in her hands the keys of his child's happiness or sorrow, life or death.

And she, Alexandra, had been the pearl for which Carter had paid this great price. For her sake he had said to Betty in those long-ago days in which, looking back, they all seemed to have been so young and raw and crude: "Make your own terms. Take what you like. But don't mention— Sandra. I'll consent to anything, but grant me that!"

She had never known it all these years. He had never told her that. It had been the revelation of her own share in this complication, those shocking words hurled at her by Betty in parting, that had spurred her into the feeling that something, something must be done.

No use to say, as she and Carter had been saying to each other during the last few weeks, "Perhaps we'll get over to Paris and see her." . . . "Perhaps next summer Betty'll send her back to us." . . . "Perhaps in a few months they'll find out that she can't stand the strain of concert work . . ."

All this was but so much camouflage for the agony of their knowing that within a few days now Patsy must learn that Daddy could *not* "'range everything," and that she must go away from her beloved California and Doris and Jean and the pony down at Uncle Peter's and take up the serious business of her life again.

Alexandra and Peter—big, gentle, silent Peter—and Carter, grown up, suffering at last, must button on the small coat and kiss the small, serious face and put good-bye presents into the little gloved hands, and so good-bye to Patsy, who had brought such changes, such new pain and new joy into all their lives!

"If my little girl had lived and this were my little girl

. . ." Sandra thought, and her heart closed on a spasm of pure agony.

Patsy's last words to-night had been on the burning topic. She had drawn Sandra's head down against her own for a final kiss, and had murmured confidently, lovingly, in the darkness of the nursery, "Did Dad fix it?"

"He's doing his best!" Sandra could only answer with a desperate little whispered stress on the last word.

Well, she thought, alone before the fire later, deep into the cold spring night, if she got Patsy a big doll—children were easily consoled . . .

Children, but not Patsy. She was not like most children; Betty was not the typical mother. Carter's love for the child, hers for him, Sandra's new-born affection for Patsy, Peter's position, the grandmother's position—all these made the situation unusual. And of course the possibility of an ambitious, cruel stepfather introduced a new and insufferable element.

"If I got a divorce . . ." Sandra thought. But even this extreme course would solve nothing. Betty would still be free, still be Betty. Carter would have no claim on Patsy that he had not now.

"If I killed myself . . ." No solution there. Even supposing Sandra to be out of the problem entirely, it would not be solved, nothing would be changed. Only Betty could give Carter any share of Patsy again, and Betty was adamant. Betty was jealous of Sandra, angry to find her friends now Sandra's friends, her old place more than filled; she would use any means of revenge that chance placed in her power.

Sandra cupped her chin in her hand and stared into the dying fire, her jaw set. There must be—there *must* be some way out.

She, Alexandra, could not go on into the future with

this bill unpaid. She could not complacently take the place of Patsy's mother in society, could not happily anticipate some day the coming of another child, with this sensitive, eager, loving child in exile, victimized by an ambitious mother and a harsh, disciplinarian stepfather. It was unthinkable; a future in which Alexandra would be dreaming over Carter's protected, adored baby son, and Carter's little daughter be alone in a foreign land, straightening her weary little back through two hours—three hours—five hours of practice in some dull hotel room! Poor little lonely Patsy, remembering the ranch and the shore, her pony, the California background that she perhaps was never to know again.

No, Alexandra would not—she could not—bear that.

There was but one light in the orderly big room; it shone down on her hair and on her long body stretched in a deep chair, her chin resting on her hand, her eyes on the fire. Hour after hour after hour she sat dreaming, and the clock struck over and over again without her hearing it. And still Sandra could find no way out.

CHAPTER TWENTY-THREE

JUST A WEEK LATER on a Sunday afternoon Alexandra and Carter were at the Country Club. Carter had been playing golf all day long, with a rubber or two of bridge to finish off; Sandra had played eighteen holes, too, after their late breakfast, and had since been amusing herself with backgammon and gossip in the game room.

It was five o'clock; the bright day had clouded over suddenly in the late afternoon, and fog was rolling in over the long line of westward hills from the ocean. An enormous fire had been lighted in the big main room, and men and women were drifting about in the welcome warmth and brightness, eating sandwiches, drinking tea, talking over the various games of the day and the various plans for the evening.

To the group that loitered on the hearth, some standing, some seated on the broad leather fender that fenced it, came Sandra and Carter together. Carter, explaining that he had been playing cards on the porch and was freezing, had a tall glass in his hand; Sandra, as usual rather silent in a group, merely smiled as she came up.

Anyone who knew her intimately might have seen in her face and manner signs of the strain she had been undergoing during this endless week. Never highly colored, she was to-day more than ordinarily pale, and the gold-brown eyes were ringed faintly in shadow. Her manner was quieter than was customary, too, and she seemed to cling to Carter, keeping near him, watching him when he spoke, following him wistfully with her eyes when he moved away.

But there was no one to notice this in the carelessly chattering group, and Sandra had only her usual nods and smiles of greeting. She was smart to-day in a white golf costume, loose long coat and pleated soft skirt of white, blouse of white and French blue, with a line of scarlet, and small soft white hat banded in scarlet and blue. Her long thin silk scarf had an edge of dark blue and bright red; the only color in her face was the line of her red lips.

"Sandra, you're beautiful!" Joe Hamilton said.

"Come, that's interesting!" Sandra answered indifferently, with an indulgent smile. A delighted English laugh drew her attention to a man standing near.

"Oh, I say!" exclaimed young Sir George Wylie, turning about from the fire. "I like that! Do you have so many compliments you can take that tone about them, Mrs. Cavendish?"

Alexandra smiled again, shaking hands with her dinner guest of a few weeks past. Both the Englishmen had been much entertained during their visit; she had seen this pleasant rosy boy a dozen times.

"How do you do, Sir George? Did you win that big rubber the other night?"

"No, I say, d'you know we lost it!" Sir George cried, with tremendous relish.

"With all those penalties!"

"Oh, rather. But how is it you're not freezing?" the Englishman asked, hospitably making a place for her by the fire. "Mr. Cavendish looks all done in!"

"I was playing in the game room with a player more in my class," Sandra explained.

"You play better bridge than Mr. Cavendish; that's it, eh?"

"Ask him," Sandra suggested through the general laugh, with a glance toward him.

"But do you know I liked what you said then, awfully," Sir George said with inexhaustible relish. "Hamilton here tells her she's beautiful," he explained at large, "and she says, 'Come, that's interesting!'"

"We don't take anything Joe says seriously," Helen Peabody told him.

"And how's my friend, the General?" Sandra asked of the other British visitor. The name made its owner wheel about also, and he answered for himself.

"Oh, how d'ye do, Mrs. Cavendish; jolly to see you! Did you get home safely in all that rain last night?"

The conversation became general; they were all standing laughing together, a dozen or fifteen men and women, some biting into sandwiches, some balancing cups of tea, some merely toasting by the fire, when Alexandra was conscious of a little excited ripple through the group, and sensed rather than saw that Betty, escorted by some man unknown, had drifted to the fireplace, and was standing within a few feet of her.

She had encountered Betty more than once in general gatherings since the day Sandra had called on her, but they were not often as close together as this.

Was Betty aware that Sandra and Carter were there? Was she deliberately joining them? Alexandra dared not glance toward her to make sure. She devoted herself nervously to the two Englishmen, the older of whom chanced at the moment to say:

"D'you know, Mrs. Cavendish, I quite can't believe you've no English blood?"

"Oh, I never told you that!" Sandra answered, her eyes wide. "I said that I wasn't English-born. My father was an Englishman."

"Well, of *course*. Trumbull was the name, you said," the General said promptly. "That'd be the Surrey family," he told his companion.

"Lady Miggy's crowd," Sir George said, with a nod, after an appraising glance.

"Exactly!"

"But of course!" the younger man murmured, staring and smiling at Alexandra. "She's like them all!"

"Your father," General Brooks said, "was Rodney. He came to California. You don't remember Rod Trumbull, Sir George, but you must have known Sir Edward?"

"I knew Cecil."

"Yes; well, that's Ned's boy. Ned was the oldest—Rod came fourth, I think. There were a lot of them!"

"I know your cousins aw'fly well," Sir George said to Sandra simply. "Flurry was in my squadron; ripping chap. He died of wounds."

"My cousins!" Sandra could only echo with a gasp and a laugh.

"I never knew you had cousins in England, Alexandra," Helen said reproachfully.

"I never knew it myself!"

"You've been quite aware of it all along, of course, but you Trumbulls are not talkers," the General said, in affectionate approval. "I think—I think your father died some time back?"

"When I was three. That's twenty-two years, almost."

"Dear me, you're young! I never knew your father very well—knew the older boys. Marvelous old place, Whynell Abbey."

"They've rented that, you know, General. Lady St. Gregory is living at Whiteangel," Sir George contributed.

"Lady Miggy is your——?" General Brooks looked at Sandra, and Sandra laughed back ingenuously.

"I don't know any of them, General."

"Why, but she's your father's sister!" he said.

"But, you see, I was only a little bit of a girl when my father died. My mother never knew his people at all."

"You're like her, you know, and you're aw'fly like Constance," the younger man said enthusiastically.

"Your father was Rodney?"

"Father was Rodney St. George——" Alexandra smiled and hesitated. "I *think* St. George," she remembered the name by degrees. "Rodney Howard St. George Trumbull."

"His mother was Charlotte St. George; quite right!"

The group about her had been transfixed with interest in this revelation; Sandra had been conscious of their complete and fascinated silence while the conversation had been in progress. They lived in a small circle of interests, knowing and caring nothing of what went on in other worlds than their own world of amusements and pleasures, but passionately interested in everything that touched themselves.

To discover that Carter Cavendish's obscure young wife, who had been his stenographer, whose mother had been a second-rate San Francisco cabaret singer, was closely connected with the English nobility caused a stir.

"You know, it's exactly like her people, never to have said a word of this!" the General said, in high pleasure. "I've known them all; we've been neighbors since the beginning of things! Lady Miggy's my daughter Annie's closest friend. Miggy—that'd be your father's sister, Margaret. Her daughter Violet married Anstruther, after the war."

"Anstruther's my cousin," Sir George said. "I say, that makes us cousins! But I mean, how very jolly!"

"I never knew Rod married," the older man said, looking keenly at Sandra.

"My mother," Sandra explained simply, "was an actress. Perhaps his family wasn't enthusiastic."

"Very likely. But you know, Cavendish, you must bring your wife home one of these days," the General said. "She'd like it. She's a Surrey Trumbull, after all, and you've got to bring her home to be vetted. They'll all be curious to see her. I shall tell Miggy and Lady Vi about it directly I get back."

"'Vetted' sounds like a horse!" Sandra protested, laughing, a little self-conscious, as pleased and excited as they were.

"Exactly! And they'll like you and you'll like them and you'll be interested in the old place," General Brooks said. "Whynell Abbey is rented; that's where your father was born. But Whiteangel is a fine old place, too, and the Grouse Over Farms. You'll see it all! How could you ever have been to England and have missed it? For you're as like Charlotte as one of her own girls."

"I've never been in England."

"Oh, then, I say, you've got to come!"

"After this," Carter's pleasant definite voice said, "we certainly will go; won't we, Sandra?"

"Sandra, you see," Sir George repeated it. "The little St. Gregory boy is Alexander."

"And Vi's girl is Alex."

"You belong to England," General Brooks summarized it. "You'll find cousins under every hedgerow, won't she, Sir George?"

"Droves of 'em, myself included," the young man agreed.

"Ah, but I belong to America by marriage," Alexandra said laughing. She looked at Carter, brown and square and hard, in his golf apparel, and beyond him got one glimpse of Betty looking on with a set white face and narrowed eyes. Betty had heard everything.

Instantly Alexandra's mood changed, although she gave no sign of it. She felt her heart stop beating and begin again at a slower pace; her world clouded over as the spring day had clouded; fog closed in about her spirit; she felt afraid. This revelation that made Alexandra important, that lent to Carter's already popular wife a new romantic interest, was gall and wormwood to Betty.

Carter was naturally pleased at the little unexpected development. He talked about it interestedly as they drove home for baths and Sunday supper, and gave his mother a glowing account of his wife's English affiliations.

"We'll certainly go over next year and see your people," he said more than once. "It might be a lot of fun! Of course, I knew the minute I saw you, Alex, that you didn't belong to Ellis Street and the office! A duchess, that's what you look like."

"Don't say that, Carter. Haven't you ever seen any pictures of duchesses?"

They were in their room alone; it was almost midnight. Carter was in his favorite deep low chair, Alexandra in his arms, with one of her own arms about his neck and her temple and the soft coil of her hair against his cheek, as they both stared at the fire.

"I loved you for piping up and saying that your mother was an actress, Alex."

"But what else," she murmured dreamily, "could I say?"

"Just the same I thought it was swell."

"I am ashamed to think how much pleasure it gives me—how proud I am, Carter—to have men like General Brooks know my family and like it."

"Well, why not?"

"I know. But it seems so snobbish."

"You snobbish!"

"Well, it felt so."

"But don't you fool yourself," Carter half roused himself to say after an interval. "It'll make no end of a difference to your gang—to Rose and Helen and Mab."

"They couldn't have been nicer to me, Carter."

"I know. But you wait and see!"

"Carter, did you see Betty in that crowd?"

"Up at the fireplace, you mean?"

"Yes. I think she was with Willy Hudson. I didn't dare take a real look."

"Sure, I saw her. I don't think she knew we were there when she came up."

"I don't think she did. But she heard the whole thing just the same."

"I know she did."

"It won't make her like me any better."

"You said something!" Carter agreed, with a laugh. "She'd give ten years off her life to have had that happen to her."

"My life seems romantic to me sometimes, Carter. I suppose everyone's life does. When you get far enough along to see the pattern. . . . I remember feeling so changed, so responsible, when Flossy got so ill, and you and I were first in love with each other, and I took her down to the ranch. I remember reading your letters down there in the frosty autumn and the smell of wood fires and the kitchen. . . . I seemed to have grown up so suddenly; I seemed so old. And yet looking back after her death and after our having been married so long, I seem to have been the youngest thing alive!"

"If you had it to do all over again, Sandy, you'd marry me again, wouldn't you?"

"I'd do everything so differently——" she mused aloud.

"But you'd marry me again!"

"Oh, Carter, yes—and yes—and yes! A thousand thousand times, my darling. Carter," Sandra added, in a voice he did not often hear from her, "promise me this: promise me that if ever we are separated, you'll remember that. That I love you, that I never can love anyone else!"

"We are never going to be separated."

"No. I hope not. I hope not. But sometimes, sometimes I get so frightened, Carter, thinking of myself away from you, not belonging to you any more, having days go by without your kissing me——"

"Why, God bless this little idiot," Carter said tenderly, "she's crying!"

"People have to pay, Carter, for happiness like ours," she said, wiping away tears unashamed, and smiling.

"How do you mean pay?"

"We've learned, Cart, we've grown up, since those days in the office, those lunches at Jules'."

"I've learned. I've learned that I can't live without you, honey, not for a minute. I've learned that I can be perfectly happy down at Pete's, walking round the place, picnicking, doing anything, as long as you're in the picture."

"You love me?" she said.

"My darling, I adore you."

"More—" she said—"more than you loved Betty?"

"More than I ever loved anyone. Differently. I'm different," he answered. "I couldn't love Betty as I love you," Carter presently went on. "Because in the first place she couldn't love anyone; it wasn't in her. She didn't want anyone to love her; love doesn't matter much to her kind of woman. Really, I mean it!

"We got married," he went on as Sandra did not speak, "just the way most kids do. We knew all the same people, we were always at the same things, her mother knew mine, all that. I remember that there were lots of presents, lots of talk; I was crazy about her, all right, or crazy about the idea of getting married, I don't know which. It didn't take, somehow. . . .

"But don't fool yourself," he continued, "I couldn't live without you now, Sandy. I had a crush on you in the old days in the office. I know you now. And I love every hair of my girl's head to-day more than I loved the whole girl four years ago!"

"Suppose," Alexandra presently began, in a rather trembling voice—"suppose I had to go away from you, Carter, for a while? Would you wait for me, would you come after me, when it was over?"

"No," he answered unalarmed, "for I wouldn't let you go."

"I might have to, Carter."

He tightened his arm.

"Not you!"

"Cart, suppose it was for Patsy. Suppose, by going away, I could keep Patsy with you?"

"Even then."

"Even then you'd want me, Cart?"

"Sandy, so much that everything else I want doesn't count."

"I might go away from you," she said. "But some day I'd come back, some day when I'd earned all this, Cart, the delight of it, being your wife. And then we'd go down to Pete's and loaf about on the shore and talk—and talk——"

"I don't know what you're talking about now, Sandy," Carter put into the pause.

"I know you don't!" she admitted with a rueful laugh. And for a long time she rested quietly against his shoulder, staring into the fire, thinking.

CHAPTER TWENTY-FOUR

THEY WERE STILL sufficiently lovers to enjoy every unexpected meeting. Alexandra, walking up Post Street two days later, jumped with surprise to feel her shoulder touched, and turned a strained and unusually tender smile to Carter's beaming face. Brown and handsome and impeccably groomed, she thought him the finest-looking man in the world, and judged all men by him.

"Carter, how you scared me!"

"Why, I *did* frighten you, darling!" he apologized, his strong hard fingers bracing her elbow now in the dear familiar way, his face beaming with the satisfaction of the man who finds the object of his search. "I was just heading for the St. Francis," he said, "going to meet you for lunch! What were you doing so far downtown?"

"I was buying—some little crayons and junk for Patsy."

They went along in the noon sunshine together, with eyes only for each other.

"Sandy, the new suit is lovely. Is that the one Mab was so crazy about?"

"Oh, but Carter, I was going to be so beautiful with my nose all powdered and everything! It's not quarter to one yet."

"You look lovely. But I'll wait for you; go powder your nose and make yourself beautiful!"

It seemed to her that they had never been so completely married as they were to-day, in this confidential, happy, easy hour. They had an inconspicuous table in the big hotel dining room, but the room was full of their friends; there was a certain dramatic element in this lunching downtown with one's husband, of which Alexandra was conscious every time she did it.

Carter was very much the boy to-day, pleased with her and with himself, eager, voluble, enthusiastic. He adored her in those plain dark things, he adored the way her mouth was made, he said; he said he was being envied by every man in the room.

They had their favorite lunch; in these happy years she had come to know his taste as well as her own. Oysters, the little button-size California oysters in cocktail glasses, and sand-dabs sputtering and crackling in butter, and dried crisps of rye bread, and fresh mixed salad.

"*Méringue glacé*, Infant?"

Golden lights welled in her eyes as she smiled at him.

"Remember when you always had to have a *méringue glacé?*"

"Because I was out lunching with my beau—to celebrate."

"Have one now."

"I couldn't, Carter!"

"But I like to buy you things."

"You buy me everything. But truly—nothing more."

"Small coffee?"

"Nothing."

"Haven't we had a nice lunch—haven't we had a nice talk?" he asked.

Her heart was too full; she did not answer.

They walked out of the restaurant together, handsome Carter Cavendish and his lovely wife. Eyes on all sides moved to follow Alexandra's tall figure, to study her smart suits, her clever hat, the color of her glowing face, the gardenias on her shoulder. Husband and wife moved slowly; their eyes were together, they were talking. And women she never had seen and never would know told one another Alexandra's story as she went on her way. She had been Carter Cavendish's secretary; he had been married before. He adored her. She was considered the most beautiful woman in society.

"How are you getting home, Alex?"

"Train, I think. Mary brought me in. I didn't tell Paul to come in; he's taking all those things back from the club anyway. But did you—" her face brightened—"did you want me to get Patsy?"

"She's to be at Mother's at four. Why not let me take you both home?"

"Oh, Carter, I'd love that! Can you get away so early?"

"I'll manage darned well that I do! Somehow," Carter told her, walking through the big lobby with her—"somehow I like being married to you to-day. Somehow everything seems all right when we're together."

He went toward his office, and Sandra wandered off to waste some time in the shops, sitting absent-mindedly at glove counters, standing in book departments with volumes opened before her unseeing eyes and puzzled saleswomen respectful at her elbows. Patsy and Betty were leaving California a week from to-day.

At three she went to the hotel to see Carter's mother, and sat with her for an hour. The older woman was unfeignedly glad to see her; she was confined to bed with a cold.

Alexandra felt a fresh pang at her heart as she saw the welcoming face. Their common trial was drawing these two women together. The day outside had turned foggy and cold, but here there was coziness and warmth, a table laid for tea.

It was good to belong in a scene as charming as this, to be "Mrs. Carter" to smiling Fanny who opened the door of the suite her mother-in-law occupied, to have the older woman fall straightway to family confidences.

"Alexandra, I'm so glad it's you, my dear. Get comfortable over there and let's talk. I've not seen you since Sunday. Carter tell you that Patsy wants to go down with you this afternoon?"

"I was so glad."

"She doesn't bother you?"

"Bother us! We simply adore having her. It's too lovely, having her want to come."

"I wish Betty weren't taking her back!" Mrs. Cavendish fretted for the thousandth time.

"I wish she weren't."

"The child doesn't want to go, you know."

"I know."

"I don't suppose she knows what she wants to do or doesn't want to do?" The older woman said it wistfully, expectantly, but Sandra could not join in the deception.

"Patsy's enjoyed being here so much," she said vaguely.

"Dear little thing!"

They were silent, Carter's mother and wife, in the pleasant intimacy of the former's spacious bedroom. The throbbing life of the hotel above, below, and about them seemed not to exist. Here were snugness, security, companionableness. Here was a background of books, rich furnishings, fineness. They seemed to appeal to Alexandra as never before. It was a great thing to be a man's beloved wife and on friendly terms with his mother. It was like wearing a title, a blue ribbon, to be Mrs. Carter Cavendish.

Patsy's entrance caused the next diversion. The little girl entered with a joyous rush. Whatever the coming week might hold in the way of pain and parting, these two days were to be hers with Daddy and Aunt Sandra, and she was happy. From her chubby babyhood she had grown to be rather a delicate-looking child in these last years; slight and tall, with dark eyes in a rather pale little face; but to-day she was radiant in a red coat with a fox collar. A red loose cap hung back from her dark hair.

"I had to bring my violin!" she said, coming into the room on her own characteristic dancing step, putting down the case and establishing herself, after a butterfly kiss for her grandmother, in Alexandra's lap. "Because Mrs. Rhodes wants me to play in the Children's Concert to-morrow."

Sandra kissed the small warm ear.

"Oh, that's so, sweetheart. I'd forgotten the concert."

"But that," Patsy decreed positively, "is the only thing I'm going to do that I don't want to do!"

"You don't want to do that, darling?" her grandmother asked.

"Oh, well," the child answered carelessly, rubbing her cheek against Sandra's, "it isn't much fun. It'll take all afternoon! Mother said please to have my dress pressed. She's not going to come down for the concert; she's going on a motor trip with the Grays, and she said she wouldn't be caught dead at a Children's Concert."

"And what are you going to play?"

"I don't know. Mother sent them a list. An A and a B, I guess," Patsy answered casually. And instantly she added animatedly, "Aunt Sandra, how's Jiggles?"

It was her dual personality again; one half of her professional performer, sophisticated and self-possessed, and the other half little girl.

"Jiggles," Sandra told her, "is adorable. I never saw a cuter little Airedale. He missed you so terribly last week that Daddy sent him down to Uncle Pete's, and even there he ran about, sniffing and whimpering and looking for you. Uncle Peter brought him back this morning."

"Oh, I love him!" Patsy cried, in a rich little wistful voice, tears in her bright eyes. "Are we going down to the ranch?"

"Well, we were going down right after breakfast tomorrow, you and I and Jean, and Daddy was coming down after his golf. But I'd forgotten the concert. If you have to play in the concert," Alexandra worked it out, conscious of the bright confident eyes fixed upon her, "then we can get in the car right afterward and be down at the ranch for dinner."

"Oh, darn the concert!" lamented Patsy. "But we can take our suitcases to the concert; and we don't have to stay the whole programme, do we? We could get away right after the *entr'acte,* couldn't we?"

"If you know where you are on the programme, dear."

"I think I end the first half—I generally do."

"Well, then we could."

"Oh, goody, that'll be only about half-past three!" exulted Patsy. "We'll get to the ranch—when would we?"

"Before six, I should think."

"Oh, goody!"

"But maybe Jean will want to see the rest of the programme, Patsy."

Patsy considered this, her face sobering.

"Oh, well, we can ask her."

She was all little-girl for the rest of that day and during the evening. She and the little dog romped about the house and ran themselves breathless up and downstairs after dinner, so that both were glad to climb into Carter's lap and rest, breathless, before the fire at bedtime.

And she was all little-girl the next morning, puttering about happily with Sandra, trying to train the utterly unimpressed Jiggles, in and out of the house like a flash of quicksilver. They shopped together, she and Sandra, lingering long and fondly in the five-and-ten-cent store, they called together at Jean's house for Jean, and they all went together to meet Gran at the train.

Sandra and the older woman and the two little girls lunched together in the shaded dining room; Patsy and Jean lavish with the biscuits and the jam, casual with the spinach. Then Patsy had to get into the white taffeta dress with the daisies embroidered on it in heavy chenille, and her dark mop had to be brushed until every hair lay smooth.

To see her expert little brown hands on the violin, even while they were still dressing her, to hear the swift ripple of the scale and the tentative tuning notes, Patsy frowning faintly, listening for the hundredth part of the tone, was to see a new Patsy, was to see a child who was not a child, and whose helplessness, smallness, genius, strangely tore at Sandra's heart.

There were other little girls milling and whispering nervously in the wings of the concert-hall stage; gauzy little girls who were to dance, self-conscious little girls who were to recite. Patsy at once became one of them, no more and no less, and Alexandra left her there and went out into the audience to join the child's grandmother and Carter and Peter, who had given up their usual Saturday golf game for the occasion.

The moment came. There were piano chords, an impressive silence following a general rustle. There was a circle of light piercing the darkened auditorium, falling upon the crimson and white stripes of a great flag, and upon roses and palms on the stage.

And into this circle Patsy walked, a small figure, an unexpectedly small and slim childish figure in flat-heeled slippers and a daisy-embroidered white frock. She smiled at the applauding audience in her friendly little way, walked to the piano, and bent her head, sounding the A softly, briefly, glancing expectantly at the pianist. He nodded presently, and Patsy nodded, too. The note was true.

To see her walk after that to the center of the stage, to see her straighten her small body and lift the instrument to her shoulder, to see her nod reassuringly at the accompanist, was not only enchantingly impressive to Alexandra and Carter but to the whole house. There was an audible murmur of "Ah, the darling!" and "Isn't she sweet?" even before the music began.

She played a double number and two encores; she could have played to them all afternoon. In the *entr'acte* Sandra and Carter went behind the scenes and found her, small and flushed and politely appreciative of her ring of admirers. They bundled her into a coat, and with the somewhat awed and wholly admiring Jean were all in the car and speeding south at four o'clock.

"And we can go down on the beach before supper, mayn't we, Aunt Sandra?"

"Let me wipe your face, darling. You're all messy."

"I always get like that after a concert. Aunt Sandra, did you know I could see you and Dad?"

"We thought you did."

"In the Tschaikowsky."

"That's what we thought."

Sandra's hand was touching the slender, moist little neck, was pushing aside the dark mane. Patsy, occupying one of the small seats, turned to embrace her.

"I love you!" she said.

After a while, relaxed and happy, she got into Carter's lap and half drowsed, half waked there for the long trip.

"Aunt Sandra, 'member you said sometimes we'd have all the girls down and make candy at the grill?"

"I do."

"Well, if I don't go with Mother next week could we do it then?"

"We surely could. But won't it—won't it disappoint Mother terribly if you don't go?"

"Oh, but I'm not going!" Patsy exclaimed jealously, tightening her arms about her father's neck.

"Patsy said she'd rather jump off the rocks at Point Lobos than go back to Paris," Jean volunteered, beaming.

"Because I said," Patsy supplemented it, laughing guiltily —"I said that I could swim around among the rocks before I drowned!"

"You'd do a swell lot of swimming down there," Carter told her, in a fond, chiding voice. But his eyes, meeting Sandra's, were dark with pain.

This was Saturday. The idle Sunday that followed seemed to Alexandra only too perilously sweet. There hung over their happy hours at the ranch the glamor that only impending change gives, the unbearable beauty of the end.

Spring had wrapped the place in lavish bloom and fragrance. The sea was blue; the sky, high and soft and blue. Larks were whirling into the scented air; the shadow of enormous oaks lay mellow across the breakfast table under the grapevine.

Peter and Carter busied themselves with the morning papers; the small girls seized upon the comic sections; Hong drifted to and fro with fresh coffee and waffles. The sun shone down warmly; shadows were a deep, trembling summer green, although the calendar stood at April. In the Sunday stillness they could smell the pines on the dunes above the sea, and hear the far-away church bells at San Carlos Mission.

Joe and Billy Hamilton came over at about noon; the men played bridge, talking lazily of golf, beginning another rubber. Sandra and the ecstatic sandy little girls returned from the beach in time to fuss at the garden grill with chops and salad at one.

"Happy days!" Carter said, wistfully.

"Too happy!" Alexandra answered.

CHAPTER TWENTY-FIVE

THEY WERE BACK in the Burlingame house on Monday night when Alexandra came to the library door and called Carter.

"Could you come here a moment, Carter?"

Her voice had a fluttered note in it; Carter looked up in surprise from the littered flat-top desk upon which he and Peter were at the—to Sandra—mysterious business of balancing handicaps for the golf tournament next month.

"What's the matter, honey?" Carter asked, on his feet. She had been with them until a few minutes ago, when one of the maids had murmured that there was "someone to see her."

"Someone to see me?" Sandra had demanded, eyebrows raised. "A lady?"

"No, madam. It's——" Katie had extended a card to her mistress, but as by this time Sandra had been walking beside the maid to the door, the two men at the desk had had no further information.

Now Carter, joining her, asked sharply.

"Anything frighten you? What's the matter?"

"Frighten me? No. No," she answered, in an odd, irresolute voice. She caught at his hand, guided him into the little reception room that was beside the front door. "It's a Mr. O'Connor, Carter."

"Who's he?"

"Well, he's——" Her voice wavered away into silence; they were in the actual presence of the visitor now.

Carter saw, rising to his feet as he and Sandra entered the room, a squarely built, handsome young Irishman with a somewhat doubtful expression on his face.

"This is my husband," Sandra said, "Mr. Joseph O'Connor, Mr. Cavendish."

"Mr. Cavendish," O'Connor said, acknowledging the introduction.

"Sit down, Carter," Sandra said, sitting down herself. The caller leaned forward in his chair.

"Did Mrs. Cavendish have time to give you any idea of what brings me here, Mr. Cavendish?"

"No, not yet." Carter spoke briefly, unencouragingly.

Mr. O'Connor rubbed his head and laughed apologetically.

"We've run into a little snag here," he began ineloquently.

"Who do you mean by 'we'?" Carter demanded, puzzled and unfriendly.

"I mean my brother and I," the other man explained. "My brother George and I. I'm an attorney in San Francisco," he went on, "but George practises in Reno."

Carter glanced at Alexandra. Her eyes were fixed on the visitor's face; her own was pale.

"You'll have to let me in on this, Sandra," Carter observed politely, patiently.

She only gave him a rather terrified glance as the other man went on.

"While my brother was looking up some data for another client last week, Mr. Cavendish, he came upon some information regarding the divorce that Mrs. Cavendish—that is, Mrs. Elizabeth Finchley Cavendish—secured three years ago."

There was a deathly silence.

"What is this, blackmail?" Carter asked scowling, after a pause.

The color rose in the other man's face.

"No, sir; it isn't blackmail. This information," Joe O'Connor repeated, "may prove very important to you."

"I can't imagine it!" Carter said curtly. "However, if you have anything to say to me about it, I'd be glad to see you in my office. Any time that suits you suits me. This is my home. I can see no necessity," he added, with a glance for Sandra's stricken face—"no necessity for troubling Mrs. Cavendish with this."

"If you'll excuse me," O'Connor countered, "it seems to me there is every reason to inform Mrs. Cavendish."

A dead silence, broken by Carter's slow voice.

"Perhaps you'll let me be the judge of that, Mr. O'Connor?"

"Carter, what does it matter how we find it out?" Alexandra pleaded, her fingers on his hand. "Please listen. *Please.*"

Carter folded his big arms on his chest, lowered a sullen look at the attorney.

"Shoot," he said.

"It is simply this, Mr. Cavendish; we find a flaw in that decree," Joe O'Connor said flatly.

"What decree?"

"Your divorce from your former wife."

Carter looked from one face to the other.

"What is all this?" he asked.

"Something I thought you should know," the lawyer said steadily.

"You mean that you came down to Burlingame to-night to tell me that my divorce was not valid?"

"I live in Burlingame," O'Connor said with dignity. "I saw Mrs.—I saw your former wife, Mrs. Finchley Cavendish, to-day," he added. "It was her idea that I should see Mrs. Cavendish and yourself."

"You talked to Mrs. Cavendish!"

"This afternoon."

A short silence. Then Carter asked:

"Perhaps you will tell me why *you* are concerning yourself in this affair?"

"I am—in a sense—Mrs. Cavendish's representative," young O'Connor answered, "although she will put it in her own lawyer's hands immediately."

Then there was a pause.

"My brother and I, when we discovered that there was a possibility of a technical flaw in that decree," the lawyer pursued, "felt it our duty to report it to Mrs. Cavendish. I did so. Mrs. Cavendish's own lawyer, Mr. Pry, being in Europe, she asked me to speak to you about it."

"I don't suppose she asked you to speak to Mrs. Cavendish about it?" Carter demanded, with a glance at Sandra.

Joe O'Connor acknowledged this merely with an apologetic movement of the head.

"But what do you mean by a 'technical' flaw?" Alexandra here asked quickly. "Carter, please, please let him tell us!" she begged as Carter made a quick intolerant motion.

"Mrs. Elizabeth Finchley Cavendish," the lawyer said, glancing at some notes in his hand, "registered at the Samarkand Hotel, in Reno, on the third of September. In the complaint she filed she swears she has been a resident of the county since August twenty-first; she was granted her decree on the twenty-first day of the following February. Judge Reubens drew the complaint."

"What does Judge Reubens say about it?"

"Judge Reubens died a year ago, Mr. Cavendish."

"But you don't mean to tell me that a matter of thirteen days in a date——" Carter began impatiently, and stopped.

"The complaint was filed under oath, Mr. Cavendish; if the facts are otherwise than stated, perjury has been committed, and falsely altering or making a public document amounts to forgery. Certainly the decree of divorce would be invalidated."

"That doesn't mean we aren't married, Carter?" Alexandra asked, in a sharp whisper, eyes on his face.

"No!" he answered scornfully, almost with a sneer. "This is some stupid, trumped-up nonsense! What did Mrs. Cavendish say to all this?" he asked the lawyer.

"Mrs. Cavendish," O'Connor answered unexpectedly, "told me that she had always known that there was a little juggling with the dates there, but that Judge Reubens had taken it very lightly, and she had thought it of no importance. I asked her if she had been somewhere else in Reno for the first two weeks of her stay; she said no, she had gone with a child and a nurse straight to the hotel. It seems that Mrs—" he glanced at his notes again—"Mrs. Elizabeth Finchley Cavendish wished to leave California with some friends late in February," he said, "and she was anxious to obtain her divorce and get away."

"Anxious enough to falsify dates?" Carter said.

"There is a good deal of that sort of thing being done," Joe O'Connor told him.

"What is Mrs. Cavendish's object in opening up this question, Mr. O'Connor?"

"Mrs. Cavendish knew nothing of it until I called upon her a few hours ago."

"And do you mean to tell me that you accidentally stumbled upon this question of the date of a divorce and followed it up out of sheer curiosity?"

"My brother really did the investigating; it was in a matter concerning another client," the attorney explained.

"In what possible way could the affair of another client ——" Carter was beginning, when Sandra interrupted.

"Carter, in a case of this sort, what do people do? Get a judge or somebody to make it legal?"

"Supposing it *is* illegal——" Carter answered, not moving his angry and resentful look from the lawyer.

"It wouldn't mean, would it, that your and Betty's divorce would have to be granted all over again?"

"Of course not!"

"Oh, I think it might," O'Connor said. "I don't know any other way around it. The decree certainly is void, and while no proceedings need be instituted against the complainant . . ."

Out of a storm of legal terms Alexandra emerged with a frightened, half-laughing, wholly nervous:

"But then, Carter, are we married?"

"Of course we're married, darling; don't be a fool. This sort of thing," Carter said, with annoyed vehemence, "is going on all the time—I'll get in touch with Gwin Jones tomorrow and have him straighten it all out in no time. And I wish, Sandy——" he added, with an eloquent glance and a faint jerk of his head toward the door.

"Oh, no, no; let me stay, Carter!" she begged. "I know so much about it now, please let me know it all!"

"I only didn't want you to be bothered with it, honey," he answered, touched by her manner and by the tears in her eyes. "There's nothing to worry about. Do I understand," he added, turning toward the lawyer, "that you have been retained by Mrs. Cavendish?"

"Mrs. Cavendish said that she was going to place it in the hands of her own attorneys, Dillon & Pry, and that Mr. Frank Dillon would probably come to see me about it at once," O'Connor said.

"I will have my own lawyer, Gwin Jones, get in touch with you," Carter added, with an air of terminating the interview. He got to his feet and stood with his arm about Sandra, his hostile stare fixed on the caller. The lawyer stood up, too. He lingered, his manner apologetic.

"I feel that you—you think this an intrusion, Mr. Cavendish," O'Connor said. "But, having made this discovery, it seemed—to my brother George and me—our duty——"

He paused, and Carter said unsympathetically, dryly:

"Well, you've done your duty."

"Thank you," the attorney said with a bow. "It was Mrs. Cavendish who felt that you ought to know immediately," he added.

"Thank you," Carter said, noncommittally, in his turn.

"Good-night," O'Connor said.

"Good-night, Mr. O'Connor," Alexandra echoed rather faintly.

Then they were alone, she and Carter in the big dim hall. They looked at each other, and Carter burst into a boyish laugh.

"Well, what d'you think of that lad?"

"Oh, Carter——" A pale reflection of his own smile was on her troubled face, but her voice was fearful. "What'll happen now? Do you suppose it's true?"

"No doubt it's true. That fellow Reubens was a crook; he figured in more than one case of this kind. But it's Betty that gets me," said Carter.

"Betty?"

"Sure. She's behind all this!"

"You don't think so?"

"I know so. Come on, we'll tell Pete!"

They were at the library door; they went in together. Peter, who had abandoned the golf-handicap problem, was stretched in a chair, reading, puffing absently at his pipe. Alexandra and Carter sat down, and Carter said:

"Listen here, Pete. Here's the darnedest break you ever heard!"

The brothers talked for a long time. Sandra, on the broad arm of Carter's chair, looked from one to the other, stared absently into the fire. She spoke not at all; she was very pale.

"Pete agrees with me that this is Betty's fine Italian hand," Carter said to her upstairs, an hour or two later.

"Betty?"

"Sure. She sicked this fellow O'Connor onto it, asked him to try to find some flaw in the decree."

"Why should she?"

"Oh, it's some game she's playing. I confess I don't understand it."

"Couldn't it be that he was simply telling the truth, and that he accidentally discovered the misrepresentation?"

"No! It's Betty, all right; she's trying to shake us down for some more dough."

"You don't suppose there'll be any publicity to it!"

"Oh, no. She's after the sole guardianship of Pats and the administration of the child's fortune!" Carter predicted. "Gwin Jones will wipe the floor up with her."

"But, Carter,"—Sandra was standing before him at the hearth, her hands on his shoulders—"it doesn't mean that we—it only means we have to—have to get a judge to do something? . . . It couldn't mean," she stammered, as he merely looked down at her with the favorite smile she so loved brightening his brown face—"it couldn't mean that you and I aren't married, could it?"

He locked his big arms about her, still smiling down.

"Well, what do you think?"

Alexandra caught her breath childishly.

"Well, I—I *know* better!"

"Do you think a date written on a scrap of paper is going to make me give you up?"

"Well, of course not."

"Well, of course not."

"It just means—legal formalities?"

"That's all."

"Nothing can ever separate us, Carter?"

"Not in this life."

"Suppose she—she refused to get another divorce?"

"How could she, you idiot?"

"Couldn't she?"

"If she did, I'd get it, and get it in record time!" Carter said.

Alexandra laughed nervously.

"But until you did, I'd—I'd have no business—here!" she reminded him, her eyes wide, the faint jerk of her head indicating the room about them.

"Oh, forget it!" Carter said, affectionate, impatient.

"If you want my profound conviction in this matter," he said later, sitting on a low chair, one socked foot on the floor, his knee crossed, his shoe in his hand, "it's that Betty thinks we're all making too much fuss about you!"

"She wouldn't deliberately——?"

"No, she wouldn't deliberately. She doesn't do anything deliberately. But she might see in it a fine chance to score against my mother and me, to say, 'Why, Carter and I are still technically man and wife, and if he wants to protect this marvelous new wife of his he'll have to come to terms.' . . . I figure it—" Carter said, removing the other pump and looking at it thoughtfully—"I figure that when she came back she was going to put it all over on us. She was completely Parisian, she was going to do wonders with Patsy's music, she had no use for us at all."

"She all but said that."

"But a few weeks of this life out here—it gets 'em," Carter resumed. "Hospitality, yachts, tennis on Christmas Day in the open air, everybody having a good time—Pete's place, Pebble Beach, golf courses—it's all darned easy. Toting Patsy over Europe to concerts and undertaking the

responsibility for a child who is leading that sort of life—
that isn't Betty's line, after all. It's just as if Betty, getting
back here, had realized that she herself is young and pretty,
and that this is her crowd. She's been squeezed out."

"Things mean such different things at different times and
in different places," Sandra agreed. Her tone was uneasy.

"The thing for you to do is forget it, darling."

"I suppose so."

"You'll probably never hear of it again; you never should
have heard of it in the first place. I'll turn it over to Jones,
and he'll see what has to be done."

"But it's a funny thing to happen, Carter," she said, when
she was brushing her hair.

"It *is* funny."

"If Betty's lawyer—if Judge Reubens hadn't died, could
they do anything to him?"

"Oh, no doubt. You heard what this cheap shyster O'Connor said. They could have him up for perjury and forgery
and God knows what. But nobody wants to start anything.
There must be an awful lot of that sort of thing going on.
It all goes to prove," Carter summarized it, in his cheerful
and confident voice—"it all goes to prove that marriages
are not made by names signed on dotted lines."

"Oh, Cart," she said, turning about in a cloud of soft
shining hair, "you never said anything truer than that!"

"I suppose in three divorces out of every five you could
find some flaw."

"A year ago," Sandra said, "just after I was so ill, Rose
Bray was talking one day, and she said something that didn't
seem to mean much then, but that I remembered—just tonight. She said, 'Sandra, Betty put something over when she
went abroad with me that time, right after her divorce. She
hadn't expected to get her decree until the next month, and
there was *something* about it—something——' You know

how dumb Rose is, Carter," Sandra digressed to remind him.

"It was a swell time to tell you that, when you'd been married a year!"

"I know. And I was so—so ill, and so sad about my baby," Sandra went on. "I didn't pay any attention."

"He said—O'Connor said—Betty was wise to the fact that Reubens did some juggling with the dates."

"Rose was disturbed about it because she thought I ought to protect my children's inheritance if I had any. She told me Betty might make trouble some day, and claim we weren't legally married."

Carter, tying the tassled cord of his dressing gown, came to take the chair opposite her own at the fire. The clock had sounded midnight, its hands moved into one, to two, but still they sat talking.

"I don't think I ever realized before what marriage really is, Sandy."

"I know."

"It seemed to me to-night when I saw that ass trying to annoy you, trying to scare my beautiful, gentle, adorable wife, trying to make you feel frightened and alarmed—it seemed to me I just had to mash his face in," Carter said simply.

Alexandra laughed, faintly and forlornly, and there was a silence.

"Carter, would it make a difference to you to know that Betty is thinking of marrying again?" Sandra began after a while.

"Betty?"

"I suspect so."

"Who?"

"I think——" This was to betray Patsy's confidence, but it might be important to them all now. "I think she intends to marry Schroeder, Patsy's violin teacher."

"Betty does?"
"I think so."
"Why, but he's married!"
"He's getting a divorce."
"Great God!" Carter ejaculated.
"He's given up his other pupils. He is to be Patsy's manager."
"The hell he is!" Carter ejaculated. He frowned, thinking. "A-h-h-h-h-h, now I begin to see her game!" he said. "She marries again, the alimony stops. That was part of the arrangement. No more two thousand a month! No wonder she wants to get her hands on Pat's legacy! God, she and that Austrian would hold high revel while it lasted! What a mess, Alex!"

"What a mess!" she repeated.

For a long while they were both silent, thinking.

CHAPTER TWENTY-SIX

IT WAS STRANGE, after this earthquake of emotion, to awaken the next morning to just the usual Monday morning pleasantness—sunshine, flower sweetness, and about her that ordered, hardly audible murmur that marks the smoothly running household. Below stairs there might have been the tinkle of the kitchen telephone, the closing of doors, the murmur of servants' voices. But up in her high, airy bedroom all these blended into the deep undertone that emphasized her sense of leisure, of comfort that was peace.

After a few minutes, however, recollection came. It brought with it a strange sense of unreality, an uneasy fear that trembled beneath the routine even of this ordinary quiet home morning; Katie bringing up her breakfast, her newspaper, her letters, the messages that Rose and Helen always had some reason to send her, the planning of meals, the study of the week's social calendar.

She went into town, lunched with Carter's mother, sat staring vaguely before her, across the linen and glass of the table, thinking, thinking.

The unreal day slipped by, the next few days went by. On Thursday afternoon the older Mrs. Cavendish, with Patsy, came down to the Burlingame house. Patsy was in frantic spirits, and whirled about the place like a small girl gone suddenly crazy.

"Aunt Sandra! We're not going away Sunday!"

"Hello, my darling." Sandra's trembling fingers were busy

with the buttons of the blue coat. "You mean you and Mother aren't leaving for New York?"

She was shaking; her hands were cold, here in the pleasant familiar upstairs sitting room with the peaceful afternoon sunlight streaming across it.

"Nope, we aren't going for a while yet."

"How did that happen, Pats?"

"Oh, I guess Dad 'ranged it," Patsy answered carelessly. "Can I—may I telephone Jean? Could Jean come to dinner?"

"If her mother will let her."

"My other grandma came up from Pasadena yesterday," announced Patsy.

"Your grandma Finchley?"

"Yes, and she and Mother talked, and Grandma cried. I guess she's mad at Mother. And then this morning Dad telephoned Mother," Patsy confided artlessly. "So when Mother said it was my regular night with Gran, and she would send me over for lunch, and Grandma said she hadn't seen me for a month, and Mother began to cry again and said, 'Good heavens, Mother, with Carter coming out here, I don't want her around.'"

"Daddy coming out?"

"He was coming out to talk."

"I think you'd better put your play shoes on, Pats, if Jean is coming over.

"So Dad *did* fix it, didn't he?"

"It looks like it."

"Alexandra," her mother-in-law said faintly, as the child ran off toward her own room, "I am convinced that something terrible has happened."

"Something terrible?"

"I am convinced of it. I am sick at heart!" Mrs. Cavendish said, collapsed in a chair, making faint, desperate gestures with her helpless, beautiful white hands.

"What sort of thing, for example?"

"My dear, Mrs. Rogers came to see me this afternoon."

"Oh, did she?"

"Sandra, have you heard anything of this?"

Alexandra, with her own slow smile, finished the folding of Patsy's small discarded garments, laid them on a chair-back, and came across to a low hassock that was at the other woman's knee. She sat down, took Mrs. Cavendish's hands in her own.

"You mean about Carter's divorce?"

"Oh, don't!" Mrs. Cavendish breathed, leaning back in her chair, closing her eyes. "Geneva Rogers says that Mrs. Finchley told her there was some question about it!" she whispered.

"Well, if there were, it'd only be a technicality."

"You do know about it, then, dear?"

"Carter and I learned about it on Sunday."

"Sandra," whispered her mother-in-law, clutching Sandra's wrist, "he'll not give you up!"

"He'll not have to give me up."

"She's after Patsy's money, that's what she is! She wants to get control of the child's inheritance!" Mrs. Cavendish said fiercely. "That's all she wants! She'll marry again and that child will never get a cent of it."

"If she *did,* Mrs. Cavendish, Patsy could ask for an accounting when she comes of age."

"Oh, Alexandra, don't talk nonsense! What good would an accounting do after it was all gone? No," the older woman said, rocking desperately, "she's dug up this thing just to annoy Carter! My boy, my darling—he never should have married her, I knew it! I cried at the wedding; anyone can tell you that. Alexandra, you must stand by him," she pleaded urgently, her loosened clutch redoubling. "You must stand by him. You're his whole world, you're everything in the world to him. This is all just nonsense—lawyer's talk."

"Darling, I will!" Sandra promised, pitifully. But even now her irrepressible slow smile broke out.

"I am going to tell him to do anything—anything!" Mrs. Cavendish said feverishly. "I am going to say, 'Settle with her, agree to anything!'"

"Ah, you're very generous," Sandra said, touched. She stooped and laid a quick impulsive kiss on the other woman's hand, locked on her own.

"I love you," Mrs. Cavendish faltered, tears in her eyes.

"I hope you do," Sandra responded simply. "We'll come out of this all right," she predicted.

"Sandra, you're so marvelous!" her husband's mother said in gratitude and relief. "But it makes me so uneasy——" she added. "Betty's mother knows about it, Mrs. Rogers knows about it. It would be too horrible if the newspapers got hold of it."

"Oh, what if they did?" Sandra asked dreamily, indifferently, her golden brown eyes fixed on space, their dark lashes half furled. "That wouldn't make me any less Carter's wife, really."

"Why do such things have to happen!" the older woman lamented. "It was like a blow to me. It seemed to shake the earth under my feet."

"All families have something like this sooner or later. Betty," Sandra said, "seems to have a gift for it."

When her mother-in-law had lamented herself away to her own room, Sandra went to Patsy's and hung up the child's discarded garments and unpacked the little suitcase. Patsy's room was always kept ready for her, with the big white dog curled on the bed, his beady eyes fixed in eternal expectation on the door, and the doll's house—the doll's house with all its tiny lamps and mats and telephones, and the little yellow fish on the blue plates—was always closed, dusted, in order.

Looking down through the opened window, Sandra could see the side garden, where sprinklers were sending long fans of diamonds through the sunset air, and the great low branches of the oaks were dripping. Beyond were the meadow and the old stables; Patsy and Jean were riding, with shouts of laughter, thunder of hoofs, and much flying of muddy clods from the soft wet earth.

A maid touched Sandra's elbow.

"Mr. Peter Cavendish is here, Mrs. Cavendish."

"Oh. Did he want to see me?"

"If you don't mind, Mrs. Cavendish."

Sandra found him in her own upstairs sitting room, standing by the window. He turned as she came in and caught at her hands; his good, round face was filled with distress and sympathy.

"Sandra!" he said, anxiously, studying her.

"Hello, Pete. I thought you were going up to the Desmonds'."

"I couldn't go. Sandra," Pete pursued, "this is a—a hell of a note!"

"Isn't it!" she agreed, standing beside him at the window now, looking down with him at the drive.

"It's broken Cart up completely."

"I know it has. But I tell him—I've just been telling your mother, Pete—that it hasn't any real significance. It only means a little legal fussing, that's all."

"You're quite amazing, you know," Peter told her in simple admiration. "Cart said you were being splendid about it."

"I can't see that there's any other way to be," Alexandra protested.

"I know. But he said you were wonderful. Betty——"

Peter began and stopped. "We went up this morning to see Betty," he digressed.

"You went with Carter?"

"And Gwin Jones. Betty had her lawyer, a man from Dillon & Pry, there too, and her mother. She——" Peter said bitterly—"she's enjoying herself hugely."

"I suppose so."

"All upset, you know; she said she had hoped that all that old 'agony'—that's what she called it—had gone out of her life, and now to have it all brought up again ... Why somebody didn't go over and take her by the back of the neck!" Peter added darkly. Alexandra laughed.

"Well, you're very fine about it," he went on. "Cart said you were. You won't throw the old boy down?"

"Throw him down?"

"That's what's worrying him," the brother explained.

"You mean,"—Alexandra sent a keen glance at her companion, looked down at the drive again—"you mean that Betty may delay things?"

"Well, she likes the sense of power; we all saw that," he admitted unwillingly. "Jones, Cart, and I went up to the club afterward and we talked about it. Betty is being temperamental; she never was so shocked in her life—that kind of thing."

"Then it isn't just a question of a Nevada court confirming the decree?"

"I'm afraid not. The whole thing may have to be gone through with again. Gwin's going up to Reno this afternoon; he'll find out. There seem to have been a good many cases of the sort."

"And it shocked poor Betty?"

"Oh, she's putting on a great show about it. Gwin swears he's sure she started the whole thing."

"Purposely?"

"He says it sounds darned fishy to him, this lawyer's stumbling on incorrectly given dates in one case while working on another. He thinks that coming back here now and finding out that everyone was getting on very nicely without her—well, made her mad," Peter concluded with his characteristic ineloquence.

"He believes Betty started it?"

"No question about it."

"Well, that doesn't alter the fact, Peter, that we have terrapin for dinner," Alexandra said abruptly after a pause.

"By gosh, you *are* wonderful!" Peter repeated.

Alexandra laughed again. But she knew it was true. She knew that she was wonderful, gloried in it. Not Betty herself had a more dramatic part to play; not Betty could rise to it more completely.

Quite suddenly she was alive again, gloriously alive, as she had been in those long-ago days when she and Carter had lunched together, when he had given her her blue bag; as she had been in those strange, sweet, cold days of wet leaves and wood smoke on the ranch, taking care of her mother. She had something real to do, to endure, to face again.

Lifted on wings, she could presently begin her dressing for dinner, she could select a gown Carter especially loved. It was a dark blue velvet, fitting closely her tall figure. She fastened the single line of pearls that had been her wedding present from Carter about her round firm throat and put the long pearl drops in her ears. She went out to meet him in the hall when he reached home, tired and depressed, and he stopped on the last stair and put his arms wearily about her and sank his face into the sweetness and softness of her arms and breast.

"God, you are lovely!"

"Tired, sweetheart?"

"Ah, Sandy, I'm so tired!"

"My poor old boy!" she murmured.

"Oh, I don't mind, I don't mind!" he said. "As long as you love me, as long as you're here when I get home!"

She went with him to their room and saw him start toward a hurried change for dinner. Then, always with that new thrilling sense of being alive, being needed, strong upon her, Alexandra descended the stairway and joined Peter and her mother-in-law and Patsy in the library.

"Sandra, you look lovely," Peter said.

"You do look lovely," his mother confirmed it. "But I feel—well, I've just been feeling too terribly to care whether I dressed or not!" she added. "I just feel—dazed."

"No use feeling that way," Sandra remonstrated serenely.

Patsy climbed into her lap, and she kissed the top of the child's head thoughtfully, staring into the fire.

"It's kind of knocked Mother for a loop," Peter explained.

"A shock . . . " Sandra conceded dreamily. "Carter feels it," she said.

"Terribly!" his mother agreed, with a warning glance at the indifferent Patsy, who was dividing, folding, doubling, measuring Sandra's long fine nervous fingers in the eternal fashion of childhood.

"We just have to see it through," Alexandra reminded them.

"That's what I say. Can't last long," Peter added philosophically.

"But it makes me so nervous!" the older woman lamented.

Carter came down; they all went out to dinner. Alexandra and Patsy did most of the talking, although she saw that both Peter and Carter were doing their best. Still the odd sense of being buoyed, being needed, being strangely happy, held her on wings.

After dinner the women went back into the sitting room,

and Carter and Peter went upstairs for a telephone conversation with Reno. They had just come down again at half-past eight, and Patsy had gone upstairs to bed, when there was a caller. Suddenly, unannounced, Betty burst into the room.

Peter was in a big leather chair near the fire, his mother half sitting, half lying on a divan; Carter, in another big chair, opposite his brother, and Alexandra, in her favorite place on a hassock beside Carter's chair, one arm across his knee, his hand upon her shoulder.

Betty was among them before anyone was even aware that the door had been opened. Behind her was the outraged and apologetic face of the maid.

"Please!" Betty said quickly. "Please sit down again, Peter; please sit down, Carter. Please—all of you——

"I *had* to see you," she added, establishing herself in the high-backed chair that completed the circle. "I *had* to see you. After we talked this morning, Carter——

"I rushed right past the maid," she added, as nobody spoke. "You'll have to forgive me. I *had* to see you."

Peter sat down again, with a puzzled glance at his mother. Carter, who had started to rise, sank back, scowling. Alexandra laid her arm across his knee again; she was watching Betty.

In the silence Carter's mother faltered suddenly, "We all feel terribly about this, Betty!"

Betty dropped her head to one side, spoke with that breathlessly earnest urgency that had marked her manner from the first.

"Well, you can imagine how *I* feel! I've had to postpone our leaving, cancel our passage and everything! It's been—it's been simply frightful!" Betty said, appealing for sympathy with a glance about the circle.

"Reggy Pry sent me to that awful old Judge Reubens,

years ago," she went on as nobody spoke. "Of course, I never dreamed he would do anything like this!"

"Well, he certainly made trouble enough," Peter observed briefly. The words sounded inadequate: they all laughed nervously.

"I don't know what you all think, my coming down like this!" Betty apologized. "But there are a lot of things, it occurred to me, that we didn't get round to discussing this morning, when you and Cart came to see me. I happened to be coming down to-night to stay with Janet Fargo, so I just asked her to send me over here for five minutes."

"Okay," Carter said gruffly, displeased and uneasy. "What's on your mind?"

"Well, I just want to tell you all that I really want to coöperate in anything you want to do to clear this silly situation up. I know it seems to have been my fault that there was a mistake, and I know—of course—" she glanced toward Sandra—"I realize the difficult position it puts—Mrs. Cavendish into," she finished.

Sandra did not change her position or expression in the faintest degree. Carter tightened the hand that held her shoulder, and Betty saw it.

"I've been talking to Frank Dillon all afternoon," she began again. "He advises me—we all feel, Mama and I, that we're just—well," Betty spread her hands, "we're all in this pickle together, and we have to take the sensible way out, whatever it is."

To Alexandra it was like a dream. This was her own familiar sitting room; the books, the flowers, the fire were all as usual. That was Pete in his favorite chair, that was Carter's mother among the pillows, looking just as she always looked, a pretty, faded woman with beautifully dressed graying hair. There was Patsy's book, face down on the rug; this was Carter next her, with his brown hands gripping her own. But what was Betty doing in the picture?

"You know me, Mrs. Cavendish," Betty said, speaking to Carter's mother. "You know that if I can do anything for anyone I'm just fool enough always to want to do it!"

"I know I used to be very fond of you——" the older woman faltered, inconsequentially, with filling eyes. Alexandra saw she was in deadly fear of Betty.

"I'm like that, you know that, Carter!" Betty went on, ready to cry, herself. "I—I've got to have everyone friends, everyone happy. After we all talked this morning," she continued ingeniously, "I began to think things over and I just had to tell you!—You know how it is, Peter, you get an idea and it won't let you rest——"

"I know," Peter said in the pause, clearing his throat.

"At first," Betty confided to the company at large, "I felt sort of mad; I'll admit it. I felt you all were trying to put something over on me. I didn't see what you were after. Frank Dillon just advised me to sit tight. He told me I had all the cards in my hands and just to sit tight. Well, I thought that was the wisest thing to do, but I see now—I guess now it wasn't. I think the best thing for me to do is just to—just to—get out. And that's what I'm going to do!"

Peter spoke, moderately: "You didn't seem willing to do that this morning, Betty."

"No, you're quite right, I wasn't!" she agreed quickly, visibly pleased to have elicited an answer at last. "I wasn't! But I've talked it over with Mama since, and Frank Dillon. I've thought it all over, Carter, and I'm going back to France and apply there for a new divorce!"

In the pause, as she stopped speaking, there could be sensed in the room the surprise of her hearers.

"Well, that's very white of you, Betty," Carter said thickly.

"Oh, no; I don't think it's particularly 'white,'" she

answered with a nervous shrug; "perhaps I'm fonder of you than you think, Cart. And then,"—this was to his mother—"then, of course, I feel as if I were mainly responsible for the whole mix-up!"

"It's just one of those things," the older Mrs. Cavendish said vaguely, almost hysterical relief in her tone. "I'm sure none of us—I'm sure we can't blame——"

Her voice trailed into silence.

"Frank Dillon will get in touch with you to-morrow morning, Carter," Betty said; "he'll tell you I'm more than willing to go ahead with the arrangements for a new divorce, whatever it may be. You've always," Betty told him winningly—"you've always been more than generous to me, Cart, and if I can be a little generous in return, why, I'm glad to be."

"It clears everything up for us, of course," he said simply.

Betty looked at Alexandra.

"And you two will be remarried just as soon as you can?" she stated rather than asked.

"I knew," Mrs. Cavendish, the elder, said in a prayerful thinkful voice—"I knew it could all be settled this way! Thank God, thank God!"

"You know, Carter," Betty remembered to add suddenly, "I never had anything to do with starting this. It must have been the sheerest accident that this lawyer—what was his name? O'Connor, was that it?—that he or his brother tumbled on the thing."

"It doesn't seem possible," Carter observed, frowning and surprised. "I don't understand it. Not that it matters."

"You *think* I did it," Betty said, her bright look traveling from face to face. "But I didn't. Honestly! I haven't the faintest idea how they ever found it."

A new voice added itself suddenly to the talk.

"But you knew, Mrs. Cavendish," Alexandra asked—"you knew that there was a flaw in that decree, didn't you?"

Betty, up to this point all generous good nature, turned to her with a perceptible narrowing of eyes, a chilling of voice and manner.

"How do you mean 'a flaw'?"

"Well, that there was some tampering with the dates. Mrs. Bray gave me a hint of it almost a year ago."

"Rose Bray?" Betty exclaimed in an incredulous tone.

"Yes, I know," Sandra said, her voice quite its usual self, but the hand that gripped Carter's cold and tense—"I know Rose talks too much," she conceded, "but Rose knew something—of something. And General Brooks—that was what made me think about it——"

"I'll tell you frankly what Rose knew—or *thought* she knew," Betty, displeased and suspicious, began haughtily. "This dreadful person, Judge Reubens, whom Reggy Pry sent me to, told me while I was in Reno that if I really was anxious to get away before the end of February—and I was —he could fix it up so I could get my divorce a couple of weeks earlier. I don't know how he did it. He told me over and over again it'd be all right. I think he said something to me like, 'You stayed with friends in Reno for a fortnight before you registered at the Samarkand, didn't you?' and I could see he wanted me to say 'yes,' so I did. He told me that was all he wanted to know, and then he had the case set for trial, and my decree was granted on the twenty-first. What Rose Bray wants to go babbing around about it for I don't know."

"She wasn't babbing; she just told me." Sandra's voice fell into silence; there was a brief pause. She sat motionless at Carter's knee, a tall, deep-breasted woman with fair hair catching gold lights from the fire, and violet draperies spreading about her. Her fine long nervous hands lay over Carter's; their fingers were interlocked. Her gold-brown eyes were wide-open, looking straight at Betty.

"Carter and I both feel that—since the discrepancy in the dates was there—it is just as well we all knew of it," she said.

"Well—I suppose so," Betty agreed, made a little uneasy by her manner.

Carter's eyes were on Alexandra.

"We waited for each other once, dear. We can wait for each other again," he said. "It's only a question of technicalities."

Sandra's beautiful eyes had something sad in them, something new in their earnest look as she answered:

"Oh, yes, Carter, yes! We can wait."

"Of course I couldn't be expected to go up to Reno again," Betty said; "that would be too unthinkable. I'll get the new decree in Paris. Frank Dillon says he'll see that the first one is set aside and as soon as I get to Paris I'll start new proceedings. I think Patsy, Mother, and I will leave immediately."

She paused; the echoes of the defiant, metallic voice died on the air. Betty looked challengingly from one face to another.

Sandra had not moved; her arm was lying on Carter's knee, her fingers in his.

"You're taking Patsy?" she asked. The words sounded with an odd significance through the quiet room; or perhaps it was Betty's instant change of manner, change of color that gave them that significance.

"Taking Patsy! May I ask why not?" Betty demanded, with a flicker of nervous laughter.

"I think you'll see there *are* reasons," Alexandra said hesitatingly, after a second. She glanced at Carter. "Until you *get* that new divorce——" she submitted.

And suddenly the hand on Carter's was trembling.

"——Until you get that new divorce, isn't Patsy as much

Carter's as yours?" she asked. "You have to settle everything all over again, about Patsy, don't you?"

Betty was looking at her steadily; both women were pale.

"Isn't that exactly," Betty demanded—"isn't that exactly what I just said I wanted to do? You don't think I want Carter back!"

"No, I don't think you want Carter back," Sandra agreed, swallowing with a dry throat. She seemed frightened by the other's manner in spite of herself.

"Then I don't think I understand you," Betty said scornfully, with a light laugh. But she was shaking, too.

"We—Peter, and Carter, and I—we won't give you Patsy again," Sandra said simply.

There was a pause. Carter's mother made a whimpering sound.

"I don't know what you're talking about," Betty said sharply, then.

Sandra got to her feet; stood on the hearth, looking down at Betty. No one else stirred.

"If your divorce wasn't a divorce," Sandra said simply, "then Patsy still belongs to Carter."

Betty was breathing a little hard; there were spots of color in her face. She did not move her eyes from Sandra.

"Oh, that's it, is it?" she asked.

"You—you trapped me once, you see," Sandra said. "Now I've trapped you."

The other woman looked around the circle, looked back.

"Oh, no, you haven't!" she said lightly. She stopped, thinking. A second later she added, "How do you mean you've trapped me? What's to prevent my getting this divorce, as I did the other?"

Carter was standing beside Sandra now; she looked up obliquely into his eyes, felt his arm about her.

"He won't give up Patsy again," she said.

"He won't," Betty predicted confidently, "have anything to do with it."

Sandra spoke only to Carter.

"We forgot her, three years ago," she said. "But we mustn't forget her again."

"Now listen," Betty said, impatiently and scornfully. But anyone who knew Betty knew from her tone that she was frightened. "Carter and Peter came to me to-day to discuss this divorce—I agreed to it. They——" She looked at them. "You can't go back on that!" she said.

"But Carter gets Patsy," Sandra persisted.

"That's funny!" Betty exclaimed, after a moment of staring bewilderment. But her laugh was not amused.

"You have a right to Patsy, now," Alexandra told her husband. She had half-turned to face him; her fine nervous fingers were resting on the lapels of his coat. "You see, Cart?" she asked.

"I'm afraid I don't, dear," he answered, looking down at her with infinite tenderness.

"Well, you see," she explained, with a little gesture—"you see, you're—you're not divorced."

"That's only a technicality, Alex."

"But it's enough of a technicality to"—another vague little opening gesture of her hands, another anxious smile from the eyes that did not move from his—"to save Patsy," she finished.

A sudden light came into Carter's eyes.

"We said there was a way out," Sandra reminded him. "This is the way out."

"But you don't know what you're saying, dear," Carter reasoned, affectionately, resolutely patient. "You don't realize what all this means."

"You don't seem to realize," Betty's hard polished voice broke in triumphantly, "exactly where all this puts *you!*"

"Oh, yes, I do!" Sandra answered her indifferently. She brought her eyes to Carter again. "That doesn't matter, does it?" she asked him.

The trembling was over; there was no sign of tears now in her quiet voice, her quiet, almost dreamy manner.

"Nothing matters—except that I won't give you up," Carter said, in a low tone, speaking as if they two were alone in the room.

"Not for long," she said. Standing close to Carter, almost against his shoulder, she turned again to Betty. "You trapped me," she said again. "Now it's—it's *you* who can't get out."

"Watch me get out!" Betty countered, with a scornful laugh.

"But not with Patsy," Sandra said.

"Try to stop me!" Betty persisted, boldly.

"I went to Betty last week," Sandra told the circle at large, with the same anxious, hesitant manner she had shown all through the talk. "I asked her if she would make a different arrangement for Patsy—would let her be with Carter part of the time—if I got out."

"You fool," Carter said, with a smiling glance into her eyes.

"I would have done even that," Sandra said.

There was a pause.

"But Betty—wouldn't," she added.

"And then I remembered," Sandra presently resumed, in a dead silence, "that Rose had told me once that Betty—Betty knew that something had been wrong—or fixed, or juggled somehow, in the date of the divorce. . . . It came to me like a flash that perhaps that was the way out."

"You!" Carter whispered sharply. "What have you had to do with it!"

"I went to see Joe O'Connor, Carter. I've known him all

my life. I had been talking to him that day we met downtown—remember? I told him."

"Why, what are you talking about, my darling?" Carter asked, looking down at her in stupefaction.

"Betty had told me, Cart—you never did, you know, and your mother never did. But Betty had told me that the reason you gave her Patsy, gave her everything she asked for, three years ago was because of me! So I—I had to——"

She made the ineffectual gesture with spread hands again; looked at him with a child's anxious expectancy of approval.

"Alex, let me get this straight, dear. Do you really mean to say you had known Joe O'Connor before that night when he walked into this room—before that day downtown when you——"

"I went to school with Joe O'Connor."

"And you—told him—— I don't see it yet."

"I told him that Mrs. Bray had told me—months ago, when I wasn't particularly interested—that Mrs. Cavendish's lawyer—the old man named Reubens—had hurried up her divorce for her, dated it two weeks before the six months were up. And then General Brooks told me that loads of divorces weren't legal."

"You—started all this!"

"I started it."

"Which I simply don't believe," Betty said, lightly.

No one seemed to have heard her. Peter could be heard drawing a long, whistling breath.

"I talked to Rose yesterday," Sandra went on, speaking only to Carter. "I told her the whole story."

"Burlingame will enjoy it very much," Betty put in. But again she was completely ignored, Carter having eyes only for Sandra as he said gently:

"But let me get this straight, dear. Let me understand. Why did you do all this—get hold of O'Connor, everything?"

"For Pats," Sandra answered simply.

"Who happens to be my child!" Betty interpolated, desperate to be heard.

"Rose remembered the luncheon—there were lots of them at it," Sandra resumed, with a dispassionate side glance at Betty. "Mab was there, and Elinor. Rose said she would swear to it—that Betty had said she wanted to sail in February, and that old Judge Reubens had been a dear, and said he would fix it.

"Joe and I have talked about it—oh, for days. In fact, Carter," Sandra told him, simply, "Joe explained all this to me. You could get the divorce, now. You could claim extreme cruelty, and forgery—and something called connivance—I think that's it."

She paused, once again looking timidly at Carter for confirmation, for approval.

"People can go to prison for those, Carter!" she said, innocently.

Betty was very white. All their eyes moved toward her, but she did not speak. She was breathing hard; her glance moved quickly, haughtily, about the circle.

"Not," Sandra said in the silence—"not that it would go that far."

"Thank you!" Betty exclaimed, with angry irony.

"You never told me that you gave up Patsy for me, Carter," Sandra said. "I—I give her back to you now. Joe O'Connor says you can make your own terms now."

"And meanwhile—what are *you?*" Betty demanded, in a tone of cold triumph.

It was the question that had been in all their minds during the amazing days since the validity of Betty's divorce had first been questioned. But no one had dared to voice it until now.

Sandra, answering it, answered only Carter. Her hands were on his shoulders, her face, glowing with devotion and confidence, and even with a sort of loving amusement, was raised to his own; dark, and grave, and trembling a little, he bent above her. He had seen her glorious before, he thought, but he had never seen her as she was now.

"Do we care?" she demanded, and there was almost a trace of laughter in her tone.

Carter could not speak. His arms were loosely locked about her, his eyes steadily fixed on hers.

"We can wait, can't we, Carter?" Sandra added.

"Forever!" he answered, clearing his throat.

"At first I thought I couldn't do this," she said, her smile suddenly dazzling through tears, her bravado suddenly shaken. "But now—now, you see——"

"Don't," he said simply.

"I won't."

"There's needn't be any fight; no one need know. But you'll keep Patsy—some of the time, anyway, Carter. That's what matters. And Cart, nothing else matters. Let her get her divorce where she will—but hold onto Patsy. Stand by Patsy now. Send her down to Pete's, let her run around at the ranch. Take care of her. And some day tell her that Aunt Sandra did this for her. . . .

"I'm going away—you see I must go away?" she whispered, her eyes only for him, his arms about her. "I'll go away until—this time—you're legally and rightfully free. But you'll come for me, after a while, and we'll smile at all this. I'm s-s-smiling now. I'm happy, Carter! I've never been able to do anything for you or your mother or Pete, dear, and you've done so much for me! I'm your wife—

every bit of me, forever and forever. But Patsy has the right of way now! I'll come back some day."

She was trying to laugh through tears. She took her hands away and turned her wet face unashamed toward them all.

"Pete, you have a handkerchief? Pete, will you come out with me into the hall? I have to speak to you——" she faltered.

Peter, wiping his eyes, was on his feet. They went out of the room together, and the door closed behind them. Carter had taken his chair again; both his hands were pressed tightly over his eyes. Mrs. Cavendish was crying. Betty, watching the scene with hard bright eyes, burst into a loud laugh.

CHAPTER TWENTY-SEVEN

ONE WEEK LATER Patsy Cavendish and her favorite grandmother came to call on Alexandra.

They found her in big rooms at that same hilltop hotel to which Cavendish had brought her as a bride more than three years before. But this time Sandra did not have the green balconies and the wide-spreading bay view; she was on the city side of the hotel now, with the pleasant wide street, and the brown-stone clubhouse opposite, just below her windows.

There were flowers about the rooms, and one leather-framed portrait of Carter on Sandra's desk. But otherwise there were small signs of her occupancy; her wardrobe trunk, packed and locked, was standing by the door, and on a table in her bedroom lay her pigskin suitcase and a smaller case, packed also, but left open for last-minute additions.

Sandra was in dark blue; her suit was severely plain, her small hat snug and plain, but the usual immaculate frills softened the creamy blouse, and the usual gardenias, fragrant and waxy, were waiting to be pinned on the soft fur collar of her dark blue coat. The May afternoon was cold and foggy out of doors, but within there were warmth and fragrance and light.

Patsy sprang into her arms, and Sandra looked down lovingly at the glowing little face. Carter's mother had been crying, and seemed frailer and more nervous than ever; a fresh welling of tears interrupted the few faltering words she attempted to say when Alexandra kissed her, and she subsided into a chair, fumbling blindly for her handkerchief.

"Aunt Sandra," Patsy demanded from her favorite position in Sandra's lap, and in the reproachful drawl of the injured child, "w'y are you going to New York?"

"I have to go, darling."

"But now, when I'm staying here, and I'm going to be down with Gran at the ranch?"

"It does seem silly. But I'll tell you, Pats—I'll write you every single week. I'll write you every Saturday night. . . . Saturday night," Sandra repeated, in a thick, low voice she tried to hold steady, while her hands busied themselves with the shoulder fastenings of Patsy's little velvet dress, "will be my bad time, do you see? I'll think then of all of you down at the ranch, and I'll sit down and write to you."

"But I don't want just letters, Aunt Sandra," Patsy said, with all of a mourning dove's soft rich sorrow in her voice, as she rubbed her cheek gently up and down against Sandra's cheek. "I want—joo—to come back!"

"I'm coming back." Alexandra suddenly took a bracing tone. "Do you know who lives in this hotel, Pats?" she asked, animatedly.

"No!" Patsy's eyes were all expectation.

"Remember little Virginia Duncan who was at Jean's that day?"

"Does she?"

"Yes, she does. And on such a horrid afternoon she might be home, doing her homework. So why not telephone the office and find out where her room is, and ask her to come down and have tea with us? And then while Gran and I are having our tea, you and Virginia . . ."

Patsy, enchanted, fell in with this idea, and the two women could take neighboring chairs and talk together.

while tea was brought, and while the two little girls did much important racing about through the corridors of the hotel.

"Carter's heart is broken," Mrs. Cavendish presently observed, touching her eyes with her handkerchief.

To this Alexandra made no answer. She merely said:

"Carter's coming to dinner with me to-night, and will take me to the train."

"I know."

"Pete is going to come in at about six."

"Pete said he would take Patsy and me home."

"She's happy," Alexandra commented, watching her.

"She's a different child. Everyone sees it. Of course," the grandmother analyzed it, brightening suddenly, wiping her eyes, "she's not an ordinary child, Pats. She's a genius. I don't think any of us realized, unless you did, Sandra, how deep the thing went with her. When Carter told her she was to stay with him, she all but went into hysterics. She cried and clung to him—it was pathetic. He said to her—this is ridiculous, dear," Mrs. Cavendish interrupted herself with trembling lips, beginning to cry again, "but one simply can't help it! I must not cry, I promised myself I wouldn't—especially as you are being so wonderful. But Carter said, 'Well, Pats, heard the news?' She got up from the floor—she had been reading one of her story books—and she said, 'No; what, Daddy?'

"He said, 'Why, you're not going back to Europe at all, Baby; you're going to spend this whole summer, and every summer, down at the ranch, riding your pony, and having Jean and Doris with you. You're not going to see old Schroeder ever again!'

"Sandra, she turned perfectly white—you never saw a child get so white—and she came over to him and said in —well, really, it was a terrible tone for a child to use; it was like a threat, it was—well, terrible—she said, 'Don't say that unless it's true! Don't say that, Dad, unless it's true! Don't say it and then have Mummy tell me that I have to go back after all!'

"Carter put his arm about her and he said, 'No, Baby, this time it's true.' He said, 'Why, Pats, did you dislike him so?' and she said, 'I hated him, I hated him!'"

"Schroeder," Alexandra said thickly, as the other woman stopped to wipe her eyes.

"She said," Mrs. Cavendish continued, "'He was mean to me, Daddy! He hit my fingers with his bow!'"

"I thought so," Sandra said slowly, a little color coming into her pale face.

"I'd asked her in the very beginning, you know, if this violin teacher was kind to her," the grandmother said, "but she told me yesterday that Mummy had forbidden her to tell anyone that Schroeder wasn't always kind.

"She clung to Carter, sobbing and laughing—it was really——" Mrs. Cavendish quite lost control of her voice again, and, smiling gallantly, was once again weeping.

Alexandra, with a trembling hand, poured tea. Seated in the high-backed chair at the tea table, her face was on a level with Patsy's when Patsy and Virginia came up for their tea. She watched the little girl closely as she tinted the hot cream and water and sugar with orange pekoe, and cut the cinnamon toast into fine strips to make the children's feast "the way you do—like a doll's party," as Patsy said.

Sandra did not speak except to say the usual, "Be careful, sweet, don't spill it," but her dark eyes, ringed with darker circles to-day, were fixed steadily on the child, as if she were trying to stamp upon her heart every detail of the animated, happy little face.

"When she thanked Carter," Mrs. Cavendish could presently resume, "she said, 'Ah, Daddy, I knew you could do it!' and he said, 'No, dear, it's Aunt Sandra who managed this.' "

She stopped, overcome, and Alexandra said briefly, "Ah, please!" and was also still.

"Sandra, what are you going to do now?" the older woman presently asked.

"What am I going to do now?" Alexandra put down her cup. "Well, I shall be in New York for a week with Helen. Then Harry gets back and she'll come to California with him, and I think I'll go to Boston and make arrangements somewhere near Harvard for some work—work in two very frivolous lines," she interrupted herself to explain smilingly. "Bridge and French. And then I am going to get some regular settlement work to do with children. Ladies in my position always do that in the third act, don't they?" she asked, with another smile.

"You're marvelous," was all that the other woman could find to say.

"And so I shall keep very busy," Alexandra said, "and the time will go by."

"It seems so unnecessarily hard on you," Mrs. Cavendish said.

"It will be hard on Carter, too, I think."

"Hard on all of us."

"There's Patsy, however; she won't have to go back to Paris and practise scales five hours a day."

"Well, of course," the older woman agreed. "I'm only thinking," she went on after a moment, "how lonely you'll be back there!"

"No, I'll not be lonely." Sandra swallowed, managed a smile. "I shan't dare let myself be lonely. I'll keep busy, thinking all the time of the day Carter comes to get me."

There was a pause.

"Sandra, what do you think Betty'll do now?"

"Why, what can she do but what we've asked her? Carter's been as generous as I knew he would. The divorce in Reno will be declared invalid, and Betty and her mother, as I understand it, sail for Paris on the *Aquitania* next Saturday. She'll start proceedings for a new divorce as soon as she's there. . . . At least," Sandra said, after a moment's thought, "I suppose she will. She might not, of course."

"Suppose she does nothing? Suppose she doesn't apply for a divorce?"

"Why, then her alimony stops. Carter's agreed to continue it, in case of divorce, but otherwise, he might not. It was generous of him; but it was clever, too. She can count on her two thousand a month, unless of course she remarries. It seems to me—it *seems* to me—she has no alternative. She'll probably set about freeing Carter at once. It may take a year—it may take longer. I don't know about those French courts."

"Well, it's all too much for me," Mrs. Cavendish complained pathetically. "I'm only afraid—I'm only afraid that it's going to be too hard on you, dear. It's going to be hardest on you!"

Peter came in, looking solemn and troubled.

"I knew you'd be smothered in flowers. I got you some of those candied fruits you liked."

"I shall have to take the next compartment for the overflow! Rose said she was sending me some books, and the Fultons said they had sent a basket of fruit."

"Let's see—you're in Chicago Sunday?"

"Only for an hour. Just comfortable time to make the change."

"Then New York."

"Then New York, and then—I was telling your mother—Boston probably."

"I'll run up and see you. I have to go East on business this summer. I may have to go again in the fall," Peter said.

"Ah, if you only will!"

"You won't go over to England and run out on us?"

"No. I'm going to wait—for England. You're sure you're not going to have any tea, Peter?"

"Nothing. It's after half-past six."

"Is it so late?" she asked, her heart sinking. Her last day—its last few hours—were flying away.

"After all, you've cousins in England."

"No," Alexandra said, going back to his question, "I'll not go to England until Carter takes me."

The hall door opened quietly; Carter came in unannounced. He was pale and looked tired and serious, but Sandra's aching heart had never found him so handsome, so big, so protecting. Patsy flew to him; he took the child in his arms and kissed her, without smiling. She was still clinging to his hand as he came across the big room to the others.

Alexandra faced him; she could smile. The shadows were very deep about her eyes now, the line of her lips was strained. But she managed a smile.

"Hello, dear."

"Carter!"

Mrs. Cavendish immediately began to bustle.

"We must go. Patsy—Peter——"

They said good-byes. Patsy clung fiercely to Alexandra; she had to loosen the hard little hands. The child was crying; Sandra preserved her own self-control with the utmost difficulty.

"Go with Gran, my darling. And remember to take good care of Jiggles when you're down at the ranch."

"I woo-woo-will, Aunt Sandra!" sobbed Patsy.

Sandra kissed Carter's mother, raised her face to Pete.

"Good-bye, Peter dear! Don't forget to come and see me."

"Nope," Peter said thickly. He stooped to kiss her, put a big arm about her.

"I'll be back before you all miss me!"

"Oh, God grant it!" Mrs. Cavendish said on a sob. She went out, and Peter and Patsy followed. Carter closed the door.

Then he came over to the davenport where Sandra was sitting and sat down next to her and locked her hand in his.

They sat so without speaking for a long while.

When the room was quite dark Sandra got up and went about touching the lamp chains, and the lights bloomed, dispelling the dusk. She drew the shades; telephoned downstairs for a dinner menu.

It was hard to order their last meal together, hard to remember from so many happy hours what he liked, hard to specialize the particular salad dressing that Victor always made just for Mr. Cavendish.

Sandra went into the bedroom and looked at herself in the mirror and saw nothing. She put the picture of Carter into the top of her suitcase and looked into her handbag. Tickets, money, and the gold penknife for which Patsy had demanded a penny, and the dark blue pen and the handkerchief and powder box and little bright brass lipstick. She knew everything was there; saw nothing.

Carter was sitting just where she had left him, when she went back. The waiter was bowing and obliging; they made a pretense of eating. Afterward Sandra extinguished all the lights but one, and they sat together again, speaking very little.

"I closed the house to-day, Alex. It's full of you. I'm going to be with Mother until I go down to the ranch."

"I suppose so. Oh, Carter—there was something——" It was the wifely note of warning to which he had grown so happily accustomed during these last years. "Peter is going over on the boat with us," Sandra said, "without letting us see him, just to come back with you."

"I don't want him; I'd rather he didn't."

"I know. But he wants to, dear, so be nice to him. His heart is simply breaking."

A silence. Then Carter said heavily:

"I suppose this is the best way."

Sandra made no answer. She sat silent, with Carter's arm about her, her head on his shoulder. The dinner table had been cleared away, the big room had an empty look—a "hotel look," she called it.

"Then you'll be with your mother to-night?"

"Yep."

"Did you think to wire them to have my drawing room made up, Carter?"

"I forgot."

"No matter. I shall go to bed as soon as he can do it. It'll be ten o'clock. I'll read," she said, "and get to sleep early and sleep as late as I can."

"Less than a year since we went together, honey."

"I was thinking."

"I'll bet you—I'll *bet* you—it won't be more than a year before I come after you."

"Less, maybe."

"And——" He spread her hand; fingered the wedding ring and its beautiful guardian diamond-and-emerald.— "And you'll know that I'm thinking of you every minute, dear."

"I'll know."

"When you come back, Sandra, you're going to have the best husband any woman ever had."

"I know that, too." A silence. "Carter, let's think about that," she presently said. "Let's think of your coming, and my getting ready to meet you. Packing a trunk again, putting last things in a suitcase. Will you buy me bags and handkerchiefs again?"

"I'll buy you things again."

"And shall we go to that same hotel where we were before?"

"You can leave that to me."

After a long while he said, simply:

"I love you so much, Alex. I hate to have you go away from me."

The utter bareness of it took her breath away and stopped her heart. Sandra could find nothing to say.

"Our room—" he said; "the books you were reading—your things hanging in your closet—the letters on your desk . . ."

"I'll come back. It'll all be more wonderful than ever, because of this."

"It's too much for me even to think about. I can't think about your coming back, about your getting into the roadster again, and going with me down to Pete's."

"But lunch at Jules' first."

"Oh, my God," he said.

"I walked over the old ground to-day, Carter. I was too nervous, too excited, to settle down to anything. I walked down past the old office, and the cafeteria where Gertrude Curtis and I used to go for lunch. I looked up at the windows of your office, and remembered how happy I was when I moved in there. I remember that wet night—do you remember?—when I was working late, and it was raining so hard, and you came back and we talked."

"I'd been in New York."

"You'd been in New York. And we thought we had forgotten each other."

"It seems like another life, Sandy."

"Doesn't it?"

"It isn't," he said heavily, "as if you weren't coming back."

"I know."

Silence.

"I suppose we're going to get through this."

"Of course we are!"

"You'll have a—a swell time for a while."

"I'll be all right."

After awhile she said:

"I walked up to Ellis Street to-day too, and looked at the outside of the Bevilaqua place. Heavens, what a lair! I didn't have to go in; I could smell it. I could imagine the darkness and the gaslight in the halls. I could see Flossy and myself going in, with packages from the bakery under our arms."

"You've come a long way since Ellis Street."

"That's what I was thinking. This suite of rooms and my drawing room on the train—everything I wear of silk and fur and lace and velvet—pearls, actual pearls. . . . 'The Stenographer's Dream,'" she said, and was silent.

"It's quarter-past nine, honey."

"Well, then, we'll get started."

"I'll pin on your flowers," he said. She looked closely down at the movements of his big brown hands against her furs. "There!" Carter finished.

"Thanks, dear."

He rang for a boy. Her luggage went downstairs, and Carter and Sandra followed. They crossed the wide hotel foyer and went out to a big car. Carter told the driver. "Ferry. Overland."

"Okay!" the man said cheerfully.

"I'm coming back on the ten-twenty from the other side," Carter said. "Can you wait for me?"

"Sure," the driver assured him.

It was all, fortunately, unreal to Alexandra. Had it been real, she knew that she could not have borne it.

They went down, through the black shadows, and the splashes of light, into the gray, foggy night streets; made the familiar turnings, were at the long Ferry Building. Alexandra said inconsequential things; she was afraid. The clock above their heads said nine-thirty; she would be rumbling eastward on the train in a short half-hour. But she did not know whether she could live through that half-hour.

"You're so kind to come all the way over with me, Carter."

"Oh, for God's sake!"

"I need toothpaste!" she exclaimed.

They walked over to the drug stand and he bought her toothpaste.

"Got your violet soap?"

"Yes. I got some this morning."

A radio was playing. Alexandra had not foreseen that. She felt as if she would faint, there in the crowded Ferry Building, with the evening crowd going over to Oakland and Piedmont.

"This waltz . . . is the kiss waltz,
Telling us both what to do . . ."

She could not bear it. She could not bear it. The lights, the confusion, Carter tender, serious, and gentle beside her.

"There may be someone you know on the train. Remember the awful Trouts last year?"

"It won't matter. I won't leave my room, probably. And there'll be Helen in New York."

On the ferryboat, sitting outside upstairs in the night dark and watching the city lights wheel about them, she said:

"This is May ninth. Six months from to-day will be—let's see, November sixth. If you should be—anywhere in the East—let's have that day for our day? Come and take me to lunch, and we'll do something—we'll drive, and see the red leaves, and then we'll dine together."

"All right," Carter agreed, gently. "I'll be there."

"I have such a horrible feeling that I'm going to cry," Sandra said, when they reached the Oakland slip and were gathering coats and hand luggage.

"You won't cry," he said.

"Of course not."

She walked beside him down the stairs with the moving crowd, across the bridge and into the big black railway shed. The observation platform of her train, brightly lighted, luxurious, was only a few feet away.

"Here," Carter said. "Give me your tickets."

He stopped at a high desk that had been placed beside the train; there was discussion of the long green slip under the bright night lights.

"They do that so that they won't have to wake you after the train gets started."

"They think of everything."

"Here you are. Hang onto these."

"Cora Treadwell told me what she does. She puts all her money into her stocking, and then puts it under her pillow. Then naturally she can't get dressed without her stocking, so she can't forget it . . ."

She did not know what she was saying; he did not hear her.

"Oh, Sandy, you're so lovely—you've always been so kind to me . . ."

Her face was very white. They got on the train, and he came with her to her drawing room.

"Will you look at the food! Dates, oranges! Did someone think I could eat a whole melon?"

"Ring for your porter when the train gets started, and tell him to put it on the ice."

"I will."

"This is a queer end to it, isn't it, Sandy?"

"This isn't the end."

"No, of course not. . . . I've got to get off. Good-bye, dear."

"Good-bye, Carter."

"Good-bye!"

He was gone. Sandra sat down. The colored maid, instructed by Carter, put her head cautiously into the room an hour later. The gentleman had said that his wife might be feeling badly.

But the lady was just sitting there staring out of the mirror-like window at the cinders on the tracks and at her own reflection. She spoke pleasantly enough to Muriel and said that she didn't want anything; she would put her hat in the bag herself later.

"I could git yo' all a cup of coffee?" Muriel said, feeling that she must do something for her dollar. The lady without turning said in a slow, rather careful voice that she didn't want anything, thank you. She went on looking through the black window into the night.

Meanwhile Carter had gone up the runway, and through the gate to the upper floor of the boat. He had not gotten so far before Peter's big shoulder was beside his own.

"I thought I'd make the trip with you," Peter said.

Carter remembered Sandra's charge. It would be a long time before the loved voice, the gold-brown eyes, gave him any directions again.

"Thanks, Pete. Glad to have you," he said.

THE END

ANNA CAINE.

GARY INDIANA.